SCULPTING THE MISTS

Betrayal Will Drink With Anyone

A NOVEL

JEFF DODSON

13725 Metcalf Ave,
#307, Overland Park, KS 66223
For more information contact
judy@knifeedgebooks.com

Cover design by Patrick Knowles
Interior design by Vanessa Mendozzi

ISBN paperback: 979-8-9874286-0-3
ISBN Kindle: 979-8-9874286-1-0
ISBN Epub: 979-8-987-4286-2-7

'The end may justify the means
as long as there is something
that justifies the end'

— LEON TROTSKY

'There is nothing on this earth
more to be prized than true
friendship'

— THOMAS AQUINAS

PART 1

ALEXANDRA & JULIE

1989 – 94

1

Alex (Entry Level): 1989–1993

I left on Monday, November 13. Took an overnight ferry in the driving rain from Dublin to Harwich in England, and then British Rail to Heathrow, where I caught British Airways to Chicago. Traveled on a US passport under the name of Kristin Norden since Alexandra Davis had departed the world in December 1988, ostensibly killed in a car accident.

I was nervous and excited but also angry at myself. Doubt was creeping back in, like water soaking through the towels I'd stuffed under the doors of my conscience to keep it out. The past three years had been pretty easy. I'd been a lookout, served as a messenger and entertained potential donors. I'd also helped hide a cache of weapons. But now I was going to help kill someone.

Cold-blooded murderer, some would say, but not me. I was fighting for a cause, the opportunity to right wrongs, and battling at great personal risk against a corrupt system to end decades of injustice. I also thirsted for vengeance. Regardless, mine was not going to be an inspiring story for the Princeton alumni magazine. Three years after graduation, I was not bringing fresh water to African villages or building schools for girls in the Amazon jungle. Nor was I blazing new paths in neuroscience research. I wasn't even on the soul-deadening pursuit of investment banking or strategy consulting riches. Anyone who heard of my path would, at best, believe me to be a tragic waste of potential; and at worst, call me a terrorist.

I arrived in Chicago, hustled downtown on the El and got to

Union Station, where I ducked into a handicapped bathroom, put on a brunette wig, added eyeglasses and penciled a faint crescent scar onto my chin. Then I checked into my sleeper bedroom on Amtrak's Lake Shore Limited to New York and asked the porter not to be disturbed. I was asleep before the train left the shadow of the Sears Tower.

In New York, I went from Penn Station to Grand Central, took a Metro North train to New Haven and then Amtrak to Boston South Station. I exited the station and walked a mile to the address. There, I found the late 1970s silver Olds Cutlass with a Massachusetts driver's license and keys under the rear seat floor mat. I drove north out of town and arrived in Portland, Maine, late on Wednesday.

I parked the car in a garage downtown and walked around for an hour, up and down streets and alleys. I wouldn't see the car again; someone would pick it up. I checked into the Whistler Inn and slid my cash into the slot in the glass that separated me from the night manager. The lobby reeked of what seemed to be a combination of mildew and fried food, the perfect odors to conjure up the warm, holiday spirit. I fell asleep quickly and awoke late the next morning, a week before Thanksgiving.

I ventured out around 17:00 to eat some greasy meatloaf and rubber vegetables in a tired restaurant near the hotel. I tried to think only about my mission, but that left way too many hours free, and I spent more time than I should have trying not to think of Brian. I was lonely and still feeling guilty about how I'd treated him. It was going on two years since we'd been together in Tokyo – seemed like so long ago.

Stop it! I scolded myself. *Think about something else! You could have had him, but you chose this life.*

• • •

I spent a couple of hours at The Arsenal on Friday and Saturday nights to familiarize myself with the place. The bar sat in the shadow of the Casco Bay Bridge in South Portland, at the end of a torn-up drive with a crumbling asphalt parking lot in the back. Only a litter-strewn vacant lot separated the cars in the lot from the bay. The surrounding area consisted of a fading industrial zone with a steel mill, small shipyard, paper plant and fish cannery. Nearby was a crumbled residential neighborhood with poisoned soil, rusted vehicles and houses with clear plastic nailed to the roof to cover one hole or another. The air was filled with pungent industrial smells.

People streamed in at the end of their shifts and after rec league games to drink, laugh and watch sports. The bartender told me that some found The Arsenal a romantic spot for "making sweet love," as he put it, in the nasty two-stall unisex bathroom. If doing it pressed up against the wall next to the Kotex and condom machines or sitting on the toilet was your thing.

I met Maeve on Sunday near the docks in downtown Portland. Before leaving my hotel, I'd jettisoned the brunette wig and dyed my blonde hair auburn. It was an overcast raw day in the thirties, uncertain if it wanted to snow or rain.

We'd never seen each other. Maeve was younger than I had expected; she didn't look that much older than me. She was five-five or so, very thin and attractive, with gray-green eyes and straight black hair that touched her shoulders. We both wore rain jackets, mine navy and short; hers, black and long. She had a stylish black fedora on her head, and I wore a black-and-gold Boston Bruins knit ski hat.

After a few minutes of walking together, the smell of the sea and approaching winter the only antidotes to the silence, Maeve spoke.

"Any problems getting here, love?"

"No."

"Good," Maeve said. "It's all set for tomorrow night. Doyle will get the call telling him the trawler will load its cargo late Wednesday night and sail Thanksgiving morning. Doyle will call his handler for the meet; still at The Arsenal, we expect, tomorrow night. If it isn't, you'll hear from me, and we'll adjust the plan."

"How will you get to me?"

"You will get three consecutive hang-up calls in your room at the hotel." She nodded at a statue down the way. "Meet me by that monument thirty minutes later. Are you clear on what you need to do?"

"Yes."

Maeve stopped walking and hit me with a hard stare. "This is not lower-division stuff, Alexandra. You'll need a varsity performance on this. It's straightforward, but you need to get it right."

"I know," I said, immediately irritated, and looked down while I made circles in the mud with the toe of my L.L. Bean rubber boot. *For fuck's sake, how hard could this be?*

"Why are you here, Maeve, if I may ask?"

Still staring at me… has she blinked yet?

"These things are complicated. Lots of planning and logistics and management of the aftermath. You are just one element in this process, love. It's very dangerous for us to do something like this over in the States, so the project needs experienced leadership."

We resumed walking in silence for a couple of minutes. Our soundtrack was the rain pelting against our coats and Maeve's hat, mixed with seagulls, and the engine of a lobster boat chugging into port. Maeve stopped again and touched my arm to turn me toward her. She fixed me with a 'don't-even-think-about-fucking-with-me' stare.

"I must tell you, Alexandra, you are a controversial, if not suspicious, person to some in the organization. And there is some worry about your being involved in this. You come highly recommended by the people you worked with over here, and you have proven to be effective and resourceful so far in Ireland, but you have only been there a short time. We decided – well, I decided – to bring you here for this, since having an American for the job is useful. This is a test for you."

I squinted into the steady rain. "Because you need to make sure I'm not just some sort of dilettante looking for the terrorist study-abroad experience? What, maybe people think I'm too young for this?"

Looking irritated now, Maeve wrinkled her eyebrows and stepped even closer to me.

"Yes, Alexandra, this is a test of your dedication and suitability for our work. However, you're not too young. You're twenty-five, after all. I'm thirty-four and have been doing this for over half my life. The fundamental question for all of us is, why do you want to do this?"

I'd answered this question for so many people so many times. What was it going to take? I shot back, "Why do you do it, Maeve?"

With steel that could hold up the Casco Bay Bridge, she narrowed her eyes and said, "For the same reason most in our world do this, Alexandra. My family is Irish and has opposed the British since the turn of the century. They fought in the Easter Rising in 1916, had loved ones, including my grandfather, killed by the British on the first Bloody Sunday in 1920, and have had relations killed every decade ever since."

I nodded, nervous, wondering if Maeve was now going to take a big knife from her long coat and slice me in half. I knew all this – except about her grandfather – but asked her because I was pissed off.

I'd heard the IRA and Irish story constantly, first from Paul Reilly at Princeton and ever since by his parents and the few other people in the organization I'd met. The Catholics in the six counties that comprise Northern Ireland had been mistreated, discriminated against and assaulted by the British their whole lives. Protestants loyal to the Crown had taken the Catholics' jobs, rights, dignity, hope and lives. The twenty-two counties of Ireland got their independence from Britain in 1922, but the fight never ended in the north.

Maeve and everyone in the leadership of the Provisional IRA hated the Brits and their unionist accomplices in Northern Ireland. They believed only sustained armed resistance would dislodge them. Their cause was a united Ireland and independence from the United Kingdom, no matter what or how long it took.

I stood silent in the rain next to Maeve for probably a minute. Angry, but also afraid that I might leak tears of frustration the rain wouldn't hide. Finally, I curtly said, "Don't worry, I will do the job. Make no goddamn mistake about it."

Maeve put her hand on my shoulder. "Look, love, both myself and the organization appreciate your passion and commitment. I believe in you. Know that. I chose you for this, after all, at great risk to me if it doesn't go well. Just make sure this is what you want. There are others here with me who could take your place if you want a rethink on this."

"I don't."

Maeve's expression warmed a bit. "Think of this as the moment right before you are ready to walk down the aisle at your wedding, and your father assures you it can still be called off if you have doubts. Because once you do this, Alexandra, your life will never be the same. There are no divorces or annulments here. Whatever you dreamed about your life becoming as a little girl in your cozy bedroom back in Washington State will no longer be possible."

"You don't think I've already thought about that?" I countered.

"Love, we're happy Paul Reilly brought you into our world back at university. People don't doubt you want to fight against injustice and stick it in the arse of the rich establishment and the British, but you can also do that by going to law school to help the disadvantaged or by doing social work."

"But I don't want to do that. I'm angrier than that."

Maeve resumed walking and put her arm through mine to draw me closer. She looked into the distance and continued.

"I came over here to oversee this operation, as I said, but I also needed to spend time with you, meet you personally, to see if you're really just a sociopath."

"What the fuck! What do you mean by that?"

"You're not a native citizen for our cause. So, are you the rare sort of naturalized Green Card or mercenary fighter for the cause or just a sociopath attracted to violence, anger and revenge? Either can work in our world; it's just a question of how one is deployed and managed."

"Well, what about Paul Reilly? Do people doubt him?"

"He's Irish, with ancestors who have fought and hated the British for generations. Nobody in the organization doubts why Paul and his parents do what they do."

The end of our business was near. We'd reached a point on the waterfront where we would separate. I said, "Maeve, if you don't mind my asking, why don't you have more of an Irish accent?"

She grinned as she pushed a clump of wet hair out of her eyes. "My parents are Irish, and generations of my family grew up in Northern Ireland, South Armagh, then Belfast. But I grew up in Westfield, New Jersey. My dad worked in Manhattan for a major French bank. His night job was first with the original IRA, but he joined the Provisional IRA in the early seventies when the originals lost their stomach for armed resistance. I went to Georgetown and married an American I'd met there. After graduation, we stayed in the US for a couple of years, then moved to Ireland and have been there ever since."

"What does your husband think of what you do?"

She shook her head and said, "That, love, is none of your business."

I just looked at her and didn't respond, thinking it was fine for her to know everything about me. She probably knew how often I picked wax out of my ears every day, but I couldn't ask anything about her. I wondered if her husband was in the organization as well, or if he was just some pansy-assed house husband content to do the cooking and fold her panties when they came out of the wash.

"So," Maeve said, "I think we're done. Good luck. You are clear that you are to get out of the country as soon as it's done?"

"Yes."

"No lingering about. Get back to Chicago and on to Berlin. I will see you there next month."

"One last question," I said. "How did this all come about? What's the bigger picture? I know the IRA gets guns and ammunition from the US, but how does Doyle fit in?"

She stood silently for what seemed a long time. *She's basically going to stiff me and say nothing, a sort of fuck you, Alexandra.* But she surprised me. "He's a tout for the Brits. He knows the details of an arms shipment intended for us that is going out of Portland this week on a boat called the *Swordfetch*, and he's tipped them. He's shagging the Brits."

"How did we find this out?"

Maeve shrugged. "The British, MI-5 and MI-6, have informers in our organization; we know that. We are always looking to root them out. But we also have people in their organizations, and they made us aware." She paused. "Betrayal will drink with anyone. It knows no nationality or friendship."

Maeve eyed me coldly, turned sharply, and headed away from the water. Walking away, only the back of her long black coat and hat visible in the fog of the desolate waterfront, I thought of the gunfighter leaving town. Going back along the waterfront, I ducked into a dingy waterside diner among the warehouses. The windows were opaque with fog, rain and steam. I brushed the rain off, removed my knit hat, sat at the counter and ordered a coffee from a waitress who looked about my age. Jen, her name tag announced. A few fishermen in yellow oilskins, just back into port, sat scattered amongst two tables.

What would Jen be doing on Thanksgiving five days hence? I wondered. Celebrating with her large family? Joining them with her husband or boyfriend? Or having a friends-giving with high school or college pals? Or would her reality be darker? Alone with just her cat, or trapped with some beer- and whiskey-drinking brute in a wife-beater T-shirt who treated her like shit?

Thanksgiving had always been my favorite holiday growing up in Timberline. Sitting in the diner in Portland, the newsreel in my mind inadvertently rolled. Right now, winter, with its oceans of snow, often four or five inches a day for weeks at a time with fog and mist, would be just on the outskirts of my hometown, ready to drive the cold starry nights away until almost May. Basketball had begun, the first games only a week away. Anticipation and excitement would be running high.

I thought about how, after practice, we'd hang around outside The Barn, our high school gym, the moon already up, my head nestled inside Brian's letterman's jacket, enveloped warmly by him and the scent of his cologne. We giggled, kissed and made out, my internal base coach usually waving him around to third before throwing up the stop sign and stranding him there. Or we'd be drinking hot chocolate with my best friend Julie, gossiping about school and imagining our happy, romantic futures together; hers with Tim, and mine with Brian.

Maeve was right that the Northern Ireland cause was not born into me with the blood of past generations. But it would do; it was something I could get behind. For I needed to be in a world where you could exercise power and not be a victim, and in a place where commitment to a cause ruled all – where betrayal was punished and scorned. And I needed to excel, to show the doubters and skeptics I could achieve and beat them, to do better and be better than they were. Finally, I needed revenge for what had happened to Julie and later to Adaoma. Nothing else would do.

Much later, almost ten years after sitting in that diner in Maine in November 1989, I would wonder what that pursuit had cost me. There were Brian and Julie, of course, but also other things: my parents, my friends, the chance for a conventional life, and maybe my soul.

2

The back door of The Arsenal faced the Casco Bay Bridge; the front, the surrounding dreary residential area. I hadn't heard from Maeve, so on Monday evening, I came in the back from the parking lot through a windowless gray metal door and walked down a dark hall past the bathroom. I took a small corner table and ordered a beer.

I could see Bruins, Celtics and Patriots games, each on one of the three large TVs: one over the bar and one on both sides of the dark red-brick walls. Aerosmith's *Angel* pumped faintly from the jukebox. Neon signs for Miller High Life, Stroh's and Schaefer beer lit the front windows, and three Budweiser signs, one not working, along with Miller Lite and Rolling Rock signs, adorned the back wall. Cigarette and cigar smoke infused the bar as if the neighborhood's paper plant had one of its smokestacks hooked directly into the room.

Jimmy Doyle was seated at the bar watching the rain batter the front windows. He'd draped his black-and-gold Boston Bruins jacket on his barstool. He looked agitated and impatient.

After the server brought my beer, I began to feel funny, so I got up and went to the bathroom. I sat on the toilet and tried to get myself together. I was sweating, and my stomach was jumping. Was I excited, scared, or just weak? Were Maeve and the organization right to doubt me?

Sitting on the toilet, I was overcome by nausea and was afraid I might throw up. I leaned back as far as I could and took deep breaths. I broke out in a cold sweat and thought I might faint. I bent over and put my head between my knees. It didn't help that the woman in the stall next to me was smoking a cigarette as she pushed, grunted and exploded, her smell overpowering.

Just leave. Maeve said it wasn't too late. "Dad, you were right. I don't *want to marry this guy and have that kind of life, after all!"* Without pulling my pants up, I quickly got down on my bare knees in front of the toilet to empty my stomach. But nothing would come.

Finally, I started to feel better. The sweating stopped, my heart rate slowed, the nausea faded, and a feeling of calm arrived. *I'm ready to do this.* I'd practiced, thought hard about it, and was committed. I needed to succeed here, or the last three years of my life would have been for nothing. *Just relax, focus and do your job.*

I exited the bathroom and returned to my corner table. It was after 22:00 the Monday night before Thanksgiving, and Jimmy's friend was late. There were open seats on each side of Jimmy at the bar, and only about half the tables had anyone at them. A couple of women sat at the bar; worn down and dressed a bit too nicely, but not nice enough that anyone would think they'd stopped off at The Arsenal on their way home from the symphony. Upscale streetwalkers or escorts from the discount bin, most likely looking for someone who wanted a quick date in a car in the parking lot, like screwing in a drive-through car wash.

A few tables pushed together close to the bar had loud hockey players who seemed to have come in after a game. A thirty-ish chubby guy in a red sweater said, "Dat major penalty on McGinness was harse shit; it gave 'em a fucking four-minute power play. Of course they gonna score. It was like the ref was watchin' da game in the dahk. And then, Jones, you let that shot go through your legs right at the end. If I'd been tween the pipes, I'd a just unfolded my dick down between my legs and nothing wooooda got past that."

"Ah, suck me, Rick," Jones said. "Next time I'm at the hockey hall of fame, I'm gonna look for your fuckin statue."

Three couples sat together at a round table in the middle of the room. One of the women, my stall mate, had just returned from the bathroom. The men were passing around a color GOLF MYRTLE BEACH brochure, and the women were reviewing a SHOPPING, SUN AND FUN IN MYRTLE BEACH flyer.

Farther away, toward the toilet and back exit, a thirty-something couple was at a table, right where they were supposed to be; a red Semper-Fi hat for him and a blue Red Sox sweatshirt for her.

I was properly dressed for the bar: worn, faded blue jeans with a hole in the left knee and a heavy black hooded sweatshirt that made me sweat through my bra. My auburn hair was going in every direction, so I took off my baseball cap and pulled it up into a ponytail that poked out the back of my hat. In doing this, I realized that the blue-and-yellow United Steelworkers baseball cap could cause me a problem if someone in here was in the union and asked me about it.

Once Jimmy's friend arrived, I would wait a few minutes and then leave out the front door. Jimmy looked harmless enough to me, but apparently, he wasn't.

I would learn only much later – years – that Jimmy Doyle wasn't in the IRA and was just hired muscle to load the *Swordfetch*, unaware of its cargo. He'd been coerced by the British into helping them; he was to place an electronic tracking device on the boat the night he helped load her. The British and Canadians then planned to intercept the ship and its weapons at sea.

Doyle hadn't wanted to help them, but the Brits gave him no choice, threatening to either let it slip to the FBI that he was running guns for the IRA or falsely allow the IRA to believe he was touting for MI-6. Doyle had a pregnant wife and a four-year-old son who needed major heart surgery. The Brits offered him money for his son's operation but still gave him no choice. They'd had him by the balls and were squeezing him hard. Unfortunately for Doyle, the Provisionals still learned about him. The Provos had an informer near MI-6 who'd heard the part about Doyle helping them that one time but not the bit that he didn't want to do it.

Around 22:15, Doyle's handler arrived through the front door. Overweight, his zipped, military-style black coat strained to contain his stomach. He had thick, unkempt salt-and-pepper hair that brushed the top of his shoulders, a large round face and a wide bulbous nose blotched with rosacea.

I left The Arsenal ten minutes later and walked four blocks to the mid-1970s Chevy pickup with oxidized red paint. The package was in the cab on the passenger-side floor under a pile of burlap sacks. I unlocked the truck and removed the parcel, roughly the size of two shoeboxes stacked one on the other. I put it in one of the burlap sacks and walked back to the bar, pulling my hat down over my eyes to keep the bullets of rain out of my face. *Hurry, don't mess this up. This isn't hard. Just stay calm and get it done.*

I didn't see anyone, so I walked to the parked car in The Arsenal lot and tried to pry the trunk latch open, as I'd endlessly practiced. My hands were shaking and despite the rain, I was sweating like I was on the last mile of the Boston Marathon. I'd practiced with gloves on every time, but it seemed much harder now. The latch wouldn't open. I tried again. No.

Dammit! Focus! Work the trunk lock and it will open. Doyle or someone else will come out the back door any minute. Relax. You practiced this dozens of times!

Again, no. *Slow down and try again!*

I heard the back door open and ducked down behind the closed trunk. Two people. Doyle and his handler? It was hard to see through the driving rain, but then I heard them… no, just some of the hockey players.

I froze, hoping they wouldn't come my way. But they were. *Fuck! They've seen me.* The burlap sack was next to me at my feet.

"Hey, sistah, you was in da bah back der, in da corner, right?"

I nodded as I looked over their shoulders, watching for Doyle to come out the back door any second and ruin the whole plan. End my career before it had even started.

"Maybe you'd like some company tonight, eh, honey? Are youse one of those kind-a girls? What do you chaaage?"

I shook my head. "Look, I'm waiting for my boyfriend to pick me up. He works at the mill and is on his way."

The bigger of the two, the less obese one, said, "Yeah, well, late night in dis parta town, a nice girl shouldn't be out here alone." He smirked. "Maybe you'd like to come wait in da cah with us. Eh, sweetie?"

I had to end this now if I had any hope of getting my work done before Doyle walked out.

I punched the talkative one, Mr. What-Do-You-Chaage, right in the nose and yelled, "Get the fuck away from me and leave me alone! Or I'll scream and say you tried to rape me. Leave me alone and walk away! Now! Right fucking now, goddammit!" I was shaking.

Finally, after grumbling, calling me an uppity twat, and assuming I was "one a dem Massholes from Boston," and telling me to go home and play with myself, they moved away. My hands and whole body were still shaking like I was nude in a blizzard in Siberia.

Okay, calm down, start again. You've got to get this done. It'll be okay. You can do this! Be patient, steady, take your time. Almost… almost. Finally! Okay, trunk's open. Good, now just put the sack in there.

I put the package under an old blanket at the back of the trunk and reclosed the lid. I quickly walked back to the red truck, started the engine and drove the two miles or so to the drop-off point. I put the keys under the passenger-side floor mat, left the truck unlocked and walked three blocks to the black Honda Accord the organization had left for me. I was supposed to immediately drive the car downtown, abandon it in the warehouse district and walk to my hotel. Instead, I drove back to The Arsenal, parked in the lot and watched the back door. I had a clear view and the rain was now down to just a drizzle. I went back to either see Doyle drive away or confirm he'd left.

His car was gone, but I waited a few more minutes, trying to relax. I was about to leave when Jimmy's handler emerged out the back door. I saw him turn toward the trash dumpster to his left, where I noticed the couple I'd seen earlier – Ms. Red Sox Sweatshirt and Mr. Semper-Fi hat. She was leaning against the dumpster with her pants around her ankles and her knees spread. Semper-Fi had his pants down and was pressed against her while she had her hands on his bare ass.

Jimmy's handler didn't stare, really, but stopped and watched them out of the corner of his eye, a few seconds of voyeurism that cost him his life. He didn't notice the woman who suddenly stepped behind him. She jabbed something into his neck and he crumpled to the ground within five seconds. What was it? A knife, I thought at first, but blood would have been spewing everywhere. It must have been a hypodermic.

Once the guy hit the pavement, Red Sox Sweatshirt and Semper-Fi stopped their 'we're-not-really-screwing' ballet and pulled their pants up. Red Sox Sweatshirt ran to a car in the parking lot and drove over. Semper-Fi and Red Sox loaded the body into the trunk. Semper-Fi jumped into the passenger seat and the couple drove off.

The other woman, the assassin, moved toward another car closer to where I was parked. I ducked down in my seat. As she climbed into the Ford, the dome light and the lights in the lot illuminated her… Maeve!

Jimmy Doyle's life had ended before he got home to his pregnant wife and seriously ill four-year-old son, so said the next day's afternoon paper. The small bomb in the trunk of his car was on a timer that I'd started, set to go off at thirty minutes, so somewhere on his drive before he got home. It detonated when he stopped, halfway home, at Dirt Cheap Gas to fill up. The fireball made dental records the method of choice to ID Doyle and precluded an open-casket service.

The blast also killed the night clerk at the gas station, a twenty-five-year-old divorced mother of three boys under the age of ten. Her death, I learned much later when I got the information about

Doyle, resulted in her boys being forcibly returned to Mexico, a place they had never been, to live with the father they had never known.

I lingered in Portland an extra day, ignoring Maeve's orders, mainly to see the news accounts of the bombing. Naturally, there was nothing related to the disappearance of Jimmy's handler. I only partly succeeded in not thinking much about the whole situation. I had proven myself to Maeve, justified her faith in me and shown the doubters in the organization, whoever they were. Doyle had brought this on himself by getting in bed with the British. As for the gas clerk, well, there was always collateral damage in war. But I couldn't think about that. Who'd have known Jimmy Doyle would stop for gas?

I didn't learn the fate of the MI-6 handler, whose alias was Bill, for several years, and then only inadvertently. He didn't die from the hypodermic stick in the parking lot; it wasn't intended to kill him. At a remote location outside Portland, Maeve spent the days before Thanksgiving torturing him.

Swordfetch departed Portland, absent a tracking device, late the next night – earlier than the British had expected. It headed into rough eight-to-ten-foot swells, the boxes of guns and ammunition taking all available space below decks. The vessel bobbed, pitched, rolled and eventually met the freighter, the *Izmir*, off the Grand Banks of Newfoundland, two hundred nautical miles farther out to sea than the original rendezvous point.

The precious cargo was moved precariously from one craft to the other, though one box, filled with Bill's body and accompanying weights, was dropped purposefully into the boiling ocean. It would be years before MI-6 would learn Bill's fate or even acknowledge his existence – no consolation to his teenage sons and ex-wife.

3

After seeing Maeve in Maine in November 1989, I moved to Berlin and began establishing my life as Petra Müller, an orphan since her teens whose German parents had supposedly lived in Africa with their daughter most of her life while they did Lutheran missionary work. Sadly, her parents were killed in a traffic accident in Kenya when Petra was eighteen, precipitating her return to Berlin.

I had a small studio apartment near Checkpoint Charlie in the Mitte district of the fast-disappearing former East Berlin. I spent six months taking intensive German classes (two years of German in college helped) and then found work as a janitor at the Free University of Berlin. At night I tended the bar at a techno club in a rundown warehouse district off Alexanderplatz in old East Berlin. I made friends and briefly dated a few guys, but nothing special.

Life was easy, but I was lonely and bored. I'd seen Maeve for less than an hour in Berlin a month after arriving from Maine the prior year, but I hadn't seen or heard from her since. This wasn't what I'd signed up for. I wanted an assignment. Every day on the way home from my janitor's job, I made myself go and check for a signal, but there were plenty of times I almost blew it off. Nothing was going to happen.

Then, in early December 1990, a year after getting to Berlin, on a heavy gray, bitterly cold Wednesday afternoon that reminded me of Timberline, I saw the signal. Four parallel slanting downward left-to-right blue chalk marks above the basement window of the designated apartment block a quarter mile from the TV tower. Late that night, I unloaded the dead drop, an out-of-commission post box at a construction site near Potsdamer Platz. Still largely an urban wasteland, the Berlin Wall had run right through the middle of it, and years later, it would become a major commercial area. A sealed envelope in the dead drop had a sheet of paper directing me to meet a train. Nothing else.

Two days later, Friday night at 18:00, I stood amidst rush-hour traffic at the appointed drinks kiosk next to platform four at Zoo Station with a coffee in my left hand and a blue coat draped over my right arm. I'd been instructed to arrive at 17:50 and remain as late as 19:00. If nobody met me, I was to do the same the next evening at a different kiosk by platform one. Tonight, I was to look as if I was meeting someone off the train from Hamburg, and the next night, it would be the train from Frankfurt.

The Hamburg train pulled in on time – this was Germany, after all – and passengers began streaming out. I had no idea whom I was looking for and assumed someone would find me. I felt a tap on my elbow from behind, turned and saw Maeve.

I didn't know whom I was expecting, but it wasn't her. I was happy and intimidated at the same time. Before I could say anything, Maeve smiled and took my hand.

"Hi, love. How've you been?"

I hadn't seen or heard from her in a year. "I'm… I'm fine," I sputtered.

"Let's take a walk, shall we?"

Maeve was wearing short black heels, an ankle-length coat of some sort of dark fur and a wide black fedora. She had a thin black leather briefcase with shiny brass fixtures and a Rolex watch on her left wrist. I could see she still had her straight hair that stopped above her shoulders and those same lively gray-green eyes.

Maeve briskly led me down several dark hallways and through various doors in the station that said KEIN AUSGANG. We exited through a locked metal door, for which she had a key. This was some sort of back exit, so there were few people around. Maeve linked her arm in mine, and we began walking toward the Tiergarten area, an enclave of high-end residential neighborhoods and embassies that began less than a mile away. Off in the distance, we heard the throngs in the big Christmas market by Zoo Station and smelled the roasting meats and nuts. I would have loved a steaming cup of Glühwein right then to settle my nerves.

"It's so good to see you, love, or Fräulein Petra Müller, I suppose I should say. How do you find Berlin? I'm told your German is fantastic, fluent with a native accent, in fact. And I hope the jobs we arranged for you are satisfactory."

"They're fine."

"Good or just fine?" Maeve asked.

They're not good, they're fine because I don't have a fucking thing to do. "They're good, Maeve, thank you," I decided to say instead. "But why am I here? I've not done anything for the organization. I'm bored and feel useless. It's been over a year."

Maeve nodded knowingly. "Everything in good time, Alexandra. We have long-term plans for you, and you're going to need your German identity and history in this city. But what do you want? What ideally do you want to be doing, now and in the future?"

"I… I want to move up in the organization. I want responsibility, and I want to learn. I want to make a difference."

"I'm sure that's true, love, but be honest with yourself. You want revenge. You're angry with the British and seek retribution – an eye for an eye, so to speak."

I didn't respond and we kept walking, our heads down against the rapidly falling snow and biting Siberian wind. The storm was powering in over the Northern European Plain from Russia, like Stalin's armies in 1945.

I turned my head to look at Maeve. "Why are you here? Are you in the neighborhood and stopping by, or is there something more specific to discuss?"

"Why, I'm here to see you, love. See how you're getting on, see what you still think about this life you've chosen."

"You mean to see if I can still be trusted or relied upon," I shot back, going from calm and cool to angry and pissed off, as if flicking a switch. *Why am I like that?*

Maeve affectionately squeezed my arm, tipped her hat up and rested her head on my shoulder as we walked. "Oh, Alexandra, if we felt that, I certainly wouldn't be here, and you would have never heard from us again. You're still new at this. This is a dangerous profession you and I have chosen."

"I know that," I said curtly.

Maeve went on, "But I hope you fully appreciate that fact. MI-5, MI-6, the RUC—" She meant the British intelligence agencies, domestic and foreign, respectively, and the Royal Ulster Constabulary, the cops in Northern Ireland. "…are all deadly serious and capable outfits. Now, so are we, but you must always respect them and take nothing for granted."

I just kept walking, my feet crunching, percussion in the symphony of snow and wind. After a bit of silence, I said, "And what the hell are you doing in heels in the snow, anyway? Your feet must be ice cubes."

Maeve laughed. "Yes, point well taken, Alexandra. My weather reconnaissance was poor. Though we don't have much farther to walk until I get to where I'm going. And you have boots, so you will be well-suited to make your way home."

"Then I'm not going with you to your destination?"

Maeve held my arm as we walked. "Now, Alexandra, much as you've grown acclimated to Berlin, you're going to be moving shortly. Back to Dublin."

I didn't expect that. I was curious, but uncertain. Was it an assignment, or were they posting me closer to home base, where they could better keep an eye on me? "Why?"

"An envelope will arrive at your flat next Tuesday with the logistical details. Where you will live and work as well as the information on your backstory that, of course, you must know inside and out. It will contain your Irish passport and other relevant documents and tell you how we will keep in touch. Oh, and it will detail your appearance."

"My appearance?"

"Yes, Alexandra, I'm afraid you'll have to cut Petra Müller's beautiful long blonde hair and color it dark brown. And don't forget to dye your eyebrows and the hair on your lady bits as well."

Jesus, is there anything she doesn't know about me? "Who am I? What am I doing?" I was like a dog fidgeting and whimpering for a Milk-Bone.

Maeve got right to it. "You will be Molly Fitzhugh. You're an Irish citizen because your parents are, but you grew up with them in Newport Beach, California. You only just left the States in the past few months to move to Dublin as a base for travel and adventure. You will work as a hostess in an upscale Dublin restaurant near the diplomatic quarter."

"And will people be able to verify that history if they check?"

"Of course, Alexandra — we're not some shambolic group of amateurs. Should someone want to check on you, and they will, they'll find the family listed in Newport Beach, and if they ring your so-called parents, your father and mother will indeed confirm their daughter is exploring her Irish heritage in Dublin and working in a restaurant."

"What about friends, school records, that kind of thing? Who other than my so-called parents will have ever seen me?"

"I doubt anyone will look that hard, love. But if they do, they'll be able to find your high school records from the McKnight Academy, an exclusive boarding school outside Santa Barbara. Though, sadly, you must have been an introvert nobody could remember well, save one teacher, Brendan Riley, who can talk all about you if needed. You also seemed to have been absent every year when they took class pictures, so they will find you only in the 'Not Pictured' listing with your robust extracurricular activities detailed."

"What will I be doing in Dublin besides working in this restaurant?"

"Your mission is to go undercover, possibly for a couple of years, and get close to Magnus Herrington, to become his indispensable mistress."

"Mistress? A couple of years?"

"Magnus is MI-5's top man in Derry, or Londonderry as the Brits call it, in Northern Ireland," Maeve explained. "We think he'll be a valuable source of intelligence for us in the future if we can get sufficiently close to him."

The wind was really cutting into me as we walked, though other than her feet, Maeve looked nice and warm in her mink coat or whatever it was. "Why do you think I can get close to him, anyway?"

"Well, as one of my colleagues quite crudely put it, he's got a powerful addiction to the fanny batter of beautiful young women."

"To what?" I asked.

"Ah, right, sorry. My Anglo English. The rough American translation, I suppose, would be poontang… wet pussy."

I looked sideways at Maeve and wrinkled my nose. "Nice, very nice. You learn new vocabulary every day. How flattering. So, he likes sex. What men don't?"

Maeve chuckled. "I always aim to enlighten, love. Magnus's wife and four young children are back in England, in the London area, and he only gets home for about a weekend every couple of months. Magnus told one of his colleagues, conveniently also one of ours, that the missus isn't very good in bed; seems she's not adventurous or lively. I can't blame her, really, if she's got him grinding away on top of her. She's also apparently had trouble losing her baby weight. Magnus told his workmates that her arse and thighs were as big as the Irish Sea and covered in an equal amount of cellulite."

"Ah," I said, "she's got lots of hail damage back there."

Maeve took this in for a second and then laughed out loud. "Good on you, love. Now I've learned a new phrase. Good god, men really are pigs sometimes, aren't they? If my husband ever talked to anyone about me like that, I would shoot him between the eyes. Now, I would want him to tell me about it straight out, but he'd better never mention it to anyone else."

I just shrugged. "So, why me to snuggle up to Magnus Prince Charming?"

"Because you're young, smart, an Irish-American California girl, and gorgeous. What's not to like? You also have no history in Ireland, so it's easier to create you out of thin air. We had another woman with him, Irish, for almost a year, but she, unfortunately, got pregnant by him, and he told her to sod off when he found out. Instead of having her make a scene, we decided to float someone else in – you – and take care of the woman ourselves."

"You, uh, took care of her?"

"We gave her some money and told her to make the best go of it she could. Don't get pregnant, Alexandra."

"Did Magnus tell this other woman useful things?"

"Oh yes. No huge secrets, but continuous bits of information helpful to us: new efforts being stepped up in Derry by the Brits, new informants they had, the cock-ups of MI-5 and MI-6 in Belfast and London, that sort of thing. They all violate the Official Secrets Act and would get him decades in prison if he were caught out."

"Okay, so he's up in Northern Ireland, and I'm in Dublin. How does that work?"

"He hates it in Derry, loyalist bastard, so every couple of weeks, he manages to find some job-related reason – his cover is with a UN agency – to come to Dublin. The restaurant where you're working is his favorite. He eats there almost every night he's in Dublin."

"And he's just supposed to see me and fall in love? Want to march me straight to bed?"

"Just about. He's lecherous and will be after you, especially if you flirt with him some. Just let him know you're a young woman looking for a little no-strings-attached fun in Ireland for a year or two before you go back to the States. He likes submissive women who are loud and carry-on in bed. I must tell you he also likes to administer a bit of corporal punishment now and again and fancies ventures up the back passage."

I just stood there, as I had in Maine, enveloped in bad weather, trying to take it all in. Finally, I said, "Ah, Romeo, Romeo, wherefore art thou Romeo? The makings of a true love story."

Maeve turned to me and took my hands in both of hers. She looked directly into my eyes. "Look, love, I'm not going to blow sunshine and Disney into your knickers. This is going to be unpleasant, sometimes grim work. But if you can be successful here, it will be a chance for us to strike a blow against the other side. And it will be quite good for your career in the organization."

"Ohhh-kay," I said. "You seem to have more faith in me than I do." Kicking my right boot into the snow, I stammered, "What if, you know, um, ah, I'm not very good in, you know, bed? He might lose interest in me."

"Oh, I can't imagine that, love. I would think you'd be quite capable in that area."

Wrong!

"But if not, you simply must learn quickly, on the job, as they say. You're going to do great with Magnus."

Maeve stopped at the top of a residential street full of large houses covered with Christmas lights. Headed no doubt for fine food, drink and warm holiday surroundings while I trudged back to my small, cold and lonely flat. I recognized this neighborhood in Tiergarten as one of the nicest in Berlin, near the diplomatic quarter. It was dead quiet. The sound of the wind, the heavy snow and stately, brightly lit homes evoked a cozy Christmas scene: Maeve, the indomitable warrior, perfectly situated in a Currier and Ives print.

"It's time to say goodbye, love. Until we meet again."

4

Magnus

It was a clear and dry Friday evening in early January 1992, a stark contrast to the storm boiling within Magnus Herrington. He'd returned to Londonderry that morning from three weeks of Christmas leave in England, the first he'd been home from work in Northern Ireland in almost two months. Though it had been great to see his four boys, aged five to eight, he couldn't say that about his wife, Jenny; things with her just kept getting worse.

He and Jenny, married nine years, had bickered the whole time. They'd tried not to do it in front of the boys but had made a hash of that. She was on him about his drinking, said it had gotten much worse since MI-5 sent him to Northern Ireland. That was right, he had to admit. She said it had made his bad temper and selfishness worse. They also had money troubles. Jenny complained they were living precariously every month – something she battled alone since MI-5 paid all his expenses while he was away.

She wanted him home on weekends more – twice a month instead of every six weeks. He could do that, MI-5 would pay for it, but he didn't want it. He wanted to spend his weekends with Molly. Though they'd been together for less than a year, Magnus was in love with her.

But a divorce would be dodgy. It would hurt his boys, and Jenny would raise hell and make it hard for him to see them. Plus, MI-5 hated messy domestic situations like divorce – saw it as a security risk. A couple of months previously, he'd confided in his boss and good friend, Bentley and raised the possibility of divorcing Jenny, but Bentley shook his head.

"That is utter bollocks, Magnus! Why not just take out your

nine-millimeter and shoot yourself between the eyes? Divorce could scuttle your career. You could end up driving a desk in some horrid job in London."

Magnus started to protest, but Bentley raised his hand to cut him off.

"You fight with your wife all the time. She's a good mum, but a bad shag. Hell, half the men in the world have that problem. You say she's gotten fat, never wants to fuck you, and lies there like a corpse when she does. Fine. Accept it. You can pay a woman to screw you every night in Londonderry if you want. And it sounds like your Molly is wild between the sheets and beautiful on top a that. What's not to like?"

"I don't know. I want to be with Molly. Jenny's gotten cruel to me, and my god, she's let herself go. Her arse is huge. When she sits on the loo, her thighs droop over the side. Sometime I'm gonna come home from Northern Ireland, and I'll see 'em touchin' the floor when she pees and shits."

Though Magnus knew he was to blame for a fair share of the difficulties with Jenny, he could neither forgive nor accept her sexual shortcomings and unwillingness to fulfill her wifely responsibilities. She claimed he was too rough, especially when he'd been drinking, and that sex wasn't pleasurable but painful. He was big for her. Magnus was six-four and weighed about nineteen stone. But her saying he was too large for her was rubbish. She'd pushed four kids out down there.

Magnus was a ticking bomb when he got back to Londonderry. Three weeks of fighting with Jenny, practically begging her for sex. He got it just once, on his second night home. Missing Molly made him angry, anxious and unsettled – a fevered pot on an intense boil.

As soon as he flew in, he went straight to his office, his United Nations cover, and managed a couple of distracted hours of work. Then, at a local safe house, he had his monthly meet with the British military commander for Londonderry and the leaders of two Protestant militia groups. Magnus opted for the Bushmills instead of the Guinness. When the meeting ended at 18:00, he moved alone to a pub down the street and kept the whiskey going.

Magnus was anxious to get his weekly routine back with Molly. Weeks when his United Nations cover work resettling war refugees from the Middle East and Africa didn't get him to Dublin, he'd meet Molly at the flat in Enniskillen, almost halfway between Dublin and

Londonderry. The flat belonged to a mate of his who went home to his young family in Birmingham every weekend.

Magnus checked his watch – 19:30 – and practically ran to his car to drive the hundred kilometers to Enniskillen. Molly should arrive at about the same time.

Molly (Alex)

At 21:30, Alex heard the elevator door open down the hall from the flat. After almost a year with Magnus, she still felt a pit in her stomach when he approached, unsure if he would be sober and pleasant or drunk and angry. The holiday break from him had been glorious – three weeks of peace and time to herself.

Alex shared what she had learned from Magnus with the Provisionals through a series of dead drops around Dublin. But save for knowledge of stepped-up attempts by MI-5 to recruit touts in the Provo's Derry brigade, gossip about dysfunction in MI-5 in its Belfast operations, and the discovery of ongoing sexual improprieties by a prominent Protestant religious leader in Derry, she hadn't learned much. Hardly enough to justify being brutally shagged by Magnus at will.

As his footsteps came down the hall, she smoothed her red wool pencil skirt over her hips and made sure her white blouse was tucked in. She was wearing black tights, no shoes and the dangling onyx earrings he'd once given her as a gift.

Magnus stumbled into the flat. *Oh, Jesus, he's in no condition to drive. Wonder if he ran over anyone on the way?* The pit in her stomach grew larger.

Magnus smiled as soon as he saw her. He wore a dark blue Harris Tweed sport coat and a pale blue dress shirt. His sagging charcoal trousers were pushed down his hips by his stomach, spilling over the top of a black belt.

Alex ran to him and wrapped her arms around his neck. The scent of the light floral perfume he loved would flood him with desire.

Still with her arms around his neck, Alex felt something in the inner pocket of his tweed coat and saw a handle poking out of the top. It was a knife; she'd never seen him with one before.

She smiled warmly, tousled his thick mane of dark hair and said, "Baby, you got your hair cut, even shorter than before. It looks good! Oh, it's so good to see you, honey. I thought about you every day." Resting her head against his chest, she added, "Looks like you got a new jacket for Christmas. It's nice. I know you love the Harris Tweed."

"Ah, yeah, got my hair cut." His breath and clothes stank of liquor and Dunhill cigarettes. Swaying slightly on his feet and slurring his words, he continued, "Can't wait to have our Christmas together, Mol."

"Me too," she purred. She put her right hand on his left cheek and grinned. "You silly, it looks like you started celebrating without me. Come over here and sit down and let me make you some tea. Then how 'bout you get into the bath and let me wash you up? After that, we can have our Christmas. I can't wait to show you what I got you!"

Magnus shook his head. "You joking, Molly?" He clumsily tried to remove her skirt but couldn't find the zipper at the side. He thrust his hands inside her blouse and grabbed her breasts, scratching one and painfully pinching the nipple of the other.

"Oww!" she yelped and pulled his hand away. "Be careful!"

"Then get this fuckin' skirt off," he slurred, "and your knickers. I've been wanking thinking of yer cunt for weeks."

She led him from the front entryway across the small flat to the kitchen table. "Okay, okay, sure." Alex unzipped the skirt and watched it fall around her ankles before removing her tights and black panties. "But sweetie, bad timing, the painters are in. My period showed up yesterday and is going strong. I'm good with making love. I don't mind at all, but I know you don't really fancy it when it's messy down there."

Alex dreaded what was coming next. He'd want to bend her over right there on the kitchen table and "git up the back passage," as he liked to say.

And she was right.

"Yeah, sweetie, I know this is disappointing, but we can't do that anymore when you've been drinking. Remember, we talked about this last month? You're not careful, and it hurts. Let's do some other things tonight, and we can do that tomorrow when you're in a better state."

"Bollocks! We're doing it. Now either get across the table or go lie down on the effin' bed."

"Not anymore, Magnus, PLEASE. Not if you're going to be drinking beforehand. I couldn't poo for a week, it hurt so bad last month. And you're drunker now than then. We can do lots of other things. I'd really like that."

"You fucking cunt!" Magnus yelled, surprising her with his volatile burst of anger. "Yer doing this for me, ya hear!"

Angry and a little afraid, Alex yelled back, ready to get into it if that was how he was going to be. "No! Who do you think you're talking to, anyway? I'm not some street whore you can pay to give you whatever you want when you're slobbering drunk. Sod off, Magnus! We're not doing anything tonight."

He went after her before she could react. Grabbed her hair with one hand, put his other around her neck, and dragged her to the bedroom.

"Stop it, you prick! Let me fucking go, Magnus!"

Alex struggled against him and tried unsuccessfully to land a punch. Though not square on, she managed to drive a knee into his groin, doubling him over and making him drop his hands from her hair and neck.

But he rose and came at her again.

"You daft cow!" he roared, fury and want in his eyes, a starving wolf. He drew the knife from his inside jacket pocket and started toward Alex. *My god, he's going to try to kill me!*

But then he thought for a second and threw the knife onto the floor. Before she could get her hands up, his fist crashed square into her nose, an express train versus a bicycle. Alex heard the bones in her nose crunch.

The blow took Alex off her feet, and she landed on the bed, the springs screaming in protest. She felt and smelled the blood everywhere. It streamed down her face and pushed up into her eyes, blurring everything. Despite the adrenaline surge, the pain was immediate, and she gasped and screamed, both hands up to her face. She rolled off the bed and onto the floor, blood still seeping out under her palms and through her fingers.

Half blindly, Alex pawed for the big black faux-leather purse she'd put in the corner by the bed earlier. *Where is it? Where is it?* She tried to wipe the blood out of her eyes with her left hand and desperately fished with her right for the purse.

There…she'd found it.

Magnus cried out, "Oh god! No! No! Molly, what have I done? I'm so sorry, my love! Don't know what came over me. Oh, Jesus, look at you. Look what I've done. Here, here, let's get you to hospital. I'm so, so sorry, Molly. Please, you must believe me. Please! I love you so!"

He bent toward Alex, his hands and open palms extended. She faced him with blood running down both sides of her mouth. It covered her hands and white blouse as well. She grabbed the .22-caliber revolver from her purse, and fired.

The first two shots hit center mass, the next two missed high, and the fifth drove into his head just above the bridge of his nose.

The headshot killed Magnus instantly, though it looked to Alex like the two chest wounds were in a race to see which one could drain the blood from him first.

She took off her blouse and used it to finally stop the blood from her nose. But then she fainted and slumped over into the growing pool of Magnus's blood. She came to a few minutes later, terrified, in pain and in a mental fog.

Fuck, fuck, fuck! What have you done? She moaned and put her forehead into her blood-soaked hands. Blood, both hers and Magnus's, was everywhere, even all over her bare legs. *The cops will be here soon. If I don't go to prison for murder, I'll be in trouble with Maeve. How can I justify killing a valuable MI-5 source because he attacked me, pissed me off, and wanted to put his dick up my ass and tear it up for, like, the hundredth time? Stop it! Think! Think!*

Magnus's eyes were open, and she thought he was staring at her, almost saying, "I'm so sorry, Molly. I… I loved you. Why did you do this to me?"

After a couple of minutes, Alex knew self-defense had to be the explanation for the cops and Maeve.

Alex saw the hunting knife on the floor near where Magnus had fallen. *I can't do that. Yes! You can. You have to. You can't fucking kill somebody over a pop in the face.*

Careful to leave no prints, she closed the knife in his hand, lifted his arm, ran the blade across her bare midriff twice, and screamed from the pain. She cut deeply enough that blood poured out immediately. Bleeding profusely and already lightheaded, Alex knew she would pass out any second. She stumbled to the bathroom, naked except for a bra, trailing blood all the way. She grabbed the two bath towels from the rack and pressed them into her wounds.

She heard sirens. Before passing out on the bathroom floor, she hoped help would arrive before she bled to death.

5

Alex: 1992, Northern Ireland

The ambulance got me to the emergency department at Enniskillen hospital a bit before 23:00. By 04:00, I'd been moved to a private room, a splint and bandage on my nose, forty-two stitches in my abdomen, with IV painkillers and antibiotics on board. I'd also needed a blood transfusion.

Before falling asleep in my hospital room, I'd insisted on being helped to the call box outside the nurse's station. I put the coins in and dialed the Dublin number I'd been told to memorize. It rang three times before someone picked up.

"Yeah."

I asked, "Hi, it's me. Are we still having the birthday party next week? I might be late."

"Yes. Did you get the ring for us to give her?"

"Yes, it's a beautiful… uh, uh…" *Oh shit, what's the birthstone for January?* I was in a panic until I remembered it. "Garnet."

"Good, okay," the person on the phone said.

Sign and countersigns completed, I told them where I was, spoke of a bad accident, and hung up. The person on the other end said nothing.

Around noon the next day, a man and woman arrived in my room and flashed badges in a blur. *So, that's why I'm in a private room. Can't be on a ward and have others hear them question me.*

The man was short. He looked mid-forties, had greasy, dirty blond hair and an almost perfectly round face like a frisbee. He walked with a waddle, like the inside half of his feet had been sheared off in a bizarre accounting firm accident. He wore black slacks, a too-small maroon dress shirt and a solid blue tie under a black waist-length raincoat. Inspector Walsh of the RUC Enniskillen branch.

His companion was Inspector Samantha Byrne of the Special Branch.

Shit! What's she doing here?

She was tall and wore beige wool slacks and a matching suit coat. Thin with no chest or hips to speak of, she was a straw in Scottish tweed. She had bright red (orange actually) curly hair, freckles seemingly covering every inch of skin, and a pasty complexion that said, "I haven't seen the sun since the Beatles broke up."

I'd heard about Samantha Byrne from Magnus. She led the Special Branch in Londonderry. Special Branch was an organ of the British government that worked closely with MI-5 and other police, military and intelligence organizations on matters deemed relevant to national interests. If you combined Special Branch and MI-5, you would have something akin to the US's FBI.

As the MI-5 lead in Londonderry, Magnus and Byrne were peers and worked together regularly. I'd never met her. Magnus said she was quite good at her job, but he detested her; said she was political, untrustworthy and uppity. He called her *C-U-Next-Tuesday*, as in, "I have a fuckin meeting with See You Next Tuesday today." Sometimes he just called her *Cunter*.

After some fake pleasantries and inquiries about my health, Walsh got right to it.

"Ms. Fitzhugh, we're investigating the events of last night involving you and Mr. Magnus Herrington. I'm sure you know he's dead. We must understand if you murdered him or if perhaps something else transpired."

I could see where this was headed. I was terrified and afraid I'd start hyperventilating.

"I… uh… I didn't murder anyone. You have to know that."

Clearly skeptical, Walsh almost smirked. "So, why don't you tell us what happened, Miss Fitzhugh?"

"He wanted sex. I told him no, then he punched me and broke my nose and then attacked and stabbed me with his knife. I was so scared, I pulled my gun out, told him to back off, but he just kept coming at me with the knife. I feared for my life. My god, I was just trying to wound him, to stop him. He was so drunk, more than usual. Jesus, I loved him!" *Slow down, don't say too much, something you shouldn't. Wait until they ask you questions.*

"Well, we'll see, won't we?" Walsh said in his short, clipped, high-pitched voice. "Let's start at the beginning to get some basic facts."

I was sweating like crazy: my palms, chest, legs, neck, feet and forehead. *Menopause at twenty-eight*, I strangely thought.

I spent the next two hours answering Walsh's questions: About my family and childhood in California, why I came to Ireland, how I met Magnus, why we began dating, and how long we dated. I'd end up answering the same questions, sometimes phrased differently, time and time again.

After a bit, I relaxed a little, knowing that most of what I was describing was the truth. I just had to be careful and consistent with certain details. Walsh, however, with his constant smirking, condescension and innuendo, was making me mad. I needed to keep my temper in check and remain cool. It was like sparring with my mother back in Timberline, back in another life. She was a formidable adversary, and you had to keep your wits about you when dealing with her.

Walsh went on. "Miss Fitzhugh, let's talk more about your relationship with Mr. Herrington. You were aware he was married and had four children?"

"Yes."

"Yet you had no problem entering into an adulterous relationship with him?"

"No. Early on, he told me his marriage was broken. Some months in, he began talking about the two of us getting married once he divorced his wife."

"And were you pushing him to divorce his wife?"

"Are you kidding? No. I thought he was moving too fast. I didn't want to get married."

Walsh wrinkled his nose and appeared openly doubtful of this. "Really? How come?"

"I came over from California for a little fun. I wasn't wanting any entanglements. Over time, yes, I realized that maybe I was falling in love with him."

Saying that was like eating a jar of raw, pickled herring – nauseating. I felt sorry for Magnus at first, in spite of myself, but I never liked him and, in the end, pretty much loathed him.

"Why didn't you push him for a divorce then, if you loved him?"

"I said I was maybe falling in love. That's different from knowing without a doubt that I wanted us to spend the rest of our lives together.

He had a real alcohol problem, and it kept getting worse as time passed."

Crying softly now, I said, "He was violent with me now and again, and I really needed to leave him because of that, if for no other reason. Yet I couldn't bring myself to be finished with him. I'm not proud of that. That I was too weak to leave. But he was really good in lots of ways. I loved being with him most of the time." I reached for a tissue on the nightstand beside my hospital bed, wiped my eyes and blew my nose.

"What happened when he drank? What was so bad about it?"

"Really, Mr. Walsh? He was an angry drunk, belligerent, like a runaway lorry gathering speed as the night went along. And he was verbally abusive. He'd say terrible things to me; call me a bitch, a spoiled brat gash, tell me I didn't care about him and treated him like shit. That kind of thing."

"Was there ever any physical abuse?"

I made a face and laughed while pointing at my nose.

"You mean other than my broken nose and the stab wounds on my abdomen?"

Snidely, Walsh replied, "I mean, were there any other instances of that?"

Fuck off, Walsh! "Yes, but usually just when he'd been drinking too much."

It's so degrading to get into this with this asshole, but I need to do it. It's the truth after all.

"Magnus had some unusual and aggressive sexual demands. And he'd get carried away and do painful things to me when he'd been drinking. I tried to get him to stop, but he wouldn't. And when you love someone, you know, you try to do what turns them on and makes them happy. I'm sure your wife does that for you, right, Inspector Walsh?"

His eyes narrowed as he squeezed his pen tighter. Of course, he next asked me, "So, what kind of practices?"

I walked Walsh and Byrne through the whole domination/submission thing with Magnus. How what started as relatively light corporal punishment for me progressed to having my ass beaten with all manner of things so that it was often black and blue. The worst occasion was when he hit me with a wooden paddle with little tacks in it. I had to go to the GP the next day for stitches and have scars now.

After describing that, I asked Walsh, "Do you want to see, Inspector? Would you like that? I mean... would you like to look at my GP's medical records from my visit?"

Walsh, enjoying this now, pushed relentlessly into every aspect of my sex life with Magnus. How often did it happen? What did he like? What did I like? Did I come when we had sex? *Are you kidding? Never!*

He stood up, ran his right hand through his hair, and began pacing around the room. "What was the issue last night, Miss Fitzhugh? You claim a sexual disagreement of some sort with Mr. Herrington?"

Down into the gory details, Walsh relentlessly plunged.

"Inspector, the broad headlines are that Magnus was desperate for sex after three weeks apart, but my period had started. And he didn't like conventional sex then; it always had to be up the back passage during my monthly."

I wondered if this was making Byrne from Special Branch uncomfortable. Probably not.

"I resolved last month never to do that with him again when he was drunk because he was brutal. So rough. No lube. He'd pin me face down on the bed and hammer away forever while I cried out in agony. Eventually, I would quietly begin sobbing, helpless with the pain, anger and degradation, Inspector."

Walsh snorted and almost laughed. "According to you, Miss Fitzhugh, you willingly gave him what he wanted for almost a year, and then last month, you just decided to stop. Understandably, he didn't like it. Did you just decide to shoot him so you wouldn't have to do that anymore?"

Yes, partially. But he'd also scared the hell out of me.

"He attacked me, Inspector, with no warning, and I feared for my life. That's why he got shot. The only reason!" I made my voice break and started to cry again. "For god's sake, I cared deeply about him. This is devastating for me."

I reached for another tissue. "But yes. I expected him, my companion, and the man who said he loved me, to respect my wishes and not want to inflict intolerable pain on me. Why don't you treat your wife that way and see if she likes it, Inspector? Or, who knows, maybe you'd like it done to you, huh?"

He glared at me and said nothing.

Finally, after another hour of revisiting different aspects of my story, Walsh sarcastically said, "Well, Miss Fitzhugh, thank you for these illuminating facts and your interpretations of them. We will likely have more questions in the coming days and weeks, but I'm done for now. We won't be arresting you immediately and will just need to see how the charges play out. Thank you for your time."

"Uh, Inspector, I've just a few questions for Miss Fitzhugh as well," Samantha Byrne interjected. These were her first words in the entire three-plus hours.

"The sphinx speaks!" Walsh said, smirking. "I'd love to hear your questions for Miss Fitzhugh."

Byrne ignored him and sat up from the reclining position in the plastic chair she'd been frozen into. She looked me in the eye and, in a quiet, even cadence, asked, "Miss Fitzhugh, do you have any friends in Dublin?"

"Uh, not many, I suppose. A couple of mates I work with at the restaurant, but no others, really."

"So, you've been in Ireland for over a year, and these are the only people you know? And did these restaurant friends know about your relationship with Mr. Herrington? Did you confide in them? Tell them you might be in love? That you'd met this great bloke?"

Where is she going with this? "I might have mentioned it now and again after I'd seen him for a drink, but no, I didn't tell them we were in a relationship. I'm a private person about that kind of stuff."

"Yes, of course. Why don't you have more friends, Miss Fitzhugh? A beautiful young woman, come over to Ireland for, as you say, some fun and adventure. Where are your mates, weekend trips to London, Paris, or Amsterdam, that kind of thing?"

Take a deep breath, stay calm. "To be honest, Magnus kind of got in the way. I mean, I spent almost every weekend with him. And you know, he kinda just wanted to be with me, just the two of us."

"I see. And that was okay with you? Spending all your time with him? You never told him you were going out for a girls' night or suggested the two of you go out with your mates? Most people in a, hmm, let's say, functioning or genuine relationship do that kind of thing. But not you and Magnus, eh? You didn't want that?"

"No, uh, I guess not."

"Magnus was a lucky man, wasn't he? You were devoted to him and focused on only him. In some ways, he was almost your job, wasn't he?"

Oh, no. Don't lose it. Keep it together! "I... I... uh, never really thought about it that way, Inspector. I loved being with him most of the time."

"Fine." Byrne nodded. "Why am I not surprised to hear that? I'd just like to explore a couple of areas in a bit more detail, if you don't mind, and we'll be finished. As you acknowledged, the weapon that killed Mr. Herrington is yours. You obtained it illegally in Dublin for personal protection because you believed you lived in a bad area and usually walked home from your restaurant job late at night."

I nodded.

"But you've never had to use the gun for any reason until last night. The only time you'd fired it was a few quick shots in an alley in Dublin with the gentleman who sold it to you. So you could get some sense of how it worked. Correct?"

"Yes."

"So, why did you bring the gun to Enniskillen? You were going to be with Magnus for the weekend. Not back at work until Tuesday night."

Shit! It never occurred to me to leave it in Dublin. A major error. If I'd left it in Dublin, I wouldn't be in this mess. But on the other hand, I'd still be stuck in the Magnus assignment for god knows how long. I shrugged. "Just forgot it was in my bag, I guess."

"As it turns out, it's good you had it with you, right? And it's lucky that having never basically shot your weapon, you still managed to put numerous bullets into Mr. Herrington, including one between his eyes."

"Um, I don't know what to say. I mean, he was very close to me, just a meter or so away."

"Right. My last question is about your stab wounds. The knife you say was Mr. Herrington's. He brought it into the flat with him, but you'd never seen it before. Yes?"

I nodded again. "Correct."

"You told us he pulled it from his jacket pocket, advanced toward you, swung it at your abdomen, and stabbed you."

"Yes."

"Okay, fine, Miss Fitzhugh. That's a hunting knife and has quite a substantial blade. It seems it's another bit of good fortune for you that he only struck you a glancing blow, although a long one, across your stomach. Several layers of skin were cut open, and there was plenty of blood, but no organ damage and no deep puncture wounds."

"Well, yes, I'm unhappy about being stabbed, but glad it wasn't worse."

"Oh, of course, of course. You said he punched you in the face, broke your nose, and advanced toward you while you had your hands up to your face after he hit you. Is that right?"

I nodded again.

"And Mr. Herrington's punch didn't knock you off your feet? You took this devastating impact and remained standing. Really?"

"Yes, I've said that several times now."

"Sorry, sorry, yes, just checking. Then you saw Mr. Herrington draw the knife from his suit jacket pocket, step toward you, and thrust the knife toward your belly. You pulled an arm down just in time and managed to divert the knife, so it only cut lightly, horizontally, across your stomach, twice, as you pushed or pulled it away. Do I have that right?"

"I don't think he knifed me lightly. Is that how you'd describe it if you ended up with over forty stitches and almost bled to death?"

Chuckling just a little, Byrne added, "That is quite lucky indeed, Miss Fitzhugh. It almost never happens that way if someone is advancing to stab you in the abdomen. People usually end up with deep puncture wounds. Not a simple slicing wound like yours. Well, anyway, good on you for saving yourself."

"Yes, good on me."

"Then, in pushing the knife away, you upset your balance, fell backward onto the edge of the bed, bounced off, and landed on the floor. Mr. Herrington kept advancing toward you with the knife, and you retrieved your weapon and shot him five times."

"Yes," I replied. "Except some of the bullets missed, didn't they? It's not like I'm some expert marksman, which you seem to be implying."

"Right. Lovely. Thank you, Miss Fitzhugh. I've no more questions at this time."

6

It was hot for June and my cell stank more than usual, a pungent mix of cigarettes, BO, the toilet, and horrible institutional food. The rats didn't seem to mind. Nine of the ten women were sweating in our bunks, while the tenth, Patti, violently dry heaved in the cell's one open-air metal toilet next to the foot of my bunk. Prison food had again upended her sensitive stomach.

She'd been sick most of the day and irritatingly puked in a loud, anguished way, her stomach and esophagus roaring to escape the cage of her insides. She'd been whimpering for a doctor since morning, curled in the fetal position next to the toilet, but the guards couldn't have cared less. We kept cold cloths on her head, tried to get her to sip some water and stepped around when we needed the toilet. I just hoped her GI track would keep it together.

This was my third month at Mourne House, the women's wing of the Maghaberry prison outside Belfast. I was in the crowded general population wing rather than the more sparsely populated political section where they kept those convicted of crimes related to the IRA. This made sense because the authorities didn't know I was in the Provisionals, though Samantha Byrne of the Special Branch seemed convinced I was.

My cellmates ranged in age from their mid-twenties to early thirties. There were four drug dealers, three armed robbers, an epic embezzler, an arsonist and me, the only killer. Molly Fitzhugh had fifteen months left to serve for the Magnus business. However, I would likely be out in a year, depending on the overcrowding situation.

With nothing to fill my time or my mind, I found myself thinking a lot about my past life as Alexandra Davis, about Julie, Brian and about Timberline, the small city in northern Washington State where we'd all grown up. I'd loved Brian Findlay – still did maybe – and

Julie was the sister I'd never had. I missed them. They were the best people I knew and had both overcome obstacles in their lives that would have broken most.

Yet I'd dishonestly cast them out in '88 and '89 – pushed them away for this new life. I didn't yet have regrets for doing this – those would come later – but I often wondered if I'd needed to do it with the sense of finality that I'd chosen.

As far as Julie, Brian, my parents and the people of Timberline were concerned, Alexandra Davis died in a tragic accident in February 1989. Her car slid off an icy two-lane road in Maine during a blizzard, careened down a steep ravine and plunged into a deep lake that drained into the ocean. Authorities located the car in two hundred feet of water in the spring but never found her body.

• • •

Just after midnight. The prison and our cell were finally quiet. Patti had stopped heaving a few hours before. She was now asleep with everyone else. I didn't sleep much since coming here – three to four fitful hours every night if I was lucky. Insomnia, very kind of her, was loyally serving my sentence with me.

Unbeknownst to them, I had become a student of my cellmates' nighttime habits: Who got up to pee in the night. Who talked in their sleep. Who fidgeted, and who slept like a stone. Which of the women masturbated, and how often. All, it turned out.

At first, discovering this was quite surprising to me, as it was something I'd only done, basically unsuccessfully, a few times in college. But over time, alone and awake with nothing to do, I couldn't help but notice my cellmates. Soon I knew which ones came quickly and which ones had to really work at it. Which ones quietly shuddered and who struggled to keep quiet, biting into the blanket or pillow as their hips bucked and body contorted. None of my cellmates ever saw me doing that. I seemed to be dead down there, fairly sure Magnus Herrington had something to do with it. The Provisionals don't mention that as a duty hazard on their recruiting posters.

At first, when it all went bad, I struggled to gain any sort of equilibrium. It was like I was again back in Timberline in the fourth grade, learning to ski, my first run on the big hill after moving from the rope tow. Before I knew it, I was out of control and picking up speed. Faster, faster. Why couldn't I just make myself fall in the snow to stop? I flew off the trail into the woods and slammed into a tree. Enveloped in dazed silence, pain, blood and the distant sounds of help on the way, it was the first bad thing that had ever happened to me. I was lucky – only a concussion, two broken wrists and fifteen stitches across my forehead, like the bride of Frankenstein.

This time, the ride was equally fast and terrifying. Arrested a week after leaving the hospital, locked up for six days in jail, released, given the plea deal, sentenced. Afterward, I had two weeks to get my affairs in order. Then was bused to the prison with other women and manhandled through the intake process. "Strip, squat, spread your knees wide, lean forward and cough," the men and butch women barked. Next, a gloved finger was roughly inserted up my vagina and butt, prison clothes were thrust at me, and then followed a nervous introduction to my cellmates.

I hadn't spoken to Maeve since our December 1990 meeting in Berlin, more than eighteen months prior. But I'd heard from her. That night in the ER of Enniskillen hospital, as I was adrift in a narcotic haze of painkillers, a nurse approached, bent down and whispered in my ear. "I have a message from Maeve: 'Stay strong, love. Stick to your cover. We are with you.'"

A day after I'd met Inspectors Walsh and Byrne, a member of the Queen's Council – a lawyer – appeared on my behalf to (unbeknownst to her) abet my lies. Paid by my *parents* in California, she was given the task of helping me thwart the efforts of the RUC and Special Branch to send me away for at least five years for the shooting and the illegal gun I owned. Unless, of course, I was willing to admit I'd been planted by the Provisionals and choose to inform against them.

Late one night, when I got back to my flat, an envelope had been pushed through the mail slot.

> You will be offered a plea arrangement for involuntary man-slaughter. Take the plea and serve your time. It will be no more than eighteen months and likely just a year. Nothing bad will happen to you in prison. We still have major plans for you. It's unfortunate how things ended, but we understand why you acted as you did.

But did they? Did that mean they believed the self-defense story? Or not? Would they think less of me now for killing an intelligence source? I hoped the note meant Maeve and the organization trusted me. Though if they had any hint I was unreliable, I'd have been dead before I ever darkened the prison doorstep.

In the end, things happened as I'd been told. I got involuntary manslaughter. Magnus had a history of chasing women, and his drinking problem was known to MI-5. Thus, the British authorities were perhaps more willing to accept my story and not dig too deeply. Samantha Byrne must have been overruled. It's as if the Brits just said, "Fine, let's keep it out of the press and be done with it. Magnus Herrington's mistress killed him in a lover's quarrel while he was drunk and beating her."

· · ·

I tried not to think much about Magnus in prison but wasn't successful. I told myself he was an alcoholic brute, that his wife and children were better off without him. But he loved his wife in his cruel, clumsy way. I'd come to realize this over time, though he said awful things about her when he was drunk. Magnus adored his kids, even when he was obliterated by alcohol. He often spewed out his guilt over missing them growing up and told me all about their hobbies, sports and school projects. He talked about quitting MI-5 and moving his family to the north of England to a small farm where they could afford a simple, quiet life.

As MI-5's guy in Derry, Magnus was an enemy of the Provisionals, but he wasn't a willing tout or traitor – just a soldier on the other side doing his job, like me, and I respected him for that.

Painful as it was, I had to admit I'd been weak. I'd killed Magnus in a terrified rage because I was tired of his verbal and sexual abuse. Though I'd signed up for it as part of my job. "No Disney in your knickers," Maeve had warned. Still, I was tired of being sexually manhandled, if not mutilated, and increasingly fearful of his unhinged drunken rages. The thought of that continuing indefinitely was just too much for me.

I thought less about Jimmy Doyle back in Maine. Until I learned differently, much later, I saw Jimmy as a traitor. He should have thought about leaving his pregnant wife and ill son widowed and alone with no money when he volunteered to help the British and tip them to our arms shipment. And the woman in the gas station, Angie Cruz or whatever her name was – well, I never knew her, and her death was an accident in some ways, Jimmy's fault maybe for stopping for gas. It was easier that way. That's what I tried to tell myself anyway.

Later, though, Patricia Maguire would haunt my dreams. She shouldn't have – she was just another justified casualty of war in an operation I was on after I got out of prison. That was what I told myself, but she nonetheless appeared regularly – a persistent and resolute woman, she wouldn't let me go. "Miss… you, miss, up there, you knows yooose going to hell for this too. I will get through those gates in heaven but not you – yooose will burn forever."

7

Julie Mitchell-Delacroix

Julie awoke crumpled on the floor outside the girls' bedroom. It was just after four in the morning, and only a dim night light pierced the blackness of the town house. She shivered, freezing. The March wind howled outside the thin walls, and the furnace had yet to kick on to raise the overnight temperature from sixty degrees to sixty-six. Getting up to go to the bathroom, she pieced together what had happened.

Another panic attack. In a precarious state, she'd gone to comfort one of the girls around ten after a nightmare, and leaving their bedroom, she'd collapsed with a racing heart and chest pains in a cold sweat. Since she'd hardly slept in three days, she'd eventually fallen asleep after the panic abated.

She knew she was in trouble and needed help. For the first time in five years, she'd fallen deep into the mental health ditch. Debilitating fear and anxiety again ruled her life. She worried about her husband Tim's safety, the effect of his absence on the girls, and her own fragile mental state. Tim's October deployment to South Korea had triggered it, and while she knew this was a reality of army life, it was his first station since they'd moved to Fort Riley from Los Angeles in '86. She and the girls had also just spent their first Christmas alone on base.

The Alex situation didn't help either. First, she'd cut Julie out of her life with that letter four months earlier, and last month – unbelievably – she was dead in a car accident. Just over ten years after her own mom had been killed by a drunk driver in Timberline. Alex's words in her November letter seared themselves into Julie's brain:

Julie, I'm writing to say I won't be coming to Kansas to spend Christmas with you and the girls. I know you will be alone with Tim deployed, but I just can't do it. I have tried and tried to muster the enthusiasm to see you again after we saw each other last year, but I think our friendship no longer makes sense, given where we're at in our respective lives. We're heading in different directions, so I think the best course of action is to appreciate our past but cut ties for the future. We are both strong-willed women, and to be honest, I just don't want to keep you in my life. I'm not going to change my mind, so please don't write back and don't otherwise try to contact me.

Respectfully, Alex

Devastated, Julie first racked her brain to think about what she could have done to cause the breach. But now Julie was thinking the issue had been something in Alex's life and was not her fault. Or was that wishful thinking? Regardless, it was a gaping wound, and now Alex was dead, so she would never understand more. Thankfully, the girls consumed most of her time and energy to keep her from dwelling on that and the reality of Tim in a danger zone.

The four girls were usually up by seven, and Julie led the weekday scramble to get her two sets of twins to school and preschool. Faith and Hope, six, were in the same first-grade class; and Charlotte and Lauren, three, only did half-days. Her phone rang as she returned home at a quarter to nine in early April.

"Hello, this is Julie."

"Hi Julie, it's Karen Mosely."

"Oh, hello, Mrs. Mosely. What can I do for you?"

"Please, just call me Karen, Julie."

Karen Mosely was the wife of Colonel Albert Mosely, who commanded the 16th regiment of the First Infantry Division. The regiment had six battalions with a total of roughly seven thousand soldiers, and Tim was one of them. Though Tim was just a First Lieutenant, he'd been temporarily assigned to take over A-Company, First Battalion with its one hundred and fifty soldiers, when its leader was diagnosed with testicular cancer. That meant Colonel Mosely was Tim's boss' boss. Both men, along with half the regiment, were currently deployed in South Korea, hopefully just until October.

"Julie, I've been meaning to get to this for weeks, but life's been crazy. I was wondering if you might be free to come over to the house today for lunch? It's important for me to meet and get close to the officer's wives in Al's battalion. I think we've said hello to each other a couple of times in the past year, but that's it. Forgive me. I've been negligent in this area."

"Oh, no problem Mrs… er… Karen. Yes, I'd love to come over. It's so thoughtful of you to invite me."

"Great, let's say 13:00 at my place."

• • •

Driving the several miles from the junior officer townhouse neighborhoods on base to senior officer country, filled with large, stately homes surrounded by moats of grass and landscaping, Julie was nervous. She didn't know Karen and wondered if she had an agenda broader than just getting acquainted. The invitation had upended Julie's morning. First, she needed to arrange afternoon childcare for her youngest girls. Thank goodness her friend Nicki next door was available.

Then she had to find something nicer than casual to wear. Military etiquette dictated certain fashion standards when "calling at the home of a senior officer." Julie sifted through the limited options in her closet and reluctantly settled on a simple black skirt once she'd cleaned the vomit off of it from Christmas Eve. Though a nightmare at the time, Julie couldn't help but laugh about it now. At a quiet point during mass, Charlotte started squirming and trying to leave the pew. Julie quietly scolded her, at which point Charlotte said, for all to hear, "The man next to us farted, and it smells."

Julie had immediately whispered, "I'm so sorry," and after mass, sought out the man, a general, and his wife to apologize profusely. As she was doing that, Faith projectile-vomited, and Julie's skirt had been a casualty. The general eyed her coldly, said nothing and walked away, but the general's wife had icily told her, "Who are our children going to learn manners from if they can't from their mother?" *What a bitch,* Julie had thought at the time, and she still felt that way. Tim had been able to call the day after Christmas and roared with laughter when Julie told him the story. "If only Faith had barfed on the general's wife; no better Christmas present for the cranky hag," Tim had opined.

Julie and Karen settled onto facing floral chintz sofas in the Mosely's living room. Pots of coffee and tea, soft drinks and a plate of sandwiches sat between them on a glass coffee table. Julie liked the décor in the Moselys' house. Nice furniture and fixtures but nothing ornate or formal. Pictures on walls and bookshelves depicted the Moseleys in their younger days with children, and more recent photos showed them as adults. A pine-scented candle infused the air with a warm aroma, and a wood fire blazed away. Julie guessed Karen was in her forties. She had an oval face, a bit of a pointed chin and auburn hair that dropped just below her shoulders and framed bright blue eyes. She wore faded blue jeans with frayed cuffs, a simple white long-sleeved blouse, and was barefoot.

Great, I'm hopelessly overdressed, Julie had immediately thought.

"It's so good to see you, Julie. Thanks for coming. You look fantastic! I'm so sorry. I should have told you on the phone not to dress up for me. Army etiquette be damned, but next time you come over, I am casual all the time here. And in the summer, when it's so damned hot, just wear tennis shorts and a T-shirt or something."

"Thank you. My stomach dropped when you answered the door, and I thought I'd messed up the 'Learning to be an Army Wife' code or something."

"Not at all. What are you drinking?"

"Coffee, please."

Karen poured a cup for Julie and chose tea for herself. "Shall we dig in?"

As they were eating, Karen explained that Colonel Mosely, aka "Al," had been in the army for twenty-five years and joined after college via the ROTC program at Michigan State. They had met in college and married right after. They'd been back at Fort Riley only a year, but this was their third time posted there, so she knew the landscape well.

Toward the end of their sandwiches, while refilling Julie's coffee, Karen asked, "How long have you and your husband been on base?"

"Over two years, since late '86. Tim, my husband, did ROTC at UCLA, then the infantry and Ranger schools, and I stayed in LA with the girls until we came here."

"How many kids and how old? Young, I bet."

Julie nodded. "We have two sets of twin girls. Faith and Hope are six, and Charlotte and Lauren are three."

"Wow, you have your hands full. How old are you anyway?"

"Twenty-four."

"How do you do it? Married young obviously?"

Julie grinned. "Yes. Tim and I went to high school together. Met in seventh grade, actually."

Karen chuckled. "Our oldest is twenty-five, and I'd like to think she could manage with just one kid now, but I've got my doubts. I've also got two daughters-in-law – one your age and another that's twenty-one. I have to admit, I'm happy not to be a grandma at forty-seven. What's your mom think about that?"

"Uh, um…my mom passed away during my sophomore year in high school."

"Oh, honey, I'm so sorry. What happened?"

"Killed in a car accident. Drunk driver."

"You poor thing. And your dad?"

Julie sipped her coffee and shook her head. "He left my mom when I was three and was never in the picture. It was always just mom and me."

Karen reached across the table and put her hand on Julie's knee. "Sweetie, where'd you live after that? Relatives?"

"No. Foster homes in Timberline."

"Where?"

"Oh, sorry. Timberline, Washington. It's a small town in Washington State near the Canadian border. Mom got transferred there before I started seventh grade."

Karen drew her hand back. "I feel for you. I was an orphan too. My mom died of cancer in '51 when I was ten, and my dad was a Marine killed on Okinawa in '45. There were no workable relative solutions, so I lived in a bunch of orphanages until I went to college."

"Wow," Julie said. "I'm so sorry."

Karen shrugged. "Well, I have a sense of these things, and I can tell you are a very capable and strong woman. Your husband's a lucky man."

Julie blushed. "That's so nice of you to say. Thank you."

"And you look great Julie – especially after four kids. You look like a model. My daughter's very pretty also, but she'd kill for your long dark hair and those lustrous cobalt eyes."

Julie laughed. "Well, nobody would have wanted to see me in junior high and high school. Flat chest, flat butt, zits, glasses and a mouth full of braces, with headgear even. Tim teases me now and says that by high school graduation, I'd progressed to an attractive librarian sort."

Karen excused herself to answer the phone and, when she returned, asked, "I heard you're going to college now?"

"Just part-time. Getting pregnant slowed my progress. But I've almost got my bachelor's. Between AP high school credits, a college summer in high school, some college in Indiana, classes at UCLA, and now K-State, I should be done next year, hopefully before we all deploy to Germany."

"Good for you. What are you studying?"

"Physics. I've always been a total math and science nerd. I couldn't play a sport to save my life growing up."

They talked a bit more about Julie's background before Karen asked, "Do you get much help from the other wives in the company with the officer spouse stuff? You know, helping out the wives of your enlisted people in the company?"

Julie shook her head. "Except for Tim, all the lieutenants in A-Company are unmarried. And I don't really know anyone in the other companies since Tim just got put in charge two weeks before they left."

Karen made a face. "Hmm. Okay, leave this with me. I've got to get you connected with the wives in Tim's peer companies. You all need to help each other with day-to-day stuff and also, god forbid, if something goes wrong over there."

Julie, a little scared now, nodded. "Yeah, sure, that would be great, thank you."

"We're halfway home; the regiment will be back in six months, assuming nothing goes wrong."

Julie furrowed her brow and asked, "What do you mean?"

Karen waved her right hand. "Oh, nothing, sorry. I'm sure everything will be fine. South Korea is an interesting place. I never expect full-on war; it's just that bad things seem to happen over there, weird things, little spats with the North Koreans that somehow end in tragedy. This is Al's fourth time in country. I'm always just a little more on edge when he's there."

Julie laughed nervously. "Well, I hope nothing goes wrong."

Karen leaned in toward Julie. "I hate to bring up such a grim topic, but it is one of the reasons I wanted to get together in addition to my tardiness in getting to know you better. What do you know about this predator lurking around the base?"

Julie inadvertently sucked in her breath. She'd wanted to ask Karen about this, but the topic set her on edge, nonetheless. "I heard there have been some rapes. A few?"

Karen shook her head. "It's worse. Seven rapes in the past six months. And the bastard's escalating. He killed the last two victims after he'd raped them. The authorities think that may be his pattern going forward but aren't sure."

Julie's hands shot to her mouth, and she exclaimed, "Oh my god! Why haven't I heard about that?"

"They're trying to keep the murders quiet. The first five rape victims were spouses of soldiers, but the two murdered women only worked on base and had no family in the area. They think it's the same guy but have no leads that I know of."

Her anxiety building, Julie chewed her lower lip – an unconscious reaction to stress.

"Also," Karen added, "be sure the wives in your company are taking precautions and being careful, using a buddy system. We don't want to panic them, but everyone needs to be reminded to take precautions. All the colonels' wives in the First Infantry Division were called to a briefing on this last week and told to disseminate the information to the wives in their units. How many wives do you have in A-Company?"

"Fifty. What does the army know about the guy?"

"Not much. All the victims had dark hair and were attacked in either their homes or walking to or from their cars in remote areas. Julie, do you and Tim have a gun in your house? I know with little kids that's tricky."

"Uh, no. Not with Tim deployed."

"Do you know how to use one?"

My God! Is it that dangerous here?

"I do, actually, Karen. Before Tim deployed, we went to the range every Sunday afternoon to shoot. He felt it was a life skill I needed. It was also sort of a weekly date afternoon. And as it turns out, I'm pretty good at it. Tim told me I'd be considered a sharpshooter if I was in his unit."

Karen sighed. "Honey, be sure you keep those skills up to date, just in case. And I'd get a gun to keep in your house. I hate to end our lunch on such a topic, but I need to get going. I don't want you to feel obligated, but I really feel a good connection between us, see a bit of myself in you. I'd love to try to have lunch or breakfast together at least once a month."

"Oh, wow, that would be great. Thank you so much."

"And—" Karen pointed at Julie. "Know I am always here for you. Call me if you need anything or are having any problems. Okay?"

Julie nodded as happy relief flowed through her. "Yes, yes."

8

The Kansas heat shimmered off the roads and sidewalks like cobras rising out of baskets, Julie thought. It was the middle of June, and the ninety-nine-degree heat and high humidity had her sweating through her white tennis shorts and yellow polo shirt within minutes of leaving home. The air conditioner on her 102,000 mile Ford Taurus wagon had quit the week before, and she hadn't yet dealt with that. Julie was headed to Karen Mosely's for a lunch with the wives of the other company commanders in Al's battalion.

Julie was in a better mental state now than in the dark months of December through March. In February, she'd found a psychologist on base for weekly sessions and also saw a psychiatrist monthly who adjusted and monitored her meds. She and the girls were able to speak by phone with Tim at least once a month. Her last panic attack had been in early February, and between the girls, her one college class and battalion family activities and duties, her days were more than full. Most nights, she fell exhausted into bed.

Julie lingered briefly at Karen's after the other wives had left. Since April, she'd seen Karen at least once a month, and Julie felt close to her. She'd taken the girls over to Karen's a couple of times and even felt comfortable enough to tell Karen about the Christmas Eve fart and vomit misadventures with the general and his wife. Karen loved the story and confirmed Julie's diagnosis that the general's wife was basically a bitch.

Karen walked Julie to her tired Ford, its windows down and cloth seats cooking. The two women hugged and Karen said, "Bye, sweetie. I'll talk to you soon." Just then, a man came toward them in the street, walking a large black Doberman with a muzzle. Julie saw that he was a muscular, compact man, about five-eight, with blue eyes and a blondish high and tight buzz cut. She guessed he was mid to late thirties. He wore running shoes, short, tight-fitting US Army black gym shorts and a sweat-soaked gray tank top.

He smiled and said, "Good afternoon, Mrs. Mosely," his thick southern accent evident. He nodded at Julie and said, "Ma'am."

"Good afternoon, Major Paltz," Karen crisply replied.

After he'd passed by, Karen made a bit of a face and shook her head. It was barely noticeable.

Julie raised her eyebrows. "Hmm, something I should know about him?"

"That's Jody," Karen said dismissively.

"Jody Paltz, he's a major?" Julie asked.

Karen laughed. "No, honey. That's Major Andrew Paltz, but he's Jody among those in the know."

Julie shrugged and said, "Why?"

"Jody," Karen began, "an army term that's been around forever. Jody is the guy back on base who sleeps with men's wives while they're deployed overseas. He's washed out of multiple combat units and has an administrative post on base now."

"Why's he still in the army, then?"

"Good question, hon. Lots of people wonder that."

9

It was Friday afternoon. Crowds thronged the PX, heading into a scorching Labor Day weekend. Julie questioned herself for not coming earlier in the week. It wasn't like she had any big shopping to do for the weekend; she and the girls would be alone at home, a few sweltering trips to the park and one of the community pools on base the only things on their agenda. Heading to their steamy car, Julie worked her usual balancing act, keeping the grocery cart moving with the four girls holding on and walking beside it.

She loaded the girls into their car seats – two in the middle seat and two in the tiny third-row, and then put the groceries in the front. Finished, she quickly returned the shopping cart to a corral about twenty feet away. As she approached the car again, someone bumped her from behind.

"Oh my gosh, excuse me, I'm so sorry," the man said as Julie turned to face him. "Wait, didn't we meet back in June? Were you with Colonel Mosely's wife outside their house? I was walking by with my dog."

"Yes, yes, of course, I remember. You're, uh, um, Major Paltz, right?" Julie caught herself just in time. She was about to call him Jody.

"How do you know my name? The colonel's wife didn't introduce us."

Julie smiled. "She told me your name after you'd walked on with your dog."

"Well, uh, Julie, is it? It's nice to meet you."

"Yes," Julie said. "Now, how do you know my name? Since, as you said, we weren't introduced."

"I'm glad to see you again, Julie. Do you and your husband have big three-day weekend plans?"

"No." Julie suspected he knew Tim was overseas. "My husband is in South Korea with the First Battalion."

"Oh, what unit? Is he an NCO?" Paltz smirked ever so slightly.

Julie shook her head. "He leads A-Company." Pointing at the Taurus, she said, "Now, if you'll excuse me please, Major, I've got to get these girls home. It's so hot."

As if on cue, Faith whined, "Mama, I'm hot and thirsty. Can we go home?"

Paltz acknowledged the Taurus. "Four girls – you're busy. They all have beautiful dark hair and eyes, just like their mother. Makes me wonder what your husband contributed," he joked.

Moving away from him, Julie said, "Have a nice weekend, Major Paltz," before quickly getting into the wagon and driving away.

10

September vanished in a blur; Julie was so busy. Tim and the battalion were now due back from the DMZ in November – their tour had been extended by a month. She knew it was best not to dwell on that and count the days, and to instead keep living day to day, but it was hard.

She'd had two more uncomfortable, allegedly 'coincidental' encounters with Major Paltz. A week after Labor Day, he was walking his Doberman on her street, saw her returning with the girls from school, and ambled over. More forced small talk ensued, and after a few minutes, Julie pled the need to move along and tend to her kids.

Then last week, he'd shown up on her doorstep in the evening around 19:00, claiming he'd been walking down her street and seen someone rooting around in her Taurus. As always, she'd parked in her spot in the carport at the side of the row of townhouses. Paltz said he'd scared the person off and asked Julie if she'd like him to accompany her out to the car to see if anything was missing. Julie firmly declined and thanked him. Then he'd asked to come in to get a glass of water, to which Julie had said, "I'm sorry, Major, I can't. I'm not comfortable with that." His tight smile had vanished, and Julie thought she saw him struggling to control a flash of anger. She quickly said, "Good night, Major," practically slammed the door and locked it, her heart racing.

After fretting about the Paltz encounters for a few days and telling herself not to be paranoid, Julie called Karen Mosely. Karen was a busy woman, and Julie didn't want her to think she was some alarmist baby, but she finally decided to pick up the phone.

"Uh, hi, Karen, it's Julie… Julie Delacroix."

"Hi, hon, how are you? Is everything okay?"

"Yeah, um, sure. I… I mean, I think so."

"You home?" Karen asked.

"Yes."

"Stay there. I'm coming over."

"You don't have to do that."

"Nonsense. I know you well enough, Julie, to know you wouldn't be calling me and hedging like that if this was nothing."

Fifteen minutes later, Karen had a big hug for Julie and was seated with her and a coffee pot at a small table in Julie's humble kitchen.

"Out with it, babe," Karen said. "What's bothering you?"

"Sooo," Julie began, "you remember back in June at your house when, uh, Jody walked by?"

Karen furrowed her eyebrows and nodded.

"Well, based on what you said, I assumed that he's been known to have affairs with other men's wives. And those were like consensual situations, right? The wives chose to have affairs with him. He didn't force them, right?"

Julie recapped her encounters with Paltz and how he seemed to be showing up in her life uncomfortably often.

"Hmm…" Karen said. "To my knowledge – not perfect information, mind you – he's been with at least six married women in the past three years. About half of them thought he was going to leave his wife for them, and the others just wanted some casual sex, but all of those situations were consensual as far as I know."

"Were these officers' wives?" Julie asked.

"Some, yes, but also some enlisted wives."

"Isn't adultery a crime in the army? I mean, why is he still on the base and in the military?"

Karen sighed. "The army isn't good with sex stuff. It's hell to be a woman in or around the army in these situations. You can't win. You're both victim and perpetrator."

"Well, as long as it's consensual with these women, then I'm not worried. He's creepy, but I can handle that."

"I also," Julie said, "heard there had been another rape on base last week. That's eight or nine women now in less than a year, right?"

"Yeah. Wouldn't surprise me if there had been more. Women are often afraid to come forward because they figure the army won't take it seriously, or they were scheduled to be transferred to a new post, so they just let it go. That kind of thing."

A pit forming in her stomach, Julie asked, "Did he murder the woman last week or just rape her?"

Karen took Julie's hand. "He tried but failed. After he'd raped her, she tried to pull off his ski mask but couldn't. He went crazy and beat the hell out of her. She's still in the ICU. It was touch and go for a few days, but it looks like she'll live."

Julie chewed her lower lip. "My god, that poor woman! She sat silent for half a minute before asking, "You don't think this guy could be Major Paltz, do you? Oh, listen to me, I'm just paranoid, I hope."

"Anything is possible, Julie. You know that. But, I don't know, why would he do it if all these other women sleep with him willingly?"

11

In early October, the phone by Julie's bed rang at 04:00. She sprang upright, wide awake as if dropped on a trampoline.

"Hello."

"Julie, it's Karen. We have a tragedy, and I need your help." Her voice was trembling, and this scared Julie to death.

"No, no!" Julie gasped. "Oh my god, Tim, Tim, what happened? No! No!"

"Julie, Julie, listen to me! Tim is fine. But others aren't, and I need you."

"Okay, okay, I'm sorry. What's happened?"

Later, Julie realized that if Tim had been killed, an officer in dress blues and a chaplain would have rung her doorbell at four in the morning, and nobody would have called.

"North Koreans took down a helicopter with a missile on the DMZ. The bastards. We have three KIA from a platoon in the battalion and two pilots not from the base."

Karen continued. "The men were from B-Company: a platoon leader, Lieutenant James, and two of his NCOs. You won't hear from Tim for several days. When something like this happens, they lock down communications from over there to control information flow until they can officially notify the families."

Julie's head was swimming. What if Tim wasn't okay and Karen just didn't know or wasn't telling her? And those poor families! *Stop it! Focus! You can't worry now!* "What do you need me to do, Karen?"

"Captain Frazier, The B-Company leader over there, isn't married, so he has no wife to lead support on base for the families of his company. The wife of C-Company's leader is out of state for at least a week with her dying father. D and E Company's leaders are both divorced. It's you and me, Julie – we are going to have to coordinate support for the families of B-Company. These are going to be some horrible days, so prepare yourself."

Her stomach jumping, Julie replied, "Alright, what should I do?"

"First, make arrangements for childcare for your girls. Assume you'll be busy all of the next few days, then half-days for a week after that. If you have an issue on such short notice, let me know, and I'll find a way to make something happen on childcare for you."

Julie began searching on her nightstand for a pen and paper to take notes. Finally, she found a pizza delivery coupon under the lamp.

"The notification to the families will likely come midday to early afternoon today. Once that happens, I will immediately call the officers' wives in B-Company. There are three of them, excluding Amy James, the lieutenant's widow. You and I will go meet with them ASAP. As the wife of a company commander, you will be their leader and point person with other base personnel for coordinating support for Amy and the wives of the sergeants who were killed. Their names are Becky Noth and Darla Bedell."

"Okay, sure," Julie said. "Sorry, but what all does this include – like anything and everything?"

"Exactly. Arrange two weeks of meals for the families, make sure their childcare is squared away, meet and help any out-of-town families that come onto base, go to the cleaners or iron clothes if needed, and buy funeral clothes for the kids if they don't have them. Whatever those families need, you make sure it happens. Keep receipts, and I will get everyone reimbursed. And delegate, Julie, you can't do all of this by yourself. Get the officers' and NCOs' wives in B-Company and your A-Company wives to help."

"Uh, okay," Julie said, hoping she was up for this.

"A couple more things," Karen said. "You and I will talk twice a day, at 08:00 and 16:00, to touch base, see where we are, and see what you need from me. Our first call will be this afternoon. Be sure you've contacted all the A-Company wives by then and gotten them organized. I will spin up other resources on base that we might need."

"Okay, okay." Julie's head was swirling as she scribbled things down.

"Julie," Karen said. "Other than caring for Tim and your girls, nothing you do as an army wife will be more important than this. The families in that platoon in B-Company need someone to take charge, someone to lead, and that is you. Sadly, the army is very good at this. It's a solemn ritual that will unfold with minute attention to detail and process. Just be sure the families get what they need, the things the scripted army process won't deliver. Julie, you can do this – don't let me down."

• • •

For Julie, the next week often felt like being a passenger on a speeding train; people, sounds, events and smells flashed by, often blurred and indistinct. Other times, it was as if she were on an airplane, a constant noise in her ears, clearly present in particular moments but unable to see outside to get her bearings and ascertain where exactly she was.

Nights were the worst. Though she was exhausted after days with the families and then evenings getting the girls fed, bathed, read to and put to bed, sleep eluded her. Each day's tears and raw emotions flung themselves at her again and again. Wives, children, parents and siblings trying to grasp what they always knew was possible but couldn't imagine happening. Some wept quietly or simply leaked tears all day, while others wailed and sobbed, doubled over with anguish.

Julie had to tune it out during the day, telling herself to focus, anticipate needs and problems and see that they were taken care of. Worries about Tim's safety and reliving her mother's death ten years prior also unsettled her and put knots in her stomach – so much so that bouts of low-grade nausea plagued her, and she found it hard to eat.

Dealing with Amy James, wife of the Lieutenant from B-Company who'd been killed, was gut-wrenching. She was Julie, after all; there but for the benevolence of god could have been her. Amy was twenty-two, from a small mill town in northern Maine. She and Billy had met in high school and gotten married when he was half-finished at the University of Maine. He'd done ROTC and gone into the army. They had two girls, three years old and six months, and the youngest would never know her father.

One evening Julie stopped by to drop off something Amy needed from the pharmacy. Amy offered tea, and Julie ended up staying and talking with her for over two hours. Toward the end of the conversation, Julie began feeling overwhelmed, afraid she would get emotional and fall to pieces. She hustled out of Amy's townhouse, drove the short distance home, paid the babysitter, checked on her sleeping girls, and then collapsed into sobs and a puddle of tears.

• • •

A couple of days later, she needed to take Sergeant Noth's sixteen-year-old daughter Sara shopping for a dress for his memorial service. Sara's mom was not up to it, and the few out-of-town relatives had yet to arrive. Julie picked Sara up at her family's base apartment building and introduced herself. Sara was pretty in a plain kind of way; about five-two, Julie guessed, thin with shoulder-length dirty blonde hair. She wore jeans, black boots and a red University of Kansas T-shirt.

Walking to her Taurus with Sara, Julie chuckled and said, "I'm sorry, the air conditioning in my car quit last summer and I haven't been able to get it fixed yet. It's still so hot here in October. I grew up near the Canadian border out west, and often we had snow on the ground by now."

Sara climbed into the passenger seat, mute.

After a couple of miles of silence, Julie asked, "How long have you lived at Fort Riley, Sara?"

Finally, she spoke quietly, "About two years. I started freshman year here."

"Where'd you live before that?"

"Georgia. Dad was at Fort Benning for three years. Before that, we were in Panama, Kentucky and Alabama."

"Wow, that must have been hard for you, changing schools all the time, having to make new friends."

Sara shrugged.

"Well, good for you. I'm sure you could teach me things about being in an army family," Julie said. "We moved here about three years ago when my husband Tim went into the army." She laughed and said, "Let me tell you, I learn new things every day. I make mistakes all the time."

"My mom said your husband's an officer, right? Over in Korea like my dad?"

"Yes. He's a lieutenant in A-Company, First Battalion."

"Did he know my dad?"

Julie's voice caught as she said, "No honey, I don't think he did. But I know your dad was a great soldier. So brave. Protecting all of us."

Julie quickly removed her tortoiseshell glasses to swipe a tear from her cheek with the back of her hand while Sara stared out the front window.

Julie asked, "Do you have any particular place you'd like to go to look for a dress and anything else you might need?"

Sara shrugged. "We usually just go to the PX or the Wal-Mart off base."

"Well, those are good places. We buy lots of things there too. But I hear there's a nice dress shop a few miles off base." Julie smiled at her. "I've not been there, but what do you say? Shall we check it out? Then I thought we could grab some lunch if you wanted."

Sara shrugged. "Sure, okay."

At first, Sara tried on two dresses and didn't come out of the dressing room to show Julie. But with the third, she did.

"Oh, look at you," Julie enthused. "That's so pretty! But I think maybe one size smaller in that would make you look even better."

Sara tried on six dresses and picked a flattering dark green floral print. Julie insisted she get shoes also since she apparently only owned sneakers, a pair of hiking shoes and her favorite, the pair of black Doc Martens boots she was wearing.

At the register, Julie quickly did a mental calculation of her debit-card balance as well as the credit limit remaining on her Visa. Which was the lesser of two evils? Enough room – just – on the Visa, she figured as she handed it over. As they were leaving the shop, Sara kind of grinned at Julie and said, "I figured I should listen to you because you dress really nicely. I can tell you have style."

"Wow. Thank you! That's the nicest thing anyone's said to me in a long time."

Still grinning, Sara continued, "But I'm a midget compared to you. What are you, like six-four? Did you play basketball?"

Julie burst out laughing. "I'm not six-four, more like six foot. And I couldn't throw, catch, kick, dribble, or shoot any kind of ball to save my life. I have always been a total geek. What about you? Do you play sports?"

She nodded. "Soccer."

"I bet you're something on the field. Fast and good with the ball, I'd guess. Am I right?"

"Yeah, okay, maybe."

"What about lunch?" Julie asked. "How about Fergie's? I love their shakes and fries and the bacon cheeseburger. That's my go-to order. Have you been?"

Sara nodded. "I love that place, though I haven't been in a long time."

"Well, it's a date then!" Julie exclaimed.

Once settled with their food at Fergie's, a hole-in-the-wall burger place five miles off base, Julie asked Sara about her younger brother, her soccer team and school. Though not expansive by any means, Sara engaged with her.

Julie asked, "So, what about after high school? Are you thinking about college?"

"I guess. My parents always said I should go but didn't know if we'd have the money."

"There's always a way, Sara. Work hard in school, and if you want to go badly enough, you can make it happen. Don't be afraid to reach out to people at the high school for help to figure it all out. And I'm happy to help, too, if I can."

"Did you go to college?" Sara asked.

"I'm going now. College was always part of my plan; I was going to go straight through when I got out of high school back in 1982. But then I unexpectedly got pregnant, so I needed to adjust my plan. I've been working at it for the last six years and will graduate from K-State next year. I have a class this semester – one next term, one this summer and the last one next fall. I'd even like to go to graduate school – a glutton for punishment, some would say, but I love school. So, you see, if you want it badly enough, you can make it happen."

"What are you studying?" Sara asked.

"Physics."

"What's that?"

"Think of it as a combination of math and science."

Julie excused herself to visit the restroom and, when she returned, asked, "So, Sara, have your friends been a help to you these past days? I sure hope so. The love and support of friends are so important."

She nodded. "They've been nice. I have good friends."

"Good. And how are your mom and brother holding up during these horrible days?"

She went quiet and, for a second, looked like she was going to cry as she reached for some fries from the large basket they were sharing. "My brother's doing okay, I guess. He and I are pals. My grandparents get here tomorrow, so that will be better."

Julie hesitated but opted to press ahead. "It's good you and your brother are close. I was an only child. So, uh, I don't mean to pry, sweetie, but how's your mom doing?"

Sara took a bite of hamburger and drank from her chocolate milkshake before answering. "I don't know. It's hard to tell sometimes. Even before this…ah, um…she isn't there sometimes, if you know what I mean."

Julie shook her head. "I don't know exactly what you mean."

Sara looked Julie in the eye. "She drinks. A lot sometimes. My dad wanted my brother and me to go live with my grandparents on my mom's side – my dad's parents are dead – before he left for Korea. But I didn't want to. Didn't want to leave my friends."

Julie reached across the Formica table for Sara's hand. "I'm so sorry, Sara. But you know that people can get help for that. It's a disease, like cancer. It's something people can put behind them."

"Yeah, well, I'm not seeing that. It keeps getting worse."

"That's so hard, I know, for you and your brother, but I'd encourage you not to judge her too harshly and help her however you can."

Sara didn't respond and reached for more fries.

"You know," Julie continued, "I never had a dad. He left when I was three, so it was always just my mom and me. And then, when I was about your age, my mom was killed in a car accident. I finished high school living in foster care."

"Oh," Sara said. "Do you miss her?"

Julie nodded, knowing this would cause some tears. "Every day. But she's always with me, and even though she left me way too soon, she gave me the tools to succeed in life. Just like I bet your dad did with you. I'm thankful for the time I had with my mom, she was the absolute best, and hard as it was sometimes, I knew she would expect me to move on and thrive without her. Sorry, Sara, I didn't mean to get emotional on you here."

Sara slid out of her side of the booth and came over to sit by Julie. "Mrs. Delacroix, can I ask you a question?"

"Of course, and call me Julie. Always."

Sara was crying now, tears rolling down her cheeks. She leaned into Julie and choked out, "Okay, so is this – my dad being killed and all – the worst thing that's ever going to happen to me?"

Thinking back on what had happened to her after her mom died and all the wreckage and trauma that followed, Julie paused as she hugged Sara tightly. "I don't know, honey. I sure hope so. Even when it's really, really hard, you just need to push forward every day and hope and believe that you deserve good and happy times and will get them, even if it takes a long time."

Walking to the car, Julie, her arm around Sara, handed her tissues and said, "Sara, would you like to be friends? I think you're great. Maybe we can have lunch or breakfast every couple of weeks if you like? You can bring your brother if you want. And if you like, I'd love for you to meet my four girls."

Sara smiled. "I'd like that."

"You can always call me, Sara – anytime, day or night – if you need anything or are having a tough time. Okay?"

12

Late October brought the long-awaited fall and respite from the daily heat. The horrible events early in the month had past, and although life was returning to its previous rhythm, those terrible days had doubled the size of the constant pit in her stomach. They'd brought back to her the realization that her life could be destroyed in an instant. Julie hadn't had time to worry about the rapist, and thankfully, she'd had no further encounters with Major Paltz. She'd added a second deadbolt lock to both the front and back doors of the townhouse and always double- and triple-checked that her windows were locked.

On a Wednesday night with a full moon, Julie undressed for bed after speaking on the phone with her in-laws in Washington for half an hour. They called once a week or so to check in on her and talk to the girls. Coming back from the bathroom, through the thin bedroom window shade, she thought she saw something moving outside in the moonlight. But then the shadow was gone. She froze and watched, but after a few minutes, she didn't see or hear anything. The wind was blowing hard, so she figured it could have just been a tree branch moving back and forth.

Later in the week, on another windy night, walking from her carport to the townhouse around 18:00, Julie heard a noise behind her, and the hair stood up on the back of her neck. She whirled around, ready to scream. Nobody was there, but the branches on a bush off to her right were moving. Was it the wind? An animal of some kind? The rapist? Or just her imagination? *Don't be paranoid,* she told herself. *It's six in the evening, right by the row of townhouses. Who would do anything with people around?*

Karen Mosely took Julie to dinner on the first Saturday in November, in appreciation for her help and great work with the families after the Korea tragedies. All four of Julie's girls were sleeping over at a friend's house, so Julie had a free evening. Karen had a commitment before dinner, so she had made a late reservation, 20:30, at a nice steak and seafood restaurant off-base.

"We're having steak and lobster tonight, Julie. The least I can do for all your help after the DMZ. I couldn't have done it without you. You performed like a champion, and those families were lucky to have you in their corner helping them. I've gotten nothing but unsolicited thanks and compliments from the families and others about you."

"That's good to hear. It was hard for me to keep it together at times. My heart just ached for those families. It still does. I don't know what I'd do if I were in that situation. It's terrifying."

Karen poured Julie a glass of Bordeaux and eyed her. "So, this being Tim's first deployment and all, how have you managed? From my perspective, you've done well and have totally got your shit together, pardon my French."

Julie winced. "Honestly, I was a mess the first four months. I had panic attacks and crippling anxiety at times."

"Oh no. Jesus. Did you get help?"

"I did," Julie said. "Started seeing a psychologist and also a psychiatrist who adjusted my meds."

"Adjusted your meds?"

Julie sighed. "This is a road I've traveled before Karen, off and on, since my mom died when I was sixteen. I've been on anxiety and sometimes depression meds for years."

"My god, I never would have known, hon. You are so put together and strong."

"I was a psychiatric inpatient for two months in the spring of my sophomore year in high school, then briefly again for a week in my senior year. I was great then until I fell deep in the ditch again in '84 when we lived in LA, but I didn't need hospitalization. That was still the lingering effect of the high school trauma. But here, I think it was just the stress and fear of worrying about Tim. What would I do if something happened to him?" Julie sort of laughed. "Some people speculated it's my kids that cause the stress, but I live for them. I love being a mom and building a life with them and Tim. And working with the battalion families has also been good, helped to exhaust me every night, so I don't fret and let my mind run riot."

They spent the rest of dinner on lighter topics, laughing and sharing stories. The women closed the restaurant, and as they were leaving, Julie reached for Karen's hand and stopped to face her. "I owe you so much, Karen. I don't know what I'd have done without you reaching out and befriending me these past months. Without you, I'd have been even more lonely and scared."

Karen gave her a hug, then pulled back, smiled and gripped both of Julie's shoulders. "We're always going to be friends, sweetie. I feel so close to you. I knew you were a tough, capable woman, and what I learned tonight only reinforced that." She smirked. "You're a badass, Julie, in the best possible way, and don't you ever forget it."

• • •

Karen's car followed Julie's until they were inside one of the base gates. Shortly after, Karen broke left at a fork for her house, and Julie went right for hers. Julie had about ten miles of driving through endless flat plains before the base housing neighborhoods began. Hers was the only car on the two-lane road, and she had her window down, enjoying the crisp air. The clear Kansas night was full of stars in every direction.

She crested a slight rise in the road, navigated an S-curve, then yelped with surprise and slammed on her brakes. A Toyota Camry with the driver's door open blocked the road. Had the driver spun out on the curve? Where was the driver? Hurt in the car or gone for help? She opened her door and stood behind it, peering toward the Camry.

"Hello, hello, is there anybody in there? Are you hurt?"

Only the sound of the wind met her inquiries.

She got back in her Taurus, locked the doors, pulled her purse closer to get her phone, and looked in the rearview mirror to back up and take another route home.

Suddenly, the driver's side window exploded next to her, shattered with a hammer. Julie screamed as an arm reached in to hit the unlock switch for the doors. Julie had glass fragments in one of her eyes but saw the man in the ski mask as he pulled the door open and dragged her from the car. He reeked of tobacco and sweat. She managed to grab the strap of her purse as he got her out of the car and threw her down on the pavement. He began dragging her toward a blue Chevy pickup hidden off the road behind a clump of trees.

Screaming, Julie managed to drive an elbow hard into the man's windpipe. He grunted in pain and loosened his grip on her. She broke away and tore off the ski mask. She didn't get far because he tripped her, and she fell to the pavement. He moved toward her while Julie turned over to face him, took the Smith & Wesson 357 Magnum revolver from her purse, and pointed it at him. The man stopped five feet or so away. Breathing hard and her heart racing, Julie gasped, "Don't come any closer."

Paltz sneered at her. "Well, look at little Annie Oakley."

He took a long knife from his coat pocket. "We just seem to keep running into each other, Julie. It must be fate. But since you ripped my mask off, I'm going to have to kill you now. Once I fuck your brains out."

Trying to still the gun shaking in her hands and her uneven breathing, Julie managed to say, "Is that why you killed the others? Did they pull your mask off too?"

"They got what they deserved, just like you will. It's too bad. All these months, I was hoping we could get acquainted and have some consensual fun, with you all alone and lonely. You're missing out because I never get any complaints from the women who want it."

"Then they must have really low standards, Jody."

Paltz stiffened at this barb, and anger briefly washed over his face.

"Yeah, I came to realize that you're one of those uptight twats. Gonna be faithful to your husband even though you know he's fucking whores every weekend over there. He's gonna bring the clap home to you."

"You're a pig. How many women have you raped over the years? Dozens or just a few?"

"And you're a smart-ass frigid cunt," he snarled, his anger scaling up rapidly. "I'm so tired of having to listen to women who think they're smarter than me, who don't give a damn what I want."

Julie's eyes were locked on Paltz. If he moved toward her, she was pulling the trigger, aiming for his chest.

"You'll be dead soon, so I'll tell you this. I've been following you for months, and you were too dumb to see it. Looking into your windows at night, watching you drive that crap car of yours all around the base and stick your nose up the ass of the colonel's wife. One night you forgot to close your bathroom blind all the way, and I saw you sitting naked on the toilet for about ten minutes, wiping your ass, and then getting in the shower. Then come out and dry off. Your tits are pathetic. And I looked in your trash too. Know what medicines you take, what you feed your kids, your brand of birth control pills."

Still training the gun on Paltz, Julie knew she was on her own, terrified but resolute.

"You know, sweet Julie, that night a couple of weeks ago outside your carport, I was ready, had my gear on, my balaclava, a gag for you, gloves, all that. There's that secluded spot down the embankment near the carport, away from the lights. If you hadn't turned around when you did, I woulda done you, and you'd have had no idea it was me. But that didn't work out, and I had to do that other woman afterward, since you had me all worked up. But now, thing is, I'm tired-a chasing you. When I saw you go to the restaurant tonight, I knew you'd come home on this road. I just had to make sure it was late enough with nobody around. You obliged, and here we are."

"Here we are," Julie said.

"Now put that gun down, bitch. And why don't you make it easier and take your pants off for me?"

Julie shook her head. "Not happening." She tightened her finger on the trigger.

Unexpectedly and with lightning speed, Paltz threw the knife at Julie, her head the circus performer's bullseye. Still on her back, she rolled to the side and saw and heard the knife whiz past her eye. Paltz immediately leaped toward her, and Julie fired. The knife had upset her aim, and instead of hitting him in the chest, the bullet hit him in his left collarbone. Paltz dropped to one knee, stunned, his hand feeling for the wound in his shoulder. Julie scooted a few feet back. Realizing she now wouldn't need to kill him with a chest shot, she stood up, walked closer, and put a round into his knee.

He howled in agony, screaming, "Fuckin' bitch, fuckin' bitch!" Too disabled to pursue her, he dropped onto his back and rolled around on the ground, holding his knee.

Shaking, panting and in a cold sweat, Julie was too shocked to move. Finally, she backed away from Paltz, stood and lowered the gun. Then she thought of her girls. *My god, what if he went after them first? What if he followed me when I dropped them off?* She left Paltz on the road and turned her car around. Frantic now, she drove to the girls' sleepover, where her screaming woke everyone up. Making no sense, she was sure, to her daughters or her friend, she put her kids in the car and drove to the Mosely's house. It was now after midnight. Julie dragged the girls from the car and, crying, pounded on Karen's door until more porchlights came on.

13

I t was Christmas Day, 01:00, and Julie was on top of Tim, her head on his shoulder and his arms around her in their bed. He was asleep. He'd been home only three weeks, as the Korea tragedy had extended the battalion's tour.

It was snowing hard, and early on Christmas Eve, after church, Julie, Tim and the girls had gone outside to build a snowman. They'd then had a snowball fight, Tim against Julie and the girls, before all making snow angels in their tiny front yard. Dinner had been steak, chicken and chocolate fondue; the girls loved it. Those rituals had emerged as a holiday tradition, and the prior Christmas, alone with the girls, Julie had barely made it through them before dissolving in tears in the bathroom. At dinner, Tim was quite a sight, a six-foot-five elf in a green and red striped costume.

Despite their excitement about Santa, they'd sat together in the small family room after dinner with hot chocolate by the live tree that practically took up half the room, its lights the only illumination. Later in the girls' bedroom, still in his elf costume, Tim read *The Night Before Christmas* on one of the two bottom bunks, his daughters draped on both sides of him while Julie happily looked down from a top bunk.

Tim and Julie drank wine by the tree after getting Faith, Hope, Charlotte and Lauren to sleep. Julie, leaning against Tim on the sofa with his arms over her shoulders, couldn't have been happier.

He softly said, "I think Santa's the closest thing to magic in the world. It just killed me not to be with you and the girls last year."

"My gosh, me too. I just cried a lot. I'm glad that we get to come with you when the division relocates to Germany next year. I'm excited for another new adventure with you and the girls."

Around 23:00, they'd arranged the girls' Santa gifts, nibbled at the cookies and carrots they were leaving out for him and the reindeer, and drank a little from his glass of milk before going to bed. There, laughing and giggling, Julie removed Tim's elf suit with her teeth. One of the things she was learning over time was that she apparently had a high libido compared to many women, even as an often-exhausted mother of four kids. As such, Tim's absence had also been frustrating for her.

Back in their bedroom, with Julie resting on top of him, Tim remarked, "It's supposed to snow all night. We should be able to try out the sleds from Santa tomorrow."

"Yep. The snow reminds me of Timberline. On so many of those snowy days and nights when I was alone and not with you, Alex, or your parents, I wondered if I'd ever get out of there and if my life would ever get better. And I thank god every day that it did. You saved me, baby."

Tim ran his fingers through her hair. "I just helped. You saved yourself, Jules. You're genius smart, kind, funny, strong and beautiful. How could you not? My life would be empty without you and the girls. And I'm thankful you forgave me freshman year when I was, as Alex put it bluntly to me, 'a total shit.' I love you, sweetie. You're all I will ever need."

He nodded off a few minutes later, and still lying on top of him, Julie lightly ran her fingers through his short dark brown hair. He'd sacrificed his lifetime of almost shoulder-length hair for the military. What a year it had been. Tim on the DMZ, the recurrence of her mental health challenges, and the horrible Korea tragedies. She'd kept up with Sara Noth regularly and had had her and her younger brother over to the house the day before to decorate Christmas cookies with Tim, the girls and her. Sara's mom was away at rehab for a few months, and Sara's grandparents were living on base, taking care of Sara and her brother.

And then there had been the Paltz business. Another PTSD-inducing incident for Julie to process and overcome. But this felt different; time would tell. Julie had protected herself and her daughters and taken an evil person out of action.

Paltz was in the brig at Ft. Riley, looking at life without parole in military prison. He'd taken that in a plea in lieu of the death penalty. In addition to Julie's testimony, once she named Paltz, investigators matched physical evidence from the prior rapes to him (gloves, the ski mask, the clothes he wore) and the victim who'd seen his face and survived also identified him. His wife had immediately filed for divorce and sole custody of his children and moved out of state. Paltz also now walked with a limp. Karen Mosely had gotten a message to her husband in South Korea the morning after Paltz attacked Julie, so the colonel could break the news to Tim and assure him Julie was fine. He'd also arranged for a call between Tim and Julie the next day.

Julie gently rolled off Tim and put on pajamas; the girls could come charging in early. She said her nightly prayer and made the sign of the cross. Back in bed and folded into Tim, Julie knew she was lucky. She'd succeeded in returning hope and elements of peace to her life after years of struggle. But she also acknowledged the thoughts that had been growing within her since the summer, crystallized by Paltz: Merely surviving, making it through every day, focusing only on Tim, her girls and getting her degree weren't enough. She was being too passive and selling herself short. She wanted a career – maybe that would include graduate school – and wanted to serve a cause larger than herself. She needed to make things happen and better control her destiny. She needed to be more like Alex in that way.

Thinking about Alex still sometimes made Julie sad. For years and years, they'd been as close as Julie's twins. Alex had literally and figuratively saved her life in Timberline. Julie still didn't know why Alex had cut her out of her life. And since she'd died, Julie would never see her again and have a chance to at least try to find out why.

PART 2

TIMBERLINE

1978–82

14

Alex

I grew up in Timberline, Washington. I loved growing up there. But later, in high school and college, I saw it differently. I realized it was a company town run by a corrupt and immoral oligarchy led by Win Blackpool. Win was the CEO and owner of Blackpool Industries, the largest privately-owned forest products and paper company in the US, with over a billion in sales and easily the largest employer in town. Ironically, most tagged me as a gilded beneficiary of the town's reality. My father worked for Win as one of his top executives, and I was friends since second grade with Fogg Blackpool, Win's son and the heir apparent to the company one day. True enough, but later I would see myself as passively complicit in the town's evil, though not in a direct way. Like I only loaded the Jews onto the trains to Auschwitz but didn't gas them.

. . .

Timberline, or TL, as it's known to most of its roughly 23,000 residents, sits almost 7,000 feet above sea level on eight square miles on the eastern side of the North Cascades Mountains. It's 125 miles north northeast of Wenatchee, 175 miles northwest of Spokane, and 15 miles south of the Canadian border. It can snow for days on end in the winter, and you can get feet of it in a week. Timberline sits in a deep narrow valley surrounded by thick evergreen forests. From afar, it appears ripped from the pages of a brochure for a European river cruise. There are views of the forest, the snow-capped North Cascades Mountains and the Little Yukon river from anywhere in town.

In addition to Blackpool Industries, small independent logging companies around TL help feed Blackpool's mills, and the Maine Dakota Western, the MDW, one of the country's largest railroads, runs through TL. The MDW operates a large maintenance base in town. There are also large fruit warehouses that relay crops from central and eastern Washington onto MDW trains headed east.

TL has three primary areas: Central, the Flats and the Highlands. Central is the main part of town, with the commercial district and residential neighborhoods unfolding to the north and east toward the foothills of the Highlands. TL's schools are all in Central: four elementary schools, two middle schools and a four-year high school. The high school is old. Two large four-story buildings built of brick, stone and wood in the late 1940s, with a major renovation and addition in the late '60s. The school sits secluded on a hill surrounded by forest with a view of the town on the northern edge of Central. The high school football and baseball fields offer commanding views of downtown TL, the river and the usually snow-capped peaks that surround everything.

The Barn makes the high school special and is an almost spiritual part of TL's history and identity. It's a 9,000-seat arena built with the original high school in the 1940s. Unlike the rest of the school, The Barn is a wooden structure not renovated in the 1960s like the high school. It's a key element of Timberline's decades-long tradition of high school basketball success. It's as if the building and the community's basketball passion were transplanted from small-town Indiana to take root among the Douglas firs of northern Washington. The Barn provides one of the best home court advantages in the state. It's always standing room only, very loud and when the building is in full throat, it shakes. The fans crowd the court and hover over it. The stands rise almost vertically on both sides of the court, and even more steeply graded balconies tower over both ends of the floor, beginning right over the backboards.

The locker rooms were decrepit. Hot, humid, poorly lit and small with no bathroom stalls; just four toilets lined up next to each other in a back corner. The showers offered chipped pink tiles and ten showerheads with bad water pressure along the wall, out in open view. PE at Timberline High could be an unpleasant experience for the girls. Showers were required after PE; if you couldn't wait to use the toilet until your next class, you were always in open view with an audience. Woe to the gal with the cruel burden of excessive modesty. The girls especially seemed to believe that the PE experience at Timberline was designed to give them a taste of prison, an incentive to aspire to productive and proper lives. That didn't work for me, and I can authoritatively say that I would much rather use the toilet in the girls' locker room at Timberline High than in prison.

Though it is one of the smallest schools in the state in terms of the AAA athletic classification (the largest), the Timberline Polar Bears are always very competitive with larger schools. Clad in black, white and gray and urged on by a rousing school song (USC's "Fight On") played by the "Best Band in the Northern Land" (two hundred members strong, all situated in The Barn's steep bleachers right above the basket at the north end), the Polar Bears had strong traditions in baseball and girls volleyball, in addition to its legendary boys' basketball: TL won boys' basketball state titles seven times between 1960 and 1977.

The guys were state champions in our junior and senior years in '81 and '82, and won seventy-eight consecutive games over that time. Most considered them one of the best high school basketball teams in the state's history. My boyfriend, Brian Findlay, and our buddy, Tim Delacroix, were first-team all-state both years, and another, Fogg Blackpool, was second-team his senior year. Tim was also a high school All-American senior year and the focus of a two-year college recruiting battle that captivated the town.

To my mother's horror, one reason I liked it, I was a varsity cheerleader in grades ten through twelve, and captain of the squad junior and senior years. I loved it. Maybe I should have led some cheers for the ladies in my cell in Northern Ireland: "Two bits, four bits, six bits a dollar, all for a cavity search, stand up and holler!"

West of Central was the part of town called the Flats, which features the worst of TL's housing stock. Tiny five-hundred-square-foot cabins packed together in a small area not far enough from the river to protect them from an average ten-year flood. The cabins were built in the Depression to house desperate men, eight to a cabin, working for the Works Progress Administration. In many ways, that legacy endures; the Flats has always had poverty and struggle in its veins. Brian lived a tough existence there with his family after his father's accident, though he said he was always proud to be "of the Flats."

A few wheezing businesses exist, barely, in the commercial area of the Flats, but the biggest employers are decline and despair. They are always hiring. The area is largely made up of abandoned warehouses, crumbling former small factories and long-shuttered gas stations. Stores were outnumbered by bars, taverns and cheap motels, where rough men and non-Junior League women drank, smoked, shot up, fought and fucked. If Michelin gave stars for ambiance and quality in the Flats, the winner would be the Gear Grinder, year after year. It was a sprawling upscale truck stop with vast parking lots, showers, a truck wash, a bowling alley, indoor mini golf, tire and repair shops, three restaurants and a two-screen movie theater.

The Gear Grinder also adeptly served sexual needs, so much so that it was known by most everyone in town over the age of thirteen as the Pussy Grinder, the Grinder, or simply Pussy's. Between truckers, locals, railroad workers and smokejumpers from a nearby Forest Service firefighting summer barracks, Pussy's was always throbbing, so to speak. Budget-priced working girls at the Grinder, the Lot Lizards, prowled the parking areas and moved from cab to cab. They usually ranged in age from late teens to late twenties, had bad complexions, ratty clothes and Marlboro Lights or Virginia Slims (Vagina Slimes in the vernacular) dangling from their lips.

My part of town was the Highlands. Named for the steep, thickly forested hills that rose on the north and east sides of TL, the Highlands was all single-family houses which accommodated about a third of TL's population. Numerous residential areas snuggled into the steep forests. There was one small area of large, expensive Tudor and Georgian estate homes dating from the 1940s and 50s, and that's where I lived.

Wherever you lived in the Highlands, you reached your neighborhood via one of three half-mile tunnels (two headed east and one north) at the base of the hills where Central ended. I was a "Northie" as opposed to an "Eastie" because the easiest access to my neighborhood was through the northern tunnel. Once through the tunnels, you rose on steep, twisting two-lane roads that cut through the evergreens with many ten- and fifteen-mile-per-hour turns. Often fog-shrouded and treacherous in winter, the roads were dangerous for anyone piloting home with too much alcohol or weed on board. Secluded areas were everywhere in the Highlands, venues conducive to innocent fun but also to the darker arts of teenage vice — drugs alcohol and sex.

Tim and Brian had the Highlands to thank for lifting them into the basketball starting lineup early in their freshman season. They were the first two guys off the bench playing behind juniors and seniors on a top-five state-ranked team. But over Christmas break, the five starters and two other subs got tossed off the team for the season. The seven guys had been drinking heavily and had the misfortune to be packed into point guard Jimmy Allen's bright green Ford Bronco when it crashed. Nobody was hurt, but on a snowy December night with near whiteout conditions, precision escaped Jimmy on one of those coat-hanger turns in the Highlands.

In what would forever be known as the Cowen Incident, Jimmy drove the starting five and much of our bench strength down an embankment and through the back wall of Pete and Joanne Cowen's master bedroom. Dan Rustin, shit-faced all-league senior power forward and passenger seat occupant ("I got shotgun!") on the fateful voyage, then opined amidst the dust and rubble, "Wow, Mrs. Cowen, uh Principal Cowen, uh sorry…Dr. Cowen, a black bra, skimpy panties and a garter belt is not high school principal lingerie. I would have figured you for a long flannel nightgown. Looks like Mr. Cowen's getting some tonight." From such wisps of fate are star basketball careers launched.

15

Julie came to town with her mom before seventh grade; by high school, we were pretty much sisters. We shared a similar sense of humor, though only people who knew Julie well ever noticed. She was quiet, painfully shy and introverted around most people. As an example, in sophomore year, this guy took Julie to homecoming, but at the dance kept trying to get his hands down her pants. She shut him down, and he called her a cock-tease in front of, like, twenty people. Everyone was staring at her, and she just stood there stoically and took it. But I didn't. The next week, I spread the rumor that a urologist friend of my parents had confidentially told them that the guy had a micropenis, one of the smallest ever seen, and that his family was trying to get experimental treatment for it at the University of Washington. I asked my classmates to make donations to help his family with the medical expenses.

I realize now how difficult it had been for Julie to come to TL. Few people ever moved into that inbred town, so she was a novelty, and her awkward and geeky looks in junior high also didn't help her. But by sophomore year, she looked great; I told her she'd grown to be "nerdy pretty."

I, on the other hand, was part of the so-called 'royalty' in Timberline. My father, Mike Davis, was the Executive Vice President and Chief Financial Officer for Blackpool Industries, one of the top three executives at the company. My mother, Angela, was a shameless nouveau riche social climber, the Edmund Hillary of self-promotion and unhealthy ambition. She expected the wives of my father's subordinates to happily take orders from her and play Tenzing Norgay on her various "volunteer" activities.

It didn't take these women long to learn that my mother's tongue was often as sharp as the blades in the company's sawmills. Outwardly my mother was "passionate about giving back" while she chaired the Junior League and sat on the local hospital and YMCA boards. But as I eventually realized, it was really about her ego, and a means to exercise power over others she felt were her inferiors.

My parents' friends were the other top Blackpool executives and their wives (imagine, the executives were all men), as well as a few of the small number of surgeons and other medical specialists in town, plus a couple of lawyers. There were no local politicians, law enforcement officials, or religious leaders in their midst, but those people were always accessible, ready to bend their will, their principles, and sometimes other things, to the needs of the largest employer and financial contributor in town.

My father grew up in humble circumstances in the north of England. He started college there, spent a semester abroad at the University of Washington during his junior year, decided to transfer, and graduated from the UW with an accounting degree in 1952. My parents met in Seattle in 1953 and got married in 1955. My mother also graduated from the UW.

Win Blackpool, the founder's son, became CEO of Blackpool Industries in 1973. He promoted my father to Chief Financial Officer, and my parents immediately sold our large house in Central and moved into the enormous one in the Highlands. There my mother oversaw a massive gut rehab. It was as if Gatsby's unknown twin sister and her husband had taken up residence in the north woods.

I'm surprised my mother came to TL with my father in 1962. Her dreams of big-city life and high society dashed, she had to develop a new life blueprint. However, doting motherhood, Girl-Scout cookies, dance recitals, coaching youth sports and fourth-grade room mother were not in that plan. I participated in all those things, but while my parents were occasional spectators, they never took much interest. They were neither doting nor warm. In their minds, status and wealth were all that mattered, the only way to keep score. Everything was a competition, a never-ending quest to prevail in the zero-sum game of life. They were all business, all day and every day, and later I wondered if greed and desire for power were the entire basis of their relationship. I never saw any physical affection between them really, but they could have been close for all I knew.

· · ·

Julie's mom, the one I wished I'd had, died on December 8, 1979, during our sophomore year.

When Julie started at Timberline High, her mom decided they would take a trip every year over Christmas and New Year's. The year prior, they had gone to New York and invited me along with them. New York was so much fun! We skated at Rockefeller Center, shopped on Fifth Avenue, saw the decorated stores, went to see the Rockettes at Radio City Music Hall and watched the ball drop in Times Square on New Year's Eve. Julie's mom treated us like queens. I'll never forget it.

Julie and her mom were going to Hawaii sophomore year. I was invited, but my parents made me go with them to Finland, where my father had a forestry conference. That morning of the 8th, I went shopping with Julie and her mom for swimsuits for their upcoming trip. Shopping done, we drove thirty minutes out of town to cut a fresh Christmas tree for Julie and her mom. It was a great day, a little foggy, in the mid-thirties and snowing, but not in a crazy blizzard way – just right for the Christmas season.

Julie's mom had packed lunch, and we built a fire, ate and had a nice time. The three of us talked about our early thoughts on colleges and how Julie's mom planned to take her to visit Notre Dame, as well as her alma mater across the road, St. Mary's. Julie's mom also good-naturedly asked me about my relationship with Brian Findlay.

"So, Alex, I missed my issue of the National Enquirer this week. What is the current status of one of Timberline High's most famous couples? Are we in dating mode or just-close-friends status these days?"

"Well, Mrs. Mitchell, we are dating."

"I thought you were still 'going together,' as you say. What, it's been about a year now? Julie does a good job keeping me up to date, especially when I turn the hot lights on her, but I wanted to make sure there was no late-breaking news. That's part of the nosy-mother job description – you know, the Mom Code. Julie really likes it when I ask her about her crush on Tim and whether she plans to do anything about it."

Julie rolled her eyes. "Mom, please! It doesn't matter anyway, since he's gone all year."

"That gives her more time to make a plan to reel him in when he gets back from Poland this May," I said. Tim's parents had encouraged him to apply for a Rotary scholarship program to spend his sophomore year overseas living with a family. Originally, he was supposed to be going to France, but a last-minute hiccup ended up placing him behind the Iron Curtain.

"That's right, Alex," Mrs. Mitchell said, laughing. "Julie needs a little encouragement sometimes – more self-confidence, like you have."

Julie stood up from the fire and shook her head. "Whatever. You two just go along and make all your plans for me for the next few months. You so enjoy your little conspiracies together," she joked.

At the Mitchells', we set up the tree and decided I would come over the next morning to have breakfast and help them decorate. That evening, Julie's mom took us to dinner at a new place north of town along the river. After we got back to town, Julie and I went to see the movie *10*. I drove her home around 11:30. A bigger snow squall had begun, and visibility was really poor. It was supposed to snow for the next three days, up to two feet.

As we arrived at Julie's house in Central, flashing red-and-blue lights cut through the almost zero-visibility from the snowstorm. A police car was in her driveway.

An officer walked toward us and, in a short, clipped tone, asked, "Is one of you, Julie Mitchell?"

Julie, bewildered, nodded. "Me."

There had been a fire, small as it turned out, earlier in the evening at one of the MDW's maintenance hangars south of town. Being the manager in charge, Mrs. Mitchell got beeped and drove down to the yard to check things out. Nobody was hurt, and there was minor damage, so after a while, she drove home.

As she was turning right onto the highway out of the MDW complex, a BMW ran a red light and broadsided her. The driver claimed his brakes failed and that the snow had made the road slippery. The police officer said Julie's mom likely died instantly. We learned later that the driver was Steve Lonsdale, a senior executive at Blackpool Industries and a colleague of my father's.

When the police officer said Mrs. Mitchell had died, everything stopped working. All I remember was Julie and me crying and lowering each other to her cold, snowy driveway, partners in a soundless, slow-motion water ballet. We could see each other's mouths moving, but all we heard was what seemed like roaring in our ears. I asked the cop to call my house. My father was out of town, and my mother came, spoke briefly to the officer, and walked over to us, still sitting in six inches of snow in the driveway. Traumatized, cold and wet, like soldiers on Omaha Beach.

My mother surprised me in this situation, to her credit. Though there were no tight, consoling hugs, no purring comfort, my mother was concerned about Julie.

"Julie, dear, let's get you out of the cold. You will come and stay at our house." She brushed the snow out of Julie's hair. "Alexandra, why don't you help Julie pack a bag and pull some things together?"

As for me, Mother was truer to form. I was still crying and kept saying, "Oh my god, oh my god, I can't believe this."

Julie staggered into her house, and as I followed her, my mother grabbed my arm and turned me sharply to face her. "Alexandra, pull yourself together, for god's sake. You're making a scene. It's not as if your whole family just died. Now go help Julie."

• • •

Someone had to identify Mrs. Mitchell's body the next morning. Brian and his mom, Annie Findlay, met Julie, me, and my mother at the morgue. When she saw Julie and me, Mrs. Findlay ran over and pulled us into an extended hug without saying a word. Uncomfortable at what she probably thought was a low-class spectacle of emotion, my mother walked away and began talking to one of the police officers.

I expected a morgue like on TV – a clinical, pristine room with hushed conversations, nice lighting, shiny new aluminum equipment and neat rows of drawers for the bodies. Only the best for the dead, as it should be. A four-star capsule hotel with exemplary, kind and solicitous customer service.

Instead, they led us into a dim, low-ceilinged refrigerated walk-in cooler at the back of the courthouse. Other things needing refrigeration were stacked against the wall on shelves and around the door. Boxes of cleaning chemicals, a four-pack of coffee creamer and sack lunches brought from home were arrayed on a shelf, and a few cases of Pepsi and Mountain Dew were stacked on the floor. The noise of the refrigeration fans meant you had to raise your voice to be heard. It smelled, too, of what I'm not sure, but not a respectful, clinical, reverent aroma.

There were a few people in the room, and I didn't know some of them. One guy was drinking coffee. Julie's mom was in the center of the small room on a table, covered. Somebody slowly pulled back the sheet and revealed her face. Julie sucked in her breath. Mrs. Mitchell looked peaceful, easily the best-looking person in the room. Pretty as ever, not even her closed-wound traumatic head injury marring the picture.

Julie nodded and later told me she'd wanted to go kiss her, touch her. But as if struck by lightning, she fell to her knees, face in both hands sobbing. I ran to her, bawling, feeling useless. All I could think to do was rub her back. Brian picked her up and carried her out of there. I wish he could have taken me, too, because as I got up, I had to consciously work to make my legs move.

• • •

There weren't many people at the funeral for Julie's mom: some local colleagues from the MDW and a couple of headquarters executives from Chicago. Also, a few friends of hers in TL, Mr. and Mrs. Delacroix – Tim's parents, Annie Findlay, Julie, Brian and me. My mother had a hospital board meeting and wasn't there. Julie's father, a Ph.D. chemist from a prominent New Delhi family, had left Julie and her mother when Julie was, like, two or three. He'd never spoken to Julie or her mom again after he moved back to India for a high-society arranged marriage. Julie had an uncle, her mom's much older brother, but he'd died of cancer a few years prior. During the funeral mass and at the grave site, Julie stood between Brian and me, our arms around her, as she chewed her lower lip and tears quietly streamed down her cheeks.

After the funeral, I pressed my parents to have Julie live with us through the rest of high school. She had nobody else. They reluctantly agreed, and Julie moved in. Though we didn't need to – our house had eight bedrooms and ten bathrooms – Julie and I decided to share my huge bedroom suite. Out went my king bed, and in came two doubles, and by New Year's Day, we'd set up shop. Much later, at the end of January, I went with Julie to her house to sort through the remains of her life. She decided what to keep and put in storage and what to give away. The Christmas tree we'd set up the day Mrs. Mitchell died was little more than a pile of needles. Both a fire hazard and, I feared, a cruel talisman of the barren and depleted life that maybe now awaited Julie.

16

Julie

The night after Memorial Day, Julie was alone in the dorm room she shared with Alex at Gonzaga University in Spokane. They were taking summer classes: college credit for Alex, and high school and college credits for Julie. They'd return to TL in late August, before the start of junior year. It was a bonus for the girls that Tim, Brian and Fogg had opted to play in a summer AAU basketball league in Spokane. Brian was already in town, and Tim and Fogg were due in later in the week. The three guys planned to live at Tim's sister's place because she and her college roommates were away for the summer.

Someone knocked on the door, and Julie looked through the keyhole.

Oh boy. She hadn't expected him. *I look awful: crazy hair, no makeup, ratty blue sweatpants and this torn green Seattle Sonics sweatshirt and braces for three more months.* She opened the door, smiling.

"Hey there, Jules. Long time no see!"

"Oh my gosh, Tim! Wow! I thought you weren't coming in for a few days. It's…it's so good to see you. It seems like you've been gone forever."

He was even taller, Julie noticed, but still had his lively brown eyes, slightly narrow oval face and long sort-a-shaggy dark brown hair. *He looks amazing!* He wore dark blue jeans, white hi-top leather Converse All-Stars and a dark blue Oxford University hooded sweatshirt.

"When did you get back from Poland? How was it? I want to hear all about it! When do your games here start? Jeez, listen to me, sputtering like an idiot. I should just shut up now, I think," she laughed.

Tim flashed the quick smile that always gave her a warm jolt. "I was only gone a year; it's not like I was away in the Gulag for five years. You hungry? I'm starving. Wanna go get some dinner?"

They settled on a bench in a small park near campus and dug into takeout Chinese. It was a pleasant summer night – sixty degrees, with a slight breeze and lots of stars. Tim sat at one end of the bench with Julie at the other, the white Chinese food containers and soft drinks between them. Julie was digging into her sesame chicken with a plastic fork when Tim interrupted her.

"Uh-uh, hold on here, Mitchell. That's a food foul. No forks on this team – chopsticks only."

Julie rolled her eyes. "Really? You eat a lot of Chinese food in Poland? I figured you stuffed yourself with sausages and potatoes the whole time. Fine, but with these chopsticks, my sweatshirt will be eating half the meal."

"Nah, Jules, you're more capable than you think."

"So, how was it behind the Iron Curtain and all? Were there like secret police everywhere? And you were in Gdansk with all the Solidarity stuff, right?"

Tim nonchalantly shrugged, one of his signature moves. "Yeah, some crazy stuff, for sure. I got caught in the middle of a mini-Solidarity riot one night, got whacked in the head by the police and concussed, and spent a night in jail with my two Polish brothers."

"My goodness, you sit there like it's nothing. Oh yeah, the Polish secret police locked me up." *Classic Tim. Cool under pressure, nothing fazes him.*

"But as you can see, I made it out of Poland with no lasting damage. And I played tons of hoops on a local club team. We kicked ass, went twenty-four and two."

"I think you could be in Antarctica and still find basketball to play."

"Yeah."

"Your experience over there must have been amazing. I'm jealous."

He chuckled. "Jules. Your turn. I want to talk about you."

No! I don't. Nothing good to talk about.

She told him about the happenings at Timberline High while he was gone, at least until she'd left. *He must know why I didn't finish sophomore year, why I've been in Spokane since March. And how do you gloss over two suicide attempts in less than a month?*

Julie searched her mind for a conversation topic other than her. "Alex tells me you bought a car? I can't wait to see it."

"Yep, lime green '72 Dodge Challenger: five-speed stick and four-hundred-fifty horsepower."

Julie kind of snorted and giggled. "Though I heard it needs some work – a handyman special." Teasing, she asked, "Did it break down on the drive here from TL?"

Tim grinned at her. "Yes, smart ass. As a matter of fact, it did. Just some minor overheating, though I need to get the radiator fixed down here."

Laughing, Julie put her hand over her mouth. "Wow, I was just kidding. Sorry, I'm sure that was no fun. How did you pay for the car?"

"My savings from working during school and summers at the grocery store. I'll still have to work back in TL to pay the insurance and gas and restore it."

She smiled, reached over and poked him in the shoulder. "Wow, Mr. Delacroix, a fancy sports car for the big basketball star. I hope you'll let a math and science geek like me ride in it sometime."

He grinned. "I'll take that under advisement."

"Tim. Is my memory bad, or are you taller?"

He nodded. "I'm taller, Jules. Was about six-three when I left and now around six-five. Now, Miss Mitchell, since we're on the subject of growth, it looks like your chest is, um, okay, let's say, taller. You look fantastic."

She bent over toward her knees and put her hands over her face. "I can't believe you said that! If it wasn't dark, you would see me totally blushing. What a cad you are, sir! Believe me, it's still nothing much."

"Oh, I don't know about that."

"I think you're definitely in the minority opinion on that. A girl broke her leg last fall, so she had to leave the cheerleading squad. And can you believe it? Alex tried to get them to consider me. Crazy!"

Tim asked, "And?"

"According to Alex, the consensus was, 'Well, let's see, Alex. Julie has no ass, no boobs, braces, and most people think she's mute and creepy. Sure, let's add Morticia Addams to the squad. She'll really help get people fired up.'"

Tim said, "Yeah, I'm with Alex. You're better than that in lots of ways."

Tim never asked Julie about the suicide attempts that night. He was either too nice or too afraid, Julie figured. But she knew he'd ask, and he did within a couple of weeks. The two of them were at Tim's sister's house one night, sitting on the back deck just off the kitchen. Brian was out with Alex, and Fogg was entertaining a gal nobody had ever seen.

"She looks like she's thirty. Did you see those tattoos?" Tim asked after Fogg had hustled her downstairs into his room.

"I think my favorite is the one on her arm that says 'Fuck Off,'" Julie commented.

"Hmm, that's a strong choice, Jules, but I like the one just above her butt, with the downward-pointing arrow that says, 'Enter Here.'" Tim laughed. "Good thing she's wearing that halter top so we can see it."

Julie smiled and sighed. "So many good options to choose from."

Tim got Diet Cokes from the cooler on the deck and sat across from Julie on the beat-up deck furniture.

"I'm so sorry about your mom, Jules. I should have told you that at the beginning of the summer. My parents told me about it when I was overseas, and I couldn't believe it. Can't imagine going through something like that."

She took a swig from her Diet Coke. "Thanks."

"So, uh… Julie, really sorry, but, uh… what happened with the… that other thing?"

"It's okay, Tim. Hours and hours of group and individual therapy now make it seem like I'm talking about going to the store," Julie lied.

His eyes drilled into Julie, waiting for her to speak. *Julie Mitchell will now attempt a very high-degree-of-difficulty dive.*

"After mom died, everything blurred together. Funeral, Christmas, New Year's, back to school. I knew mom would have wanted – no, expected – me to carry on. Get good grades, plan for college, and enjoy life. All that. The social worker suggested I just think ahead a day at a time. Work to stay busy one day, and then wash, rinse, repeat the next day."

"Okay," Tim said, "so far, so good, right?"

"Not really. It got a little easier to do that, and January went by pretty okay. I went to the games and movies, hung out with everyone, and Alex's parents let me keep living at their house. I don't know what I'd have done if I couldn't live with Alex. I still got hit with sadness and fear. I would cry in the shower or into my pillow while Alex slept across our room. I set a goal to only let myself fall apart three times a week max. But I was doing okay, getting on, and knew I just had to keep going."

Tim stared silently and looked disconcerted. Julie wondered if he was feeling bad for her or if he thought she was toxic – afflicted with a disease he didn't want to catch.

"In February, things changed. It got harder to keep moving forward, like walking on marbles. I started going backward."

"Why?"

Julie had to catch herself and think about her answers to questions like this one. *Nope, not going there, not within one hundred miles of it. My friends will never know.* She got up and started pacing around the deck. Tim's silence and focused intensity were too much to take at point-blank range.

"Some things happened that kind of threw me."

He wrinkled his eyebrows together. "Like what, Jules?"

"Oh, just stuff I didn't expect." *Oh my god, I can't lose it in front of him.* She wasn't going there – to that night. No way.

"Right after mom's accident, there were times when this big black wave would roar up out of nowhere and send me reeling. It was like I was being thrown and turned over through the water. I couldn't see through the black, couldn't get my balance or breath and couldn't get the roaring out of my ears. The wave had been gone for a few weeks, but it came back in February."

Tim appeared intense now, almost like he was in a game, locking down his opponent on defense, not letting them get past him with any verbal crossover dribbles. Julie despaired, *He's thinking: My god, she's a nut case!*

She forged ahead. "This wave and the blackness just swallowed my energy, and a sort of hopelessness hung over me every day. I was sinking, and each day seemed worse than the one before. I felt weak, worthless, and that's what I couldn't get out of my head."

"I don't get that. You knew that wasn't true, didn't you?"

"Part of me did, sure, but part of me insisted it was. And that darker side kept getting stronger. Like it was in the weight room every day, working out to make it easier to crush me. Every morning I'd give myself a pep talk, tell myself I would not surrender to the negative thoughts. 'Suck it up,' I'd scold myself, 'your mom would be ashamed of you,' and then I would hate myself by midday when I sank back into the dark."

"Holy shit, Julie! Why didn't you talk to somebody, get someone to help you?"

Yes I should have, but who? I felt I'd already called enough attention to myself after my mom."

Tim raised both hands quickly. "Sorry, sorry."

"I had dreams every night that made me afraid to fall asleep. Full of blood and death. In one, I was in a car accident and dying with blood everywhere. Sometimes mom was in the dreams, sometimes

Alex and Brian and you; and other times, there were people I thought I knew but couldn't identify. They shouted, 'Hang on, Julie, hang on!' In one dream, someone attacked mom and stabbed her. I found her covered in blood that just kept spreading. I woke up in a cold sweat, not knowing if I'd saved her or not."

Julie stopped. *Wow, maybe too much information.* Had he heard enough? *Fight or flight, Tim?* Julie held her breath, thinking she would soon turn blue.

Finally… finally… he spoke. "Julie, keep going, please. It's okay."

As much as she'd told herself she wouldn't cry, couldn't cry, tears began leaking out. Squeezing her eyes closed just sped them up.

"In February, the dreams rolled in every night on that black wave. I'd try to stay awake, but eventually, I'd nod off, throwing the door open for my nightmares. I'd been Catholic my whole life, but after mom died, I swore off religion. How could what happened to her be a part of some larger cosmic plan?"

"I get that," Tim whispered.

"The black wave kept squeezing my guts and hammering my brain. I was underwater. Every day."

Julie was barely whispering. The tears kept coming, dropping onto the wood deck before she wiped her eyes with the back of her hand.

"Every night, I cried into my pillow. 'Please help me! Please, please help me! Help me find a way to get through every day.' I didn't know whom I was pleading to. God, Buddha, Allah, the Avon Lady, I didn't care. I would have, you know, bought from anyone who could've helped."

Her throat was so dry. She went to the cooler and grabbed another Diet Coke.

"On that night, that Friday in February, Alex and Brian were out at the midwinter dance. Alex was mad that I didn't tag along with the group, but there was a pre-dance dinner at Fogg's, and I just wasn't up for it."

Tim put his hand up to slow her down. "So, you were home alone?"

"I thought I was, but Alex's mom was home. Her dad was out at some business dinner."

"So, you're in Alex's house, just you and her mother. Were you hanging out together?"

Julie smirked. "You're kidding, right? Even when Alex was home, we never did that. I was alone, and her mom was somewhere in that massive house."

"Fine. Then what happened?"

"My dream was different that night. I was in a bathtub full of hot water, wearing my yellow flannel pajamas, hiding from someone outside who was looking into my room. Then he was in the house, headed toward the bathroom, where he found me. The blade, the largest in the kitchen, sliced into me just below the palm of my left hand. Whoever it was must have known they would need to drive in hard to hit the artery. And since I was in the bath, my skin was soft, open, eager for the tip of the blade. Blood rushed out of me. It felt peaceful, and I began to, like, float and get tired. But I'd not closed the bathroom door all the way. A fortunate mistake."

"Then what happened in the dream?" Tim asked.

Julie again wiped the tears off her cheeks, this time with the palms of both hands. "Ah, but you see, that night, it wasn't a dream. I was the attacker, the intruder."

Tim's mouth dropped and froze open. "Oh, fuck!"

"Something… luck, god, I don't know…brought Alex's mom into the bathroom. She dragged me from the bath. Blood was all over the pajamas, making it hard for her to find the source. But she did, held my arm in the air, and pressed a white towel against my half-attached wrist. She was coated in blood. It was in her hair, all over her clothes, dripping from her eyebrows. Some had squirted into her eye."

Tim started to say something but cut out in mid-sentence.

"The front door must have opened next because Alex's mom thought it was her dad. She called, 'Is that you? I need you in the hall bathroom right away.' But it was Alex, home early. I was fading out, but I remember her standing outside the bathroom door screaming, 'Oh my god! Oh my god!' Then her mom said, 'Alexandra! Alexandra! Listen to me! Go next door and get Dr. Nickles. Now! Now! Run!'"

Tim was pale, sweating, and also got up to pace around.

"Sounds were more distant, and my vision was blurry. The next time I opened my eyes, Dr. Nickles was there. My blood had found him too and also covered the white tile floor. Alex told me later that the doctor said, 'There's no time for an ambulance. She'll bleed out if we wait. We need to get her into the car and to the ER.' He told Alex's mom to drive and had Alex get in the back seat to help him with me."

Tim looked stricken, Julie saw. Stunned at the destruction, like he'd just seen a chemical plant explode.

Julie sighed. "So, that's pretty much it. I have Dr. Nickles, Alex's mom and Alex to thank for my life. Her mom fought to slow the blood loss, buying me time even though she was losing the battle. I was almost gone when Dr. Nickles came rushing in from next door."

"What did he do?"

"He plunged into the messy field on my arm and twisted his fingers around tendons, bones and vessels to crimp the magic spot that kept me alive. Then he guided Alex's fingers to the same location for continuous pressure, picked me up in his arms, and hustled us to the car."

Silence from Tim as he sat back down.

"I drifted in and out of consciousness. All I remember from that car ride was the smell of blood. It was so strong. Alex said the blood had that metallic smell like the oil they used to lubricate the big industrial log saws in the Blackpool mills. She thought she was going to throw up in the car, but she wasn't going to release the pressure on my artery."

Julie wondered if all this was too much. As if Tim thought he'd asked her what she thought about the weather, and she'd launched into a three-hour meteorology presentation.

She looked at Tim as he ran both hands through his hair. Was he sympathetic or repulsed? Doubting how anyone could be so messed up to do something like that? She couldn't tell, but he wasn't rushing over to comfort her.

Julie continued, "You know, Alex's mom is not the warmest or most encouraging person, but she's a very capable woman. That night she was apparently a Formula One driver. Alex said she was going almost a hundred and ten once we came out of the Highlands and hit the straight avenues outside the tunnel. Dr. Nickles told me later that she was the picture of intensity and focus and very cool under pressure."

More silence from Tim. Was he processing this? Thinking about it? Formulating questions? Wishing there was an ejection handle on his deck chair?

"At the hospital, they sent me to surgery right away. I felt grateful but embarrassed and pathetic for causing all the bother. In addition to saving my life, Dr. Nickles saved my hand. Another stroke of luck was that Alex's neighbor was a vascular surgeon who had treated combat casualties in Vietnam. A nurse told me later that ninety percent of surgeons would have had to amputate because of the extensive damage."

Tim took a deep breath and slowly blew it out.

"I was very lucky. Less than a minute from dying at Alex's house before Dr. Nickles got there, one of the ER doctors estimated." Julie smiled weakly. "I'll have to wear long-sleeve shirts forever, but that's a good trade-off for my life and keeping my left hand, don't you think?"

"Uh, yeah," Tim said. "Course."

"I have quite a scar you haven't seen yet. Twenty eyelets of thick bootlaces from just below my palm to halfway down my arm."

She pulled her sleeve up to show him, and though he didn't say anything, Julie thought the stark, intrusive ugliness of it surprised him.

"But, um, sorry, Julie, if you don't mind, that wasn't the end of the story, right? What happened later?"

Well, that sounds a little prosecutorial, but just focus and finish.

She took a deep breath and sighed. "No, it wasn't. I left the hospital after about a week and went home to Alex's. At Dr. Nickles's suggestion, I saw a psychologist. We spent a few sessions together, but he mainly did marital problems, and we just didn't connect. I didn't know what to make of what I'd done. Would I start to feel better because something like that was a cathartic experience? Or would I get worse, become like a leaky Hanford reactor, poisoning everything around in addition to myself?"

"But Alex and Brian said you seemed pretty okay."

"I wasn't. Just did everything I could to hide it from them. I was a sympathetic figure to students and teachers at school when I was an orphan, but in their eyes, when I got out of the hospital, I was crazy and unstable. A Carrie and Lizzie Borden mix in tortoiseshell glasses. People spread rumors of drug and alcohol problems and an eating disorder, but none of that was true."

Tim shook his head. "What bullshit."

"I was also a topic of conversation among parents in Timberline and quite an embarrassment to Alex's mom, I'm sure. All of her achievements, her years of careful construction of Alex, and the determined cultivation of her own image, all tainted by an unwanted linkage with me."

Tim shifted around in his chair but kept looking directly at her. "You left the hospital, moved back into Alex's house and room. Then what, Jules?" *Still kind of doing the Perry Mason thing.*

"Ah yes, the denouement. The black wave, the bad dreams, the feelings of hopelessness, all quickly moved back in with me. 'Did you miss us?' they seemed to say. 'Would you like to see the slides from our trip to the Grand Canyon? Well, don't worry, Julie, we're back and will never leave you.'"

Tim furrowed his eyebrows. "Wow."

"In mid-March, two weeks after I'd gone back to school, I was in the cafeteria carrying my lunch tray, and these two girls saw me."

"Who?"

"A couple of seniors. One said, 'Oh no, only plastic silverware for you, Mitchell.' Then the other chimed in with, 'And you'll need more napkins, lots and lots of absorbent napkins.' Then they burst out laughing, and people around them heard it all and some laughed."

"Did you know them? Why would they say that?"

"Not really, and who knows? I should have just let it roll off my back and kept walking. But something in me just, I don't know, broke. 'This is how it's always going to be,' I told myself. I mean, they were seniors; I hardly knew them. Was this what everyone thought, how everyone in school was going to be for the next two years? Would I be reminded of it every day?"

"No, that's not what everyone thought," Tim said. "Not your friends."

"Yeah, but I didn't have many friends. I never did, really, other than the few of you. So, I set my tray down on the nearest table and ran out of the cafeteria. I didn't know where I was going or what I was doing. I just had to make everything stop. I ended up in the kitchen and grabbed another big knife, something with me and knives, apparently. I'll understand if you never want to carve a Thanksgiving turkey with me."

"I was just thinking that." He smiled. "I'll cook."

"The kitchen ladies screamed and called for help. I ended up sitting on the floor in the corner holding the knife, lost in some sort of catatonic state. I didn't use the knife on myself or anyone else, though I apparently put on a nice show for everyone peering in the cafeteria windows. It's like there was a sign: 'The bear exhibit is closed for maintenance today, but Julie Mitchell is just down the way and open for viewing.' I'm sure many of them thought, 'That clinches it. That chick is REALLY crazy!'"

Tim sat and looked at me, silent.

"That was the end of my sophomore year. People at school made some calls, and that night, Alex's mom drove me to the big medical center here in Spokane. I don't think she said ten words to me the whole trip. I just sat in the passenger seat, lost in space. She later told Alex she thought I'd be gone for quite a while."

Julie looked at Tim. Was he transfixed or thinking, *I can't believe how messed up she is?* His eyes didn't dart around; his head didn't move to look at noises from the cars driving past.

"A doctor met us, and at like three in the morning, they admitted me to the psych unit. I was an inpatient for over six weeks."

"What was that like?"

"Awful. First, I spent days in a drug-induced haze as they experimented, looking for a workable Goldilocks combination of drugs for me. There was also individual and group talk therapy, lots of that."

Julie didn't tell Tim she couldn't have visitors and was alone with her fears and sadness every night. No fellow troubled soul shared her semi-private room. Her only company was the distant rants and screams from others on the floor who apparently had it worse than she did. Sometimes she saw the staff restraining people, but that only happened to her once.

"In the hospital, I got into the habit of watching Ted Koppel on *Nightline* with his daily update on the Iran hostage situation. You know, I felt a connection with those people and that terrible Desert One fiasco. Just as the US government's attempt to stop the siege ended in blood and failure, so did mine. I watched Ted every night in my room on a black-and-white TV with an unstable picture… kinda fitting, I suppose, huh?"

Tim visibly winced.

"Ted delivered his nightly update on the hostage crisis with no end in sight. And that's how I felt. Counting from when my mom died in December, it was like Day 125 of my own hostage crisis, with no rescue for me either. At least the people in Iran had each other. But like them, I felt powerless to change my circumstances, to rescue myself. All I could do was to survive and try to tell myself, sometimes amidst nothing but bleak, scary blackness, that I had a future and would someday get to it. I could talk to Ted Koppel every night, but he couldn't hear me."

"When did you get out?"

"Early this month, they moved me into a supervised halfway house. Nuts-to-Go, some called it. I lived with a roommate, checked in three times a day, and continued the group and individual therapy sessions. I left there last week, almost free and clear. I'll have weekly sessions with my psychologist all summer."

Exhausted, Julie held her hands out. "Sorry about the tears. But that's it, the ugly truth." *Well, some of it, but I'm still not going there, to that other night. Not now, not ever.*

Tim stared at the ground for what seemed like forever, not looking at her. She asked herself if he would be brave enough to venture inside the yellow crime scene tape to let her show him she could be normal and continue to get better. Or would he just melt away? *Please, please, Tim, give me a chance!*

She was holding her breath again. Finally, with maybe not as much affection or conviction as she was hoping for, Tim leaned over, helped her up out of the chair, hugged her and whispered, "You're gonna be fine, Jules. It will be okay."

17

Mike and Angela Davis

Walking into the house, Mike Davis removed his maroon tie and charcoal pinstriped suit jacket. Mike was five-ten, thin with blue eyes and curly, always-ruffled blond hair topping a weathered square face.

Hearing the door open and close, Angela Davis hustled down the sweeping Gone-With-the-Wind staircase and greeted him in the living room with a hug and kiss.

"It's so good to see you! How were the flights? When you called from Chicago saying there were storms, I was afraid you'd be stuck there overnight."

"The flight was an hour late out of LaGuardia and then two hours late out of Chicago to Seattle. But the car was waiting to take me to meet the helicopter at General Aviation, and the trip from there to Timberline was fine."

"I know Win has the Gulfstream in Japan, but where was the Falcon? Why did you have to fly commercial?"

"Lonsdale has it in Quebec. A couple of his HR guys are with him, and they're doing their part of the due diligence on the sawmills."

"How was New York? You were so busy all week, we've hardly had time to talk. What did the banks and rating agencies say? I've been thinking about this all week."

"We'll get the acquisition financing done. Just a question of terms."

"Win's so lucky to have you arranging all this stuff," Angela said. Moving out of the living room, she beckoned to Mike. "Let's go catch up over a drink in the library."

"I didn't want to bother you in New York, but we need to talk about Alexandra and Julie."

Mike walked over to the bar in the library. Floor-to-ceiling windows offered the panorama of the sun dropping into the west over Timberline, the river, the forests and the mountains.

"What are you having, Ange?"

"Maker's Mark and Coke, please, thanks."

Mike and Angela kicked off their shoes and sat facing each other at opposite ends of the dark brown leather sofa in the library, each with one leg stretched out toward the other. Angela lightly rubbed Mike's calf.

"Before we talk about Alexandra, what are we doing tonight, Ange?"

"Nothing. Tomorrow night is the July Fourth dinner and fireworks at the country club. The fireworks won't be as big as last year's when they were bidding goodbye to the seventies."

Mike nodded. "Okay. Alexandra and Julie."

"When Julie went off to the hospital in Spokane, you seemed okay with her living with us through the rest of high school. I mean, she has nowhere else to go, and she and Alexandra are so close. But you've seemed ambivalent about that for the past month or so. Has something changed, or am I reading you wrong?"

Mike pursed his lips and said nothing.

"I mean, you know Alexandra is expecting this. In her mind, there's no question. And they're due back from Spokane in six weeks to start junior year."

"Ange, where would Julie go if she didn't live with us?"

Angela sipped her drink and set it down. Talking with her hands, she said, "I have no idea. I suppose she'd have to go into the social service system. Other than Alexandra, her only close friends seem to be Brian Findlay and Tim Delacroix, and she certainly couldn't live with them. We'd be kicking her into a foster home of some kind."

Mike nodded. After a few seconds, he said, "Maybe we should do that."

"Really, Mike? Why on earth would we do that? I mean, look, obviously, Julie has issues, and I don't really understand what Alexandra sees in her, but the girl is an orphan. She has nowhere to go. And she's Alexandra's best friend. My lord, they're like twins."

"I am aware, Angela, okay?"

"Julie will be crushed, but just go away quietly. But Alexandra will go nuclear. She'll never understand. And as you know, our relationship with her is steadily getting worse. How do you think this will help that?"

Mike put a hand up. "Alexandra is just going to have to deal with it. Life isn't always fair."

"What are you not telling me? Something is going on. What's happened?"

Mike picked up his drink, stared into it for about thirty seconds, then took a long slug.

"Mike? Hello, are you there?"

"Look, Win heard, I assume from Fogg, that we were planning to take Julie in through high school, and he's not happy about it. He first mentioned it back in March, but I kind of just ignored him, thinking he wouldn't make a big deal about it."

"Why would Win care? Does he want her to live with them? What are you not telling me?"

Mike put his drink down, rotated on the sofa, and put both feet on the floor. Bending forward, he dropped his face into both hands and rubbed his temples. Angela slid closer to him.

"Mike! Mike, what the hell is going on?"

Finally, he lifted his head and leaned back into the leather cushions.

"Ange, remember when you and Alexandra went east that week in February?"

"Yes. You and Julie were here at the house. She didn't want to go with us to watch Alexandra look at colleges."

Mike got up, walked over to the bar and fixed himself another scotch. He nodded at Angela. "Another?"

"No thanks, I still have half a drink left."

"You left Friday morning, and that afternoon Win and I met with the guys in from Japan to talk about renegotiating the logging deal. All of us went to dinner after. We finished about nine, and Win told me to meet him at his house at ten to debrief."

"And Julie was home or out?"

"I had no idea what her plans were that night. You realize I hardly know her."

"Oh, come on, she's been Alexandra's best friend since the seventh grade."

Mildly irritated now, Mike shot back, "Go right ahead and be high-and-mighty about it, Angela. But I've never noticed you being terribly close to her, either."

Angela took a breath. "No, you're right. Sorry."

"Well, uh, anyway, I got to Win's about five to ten. Went in through the side door off the kitchen. Fogg was in the kitchen signing for a bunch of pizzas and said he was with friends in the basement in the East Wing."

"I bet Julie was in the basement," Angela noted.

"Fogg said he hadn't seen his dad, but I guessed Win might have come in from the garage and gone into the game room. So, I went back there.

"Mike, what does this have to do with Julie not being able to live here?"

"Angela, please, I'm getting there," Mike implored as he returned to the sofa.

"Sure enough, Win was back in the game room. He seemed surprised to see me like he'd forgotten he'd told me to come over. And, uh, he was pulling up his pants and adjusting his belt when I walked in. He just stared at me for maybe fifteen seconds, and his eyes went stone cold. I heard a noise over by the fireplace and turned to look."

Angela was sitting rigidly straight, eyes open wide. Awaiting the diagnosis: malignant or benign?

"The sound I'd heard was this woman, a girl actually, throwing up. She was on the floor, covered with vomit, leaning against the stone fireplace wall with her pants and underwear around her ankles. This… this girl was crying, and she looked awful. Blood was running down from the back of her head. Her left eye was swollen shut, and that whole side of her face was swelling like some kind of black and purple balloon. She almost looked dead."

"Oh, no, no, he wouldn't have," Angela said. "This girl…"

Mike rubbed his face with his hand. "It was Julie."

Angela closed her eyes tight and kept them that way, like she'd mistaken Super Glue for eyeliner. Her hand only partially covered her gaping open mouth.

"But, but why? Why would Win do that? It's evil. Jesus, she's sixteen years old! She's one of his son's friends. We know Win's done some horrible things in his life, but this, this… It's monstrous."

"I don't fuckin' know, Ange. We know how he is, his track record and all. But this, I was practically in shock."

Angela replied, "Win was always nice to Julie and so concerned about her after her mother died. He offered to help her with a summer job."

Mike helplessly raised his hands to his side. "Win claimed he'd gotten to know her in the past couple of months, and she kept coming on to him. Said she wanted it."

"Really, Mike? Give me a fucking break! No sixteen-year-old girl would want that if she was in her right mind. And certainly not Julie. Christ, she's afraid of her own shadow!"

"Shit, Angela! I'm not saying Win was right. Obviously, it was bullshit! It's not like I encouraged him or knew he would do it. It was done when I got there. I'm not the fucking enemy here!"

Angela rose from the loveseat and started pacing around the library, incredulous and almost panicked, talking with her hands turning in circles like a Dutch windmill. "God, I don't even know where to begin, but, okay, then what happened? What did Win do? What did you do? What happened to Julie?"

Mike looked down at the floor with his scotch back in his hand. Finally, he spoke. "I said, 'Jesus Christ, Win, what have you done?' He pointed his finger up in my face and said, 'Mike, not another fucking word. Hear me? You know what to do. Make sure this is taken care of.' And he went to the garage, got into the Porsche, and drove off. He's never mentioned that night since."

"Leaving you to clean up the mess, as always. My god, what if someone had walked into that room? Fogg, his friends, his wife. Was Jessica even home?"

Mike nodded. "When I got there, Fogg said something like, 'My mom's around somewhere. Want me to tell her you're here?' I said no, I was just there to see his dad."

"And what did you do?" Angela challenged.

"I had to get her out of there, right? I helped her pull up her pants, picked up the torn clothes, and got a towel to mop up the vomit and blood. She was moaning and kind of in shock."

"Goddammit! I can't believe he put you in that situation to deal with the whole shit storm."

"I picked her up in my arms and carried her out the door by the garage. Then I sat her in my passenger seat and got the hell out of there."

He stopped and took a drink. "After half a mile or so, I pulled off the road by that sharp hairpin turn. I wasn't thinking straight. I kinda freaked out and just shut down for a bit. Julie was moaning and crying, drifting in and out of consciousness. She threw up again, and her face was just hideous."

"And? Did you take her to the hospital? Did you call the police?"

"Think about that for a minute, Angela. She needed an ER, but how do you keep something like that quiet? Way too many questions and maybe more blowback than Win and I could contain. It's not like I could say she slipped on a bar of soap in the shower. As for the cops, you know they're totally in Win's pocket. Nothing would have happened to him. The only people certain to suffer would've been Julie… and us. Win would say she was the aggressor, a slut who came onto him, and that it was consensual. She'd have to leave town."

"Bullshit! Who would believe it wasn't Win's doing?"

"Maybe nobody, but that's no guarantee of justice in this town."

Angela, disgusted, waved her hand at Mike.

"Okay, Ange, you want to go to the cops? We still can. It's only been a few months. If Julie wants to press charges, I could tell the cops and the DA what I saw. But are you ready to give up this life? To leave town? To maybe go back to struggling to pay our bills every month like we did when we started out?"

Angela stood, not knowing what to say, angry, frustrated and fearful.

"Win would ruin me, make up shit, make it look like I embezzled money or something. I'd be lucky to work again. And you sure as hell wouldn't be sitting on any more hospital boards or leading the Junior League. And we wouldn't be going to the fucking fireworks at the country club."

"Shit." Angela picked up her drink from the end table. "Okay, you're right. We're in a tough spot here. If we go to the police, it will ruin our lives and Julie's too. Why put her through another trauma? Wouldn't accomplish anything. But still, Julie needed medical help. What did you do?"

"I decided to take her to Nate Burns."

"Oh, Christ, that butcher. I think he got his medical degree off a matchbook cover."

"Well, he's quiet and discreet and on the Blackpool payroll. I figured he was my only option."

Angela just shook her head.

"Dammit, Angela! You're just sitting there in judgment. What would you have done?"

"Look, Mike, I understand it was a horrible, unimaginable situation. But I would've taken her to a hospital in Spokane. Even better, I'd have ordered up the company plane and taken her to Seattle or Portland. It's not like Win would have complained. He told you to take care of it."

"Well, Angela, hindsight is always perfect, right?"

It was dark outside. The entire Davis house was pitch black, save for the two small Tiffany lamps illuminating Mike and Angela in the library. Insufficient light amidst the dark.

"Okay, you took Julie to see Nate Burns."

"No." Mike held up both hands in front of Angela like a flashing stop sign. "When I told her I was going to take her to a doctor to get help, she got hysterical. Said, 'No, no. No doctors!' I couldn't believe it."

"Why no doctor?"

"She felt everyone in town would know what happened and blame her. Nobody would believe her."

Angela sighed. "Sadly, she was likely right, but still was in no condition to know what was best for her."

"I told her she needed a doctor, not to worry, nobody would know."

"Why didn't you take her to see Burns, anyway?"

"She kept getting more and more upset. Crying. Screaming at me. Said she wanted out of the car, said if I didn't stop and let her out, she would tell the police I raped her. I tried to calm her down, but it was no use." Shrugging helplessly, Mike said, "So, I let her out of the car, just outside the entrance to the north tunnel on the Central side."

"Oh my god, Mike! What were you thinking? Why? Why? Fucking unbelievable!"

"You're right. You're right, okay? I panicked. I made a mistake. I wasn't thinking clearly. She was hysterical. I've never seen a woman in that state."

"I'd hope not," Angela said tartly. "Okay, you just left her outside in the snow, left her to die, maybe? Obviously, she didn't die, so what happened after that?"

"I don't know exactly. I got a call at the office the next morning from Brian Findlay's mother. She told me she'd seen Julie in town the night before and she hadn't been feeling well. So, she took her home to spend the night at their house. She told me since you and Alexandra were out of town and she figured I was busy, she'd let Julie stay there if she wanted until she felt better."

"Did you go over the next day to see Julie? And what did you do all morning before Annie Findlay called? Just assume Julie was dead outside the tunnel where you left her? Finish up your Father of the Year application?"

Mike was angry. "Don't be a bitch, okay? I don't like this any more than you. No, I didn't call Julie or go over to check on her on Saturday, and I didn't do anything before Brian's mom called me."

"This story just keeps getting worse. And you still didn't call me. Why on earth not?"

"I'm not proud of any of this, okay? I'm sorry."

"Did you apologize to Julie? Or did you just pretend it never happened?"

"Come on, Angela, that's unfair. Sunday morning, I picked her up at the Findlay's house, and we took the company plane to Seattle, the UW Medical Center. I had specialists in three departments look at her concussion, eye and face. We flew back that night, and Julie told me Brian's mom and another woman had driven her to the hospital in Wenatchee Friday night after it happened. The doctors there found significant damage but nothing permanent, and the people at the UW said the same. Said she'd maybe need surgery at some point for the broken cheekbone, but they weren't sure.

"Did she go back to the house with you?"

"No. She wanted to stay with the Findlays. Said she'd prefer to come back after you and Alexandra came home."

"Did you talk at all with her about that night?"

"Yes. On the plane, I told her I was very sorry that I'd given in and allowed her to get out of the car Friday night. Told her I'd panicked, not an excuse, but I wasn't thinking straight. I said I was very thankful she'd found Brian's mom, or she had found her."

"What did she say?"

"Nothing," Mike said. "She just thanked me for taking her to the doctors in Seattle. I was surprised you and Alexandra didn't seem curious about her explanation for her injuries when you got back. I mean, slipping on the ice?"

"I wouldn't have had to make guesses or ask questions if you'd told me what the hell had happened. I guess I was wrong to assume that you might have said something if she'd been raped and beaten up."

Exasperated, he shook his head. "She must have told Alexandra everything."

Angela thought for a moment. "I don't think so. If she had, we'd have heard about it immediately. And we'd have had to imprison Alexandra in this house to keep her from telling Fogg what his father had done. I'm sure Julie felt keeping it to herself would help keep it quiet."

Mike took this in.

"Mike, do you think Win would have mentioned the whole thing to Fogg in some perverse macho father-son bonding thing?"

"Oh no," Mike said. "No way. But what does Brian Findlay know? Nothing, everything, or a little?"

"I don't know," Angela said. "Annie Findlay has to know Julie was raped, but maybe Julie didn't tell her by whom, and maybe Annie didn't share the rape detail with Brian."

"Let's hope not," Mike replied.

"Anything else, Mike?"

Still standing, Mike scrubbed his face again with both hands. "Yes. When we got back from the UW, Julie said in this flat, defeated kind of way, 'Nothing will happen to him for doing what he did to me, will it, Mr. Davis? Because you're not going to say anything about this, to tell what you know, are you?'"

Angela drew her breath in as if preparing to go for a deep dive into the black ocean. "What did you say?"

"What could I say? I wasn't going to lie to her. I shook my head and said, 'I'm so sorry, Julie, but I just can't.' I wasn't proud of that."

"Christ, Mike, no wonder she tried to kill herself. Are we monsters?"

He shrugged and partially raised his hands.

Finally, Angela sighed. "I see why Win doesn't want her living with us. I'm sure he'd like to get her out of town."

"You're right. Win asked me if I could talk her into going to boarding school somewhere, said he would pay for it, of course."

"Yeah, that worked out so well for Fogg, didn't it? He didn't even make it through his freshman year at Groton."

"He got kicked out for cheating and selling drugs. I doubt that would be an issue with Julie. But I asked her if she'd be interested. She saw the offer for what it was and declined. Said such as it was, Timberline was her only home, and she wanted to finish high school with Alexandra and her other friends."

"I understand that. Julie's not the adventurous, courageous sort."

"Win isn't going to let this go, Angela. If we let her keep living here, it will be waving a red flag in front of the bull whenever he hears her name. It's like a weird loyalty test with him."

"I know. I'll call social services next week to get the ball rolling."

"You think Julie will ever tell Alexandra what happened?"

"If she does, there will be hell to pay."

Mike said nothing, lost briefly in thought.

"Mike. Is there something else you're not telling me? Because now is not the time to be withholding information. It's full confession time."

About thirty seconds later, Mike wrinkled his nose and made a face. "Yeah. Lonsdale killed Julie's mom last December."

"Well, I know he was driving the car and hit her in that accident, but…"

Mike shook his head. "He was blind drunk again. Like three times the legal limit. But this time, it wasn't so easy to cover it up. It happened in town, and Julie's mom worked for the MDW. They were really unhappy. Had their insurance and security people from Chicago snooping around to see if it was anything other than an accident."

"Jesus," Angela whispered. "You said Win told Steve after that business last year that he'd have no more chances. That he'd had enough of cleaning up Steve's messes all around the country: DUIs, drunken assaults, serial adultery and what, like a half dozen sexual harassment settlements?"

Mike nodded. "The MDW is a force in this town. Not like Blackpool, but still influential. You don't just kill one of their executives and sweep it under the rug. This had lots of exposure for Win and the company."

"That girl last year died too because of him," Angela said. "That's not nothing."

"No, but it wasn't like this. That was a nineteen-year-old girl working a paper machine in the Oregon mill who carried on an affair with Lonsdale for six months. He got her pregnant and fired her. Then she died during a botched abortion by Nate Burns that Lonsdale forced on her."

Angela sighed. "God, he's a butcher. I wouldn't let him treat me for a hangnail."

Mike snorted in accordance.

"So, how did Win fix the business with Julie's mom?"

"You mean, how did I fix it? I know, I know. I should have told you, but the fewer people who knew, the better."

Angela was fuming again, so Mike rushed out with the rest of the story.

"You know, Jill, the police chief's wife, has been steadily declining over the past couple of years with the ALS."

"Yes," Angela said, "everyone knows that."

"Well, since Jill is in no shape to, as the chief says, 'perform her marital duties,' he'd taken a mistress in Wenatchee. He put this woman up in a house, bought her a car, jewelry, all kinds of stuff, the usual drill."

Angela pursed her lips, knowing the moral rot of the situation had already spread like the flu, again infecting the two of them.

"With the mistress and Jill's medical bills, the chief had serious money trouble. The daughter's college fund was gone. He was under pressure at home, and Win was pushing him to clean up the Lonsdale mess and thwart the MDW. Right away, he started making noises to Win about needing some money if he was going to 'unfortunately' lose Lonsdale's blood alcohol readings from the night of the crash and to also silence the officers at the scene."

Angela leaned back into the couch cushions and folded her arms, not surprised.

"Win told me to fix it. I explained to the chief we couldn't just cut him a check or give him bags of cash. We decided the company would make a quiet contribution to the Police Union's welfare fund, a way for the chief to funnel something to the guys at the accident scene. And for the chief…"

"Wait, let me guess." Angela moved her hand to her forehead. "The scholarship Blackpool gave to the chief's decidedly average daughter for college a couple of months ago was his payoff."

"Yes," Mike said. "A four-year full ride. That was my idea."

18

Julie

Julie knew why Alex's parents were punting her into the foster care system. Her presence made Mike Davis uncomfortable, and her troubled life situation, an orphan with mental health issues and one maybe two suicide attempts, undoubtedly embarrassed Angela. To Mike and Angela, she was like black mold, something they needed to remediate from their house and their lives as quickly as possible.

Julie watched Alex rage about this injustice for weeks. She'd taken to calling her mother a "heartless bitch" on multiple occasions. That infuriated Angela, but Alex didn't care and kept using the term.

Alex had no idea what had happened to Julie that night at Win's, neither did Brian or Tim. Julie would never tell them. No one knew except Win, Mike Davis, probably Angela, Annie Findlay and Gloria Rodriquez, the Findlays' neighbor and a nurse Annie had reached out to in the aftermath. Annie Findlay had promised she wouldn't tell Brian that Julie had been assaulted. Brian had not asked Julie about it or mentioned to Alex that he wondered if Julie had really just taken a hard fall on the ice that night, as she claimed.

Julie was out of the Davis house by late September 1980, her junior year, and placed by local authorities with a foster parent, Roberta Zerepick. "Aunt Roberta" owned the Timbers, what she called a bed-and-breakfast, but what was really a rundown, fifteen-room, three-story hotel in the Flats. Roberta had apparently hosted foster kids off and on over the years, but that fall, Julie was her only resident. Roberta lived on the top floor, and Julie had a room on the ground floor, down a hallway with a lone bare lightbulb. She shared her bathroom with the lobby, and it had a toilet, a small sink and a metal shower with bad water pressure. Soon Julie realized the people who used the hotel rooms did so on an hourly basis.

Julie hardly slept during her first weeks of living there. Sad and depressed, she jumped out of her skin at every creak and odd noise in the quiet of the wee hours. She bought two deadbolt locks for her door. Win Blackpool re-entered Julie's dreams on occasion, and like rosary beads, she furiously worked the coping skills learned on her psychiatric journey to stay out of the abyss. She went from talking to her psychiatrist in Spokane by phone every week to three days a week. She fought and fought to stay above the waterline, and after a few weeks, her mental outlook began to improve.

Since Alex picked her up every morning for school, Julie asked if they could leave earlier so she could hit the early-morning mass at church. Every day before school, Julie prayed for mental stability, fortitude and the strength to stay positive. She prayed to hear from her mom in some way, for her presence to appear and provide reassurance she hadn't been abandoned. Alex went in with her sometimes, holding her hand or putting her hand on Julie's back when she kneeled. Other times, she sat in the car blasting her ELO or Def Leppard cassettes.

By November, Julie knew Roberta was a heroin user, losing the ability to function as her addiction gained traction. Like her guests at the Timbers, Roberta had become a prostitute. One of the call girls who worked at the hotel told Julie that Roberta was so far gone she took her fees in product rather than cash.

On Christmas Eve Day, Alex came to the Timbers with Julie. They'd been out shopping, and Alex was going to early evening mass with Julie. Alex wasn't religious, but she didn't want Julie to have to go alone on Christmas Eve. They had come by the Timbers for Julie to change clothes.

Alex walked in first. "What the hell?" A dozen bodies littered the lobby like felled bowling pins – on the couch, in the chairs and all over the floor.

"Ah, right, should have given you a heads-up." Julie sort of chuckled. "Told you there'd be people zoned-out all over the lobby. Roberta's customers. The hotel's been busier than usual this week, with the holidays, I guess. Maybe she's running a special."

Alex stood, speechless. Julie tried to put her at ease.

"At first, I found it really shocking to see people like this every day, but it's usually only two or three. And they're always so out of it. And most of the girls, not Roberta, look out for me and keep any bad people away. The ones that don't shoot up kind of look out for me."

"Great, Julie, you've been adopted by hookers."

Julie and Alex went to her bedroom, and, walking in, they both gasped. Naked and high, Roberta was giving a guy a blowjob on Julie's bed. Spray-painted on her bedroom wall was *Roberta Takes It up the Ass for Crack*. The needle tracks and sores all over Roberta's arms and legs shocked Julie.

Roberta saw Julie and said, "Oh, hi, honey. I didn't expect you home so early. Do me a favor and just go to the kitchen and let me finish up here. Won't take long."

Alex and Julie backed out of the room.

"What the fuck!" Alex seethed. "I'm calling the cops."

"No, Alex, please, don't. It's okay. I'll try to clean the paint off tonight."

"That's the problem. It shouldn't be. You should be raising hell. My fucking parents, I hate them!"

"Don't say that. Really, it's okay. I'm hardly ever here, anyway. I'm either at Tim's or your place, or we're all someplace else."

Exasperated, Alex asked, "Can't you move in at Tim's?"

"His parents have offered a couple of times, said they'd even go to court to try to become my guardians. But you know, that's just too weird. I'm his girlfriend, not his sister, and I don't know; staying there might mess that up."

Alex threw her hands up in frustration.

"My therapist in Spokane wants to intervene with social services. She says it's a terrible environment."

"No shit! Do you need a Ph.D. to decide that?"

"But I don't want her to get involved. I don't really tell her all the details because I don't want any more trouble. And I lie to my social worker; tell her everything's fine. I make sure we always meet in her office"

Julie was just trying to keep her head down, her eyes and ears shut to get through each day. Putting one foot in front of the other, one of her primary coping skills. Julie also had money from her mom's insurance and could have tried to access that through her court-appointed guardian to live on her own. But she wasn't yet ready to be alone, no matter how bad her situation was. She'd come across a Finnish proverb that said, "Life is all about finding an acceptable level of unhappiness."

"Aunt Roberta" died of a heroin overdose in June 1981, during the last week of Julie's junior year. Two of her customers found her in the alley behind the hotel, naked from the waist down, scabs and needle tracks all over her body, with a hypodermic stuck in her emaciated rear end.

When Julie told Alex the news, Alex's first comment was, "Well, good for her! That's the nicest thing she ever did for you."

Given a second chance, Washington State did better, placing Julie for her senior year in the home of a deacon at the local Catholic church and his wife. Their children had long since grown and moved away, and they were happy to take her in. Immediately, Julie knew they were kind, generous, interested and loving. *Maybe things will start looking up for me*, she mused.

19

Alex

MAY – DECEMBER 1981

May, almost the end of junior year, and on the third Saturday of the month, I needed to be in Spokane for some sort of all-day student government conference. I was going to be the senior class president of Timberline High in the fall. Brian was going to be the student body president, but he was bagging this conference to work. My car was in the shop, but as it turned out, my mother had some people she wanted to meet next time she was in Spokane, so she agreed to take me.

My mother was fifty-two at the time and an attractive woman. She was thin with light brown, shortish hair that framed perpetually furrowed eyebrows and pursed lips. Her features were harder and more chiseled than mine. Angela was always a sharp dresser. I'd lived with her my entire life, and I could probably count on two hands the times I'd seen her in workout clothes, an old sweatshirt with holes, or even, god forbid, pajamas. She always wore her clothes for the day until she went to bed. My mother, the department store mannequin. That day she was wearing a charcoal tweed skirt, matching blazer, white blouse and short black heels.

The trip down was fine, peppered with occasional light conversation followed by forty to fifty miles of silence. I worked haphazardly on homework and listened to my cassettes with headphones. Perfect.

We were over an hour into the return trip to TL, early evening and the silence lulled me. Alas, it was too good to be true.

"Alexandra," my mother began, "Julie is soon to be a senior in high school, and I never hear her talk about her college plans. What is she thinking about? Did her mother even go to college?"

"Uh, duh. She was a manager at the MDW. She graduated from St. Mary's."

"Never heard of it," Angela sniffed.

"It's a women's college affiliated with Notre Dame. Notre Dame is co-ed today, but in the sixties, the men were at Notre Dame, and the women went to St. Mary's across the road."

"Well, Notre Dame is certainly a respectable school. Not elite, but okay. Why doesn't Julie go there? Or would she not get in?"

What's this all about mother? Why the sudden interest in Julie? Are you finally feeling just the smallest shred of guilt for kicking her out and making her live in a shithole crack house? Or are you just counting the days until you can hopefully see her go far away to college?"

"Alexandra! Watch your language and tone. I'm no longer having that conversation about Julie's living arrangements with you. Anyway, I'm always interested in hearing about your friends' plans, what colleges they might be able to get into and that kind of thing. You tell me Julie is really smart, that she scores around the ninety-eighth percentile on standardized tests. She should have good college options. I think it would be good for her to get far away from this area."

"Do you want to know her bra and underwear size next?"

"Don't be crude with me. Nobody would ever know Julie was smart. She just takes up space in a room and doesn't say anything. Doesn't contribute, shape the conversation, or make a forceful impression. And since her father is from India, she doesn't look as white as most people in this town, so it's especially important she makes a good impression. Now, she always dresses well. I'll give her that. But one of my friends half-jokingly asked me if she was mute. I was embarrassed for her and for me. It makes me nervous taking her places with you, Alexandra."

I rolled my eyes and shook my head.

"Look, I know Julie's had some speed bumps in life – her mom and that other business. But challenges present themselves all the time, and people pick themselves up and don't let circumstances define them. They set goals, they make a plan, and they go out and achieve something."

"That 'other business,'" I said, using air quotes. "Unbelievable! You mean a suicide attempt and months of psychiatric hospitalization?

Wouldn't that make anyone a little shy or reserved? You hardly even know her, anyway."

"Fine, Alexandra, but I know what I see."

I shrugged and sat back in the passenger seat. "Well, go ahead and see what you think you see."

Angela eyed me coldly, brisk vapors of condescension coming right off the glacier. "Perception is reality for most people, you should remember that. That's just the way it is in life."

Not able to let it go, to let Angela have the last word, I shot back. "Julie plans to go to college. She just doesn't have her list of places yet. Look at Tim and Brian. Tim won't know where he's going until he decides on a basketball scholarship. And Brian hasn't really thought about where he'll go if he doesn't get an Annapolis appointment."

Angela blew a short gust of air out of her pursed lips. "I hardly think Tim and Brian are people Julie, or you for that matter, should be looking to as an example. I mean, they're nice boys and smart perhaps, but Tim's father drives a beer truck, and his mother's a secretary, for god's sake. And Brian's family, good lord, they're white trash, living down there by the river, taking food stamps and welfare."

I took that in, briefly lost in thought…

**WIFE OF PROMINENT LOCAL EXECUTIVE STRANGLED!
BODY FOUND IN OUTHOUSE PIT NEAR SPOKANE;
POLICE HAVE MANY SUSPECTS.**

Furious now but telling myself to keep my wits about me, I finally said, "I don't think of them that way. Their parents are always very nice to me, and I really like them. Well, not Brian's dad so much; he's a different person since the accident."

I saw no reason to tell my mother the extent of his damage. When Brian and I were in seventh grade, his dad Roger had been leading a logging crew for Blackpool during torrential October rains when the hillside gave way and buried him and two others in a landslide. Roger saved his men, but the slide destroyed him, wrecked his spine and legs. Months of hospitalizations and surgeries couldn't help much. Permanently disabled, he had a wheelchair but spent most of his time in pain lying on the sofa – angry, drinking and quaffing narcotic painkillers. His inability to work and medical bills drove the Findlays into crushing poverty. The bank took their house in Central, forcing the family, including Roger, Annie, Brian and his three younger siblings, to move to their tiny hovel in the Flats.

Still up for battle with my mother, I continued, "Besides, what you do for a living doesn't define the kind of person you are."

Angela rolled her eyes and looked at me. "That's just naïve, Alexandra."

The landing crafts of Angela's second wave were now rolling up to the beaches.

"About Brian. He's a nice boy, but you certainly don't plan to just keep following him around all doe-eyed after high school, do you? Like Julie does with Tim. Giving up your own ambitions or ideas to just be Mrs. Brian Findlay? God, I hope you choose to do better than that."

It was then I had some appreciation as to how crimes of passion got committed. I wanted to roll down my window, reach over to the logging truck we were passing, break off a heavy piece of lumber, and crush her skull with it.

"You don't know shit, mother. I'm surprised you can see out the front window with that huge bejeweled scepter stuck up your ass. I know it will horrify your snooty minions, but what if I love Brian? What if I marry him? But even if I do, I'm still going to an Ivy League college, and I'll be successful in whatever I do after that."

She reflected on this and sighed. "I hope you're right. I would hate to see you settle for marriage and motherhood, with Brian or someone else for that matter, because you don't have the courage or the work ethic to do anything else. To see you decide to just spread your legs rather than use your brain."

I turned the radio down and looked at her. "Does your comment mean you're not a fan of motherhood? Do you not see anything of value in it?"

She pursed her lips and wrinkled her nose as if reacting to sewer gas.

"Motherhood is nice in ways, but it's mainly an obligation. It's something you need to do as well as you can if you find yourself in that circumstance. But it's not a particularly prestigious or noteworthy vocation. Anyone with a uterus can do it."

I thought about that.

JUNE CLEAVER NOW PERSON OF INTEREST IN OUTHOUSE SLAYING - WALLY AND BEAVER SHOCKED

I was kind of enjoying this now, as I seemed to have landed a shot. "I don't agree. It's probably the most important thing for your children, isn't it, MOTHER? Because life can be hard for a child if you don't have someone who thinks motherhood is really important. Someone to set expectations and get you on the right path, yes, but also someone to love and take care of you, to pick you up when you're down. To ease, rather than feed, your insecurities and fears. Don't you think?"

She was quiet as we passed another logging truck. Back in the right lane, she said, "I'm not going to argue with you, Alexandra. I think I know quite a bit more about the subject than you."

Out of the corner of my eye, I imagined I saw a highway sign: Timberline 3,431 miles.

• • •

Fall of senior year, Brian and I were Homecoming King and Queen. Homecoming was at the last football game in October, and it was snowing hard at halftime as the homecoming court rode in six convertibles around the track at the football stadium. There was an unzipped sleeping bag in each car that we spread across our laps to try to keep warm.

I was freezing in a black dress and sweater, having changed out of my cheerleading uniform in the girls' bathroom when halftime began. Brian was wearing a sport coat, white dress shirt, jeans and cowboy boots. The sleeping bags didn't help much to keep me warm, but thankfully the cars moved around the track, like the pace lap of the Indy 500, I'd joked.

My parents missed it, of course. My father was in Montana at a Blackpool sawmill that had operational problems. As always, my mother didn't give a reason for not coming. She just didn't want to admit that she couldn't see herself sitting in the stands socializing with people she viewed as her inferiors or watching her daughter do something she deemed frivolous and degrading – "air-head-ish," she told me more than once.

I was a varsity cheerleader for the third year, and while that was always painful during football season (1-8 sophomore year, 2-7 junior year and 0-9 senior year), it was the best thing ever during basketball season. The guys had gone 34-0 and won the state basketball title as juniors. The town was in a frenzy, with 9,000-plus people packing

The Barn for every game. Brian and Tim were first-team all-state as juniors, and Tim ended up as Washington's Mr. Basketball.

Lots of people, I think, look forward to leaving home for college; they are tired of high school and want to take their next step in life. I was one of those people, but as much as anything, I was sick of my parents and couldn't wait to get away from them. Our relationship was a drought that had seen only minimal life-affirming nutrients throughout high school. It was arid and dangerous tinder.

20

Alex

It was a sunny Monday morning in early June, and Julie and I were high school graduates! It was in the low seventies, with a sunny blue sky and puffy clouds. The forest's evergreens smelled like the arrival of a short but fantastic summer, as did the freshly mown grass. We sat in the press box of the high school football stadium, the last gasps of freshman PE for the school year playing out before us. Man, they looked young and clueless!

We'd graduated the previous Saturday afternoon and had come back to clear a few remaining things out of our lockers. Finished, we wandered to the football field and, finding it in use, ended up in the tiny wooden press box, prime witness to years of futility in football.

Even now, done with school, Julie had, as always, invested more care than me in her appearance. She was wearing dark indigo jeans, new white leather Adidas sneakers and a pale blue button-down blouse with a white collar. I had faded blue Levi's with a big rip in the left knee, a red polo shirt and ratty, black, low-top Chuck Taylors with yellow paint splotches and no socks.

We sat in silence for a while, watching the freshmen labor through the end of the spring track and field unit. I reached out and squeezed Julie's forearm.

"Hey, why so quiet?"

I didn't think she heard me because she just kept staring down at the field and biting her lower lip. But finally, after maybe half a minute, she swallowed hard.

"I'm pregnant, with twins."

I imagined this was what it was like when a bomb went off in your midst: surreal, disorienting and terrifying. I sat silent, my mouth hanging open.

Julie poked me in the arm. "I've rendered you speechless, probably for the first time ever."

"But...but...how?" I sputtered. "You and Tim weren't even having sex."

"I'm the cautionary tale, right? The person your parents and health teachers warn you about. 'She didn't plan to have sex, but things got away from them just one time, and now she's pregnant.' I could star in one of those ABC Afterschool Specials."

"That's not funny, Julie."

"Did you and Brian ever have any, you know, close calls?"

I shook my head. "We've only done it once, last year, right before Christmas. It wasn't as fun or easy as I thought it would be. Let's just say I wasn't any good at it. It was embarrassing. So I told Brian I wanted to wait until we got to college. He was disappointed, but he understood. Said my new nickname for him could be 'Blue Balls.'"

Julie wiped a small tear from the corner of her eye with her fingers.

"Ah, sweetie, Julie. I know this is unexpected, but if anyone can make lemonade from lemons, it's you and Tim."

She shrugged as more tears flowed down her cheeks. She needed both hands now to wipe them away. In a halting voice, she sputtered, "Yeah, I've had lots of practice at that, huh? And, uh, um, I really don't know where Tim will come out on all of this."

"What do you mean? He knows, doesn't he? When did you learn all of this?"

"Of course Tim knows. It happened in early March, and then I was late, and you know that's never happened. I run like a Swiss watch. I got someone to buy me like ten home pregnancy tests, and they were all positive. So, a week later, this person drove me to Wenatchee to see a doctor because, you know, I couldn't go to anyone in this town. You could see the headline, 'Weird girlfriend of beloved local basketball star pregnant, set to ruin his life and college career.'"

"Who took you to Wenatchee?" I asked.

"Annie Findlay."

"Really? Did Brian know?"

"No."

I learned later that Brian's mom, Annie, had become a sort of surrogate mom to Julie – something I didn't know. I also learned it was Julie who'd pushed Annie to address her drinking problem our senior year and did a bunch of things to offer support.

Annie was warm and affectionate, the kind of person who made you feel special and always seemed happy to see you. She greeted each day with the resolve to be positive and energetic, to enjoy whatever small pleasures or victories came her way. She did better than most would have for a long time. But by our junior year, her husband's pain and disabilities, his verbal abuse, and the family's crushing poverty had torpedoed her.

Thus, Annie embraced the bottle. It was a clandestine affair initially, stolen moments when nobody was looking. But secrecy became the casualty as Annie's passion built, and the existence of her dangerous new lover was eventually evident for all to see. Most days, she was upbeat and upright, seemingly full of the Lord-doesn't-give-you-anything-you-can't-handle spirit. Nights, however, she retreated outside to the back porch of their tiny house in the Flats. There she would quietly weep and drink herself into an anesthetized state, her pain and demons inexorably shrinking her family presence like air leaking from a balloon.

Idiot that I was, I offered Julie a simple prescription. "So, now you just move to Berkeley with Tim, and the two of you will start your life and family together early. Right?"

She shook her head and again bit her lower lip.

"I don't think so, at least not right away. This is all too much for him now."

"And it isn't for you? Jesus. What, he wants you to wait a couple of months and then come down?"

"I don't think he wants me down at all. And I'm not going to force myself on him."

"What the fuck? He's being a total shit."

"I'm looking into some things."

"An abortion?"

"Alex! Please, how long have you known me?"

Julie had told me that Annie and I were the only people that knew of her situation in addition to Tim, though she wondered if he'd told Brian. Two days later, we met again in the high school press box in the early evening. There was nobody around. It was breezy, and in the fifties, the lights of Timberline, the mountains and the river spread out before us.

"What do Tim's parents think? I can't believe they'd be telling him to just abandon you and his kids?" I asked.

Quietly, almost in a whisper, Julie said, "I don't know if he plans to tell them. At least not now."

"What the fuck! He's nuts. He thinks he can keep a secret like that in this town?"

"Well, maybe he can if I leave town in the next few weeks."

"For Portland? To go to Reed, like you planned?"

"No. I'd have to live off campus, just me and the babies. They have no housing for people in my, say, situation. I could afford it – I have my mom's insurance money – but it doesn't seem like my best option to go there without support."

"You could stay in Timberline."

Julie looked at me like I'd lost my mind. "God no, Alex! You, Brian and Tim, will be gone, and I'm going to stay in this town where the worst things that ever happened to me took place? And where lots of people just think of me as 'that girl who tried to kill herself,' and they'd now think I was just trying to trap their basketball hero?"

Julie dropped her chin to her chest and closed her eyes tight. I was afraid she would start sobbing. But finally, she whispered, "I don't have many choices, Alex. But I've decided to keep the babies and not adopt them out. I don't know how I'll make it work, but I'll find a way."

"Okay, then I'm all in for you. We'll find a living situation for you that works."

Julie wiped her eyes again, sniffled a couple of times and raised her head to look at me.

"My mom's best friend from St. Mary's is now the Dean of Admissions there. She's kept in touch with me since mom died. She found a full-tuition scholarship that I could get, even as a part-time student. St. Mary's gives me probably my best living option."

"What's that?"

"There's a complex on campus where retired priests and nuns live. There's a one-bedroom apartment in the building I could live in. Go to school full time this fall semester. I'm due in December, and then if I can make it work, maybe take a class after December. My mom's friend said she could arrange help with childcare from people on campus and get me a job at the front desk of the building, so I'd have some money."

"You've never been to Indiana."

"True, but I was close, since mom and I lived in Chicago before we moved to TL."

"You know, I ran into Tim downtown last night and called him an absolute shit. Told him he was being a pussy for not stepping up."

Julie shook her head. "He's not a shit. He's just not able to deal with this now. And that's why I can't go to Berkeley with him. I wish I could, but it doesn't feel right. If I'm not wanted, I'm not going to force him to do anything. He has to want me. Who knows, maybe later, but the timing or whatever is not working now."

I leaned over and put my arm around her. "You're going to be fine, and we're both going to have great lives."

Julie sniffled and shrugged. "Do you know what I want?"

"What?" I asked.

"I want to graduate from college and have a family. I want to go to bed at night, not afraid of what or who might be lurking outside my window. I want to get up in the morning, not worrying about what bad things might happen next. And when my mind tells me my world is nothing but blackness, I want peace and hope."

I dropped my head onto her shoulder and said, "You'll get that. You're one of the toughest people I know. I will love you forever and always be with you. Never forget that."

PART 3

Middle Management

1994

21

Ireland and Northern Ireland

March 1994, and I'd been out of prison for a month. Molly Fitzhugh came down to Dublin immediately after her/my release. I was working in an upscale pub, McNulty's, near Trinity College. I was sleeping on a sofa in some flophouse the organization had arranged in a dicey part of town.

I likely only had a couple of months more in Dublin. I would leave Ireland and resurface in Berlin as Petra Müller. Same flat in the Mitte district but a different job, this time a junior management sort in an advertising firm. I would be moving up in the world! In Germany, I could finally return my hair to its natural blonde state. No more improvised prison dye jobs using shoe polish and other primitive things assembled from the commissary with the money my "parents" put in my account every month.

I needed to be in Dublin for a while so the authorities would lose track of me. Would've looked odd for someone just out of prison to fly off to Germany.

It was sometime before 21:00 on a Friday night, and McNulty's was loud, crowded and happy. Heaving, as the English would say. Lots of couples flirting, groups of friends laughing and everyone dressed well. Nobody looked lonely like me. I was behind the bar, looking down and pouring a Harp off the tap, and when I looked up, I couldn't believe it. I almost spilled the pour.

Maeve, smiling wide and staring right at me.

Still those sparkling eyes and straight hair that didn't quite touch her shoulders. Wearing a red wool shawl-collar sweater and a black skirt, she was also sporting big dangling costume jewelry earrings

135

and her ever-present fedora, this one black wool felt with a red stripe around the base. *That woman is always dressed well. She reminds me of Julie in that way.*

I hadn't seen her since Berlin in December 1990, over three years prior. I was afraid of Maeve, that fierce, mysterious, competent woman, but I also longed for her approval. I wondered, would we ever get closer?

Maeve leaned toward me to be heard amidst the good times. "Excuse me, love, the jacks, where?"

Too stunned to speak, I mumbled, "Uh…um…um…sorry, what?"

"I need the toilet. Where's it at?"

"It's, ah, back behind the bar. You go down the stairs, and then it's there."

"Cheers, love. I was sure you'd know. That's where I'll be then."

What did that mean? *"That's where I'll be then."* What was I supposed to do? This couldn't have been a coincidence, could it? Was she bringing me a message? Did she want to talk? Would she come back, have me follow her outside? Or should I follow her now? I'd just sounded like an idiot: Yeah, um, uh, uh. Damn! Yes. I'll go on break and go down to the bathroom. Just see what happens.

The ladies was a two-stall setup, both occupied when I stumbled down the stairs and through the door. Maeve was first in line, and as I got in behind her, she smiled brightly. A good sign, I hoped. Maybe she'd wanted me to follow her down.

"Ah, look at you, love. Decided to join me, I see. My husband's always telling me I've got a tiny tank. Every time we go out, I need to make at least two trips to the jacks."

The women in one of the stalls exited. Maeve went into the stall closest to the chipped white tile wall, and I entered the other when it freed up. I sat down and peed. Why not? I didn't know what else to do. Maeve was peeing, too.

Since these were American-type stalls rather than the full floor-to-ceiling European setup, Maeve passed me a note between the small space in the back where the stalls didn't quite touch the tiled wall.

> Great seeing you, love! Proud of you for getting through the prison bit. Brill work. Will have you settled back in Berlin within a month. Soon we will get caught up on everything. But we're in a pinch now, a bit of an emergency – unexpected really – that's why I'm here. We need your help with an urgent

situation tonight. Not ideal, but you're available. It's very short notice, and we need a young woman. Below is a map of the area around the St. James Gate Guinness brewery. After work, follow the map and retrieve the instructions as indicated. I don't know any other details, so can't tell you more than this. Good luck, love. Burn this note once you get back to the bar. Wait a bit here before leaving the stall to let me get outside. Can't have people seeing us coming out of the loo together.

Maeve flushed and left. A dead drop. I needed to go unload the dead drop. I returned behind the bar, and Maeve was gone.

I left McNulty's at the end of my shift at 22:00 and began my circuitous, multi-transfer bus journey toward the brewery to make sure nobody was following me. By 23:30, I'd left the buses and walked to the appointed intersection. It was raining, cold and foggy, with temperatures in the low forties Fahrenheit.

It was a mixed area, residential and commercial, but no traffic at that time of night. I was nervous, sweating like I was in a sauna. I smelled of BO, and the rain hardly put a dent in it. *Where is the dead drop?* I looked at the map again, but the rain was making the ink run. *Why didn't I bring an umbrella? I'm an idiot!* Nobody was around, but still, I couldn't be seen wandering about looking at a map. Ah, over there across the street, I saw it.

Next to a phone box was a blue trash dumpster sitting near the street at the side of the Indian restaurant Tandor Palace. I looked around, didn't see anyone, and walked to the dumpster. The rain jumped off its metal lid and kicked back into my face. I took out my small flashlight, lifted the lid and scanned the top layer of trash. There! An empty Boots store-brand one-kilo-sized detergent box, and inside a tiny package wrapped in a waterproof cover.

I had to get out of the rain to read the note. Three blocks away, I found a covered bus shelter with a light and nobody waiting. It was midnight, and the note told me I had to be downtown next to the main post office on the River Liffey by 01:00. Not much time to weave around and make sure I wasn't being followed. I was roughly two miles away.

I was to meet Max, a guy who'd be wearing a red Chicago Bulls baseball hat. There would also be Paul, with a blue raincoat and black Guinness knit hat, and finally, Otto, who was bald. The note offered nothing else other than a password sequence.

● ● ●

I was at the post office on time. I'd had to run the last mile from where I got off the bus. The rain had stopped, and I was panting when I saw my dates. I walked over.

Max did the talking. "Lady. I don't think the trains run this late. Did you walk?"

That was the right question, so I gave the coded response. "No, there are still bus routes running this time of night, but it can be dodgy."

Max nodded. "Welcome, Molly."

"What's going on?"

Max took his Bulls cap off and started picking his nose. That was just gross, not a coded message. "You don't need to know. Better for you that way. We need you to do one thing. We goin' to a house outside Dublin. You gonna pound on the door and wake up the woman inside, Patricia Maguire."

"Okay, then what?"

"You to tell her you go to university here with her son Brady and he gave you this address. You say Brady's been in a nasty fight outside a pub and is cut up bad. You wanted to take him to hospital, but he refused. Said he wanted his mum's view if he should go. He's at a friend's house, and you want to take her there. You have the friend's car outside. Then get her out to the car, and that's it. Nothing more for you, so then push off and be on your way."

The four of us, Max (young, freckles, red hair), Otto (short, muscular and bald), Paul (tall, lanky and a bad complexion), and I climbed into a green two-door Ford hatchback and headed west out of Dublin. Thirty minutes later, we were in a neighborhood of tiny cottages astride narrow alleys just off a small commercial square. Two pubs were open about a hundred yards away, but nothing else except the Garda station across the commercial square. Great. The Garda was always open.

I pounded on the designated door, waited for the woman to answer, and told my story. She was maybe in her thirties with short hair, like plastic wrap had stuck to her head. She was five-five, I guessed and overweight with an owlish face. She got her coat right away, muttering all the while. "Ah, Brady, always getting in scrapes, worrying your poor mother. I'm always on my knees praying for that boy."

It was dark, no streetlights, but as we closed on the car, she saw Max, Paul and Otto and stopped. "Oh mercy, oh mercy," she whimpered and crossed herself. She tried to pull away, but I had my arm through hers and dragged her along toward the car.

"Good ole Mother Mary gonna be no use to ya tonight, Pat," Paul snarled.

"Hi, Pat, get in the car, please," Otto quietly suggested.

"Why? Where we goin'? Let's just talk here. Come in, and I'll make some tea."

Otto shook his head. "Get in the car, please, Pat."

Visibly shaking, the woman walked slowly toward them. Paul grabbed the arm I'd been holding and pushed her toward the car. I stayed behind the boot, between Paul and the woman on one side of the car, and Otto and Max on the other.

Paul opened the hatchback's front door and tilted the front seat forward to put the woman in the back. Apparently, he had a knife in his inner coat pocket because she suddenly grabbed it and stabbed him hard in the thigh.

Paul screamed. The knife stuck deep in his thigh, like a fork into a moist Thanksgiving turkey, and he fell to the ground. I saw blood oozing, illuminated by the car's dome light. He rolled around in agony, making a hell of a racket.

The woman took off running, screaming, "Help, help, help me, please, somebody! Oh Mary, please, somebody help, help!"

"Fuck!" Max uttered.

"Abort! Abort!" came from Otto. He seemed to be the boss. "Get in the car, everyone, and let's go."

I didn't know why, but I chose not to hear him. The woman hadn't gotten far. She was neither fit nor fast. As she ran, her billowing ass looked like a bunch of kittens fighting to get out of a burlap sack. Without thinking, I took off to run her down. She was a block ahead of me and headed straight for the Garda station. Thank god there were no drunken pub crawlers out on the street.

I closed on her, a lion reeling in a doomed zebra. I figured Otto, Max, and the car would be gone when I caught her. She'd scream, make a scene, and the coppers would find Molly Fitzhugh, just out of prison for manslaughter. Then I'd be screwed. Back to prison for god knows how long. Or worse, the Provisionals would silence me forever.

But I didn't care. I didn't know what this woman had done, but she wasn't going to mess up a mission I was on and make me look bad.

She was slowing, losing her wind. My plan was to grab her, hold on to her, calm her down, and hope the others hadn't left me. But my momentum took me into the back of her, and I ended up tackling her to the pavement.

We both went down. I hit my forehead hard on the road.

She was crying. "Please, please, don't let them take me. Don't let them kill me! They're here to kill me, and I didn't do nothin' wrong. My children, my wee uns."

I tried to get my hand over her mouth to get her under control. Out of the corner of my eye, I saw several Garda officers exiting the station a couple hundred yards across the square. Three of them began jogging our way. *Great.*

Hopefully, they'd just think we were two drunken fools who'd fallen down.

"Shut up!" I whispered to the woman. "Calm down."

But I couldn't keep her quiet. I had to get her off the street. I pulled her up harshly and dragged her away to one of the residential alleys. Good thing the streetlights were out. Lying on her at the top of the narrow alley, both hands clamped over her mouth, it took every bit of my strength to keep her down and limit her thrashing.

The Garda officers came closer, now standing on the street only about twenty yards from us. One of them lit a cigarette. *For chrissakes, why not just go get some doughnuts and eat them here, too?* My head throbbed, and I was getting nauseous, fighting to keep from throwing up. Vomiting would turn the searchlights onto us, like ill-fated World War II allied airmen thwarted in their escape from Stalag Whatever.

Finally, one of the Garda said, "Ah, probly jis a couple of pissed eejits wandering through. Let's go." *Why rush off? You sure you don't want another cigarette?* The coppers walked back to the square, climbed into two squad cars, and pulled away in opposite directions.

Otto, Max, and Limping Paul walked up after the Garda left. Paul had gotten the knife out of his thigh and was holding a rag against the wound, but blood continued to ooze. They dragged the woman to her feet, and Paul punched her square in the face.

Broke her nose; pushed it over to the side. Blood was already flowing. I knew how that felt and thought it unprofessional of Paul to hit her. That wasn't needed to subdue her. He was just pissed off about his leg, but he was careless, leaving a knife within the woman's reach.

I shoved him. "What the hell are you doing? There was no cause for that. It's your fault. You let her get away."

"Shut up, cunt," he hissed.

"Fuck you, incompetent bastard!" I screamed back.

Otto spoke firmly, with a gravel-like undertone of menace. "Molly! Calm down! Things go wrong all the time in this business. We deal with it and move on. And good work here, good on you."

"Yeah, calm down, you little twat," Paul spat.

Otto walked over to Paul and got in his face. "That's enough," he whispered. "Not another fuckin' word. Understand? Now get the hell out of here. You're not coming. You can't drive with your leg messed up. Find the doc and get it looked at."

Paul protested, but Otto shook his head. "Don't. Don't. Control yourself and walk away. Now. Ya hear me? Just go. Don't make me tell ya again."

Paul limped off with a "fucking bitch" parting shot for me.

"Wanker!" I shouted back, giving him the finger.

Max ran to get the car and brought it over. Otto and Max sat the woman in the middle of the back seat, the two of them on either side of her.

"I guess you're not finished, Molly," Max said. "You're driving. Let's go."

Dazed, I got behind the wheel. I drove north out of Dublin toward Belfast on the M1. I said nothing, but listened carefully to try to understand who this woman was and who these other people were.

I guessed I had a concussion from hitting my head: Splitting headache, a bit of double vision and some disorientation. Within thirty minutes, I had to pull over and be sick. I barely got to the side of the road, and my door opened in time before torrential vomiting emptied my stomach. An hour later, fighting debilitating nausea, I pulled over again in a cold sweat and vomited and dry heaved for what seemed like forever. I was splayed on the ground on all fours in the mud before I was able to shakily get back in the car.

The woman knew Otto, it seemed.

"Otto, what you thinkin'?" she pleaded. "Please, please, we grew up together in the Shank, our families surrounded by Unionists—." *West Belfast, a largely Protestant area, off Shankill Road.* "Otto, where you takin' me? Me wee uns, I can't leave 'em. I'm all they got since Benny passed; been three years now. Who will care for my babies? Oh, Jesus, Mary and Joseph, me wee uns."

Max had heard enough. "Christ, Otto, can't ye shut 'er up?"

"Stay out of it," Otto growled.

The woman droned on and on, getting more hysterical with each sentence.

Finally, Otto couldn't take it anymore. "I'm not happy 'bout this, Pat," he quietly said. "Not my idea. This coming right from the top."

"Why, god, why? I didn't do nothing, Otto!"

Max couldn't help himself, despite Otto's command to keep silent. "Then why you hidin' down in Dublin, Pat? Stealin' out of West Belfast two weeks ago and leavin' your precious we uns behind with your sister, if you're so worried 'bout 'em?"

"My other sister was ill. I come down here to help her and to see my Brady. Nothing wrong with that. I haven't done nothin'!"

"Ah, Pat," Otto said, almost sadly, "your sister don't live in that Dublin house. It's a friend of yours. And you know why we're here. You're a goddamn tout for the Brits. For the RUC. At great risk to me, I even gave you an effin warning last year. Remember? Outta respect for havin' grown up wit ya off the Shank. Your neighbors in Divis." *Divas Flats, a West Belfast housing project full of low-income Catholics off the Falls Road* "Seen ya helpin' that British soldier, taking 'em into your flat."

"Otto, he been shot and crawled to my doorstep and knocked on the door, moanin'. He wasn't any older than my Brady. I couldn't let him bleed to death, for god's sake!"

"Pat! Then when I seen ya last year, I took that radio transmitter your neighbors said the Brits gave you, but you got another one. Jesus, Pat. I know you got money trouble with nine kids and bein' a widow, but how could ya do this? To your own people? Now you gonna pay a high price, and there aint nothin' I can do. Oh my god, Pat, what have you effin done? I'm sick about this."

Pat was sobbing, wailing, really. "Oh, god, Mary, Mother Mary, help me, please. It's not true. It's not true! Otto, please! Otto! What will my wee uns do? Brady, he's twenty and off at university. He'll be okay, maybe, but Mary, Otto, my baby Mary, she's only six. Ma'am, you up there, driving, tell 'em, tell 'em how horrible it would be for a little girl to grow up without a mother or father. Please! And my other seven are less than fifteen."

Another wave of nausea hit me, and I had to fight pulling over to throw up again. The smell of vomit on my shirt from earlier wasn't helping, nor was the fact we had a veritable farmers' market of BO in the car. Was it the concussion or the thought of what I'd gotten myself into making me sick? What I'd allowed to happen? Taking deep breaths through my mouth helped a little, and I opened the window wider for more fresh air.

We'd crossed the border, I was pretty sure and passed Drogheda and Dunleer. I was back in Northern Ireland, South Armagh. I didn't fear the police because this was what the media liked to call Bandit Country, a bastion of the Provisional IRA. It was common knowledge that neither the cops nor the British Army would venture there after dark. Since the Troubles kicked up in the early seventies, something like one hundred and twenty-five British soldiers and over sixty cops had been killed by the locals or the Provisionals.

Pat regained a bit of composure. "So, if you just gonna kill me, Otto, why not do it and leave my body in the street in West Belfast? Isn't that what you lot do with touters? To teach everyone a lesson. I seen those shovels in the back of this car. You're going to kill me and bury me so my kids can never find me, aren't you? Because killing a thirty-six-year-old widow with nine children would be too much for anyone to take your side, wouldn't it? That would be unspeakable, even for the murdering godless Provisionals."

Pat started to cry again. "Oh, Otto, Otto. You'll burn in hell for this. What would your poor mum think if she was alive to know you's doin' this? She used to take you and me to mass when we was little. Remember? And you—" She pointed at Max. "And you up there driving, you both goin' to hell too. Just as certain as the sunrise. You'll burn forever. You'll never see your loved ones and the beauty on the other side."

Just before 04:00, Max told me, "Stop up here and get out. We don't need you from here. I'll drive."

I pulled over, numb and disoriented. The woman was shrieking again. "Help me, miss, help me. Oh, please help me! You gonna burn with Otto and this other fella if you don't. Don't leave me! Please!"

As I was exiting the car, she grabbed hold of my arm and dug her fingernails in deep, her parting gift to Pontius Pilate. She drew blood. Her eyes lined me up like the barrels of two Glocks.

"Don't, don't," she whimpered. "Miss, save yourself and help me. Stop this! Save yourself if you don't care about me!"

Like an escaping prisoner caught in a searchlight, I didn't move. I couldn't move. Her eyes!

Otto gently tapped my shoulder and pushed a bit. "Move on, please, Molly. Good on you tonight. You done good."

I forcefully removed Pat's clinging hand from my flesh and stepped back.

I took ten or twenty steps away from the car. As Max went around the car to get in the driver's seat, I beckoned him over. "I know we're in South Armagh, Max, but where? And what do I do next?"

He pointed down the road in front of the car. "Crossmaglen is ten kilometers down that road. You can hitchhike into Dundalk from there, where you can get a bus back to Dublin. Or you can walk to Dundalk from here. It's a bit over twenty kilometers."

Max started walking back to the car, but stopped and turned to me. "Good work tonight. This is unpleasant business, not something we would usually do, but the man himself on top, the Officer Commanding, handed down the orders."

I rubbed my face with both hands. I knew the answer but felt the need to ask, "What's going to happen to her?"

Max came over to me, took off his Chicago Bulls hat, and leaned in close. Long hairs stuck out of his nostrils, and his breath just about knocked me over: Cigarettes (Marlboros), Irish whiskey (Bushmills) and terrible food (Chinese). He made a small pistol figure with his thumb and index finger.

"OBE," he said.

"What? I don't understand."

"One behind the ear, from Otto."

The car drove away, a hearse with oxidized green paint missing three of its four hubcaps. I could see Pat through the back window launching her final, futile appeals to the jury. I was standing at the side of what was barely a country road, a path, really. I couldn't move, couldn't function. Everything was spinning and roaring in my head.

I sat on the grass, pulled my knees to my chest, and rested my head on them. The sun would start up in an hour or so, a pretty new beginning over the peaceful countryside. Yet a few miles away, Pat would cry and moan as Otto shot her in the head. Then he would bury her in an unmarked grave. No more sunrises for Patricia Maguire.

I could remember crying only three times in my life. The first was in the fourth grade after my ski accident. Then in high school with Julie. The third time was that unspeakable day in Africa in the summer of '85.

But now I started and couldn't stop. Gasping, racking sobs tore through me as I poured tears onto that grass road in Northern Ireland. What had I done? That poor woman and her children. What was I doing in this kind of life? What was the matter with me? Then a painful, stabbing thought: Jesus, was I just an unfeeling, cold-hearted, ambitious bitch like my mother?

Otto or Max had called to abort the mission back in Dublin, but I had to run her down for some reason. Why? They'd have gotten her anyway, another time, but I would have been back in Germany and wouldn't have her blood on my hands. Her howls burrowing into my dreams like plutonium into groundwater, her life intermixed with mine forever. Yes, she was a tout, a traitor, a spy for the British. But what she had done didn't seem bad enough for this. Bad enough to make orphans of nine children.

I had no idea how long I'd been on the ground, folded like a lawn chair left behind at a picnic. Finally, I tried to compose myself and think about the future. I reminded myself I was fighting a war, one that entailed blood, death, sorrow and loss. But as much as I tried to only look forward, I couldn't.

Gatsby stared at the green light at the end of Daisy's dock every night, certain evidence he was sure, of a new and better life. But looking at the light, Nick Carraway knew better – that we never leave our pasts no matter how much we want to. I struggled with this every lonely night - Brian, Adaoma and Julie the currents dragging me into the past.

22

May 1994, and I was on the overnight train from Berlin to Vienna. Though a nine-hour trip, mostly through the Czech Republic, it was more anonymous than flying. Petra Müller was staying home and wouldn't be seeing Maeve. Klara Steinmetz was making the journey instead.

Klara, a German citizen from Dresden, moved to Hamburg after the wall fell. She sold medical devices for a small Polish company and most assumed her bright smile and beautiful head of loose black curls (a wig this time, but as always, I'd dyed my eyebrows) helped her convince doctors and hospitals that they needed her company's line of surgical plates, rods and screws.

Petra Müller finished work on Thursday night at the ad agency. Then I ran back to my flat for my bag and ducked into a seedy hotel bathroom near the train station to transform into Klara. I boarded at Hofbahnhof a half hour before the train left at 23:30. My couchette's seat and footrest had already been turned into a twin bed.

I was a bit apprehensive about going to meet Maeve for our Terrorist Girls Weekend.

It had been good to be back in Berlin; in small ways, it kind of felt like home. The Provisionals got me back to Berlin within a week of Patricia Maguire. They took real heat for Patricia in Ireland and Britain once news and speculation seeped out. She'd been missing for two months, and nobody thought she was off on a bender or had run off to Asia with some unknown boyfriend. Most assumed she'd met an unfortunate end. Her rumored flirtations with the Brits had apparently been no secret to those in West Belfast, Divis Flats and other Catholic areas around the Falls Road. I was glad to be gone, hoping – foolishly, as it turned out – I wouldn't be reminded of her and my bloodstained hands.

I wasn't sure what Maeve had in store for us in Vienna. Would I see her for thirty minutes like before, or would we have a more substantial interaction? Would she just give me another assignment, or could I get a bigger picture of how I fit into what the organization did? What department was I in, after all? Did I have peers who did similar things, or was I a unit of one? Regardless, I wasn't holding my breath for team-building sack races.

I'd been sleeping much better since returning to Berlin, but not that night on the Inter-City to Vienna. Lying in my couchette in dark blue flannel pajamas watching the night fly by, I wondered how many others on the train were alone like me. Bob Segar's *Night Moves* drifted from my mix CD into my earphones. Before the verses finished, I was softly crying, couldn't help it. My vision blurred, and tears rolled down. What was the matter with me?

I was back in Timberline with Brian. In the woods on a blanket making memories under those dark star-filled skies. I drank in the smell of his musky cologne while snuggled into his letterman's jacket. God, I loved that jacket! Black wool with white leather sleeves, the TL logo and the polar bear mascot stitched on the front. It was also like a fighter pilot's, festooned with commemorative patches from basketball tournaments where he'd played far from Timberline: Los Angeles, Portland, Seattle, even Philadelphia.

To sharpen my sadness, the fates next sent the Eagles' *After the Thrill is Gone* into my headphones. As if they were asking me, "So, you thought you wanted this, but now you're not so sure? Is it worth all you've given up?" I missed Brian desperately at that moment, much more than I did when I'd sent him away at the end of '87. I couldn't believe how badly I'd treated him. I hated myself for that. I'd been a bitch. Cold and uncaring. For the longest time, I'd tried to convince myself I did it to protect him, to save him from the life I planned to live. But as time passed, that lie wore thin. The truth relentlessly pushed up at me like weeds sprouting through cracks in the concrete, weeds that no amount of poison could keep down.

I did it because I thought I didn't need him, wouldn't need him, didn't think he'd help me live the life I wanted – the one I needed to sate the anger boiling within me. I figured there would be other men to share my life with. While there had been others, they weren't the one I now knew I wanted. Brian loved me unconditionally, and

I think that no matter how dangerous or unconventional my life, he would have followed me anywhere. Like Maeve's husband. But now that was all just old discarded news, ancient history. More of my past that I needed to let go.

He was probably married. Thinking that jabbed at me like an old sports injury. He might even have kids, but for some reason, that didn't inflict the ache the idea of a wife did. I wondered if he was still in the Marines or if he'd gotten out. It was never his plan to make that a career. I knew he'd made it through the Gulf War in '91. I'd simply had to know, just couldn't put it out of my mind. So, in February '92, during the Magnus Herrington business, I called his parents' house in Timberline from a Dublin call box. His mother answered, and I immediately hung up. I tried earlier the next evening, before I thought his mom would be home from work, and got one of his younger sisters. I didn't identify myself and asked for Brian. She told me he lived in California but was moving to Boston to go to graduate school at Harvard. I thanked her and hung up. No message.

I was in love with him for the longest time. I figured we would date through college and then get married. What happened? Had I made a mistake in trading that life away for this? I gave up trying to get myself together, couldn't pull it off, and just kept crying, Pacific Northwest rain drizzling onto my pajamas.

23

My two-star hotel was in Vienna's 13th District near Schönbrunn Palace. It was Friday afternoon, and I was to meet Maeve for dinner at an apartment in the 2nd District, downtown off Stadtpark, near the Intercontinental Hotel. I arrived at 19:00 sharp. Maeve answered the door, said, "Hello, love," and reached her arms around for a very quick hug. I didn't expect that!

The apartment was tiny, clean and functional. Black, white and brown décor, well-lit with various lamps and tracks of overhead spotlights, a bathroom and one bedroom. Something was in the oven and smelled good. I hadn't eaten since morning.

"You look good as always, Alexandra."

I nodded and shrugged my shoulders. I was still Klara, wearing a black pencil skirt, gray blouse and earrings. Maeve was in a light wool, dark blue, chalk-stripe suit with dark blue stockings and matching heels kicked off near the coffee table. She had diamond earrings, a large ruby pendant, a Rolex on her left wrist and the ever-present color-coordinated fedora sitting on the small dining room table.

"I hope you didn't dress up for me." I chuckled.

"No, love, I came from a business meeting, but I am looking forward to our dinner much more. I'm cooking for us – Coq Au Vin, vegetables, a salad and mousse for dessert. And wine, of course." She laughed.

She checked the food, poured me a glass of Bordeaux and refilled her glass. She moved to the couch, sat and motioned me over. I sat down and Maeve pulled her legs up beside her on the sofa. Nervous, I did the same.

"I shouldn't ask," I began, "but I can't resist. Two of the three times I've seen you, here and in Berlin, you've been all dressed up. Is that for our business or just part of your cover?"

"Neither, Alex. It's my day job, my other career. You'll keep hinting around and asking, so I'll just tell you. I work for a low-profile private multinational Dutch investment firm. I run their businesses in the UK and Ireland."

Surprised, I offered, "Oh. Do you do that job from Dublin or London?"

"Dublin, though I spend lots of time in London and Edinburgh. They wanted me based in London, but I told them I wasn't moving my family. The Dublin setup was part of the deal when they recruited me."

"How long have you worked for them? Do they know about your, uh, night job?"

"A while now. They hired me away from a Bahrain private bank, whose business in the UK and Ireland I also ran from Dublin. And no, they, of course, have no idea about my other career."

I asked, "Does your husband work?"

Maeve quickly shook her head, mildly angered. "That's none of your business. No details about my husband or family – that clear, Alex? I'm blessed with a great marriage and family, and given my line of work, I do everything I can to say as little as possible about them."

"But your husband knows what you do, right? Oh, sorry, maybe I shouldn't have asked that."

Maeve took a drink of wine and said, "Yes, he knows what I do. He knows everything about me."

I nodded and took that in.

As we sat down to eat a half hour later, I hoped Maeve had an agenda of some sort. Perhaps she'd help me understand what she had planned for me career-wise.

"Fantastic work, love, back in Dublin with Patricia Maguire on such short notice. You really impressed Otto. He's someone with lots of weight and influence in our organization."

A good start.

"As for Magnus Herrington, good on you for getting through the prison time with no issues. I must tell you, though, some in the organization found it unfortunate that whatever your differences with him were, you had to kill him. I thought this myself."

Shit!

"But if someone is trying to kill or rape you, self-defense is under-standable. I told the organization you were a high-potential asset for us, and we needed to give you the benefit of the doubt."

So, not a fatal blow for my prospects, but does Maeve still harbor doubts about me?

"Alexandra, I asked you to Vienna to have a conversation about what I have in mind for you in the future. I'm going to take a risk with you, and offer you a major new responsibility."

My mouth was so dry. Instead of gulping my whole glass of seltzer water, I forced myself to calmly take a sip of Bordeaux. "Okay, thanks."

"Love, I run operations for the Provisionals on the Continent, a sort of President of Europe, if you will. Nothing happens over here without my approval and oversight. I lead a small organization, and nobody on my team knows or interacts with anyone else in my group without my permission. My remit includes active measures…"

Likely bombings and killing people.

"…weapons procurement, intelligence gathering, and all coordination with functions and elements back home."

I was fascinated that the Provisionals had so much formal structure.

"And I am one of just a few members of what we term the Army Council. Think of it as the leadership team for the Provisionals."

"You know Gerald Morrissey?" I asked, immediately admonishing myself for such a stupid, keen-grasp-of-the-obvious question about the head of the Provisionals.

Maeve laughed heartily. "Love, please! We've known each other practically our whole lives, since third grade. And our families have fought for the cause since the 1920s."

Hoping to move on from my stupidity as quickly as possible, I asked, "How do you see me fitting into your group?"

"We need new capabilities in Europe, things previously not handled well, I might add, on an ad-hoc basis out of Northern Ireland. The first is counterintelligence – ferreting out touts, primarily our own people but also others we work with who are against us."

"That's what you see me doing?"

"No. That will be someone else. I see you filling our second need over here, active measures against those counterintelligence has identified.

"You mean uh, um…"

"You will kill them, love. You will be an assassin, right at the coal face of our work, the tip of the spear, as those in the military like to say."

What!? Shit. Ask me to list fifty jobs she had in mind for me, and this wouldn't have made the list.

"What do you think, love? Do you want to do this? This will be a high-profile remit."

"Um, ah, thanks. But why me?"

"In the past five years, you've had no trouble killing people, either directly or as part of a group. Maine, then Magnus, and most recently, Patricia Maguire. You've a certain single-minded ruthlessness about you. You remind me of myself in ways."

I was mainly happy to hear this; I hadn't expected her to tell me I reminded her of herself. Though it gave me pause to hear she thought of me as a remorseless killer.

My head was spinning. I practically lunged for my plate to scoop up some chicken and rice to buy time to think. Was I going to do this? *You either take this job, or you've no future in the Provisionals. They'll never trust you again and will likely kill you. Besides, isn't this what you want? What you've been working for? To get into a position to get back at the Brits for what they did to you? And maybe, hopefully, even to be able to settle a personal account from back in Timberline.*

"Will you join me to do this?"

Finishing my slow chewing, I grinned. "Yes! Can't tell you how much I appreciate your faith in me."

We finished dinner, and as we were doing the dishes, Maeve explained she was counting on me to work alone as often as possible. My job would always be to take great care to spare innocents and to conduct 'low-signature' actions at all times. Public mayhem traced back to the Provisionals in foreign lands wouldn't be good, unless it happened in the UK.

The dishes cleaned and put away, Maeve and I went back to the sofa. We sat at opposite ends and put our feet up on it.

"I'm curious," I said. "I know Patricia Maguire was a tout, but I don't know – do you think the punishment fit the crime? She was a really low-level tout from what I gathered from conversations that night."

Maeve took a deep breath and sat looking at me.

Christ. Have I stepped into another taboo topic with her?

"This is a war, Alexandra, and as in any war, decisions are made by people at all levels. There is also collateral damage, and, unfortunately, there are war crimes. The British, the Israelis and the Americans don't have clean hands in these matters either. The Maguire decision came straight from the top, a direct order, with no opportunity for discussion."

"Gerald Morrissey? Why?"

Maeve fixed me with a stare. "I'm just going to say he didn't technically give the order because he isn't officially in the Provisional IRA anymore."

She dipped a spoon into the large bowl of chocolate mousse between us on the sofa, took a bite, and handed the bowl to me.

"Leaders of any organization must always focus on the strategic context, sizing up challenges and opportunities, as well as anticipating what might be around the corner. Some people on both sides would argue that Britain and the Unionists ultimately need to come to some sort of political peace in Northern Ireland. Many are violently opposed to that. People on one side will only accept a united Ireland, while the other side insists on a Northern Ireland firmly rooted in the UK, with no rights for the Catholics. Those people will never settle for less."

I passed the mousse back to Maeve. "And?"

"You're evil feeding me this," Maeve teased. "Some suspect Gerald Morrissey may sell out for a peace deal one day. He denies it, but he needs to protect his flanks now and again and show that he still has the steel in his spine to wage war."

"Okay, but why Patricia Maguire?"

"The Maguire situation offered a chance for particular ruthlessness, a real messaging opportunity. Also, some in the organization may eventually split to form their own more violent version of the Provisionals that will never accept a peace deal. To head that off is another reason to keep up the fight."

"Did you support the Maguire decision? Would you have ordered the same?"

Maeve smiled at me. "You have performed like a champion for us and for me. I'm proud of you: Maine, Magnus Herrington, prison, and then Maguire. You're a warrior. You have the potential to do bigger and better things for us."

She didn't answer. No surprise. She's a bottomless trove of secrets.

Sitting there in quasi-sisterly communion with Maeve, my leader and mentor, I was proud to be a key person on her elite team. I hadn't felt this close to a woman since college. I wanted – no, needed – a friend. Could it be her? At that moment, I was happy, as happy as I'd been in months, thoughts of Brian and what I'd given up banished, at least for a time.

"Hand me that mousse again, will you?" she asked. "I'll have to starve myself for the next two days after all this food. I must be careful, or I'm going to end up with, what did you call it in Berlin? Oh, right, hail damage on my arse. I need to keep my husband coming to bed every night. That's no worry for you, though, so you're the one who should be eating this. You must have men chasing you up all the time."

I shook my head. "I never pursue anything much anymore."

"Love, let me give you some advice. You need a good balance between the personal and professional. For me, being alone would be awful. You need someone to make a life with, have kids if you fancy. Someone to share the fun, the struggles and the inside jokes. A partner to dream about the future with."

I dropped my eyes and shook my head.

Maeve leaned in, her sparkling, urgent eyes boring into me. "Alex, a cause you're passionate about is key, but it's not the only thing. Love is important. The world's a cold and lonely place without emotional intimacy, especially in our line of work." Chuckling a bit now she added, "and let's face it, sometimes you just need a vigorous shagging from someone who knows how you work."

I wrinkled my nose. "I'm not so sure."

"Really, Alex? Don't underestimate the benefits of someone you care deeply about, just throwing you down and fucking your brains out now and again."

I made a face in mock horror. "Well, you're lucky."

Maeve went to the kitchen to open our third and final bottle of wine and returned to the sofa. She filled our glasses before sitting down. "Alex, I know you've had plenty of sex, but have you ever been with any blokes you really fancy?" She chuckled. "Even if you didn't fancy them, did you at least like the sex?"

I sat silently for probably thirty seconds, thinking back over time. Then, encouraged by way too much wine, I sighed and said, "Sex hasn't been great for me for a long time. Let's just say it never ends with fireworks exploding in the night sky. I'm not sure I even want it anymore. I've just maybe given up."

Maeve put down her wine glass and squeezed my knee a little. "Ah, love," she urged, "don't be one of those women who can't come or who hates sex. You need to fix that. Maybe it's a medical issue? Or psychological. Either way, get some help when you get back to Berlin. Hopefully, you can pack away miserable Magnus Herrington and move on from it."

I offered more silence.

24

Maeve left around 02:00 to return to the Imperial Hotel. Alex slept for two hours, then set off as Klara on a circuitous route, on foot and by U-Bahn, to get back to her own hotel, arriving at 06:00 on Saturday. She slept until 16:00 and woke to prepare for the meeting Maeve had set up for her with a man named Pavel.

As Klara, she left her hotel at 18:30. It was still about seventy degrees as she began what the CIA would call an SDR, a surveillance detection run. Klara didn't think anyone knew who she was but nonetheless figured three to four hours for her SDR would still be prudent. She rode buses, changed U-Bahn trains rapidly, crossed streets abruptly, and looked in store windows to see if someone else was crossing the street. She added and discarded hats and various other things along the way.

Convinced nobody was watching her, that she was "black" in spy lingo, Klara ducked into the ladies' toilet at St. Stephen's Cathedral at 21:45, right before it closed for the night. Klara's black wig with big bouncy curls went into her big purse, and a redheaded wig with long, straight hair took its place. Three deflated cushions also came out of the purse. Klara blew them up, put them on, and *voilà*"! The redhead was now pregnant with massive breasts and a stomach looking ready to drop any day.

The woman was now Inge Marstellar. She waddled out of the church with Klara's wig and clothing zipped into a hidden pocket at the bottom of her purse. Inge was an Austrian from Graz, making a last getaway trip to Vienna before having her child and embarking on a dreary life of single motherhood. The picture on Inge's Austrian passport didn't do her justice.

Maeve had briefed Alex on the meeting with Pavel during dinner the previous night. He was Russian and with the Sluzhba vneshney razvedki Rossiyskoy Federatsii, the SVR, Russia's foreign intelligence service and successor to the First Directorate of the KGB from Soviet times. Maeve and Alex had role-played the meeting with Pavel after dinner in the apartment. Inge Marstellar would be alone with him.

Around 02:00 after another SDR, Inge arrived at the meeting site, a Catholic church twenty-three kilometers out of Vienna. She stood at the bottom of the steps in front of the church, its doors barely visible in the inky black. There was no moon, and the streetlights around the square were out, likely broken, though Alex couldn't suppress the thought that maybe somebody had shut them off.

The silence was oppressive – not a sound anywhere. Alex irrationally thought the whole neighborhood could hear her breathing. She started down the small alley on the left, which would take her around to the back of the church. She heard the echoes of her flats on the cobblestones and cringed. They might as well have had a string of cowbells attached to them. She removed the shoes and put them in her voluminous purse.

Halfway to the back of the church, Alex heard a sound behind her; someone maybe bumping into something. She whirled around, then darted into a doorway and pressed herself against a closed door. *Why didn't I bring a gun?* The sound continued faintly. Should she abort the meeting? If she did, she would look stupid to Maeve. All the good feelings from the dinner last night would be gone, and she'd have angered Maeve, something she always feared.

Still shoeless and casting glances over her shoulder, she shuffled down the alley and walked to the small fenced graveyard behind the church – *of course there's a graveyard* – trying to avoid the broken and crumbling headstones. She opened the gate. It screeched like a cave of disturbed bats. She felt her way, having been told to carry no light of any kind. Random stones tore at the bottom of her stockinged feet.

Suddenly, she was face down on the ground with the wind knocked out of her. Something had hit her. Frantically looking around, still on the ground, she didn't know what was going on. Oh. *Fuck! Idiot!* She'd just tripped.

Warily, she got up and brushed off the grass and dirt. Her knee hurt; she'd landed on a protruding stone. Finally, convinced she was alone, Alex picked her way for another ten yards. She reached an unmarked back door to the church. An empty Heineken bottle stood in the right corner. The signal to proceed. She knocked slowly four times, the first two hard, the second light taps.

No answer. *What?* Did the meeting get canceled? Was the time wrong? Was she being set up? Was someone following her, after all? Her mind running riot, she stepped back from the door and looked around. Silence. Were the Russians here to ambush her? The British? God, was she going to be killed or caught? Sent back to prison? Probably they'd just kill her but maybe torture her first.

Just calm the fuck down and get a hold of yourself! She was about to knock with the signal again when an old priest finally opened the door.

This can't be right. This is screwed up.

"Guten Abend, Fräulein Marstellar. Willkommen."

Alex nodded, but said nothing.

"Ich heisse Pavel." *I am Pavel.* "May I call you Inge?"

He was much older than she'd expected, sixties, she guessed. She wondered if he'd been in the spy business forever. If the Ghosts of Spy Adventures Past, people like Penkovsky, Burgess and Philby floated over the Glienicke Bridge and visited him at Christmas.

Alex grinned slightly. "Schöne Kleidung. Father Pavel." *Nice clothes.*

He laughed out loud and, in German, said, "What do the Americans say? When in Rome…"

Suddenly Alex wondered if he knew she was an American and how much else he knew about her. Maeve wouldn't have told him that, but maybe someone else did. Maybe the Russians already knew everything! Her heart started racing again. *Just stay calm and go with it.*

Pavel was about six foot, with bright blue eyes like Alex's (though not that night, thanks to her brown contact lenses). His bright white teeth were better than she'd have expected from someone who'd spent most of his life behind the Iron Curtain. *Spasibo*, thanks to Boris, the KGB dentist. Pavel also had a nice head of salt-and-pepper hair. Take the priest's clothes away, put him in jeans, a button-down corduroy shirt and cowboy boots, and he'd have been right out of a Ralph Lauren ad.

They sat in a small room off the cathedral. Pavel had made tea. Alex briefly considered making a nervous joke along the lines of "What, no vodka?" but wisely kept her mouth shut.

• • •

Sunday morning, on time at 11:00, the Inter-City train pulled out of Vienna Südbahnhof, bound for Berlin. Inge Marstellar had finished her meeting with Pavel just before 03:30. Another three-hour SDR took her back into the city center and a route back to her hotel after resurrecting Klara Steinmetz in a public toilet stall.

Klara slept as soon as her head hit the pillow sometime after 07:00. She awoke at 10:00, showered, checked out and taxied to the train station. She grabbed a coffee at a platform kiosk before crashing into her seat, tired and exhausted, thankful nobody was near her.

Alex had had an exhilarating weekend that went beyond her best expectations. A sense of mission and how she fit in was now clearer. The Provisional IRA had important work to do that would improve the lives of hundreds of thousands of people in Northern Ireland. She felt closer to Maeve now, thought maybe the woman cared a little about her and would mentor her. Maybe even she could become sort of a friend.

Alex would be back in Vienna in late September to see Pavel and execute the first phase of a new cooperation. The SVR wanted a hundred false Canadian, US and Irish passports, and the Provisionals could get those more easily than the Russians. Pavel wouldn't say why they needed the passports, but Alex guessed the SVR wanted to sell them to the emerging oligarch class to supplement the official SVR budget or the unofficial personal budgets of certain of Mother Russia's more corrupt intelligence officers.

In exchange, the Provisionals would get five applications of poison, varied substances and delivery mechanisms, most of the SVR's choosing. The Russians, Americans and Israelis were the best in the world at poisons, and each had a kaleidoscope of sophisticated options, a veritable Sears Catalog of Death, for the choosy assassin. These would be some of the assets for Alex's new activities, arrows in the quiver.

Alex thought she'd done okay with her first negotiation. Maeve told her she had to get at least three poison applications for one hundred passports, but instead, she got five applications for just seventy-five. She'd persuaded Pavel that the Provos could get cruder poisons from others – less sophisticated, yes, but workable nonetheless. She told him it was in the SVR's interest to be a sole supplier to best guarantee future access to passports and anything else the SVR might need. Besides, it was likely no big concession for Pavel. In those days, there was probably more poison than bread in Russia, warehouses of it awaiting monetization.

Initially, Pavel was skeptical the Provos would need poisons for certain "active measures" in Continental Europe. He'd asked, "Who do you need to kill over here?"

"There aren't many," Alex said, "but there are some."

He sighed. "Yes, it is always true. There are people to kill everywhere. Sie sind wie Unkraut." *They are like weeds.*

25

A week before Christmas 1994, I was in Poland, summoned for an urgent meeting with Maeve. Klara Steinmetz had checked into a dingy two-star hotel five miles from the new high-rise Marriott in the center of town, Maeve's lodgings, no doubt.

We were to meet at a spa/sauna about a mile from the Palace of Culture and Science, an ugly, semi-phallic Stalinist scar jutting into the sky in the center of the city. Officially, it was a "gift" by Stalin from the Soviet Union to the people of Poland in 1955. Unofficially, Warsaw's unappreciative residents had other names: Stalin's Syringe, or Nyet Chuj Stalina (not Stalin's Dick), or Chuj Trotsky (Trotsky's Dick). Sarcastically I thought maybe that was why Stalin had Trotsky killed with an ice pick in Mexico City in 1940.

I did my SDR for about three hours before taking a bus to the center of Warsaw and heading to the meeting with Maeve. After the bus, I had about two miles to walk. It was pitch black by 15:00, in the low twenties Fahrenheit. Dense fog suffused everything. I could only see a foot in front of me.

Seasonal decorations were minimal in this part of town, with occasional trees in lighted storefronts and white or colored lights around apartment windows here and there. The air was thick with the pungent odor of brown coal, Poland's key power source. The faint whiffs of chestnuts being roasted by street vendors hardly put a dent in it.

I arrived at the spa, if you could call it that. Really, a small storefront with see-through curtains pulled across a dirty front window. I looked around and listened. I neither saw nor heard anyone nearby, so I went in. A wrinkled woman, like a bathroom attendant wearing rags, smiled at me, said nothing, and had me follow her down a hallway to a locker room. She pointed to the lockers, showed me a series of doors across the hall and in German said, "Vier," while holding up four fingers. I nodded, and she left. I undressed, wrapped myself in a towel, and went to the toilet, hovering over it since there was no seat.

I walked across the hall, pushed on door number four, and entered a ten-by-ten room. Maeve sat on a wooden bench amidst thick steam with strong hints of eucalyptus. That felt good, both the steam and the sight of Maeve. She smiled and patted the bench next to her.

"So good to see you, love."

"You too." This was the first time I'd seen her without one of her fedoras, and it was certainly the first time I'd seen her wrapped in a towel.

"I appreciate you coming on such short notice. I had to find some banking business in Warsaw out of nowhere. Fortunately, a New Zealand entrepreneur bought a decrepit privatized brewery here a few years ago and is making a good run of it. He agreed to meet me to discuss cash management and currency hedging."

She reached down to an ice bucket at her feet and pulled up two glasses and a bottle of vodka, pouring us each a healthy shot. She smiled, and we clinked glasses and drained them. She refilled them.

"What's up?" I asked.

"A duty and opportunity have arisen, which we have you to thank partially for. I'll get to that, but first, good on you for the Gerry Conley business in Amsterdam."

I nodded. "Thanks."

"Succinylcholine?" Maeve asked. "From our Russian friends?"

"Yes."

Succinylcholine paralyzes all skeletal muscles, so when the diaphragm stops moving, breathing ceases. If injected by IV, this leads to loss of consciousness and death by cardiac arrest within minutes. Unless a biopsy of brain tissue is done after death, the poison is undetectable, and it will appear the person died of natural causes, a heart attack.

Gerry Conley was a low-level foot soldier in the Provisionals who'd thought it wise to tout for the Brits to get a fellow Provisional arrested because he was fucking his wife. He fled to Europe once he realized what he'd done, and hid out for two years. Maeve's other people had found him working construction in Amsterdam, and I'd killed him, the first scalp in my new role. I'd chatted him up in the bar, gone back to his room with him, and slipped something into his drink to knock him out. I'd then injected the poison inside his rectum to lessen the chance of anyone finding a needle mark on him.

The steam was thinning, so Maeve walked across the room, bent over and poured a bucket of water over the rocks, inadvertently letting her towel slip to the floor.

"My god," I burst out, "what's that? Is that a scar?"

She looked back at me and said, "Yes, it is, love."

It was a dark, ugly, racing stripe about the width of a piece of masking tape that started at the top of her left butt cheek and didn't stop until it was a few inches down the back of her leg. There, it bent like an elbow toward her inner thigh and curved back up.

"What the fuck happened? Are you okay?"

"Yes, it happened years ago."

"It?" I asked.

"A gun battle with the British Army."

I was incredulous. "That's all you got, really?" I laughed. "You're not going to tell me any more than that?"

Maeve sat beside me on the wooden bench, the towel in her lap. The steam hissed and spewed, drenching us in sweat. I could feel scented eucalyptus and evergreen overrunning my nostrils and sinuses.

Sighing loudly, she said, "Okay, love, I'll run through this quickly for you."

As she laid it all out, I sat there dumbstruck, too enraptured to even wipe the sweat pouring down my face with the towel.

My parents were originally from South Armagh and then moved to Belfast. I mainly grew up in America, as I told you before, but spent summers as a girl with my aunt, uncle and cousins in Belfast, the Andersonstown area. My brother and I would come over, starting when we were about eight years old.

Beginning about seventh grade, my cousins and I started helping first the IRA and then the Provisionals. Little things. We'd serve as lookouts while we played outside, blowing whistles, or banging pots and pans or garbage lids when we saw the RUC or British Army coming round to surprise people. As we got older, we'd act as couriers and such, bringing messages and food here and there, sometimes even guns and ammunition.

After my sophomore year at Georgetown, in July of '74, I was back in Belfast, this time with my cousin and brother, who'd moved to Belfast to join the cause full time. Tommy was three years older than me.

On a Sunday afternoon, we were walking down a dead-end street off Falls Road, with no plans to do anything but visit a friend of my brother's. It was Catholic, Provo territory. Out of nowhere, two British Army wagons came roaring down the road toward us, and we ran. Turns out the British Army, the supposed protector of all the citizens of Northern Ireland, was working with the RUC and unionist militias, helping them kill Provisionals. Bastards, the whole lot. This was an assassination squad; apparently, my brother and cousin were on an RUC hit list. A tout in the Provisionals had given them up and told the RUC where to find them that day.

We'd almost made it to Tommy's friend's house at the end of the street, one of a bunch of multi-flat attached homes. The army wagons pulled up and started shooting at us as we ran inside. Six soldiers started toward the house, and one each remained with the wagons. There were ArmaLite machine guns, M-16s basically, and nine-millimeter pistols in the house, so we got inside and started firing at the soldiers. Tommy gave me a pistol, smiled and said, 'You've practiced for years. Now it's time to shoot and stick it to the bastards. You'll be okay.'

The soldiers staying with the wagons fired tear gas canisters that shattered the front window. The other six soldiers, wearing gas masks, charged the house; two fired with machine guns through the front window to cover the four, who headed to the front door with a ram to knock it down. My cousin dropped the two machine gunners with his ArmaLite. That left six soldiers, the four coming through the door and the two back at the wagons.

The tear gas was spreading, we were choking, and it was getting hard to see. We covered our faces with our shirts, but it didn't help. Tommy's friend pushed us to the back of the house, toward a door off the kitchen. He was in the lead, I was behind him, and my brother and cousin were behind me, facing backward, covering us.

The four soldiers in the house lost track of us for a few moments in the tear gas. Then they saw us heading to the back of the flat.

My brother and cousin shot two of them in the head: kill shots. But the other two fired and hit my brother in the shoulder and my cousin in the leg. They were down, but alive.

I screamed, "No! No!" because I could see what the soldiers were going to do.

They stepped up, kicked their ArmaLites away, and shot Tommy and my cousin in the head.

I couldn't believe it. Maeve was retelling this as if she was giving someone a route to the neighborhood pub: "Walk down the high street two blocks, turn left on Doherty Street, and the Smiling Wolf is there on your right. Then you shoot him between the eyes."

She continued.

Everything was in slow motion. All I remember is running toward Tommy and the soldier standing over him, gloating. I had the nine-millimeter, a Sig Sauer, in my right hand and came up behind him. I put two shots into him, the gun practically flush against his head. Blood and brains were everywhere, dripping off me.

I was deaf for a moment. Then I turned and ran toward my brother's friend and the now-open back door. Next thing I knew, I was face down on the floor, my entire body on fire and convulsed with pain. I could feel liquid, blood running down my legs and inside my pants. This is where I die, I thought. But my brother's friend still had an ArmaLite and dropped the remaining soldier who'd shot me.

I survived, but Tommy and my cousin were dead. I'd taken three forty-five-caliber pistol rounds in the back of my leg just below my arse. The bullets traveled upward and hit my intestines, among other things. I was bleeding out fast and going into shock. My brother's friend saved my life. He tied a tourniquet around my thigh to slow the bleeding and dragged me out of the house before more soldiers arrived.

I was lucky. My brother's friend carried me to a Provo safe house nearby. Calls were made. A surgeon came within fifteen minutes and performed crude surgery to stabilize me. That night, heavily sedated, they drove me out of Belfast and across the border into the Republic. I ended up in hospital in Dundalk under an assumed name. My parents came over from the US.

I was there for three weeks and had four additional surgeries, two of an emergency nature. I recuperated in another safe house for four more weeks and then flew home to New Jersey.

I couldn't attend the funerals of my cousin and brother, partly because of my injuries but mainly because the Brits didn't know I existed. If I'd gone to the funerals, they'd have known about me, and put a name, face and family together.

I did physical therapy my entire junior year at Georgetown and still made the Dean's List and Phi Beta Kappa. I was stuck in a wheelchair during the first semester because I couldn't walk more than twenty meters on my own. Most people said I'd never walk normally again, but I proved them wrong. I couldn't use the loo for fifteen months; my toilet was a catheter and an ostomy bag. I got an infection and sepsis from the catheter and almost died right before Christmas and spent another month in the hospital on my break.

I wiped my face with a towel. Finally, I said, "I, I, um… I could ask you questions for hours about this."

Maeve held her hand up. "I've said enough, love."

"Just one more question. What happened to the tout?"

I thought I saw an almost imperceptible upturn or grin at the corner of her mouth before she said, "I killed him."

Maeve was nothing if not hands-on, like Darth Vader, I already knew. "You?" I asked.

She poured us yet another vodka shot, drank hers down and nodded. "I suppose it was my summer internship that next year. Some people work in marketing or consulting, but I plotted and killed the tout responsible for the death of my brother and cousin."

"How?" I shot back.

"By Christmas junior year, when I was in hospital in New Jersey with sepsis, the Provisionals had found the tout. They sent word to my father and asked him if I wanted to settle the score, and I did. They gave the tout different work for a few months so he couldn't do any more harm and waited for me to finish my junior year at Georgetown."

"Aannnddd?" I said.

July '75, just over a year later, I was back in Belfast. I was walking better by then, but nowhere near normal. I still had bags of pee and poo stuck to my body, but I had been thinking for months about the tout. It was simple, really. He lived outside Belfast in a small village and, every Friday afternoon, went fishing at this isolated spot twenty kilometers out of town.

I waited for him one warm summer evening in a ditch across the road from where he always parked his car. I could hear the river down the embankment from his car. When he came back to the car, I ambushed him and shot him behind the ear, just like I was supposed to. Didn't say a word to him, left him lying in the road. I'd carried a big knife with me, too. My plan, right up until the last minute, really, was to shoot him, to disable him and then cut his throat and talk to him about my brother and cousin while he bled to death.

I quietly asked, "Why didn't you do that?"

Maeve, staring straight ahead at the wall, said, "I decided it would have been unprofessional. I'd have been giving into my own vengeance rather than enforcing the code and procedures of the Provisionals."

Then Maeve surprised me. Turning to look at me, with thick emotion in her voice, she said, "Alexandra, my mum was never the same after my brother. She cried every day for months. 'Oh my Tommy, my Tommy,' she would wail. To me, her agony was like the tear gas the soldiers had shot into the flat. I choked on it every time."

"I'm so sorry."

"Love, my mum's family was hardcore Republican. They'd fought for the cause for generations. Mum's grandfather fought with Michael Collins in the uprising in 1916, and she'd had other relatives fighting for Ireland against the British since the eighteenth century. She never got over Tommy, though. Lived enveloped in grief for the rest of her days, and none of us could do anything to help her."

Like snapping off a light switch, Maeve was back in the present. "Now, love, let's get about our business before we melt away in here. You're going to make another visit to Pavel. We need a special potion from him. It's up to you to decide what exactly that should be."

"Okay. What's it for?"

A smile crossed Maeve's face. "We've found Sally Horrigan, one of the most notorious traitors in the organization's history."

My eyebrows shot up, and I drew in a quick breath. A jolt shot through me. *Revenge at last!* "Really? How?"

"Much of it, thanks to you. After your PLO friend tipped you about her and the Brits, that gave us the path we needed. She needs to suffer, die in agony. I'm sure you'd agree."

"Oh, yes."

"That's why you're going back to Pavel. This can't just be, 'Oh, look at that, she had a heart attack' or 'She got mugged in an alley, got shot or stabbed, and died.' I don't want to know any details from this point on. I trust you to take care of this and have told the leadership you will get it done."

"How soon does it have to be done?" I asked, my mind already racing.

"The sooner, the better, but I've told the leadership this isn't something you just throw together in a week. Told them it could be months. Of course, if Sally gets wind of us and we lose her, that's not a good thing for you."

"Where in Europe is she?"

She shook her head. "She's not. She's in the US. St. Louis."

"Why me then, if she's not in Europe?"

"This is a special case, love, a festering wound for the organization for a decade. We need a very capable American, and that's you."

26

Christmas Eve 1994, and I was back in Vienna. Well, actually, Inge Marstellar was back in Vienna. Inge had had her baby, thank god. I hated those cushions stuffed up under my shirt and in my pants. Inge still had straight auburn hair, and now also nice breasts, butt and stomach returned to their original forms.

I'd messaged Pavel the week before, two days after I returned to Berlin from Warsaw. I'd requested an urgent meeting as soon as possible.

We met at 23:00 at the iconic Ferris wheel in the Prater. It was a bright and clear night but very cold. There were hardly any people waiting to ride, so Pavel and I had an enclosed car to ourselves. The clerical collar was his only visible priestly vestment, poking up from his buttoned coat. We again spoke in German.

"Fröhliche Weihnachten, Pavel." *Merry Christmas.* I smiled.

"Und dir auch, Inge." *To you also, Inge.*

"Still in your priestly clothes, I see, even outside the church?"

"I helped give the early mass at St. Stephen's tonight."

Not believing he could really be a priest, I asked, "Bist du wirklich ein Priester? Nein." *Are you really a priest? No.*

He spread out his arms. "Gott ist geheimnisvoll." *God is mysterious.*

Pleasantries done, Pavel asked, "What can I do for you, Inge?"

I told him what I wanted.

He pursed his lips. "Not even the Chinese have this. It is only us, the Israelis and the Americans. People will immediately suspect us, and there will be hell in the media and governments."

I shook my head. "It's unlikely anyone will ever know about this operation. But if people are suspicious, we plan to make it look like the Mossad did it. We can make people think they had a motive. If they look anywhere, it will be there. You'll have to trust me."

Pavel took this in. "I assume you have something more than passports to offer us for this?"

I reached into my purse and handed him a single sheet of paper, a list of twenty items. "The SVR has a traitor stationed somewhere in western Europe who has been passing highly classified military and intelligence secrets to the British, MI-6. You have been looking for this person for over a year with no success."

The Ferris wheel was near the top of its arc. Pavel looked out over a cloudless Vienna Christmas Eve, perhaps hoping he could find the person's identity in Santa's sleigh and not from me.

"And the Provisional IRA knows who this person is, Inge?"

I nodded subtly at the paper I'd given him. "The first ten items on that list are documents and information you know have been lost to the west. The next ten items are also things that have been passed along, though until now, you didn't realize that or couldn't confirm it. I will give you the name of the person and additional proof when I receive what we need."

Pavel folded the paper and put it into an interior pocket of his overcoat. "I will, of course, need to pass your request upward in my organization. It is not my decision to make. When do you need the material, assuming we are willing to provide it?"

"As soon as feasible."

"Where and how would we deliver it to you?"

"In Canada, and that is non-negotiable. You can pick any place in Canada, though, and the package needs to be very secure."

"Well, obviously." Pavel was noncommittal, as expected. "I will have an update for you in two weeks."

Our car had returned to the bottom of the wheel, and I thought our ride was over. Pavel had other ideas. "Let's keep riding, shall we?"

"Okay."

Pavel indicated to the attendant that we would ride again. His eyes bright and lively, he asked, "So, will you return to Graz tomorrow or elsewhere, for this blessed season?"

I smiled. "Elsewhere."

"I thought as much. Somewhere outside of Austria, I suspect, but you won't answer that."

I nodded. "I won't."

"Do you have a family to go home to, Inge? It would be terrible to be alone this time of year."

I didn't answer and averted my eyes to the floor. After a bit, I asked him, "How about you? Do you have a family? A wife?"

"A wife?" He laughed. "Inge, I am a Catholic priest. No wife, but brothers and sisters, nieces and nephews."

I made a face. "Really? A Catholic priest in the SVR and the KGB before that? How does that work?"

Pavel smiled, turning again to look out over the skyline and Vienna's snowy landscape. "I was a priest before I got into this, um, line of work. I grew up in the southern part of East Prussia, now part of Poland, as you know. The Nazis killed my parents in 1944 and my siblings and I ended up orphans in what became West Germany. The church ordained me in 1957 and I served a small parish near Stuttgart. The KGB found me in 1960 and persuaded me to join."

"Why? How could you support a government that outlawed religion?"

"I initially believed the Communist cause was just, protection against the return of fascism and Nazism. I wanted to improve the suffering of the less fortunate, end destructive class divisions. I thought the Stalin years an unfortunate aberration and had great hopes for Chairman Khrushchev to reignite the spirit of the revolution and the people. As for religion, Communism was never going to kill it, and I was able to ignore that part. Kind of like most Catholics do with birth control."

I laughed.

"We made good progress with Khrushchev but then slipped back into stagnation with Brezhnev and the dying old men who came after him. I began to lose faith in the cause of Communism and class struggle. Even though I was a colonel in the KGB, I decided to leave, to retire and fade away, in the late seventies."

"Why would you leave and give up all you'd worked for? The work wasn't any different, was it?"

Pavel sighed.

"No, Inge, it wasn't. I think ambition, skill and hard work will take you far in life. But over the long arc of the journey, achievement and personal advancement are not enough. It took me a long time to understand this. You need to believe in what you're fighting for. Really believe you are making a difference and that all the sacrifices and moral tradeoffs are worth it. This is something you might want to think about, too, as time goes on."

Later, these perspectives would often intrude on my thoughts.

"It's fine to rationalize and talk about casualties of war, tell yourself it's all part of the struggle. But that won't help you when you can't sleep at night and are eaten by self-loathing and guilt. We all go out fighting for our causes every day, but it's not like Stalingrad, where life's calculus was brutally narrow. Fight or die, and you didn't have the luxury of thinking about anything else."

"But you can always go to confession, Father." Later I kicked myself for being a smart ass.

"So can you, Inge. Like any organization, there are people in our line of work whose passion for the cause has been constant and will always burn. Your Maeve is like that, I think. I believe the British killed her brother or sister or something like that years ago and almost killed her too. Is something like that also your story, Inge?"

"So, you retired in the late seventies and yet here you are, Father."

He nodded and smiled. "My retirement was short. Gorbachev's people convinced me to return to run Spain for the KGB. And now, ten years later, we are in a new chapter. Nationalism and corrupt oligarchs are replacing Communism and criminal senior party members. But this is again a cause I can support. I am energized to help build a new Russia."

"Then you will be helping support democracy in Russia, Pavel?"

He burst out with a hearty laugh. "That will never happen in Russia. People are kidding themselves. Those roots will never grow in our cold soil."

Our ride finally over, Pavel and I parted ways outside the gates of the Prater.

He waved and said, "Wiedersehen, Inge. God bless you."

PART 4

Alex & Julie

Beyond Timberline

27

Alex

I applied to Harvard, Yale, Princeton and Columbia and got in everywhere – miraculously, I now think. Discussing me, I suspect the admissions offices said, "Shit, we'll have to take this Alexandra girl from Timberline now; our ten preferred female-snowbound-geographic diversity candidates just pulled out." Ivy acceptances in hand, my mother was finally able to spread her peacock feathers (even further).

I could just see her. "Carolyn, it's great that Joanie's going to go to Western Whatever State. Yes, Alexandra is going to the Ivy League. Well, thank you, but that's exciting news for Joanie, too. All schools are great, and the kids know the best fit for them." But if Carolyn looked deeply into my mother's eyes, she would have seen her spiking the ball, doing her touchdown dance while heaping scorn on hapless, average Joanie.

Thinking it would be nice to get out of the wet, cold and gloom, I didn't tell my parents, but also applied to the University of Miami, the University of Florida, Florida State and the University of Texas. All four places offered me a full ride for four years. This caused a stir when mail from them started arriving at my house. Were my parents over-the-moon about these offers? Yes, but not in the way you'd think. It was as if I'd told them I was skipping college to be a groupie for a Bee Gees cover band and was going to pole dance on the weekends.

I chose Princeton. Did I cave in to my parents' expectations, or was the whole Ivy thing something I wanted, too? I didn't know and still don't.

My parents dropped me at Princeton in August '82 for freshman year. My father tried to commandeer one of Blackpool's corporate jets to take us east, but Win said no.

Trouper that she was, my mother managed this crushing disappointment with aplomb. Talking to other parents at move-in, she said things like, "I was afraid we were going to get here late. There was a problem with the Gulfstream, so we had to fly commercial in first class. The traffic down from Newark is so much worse than from Teterboro."

Or, "Coffee? Oh, no, thank you. We have to take a car up to Teterboro to meet the Gulfstream since it is taking us back. We don't need to be stopping on the way because I drank too much coffee." This was a complete fabrication; they flew back commercial.

My freshman dorm room was in this great gothic residence hall, and F. Scott Fitzgerald once occupied my room. I was psyched! My roommate was Eleanor Dorsett from the heart of Mainline, Philadelphia. She grew up on a three-hundred-plus-acre estate and had gone to boarding school at Miss Porter's in Connecticut.

Eleanor was a descendant of one of the founding families of US Steel, a partner of Carnegie. Her mother, Victoria, did the highest of high-society social work. Her dad, Phillip, didn't work and saw no shame in that, according to Eleanor (never El or Ellie, always Eleanor). Her dad played golf and squash, flew his helicopter, and, I would later learn, fucked and cast aside a continuous stream of mistresses as if they were his estate's lawn clippings.

Eleanor grew up with a nanny, butler, maid, chef, tutors and a very discreet but well-armed 'driver.' Think Oddjob for the Episcopalian set. Her family lived off a mid-nine-figure trust fund. Needless to say, they made my preening, keening, sorta-wealthy, nouveau riche parents look like migrant farm workers.

Eleanor's parents were very nice on move-in day (Oddjob did the heavy lifting), and on their many visits throughout the semester, they always seemed genuinely happy to see me. Always interested in me, asking if I needed anything. Unfailingly polite, low-key, and even, I thought, modest given their station in life.

Unfortunately, my relationship with Eleanor, while not bad, wasn't close. Her male and female friends, of whom she seemed to have many on campus, were all fluent speakers of northeastern plutocracy: boarding schools, equestrian circuits, polo, debutante balls, world travel and smooth conversations with their friends' parents about summer homes, critiques of the world's most exclusive resorts, sailing and charity galas. Many of Eleanor's friends were super smart and studied stuff in high school I'd barely heard of. They all viewed me, at least I felt they did, as little more than a rube carpetbagger, and patronized me accordingly. I felt inferior to most of them, which poured self-loathing and rage into me like the molten steel that used to stream from the Dorsett/Carnegie Bessemer furnaces.

Eleanor told me she was supposed to have roomed with a friend from Miss Porter's, but there had been some sort of mix-up, so she'd ended up with me. Her family, at one time, built world-class steel mills but apparently couldn't control roommate assignments at Princeton. Or so I thought. Right before finals in December, the housing office informed me of my new residence hall and roommate assignment for the second semester. Eleanor had fed them a litany of lies about my shortcomings.

According to Eleanor, despite her magnanimous "best efforts," she just didn't feel I was receptive to changing and "meeting her halfway." What a twat. And she was concerned about my "health and well-being," the great humanitarian that she was. Nobody at Princeton was interested in my response to any of this. In fact, I was "advised" not to make a big deal about it, lest the school feel the need to "look into Eleanor's (completely false) drug use allegations" about me.

One thing I learned about Eleanor's world in our brief time together was that when you had as much money as her family, you never thought about it. It was just there, always, like the air, water and trees. Though considered wealthy by Timberline standards, my parents were always talking about money and status. Who was gaining, who was losing within the Blackpool executive hierarchy. Had my mother been purposely snubbed at the country club Christmas party by someone she viewed as an inferior, or was it merely a misunderstanding?

Princeton helped me realize that my parents lacked the grace, manners and ease of the old-money super-wealthy. Also lacking was any genuine sense of noblesse oblige. I came to believe that my parents idolized and lusted after only wealth and recognition on the island of Timberline. I began to see that almost all of my family's Timberline status – the nice German cars, the flights on the corporate jet, the country club membership and the palatial house – were solely tied to Blackpool Industries and, more accurately, to the whims of Win Blackpool. My parents perhaps even lacked what my aspiring Wall Street friends called FYM – Fuck You Money.

. . .

First-semester finals over, I was in my now-former room picking up some last few things when Eleanor walked in. She nodded at me but said nothing. I'd been hoping I'd see her before I went home for Christmas.

"You know, Eleanor, if you wanted another roommate, you should have talked to me about it. If you had issues with me, we could have discussed it, and I'm sure we could have figured something out."

"I was never supposed to room with you anyway. The housing office messed it up."

"So what? That's no excuse for making up lies about me with the housing office. Drugs? Give me a fucking break! You're the cokehead, not me."

"I don't know what you're talking about. I never told the housing office anything. You must have misunderstood, or it's just something you made up, some kind of weird self-defense mechanism."

The lying bitch!

"This is for the best, Alex. You and I were never going to get on. I mean, really, you don't belong here. Princeton is a foreign world for you. All my friends can see it. You don't fit in socially or academically. You're just an eager pretender. Some of my friends think you'll be gone at the end of this year."

"My grades are probably at least as good as yours, Eleanor."

She shrugged. "Maybe, but my grades won't matter. Princeton would never throw me out. But they will throw you out."

I couldn't believe it. She was completely serene as if dismissing a maid from her estate.

. . .

In February of second semester, around midnight, I was leaving an off-campus bar with my new roommate, Adaoma Badero, from Lagos, Nigeria, when we ran into Eleanor and a group of her friends.

She smiled. "Oh, Alex, so good to see you. I've been thinking about you," she purred with patronizing sweetness. "How have you been? Our old room is kind of lonely without you."

"Uh, I'm fine," my anger immediately flaring. I introduced Adaoma to Eleanor and the others.

"Uh, we were just leaving," I mumbled.

"Oh, too bad. It would have been so much fun to catch up. Let's all of us get together again sometime."

With all that sugary sweetness, I wished her diabetes and all its nasty complications on the spot.

It started to pour rain as Adaoma and I walked back to our dorm room. I was silent, seething. Adaoma broke the silence.

"Ah, so that's the famous Eleanor. As my mates at boarding school in England taught me, she was 'grin-fucking' you. You know, Alex, instead of getting pissed off, you could have given the same thing back to her."

"I know. But she's a cunt, and I couldn't bring myself to do it. Besides, it's easy for you," I teased, "Miss Fancy English Girls Prep School."

"Yeah, hardly. I was one of two black girls in my class, along with five Indians and ten girls from Hong Kong in a class of one hundred. We were the diversity."

I moved closer to her so our shared umbrella would better keep her dry.

"Lots of those England girls were bitches. They used to say they'd never seen anyone as dark as me, and they'd tease me, saying I had a big ass, huge boobs and a big flat nose."

"What'd you say?"

"I'd laugh and say, 'Yeah, but I also have a big brain.'"

I snorted. "I'd have just told them to fuck off."

"Alex, life is good for people like us. We don't live in a refugee camp, we have family and friends, and nobody is shooting at us. Why let yourself get wrapped up in anger?"

I shrugged as we walked in the front door of our dorm.

Adaoma means "a good and virtuous lady" in the Efik language, and she was certainly that. Adaoma was the oldest of seven siblings. Her mother, who was French of Algerian heritage, was an infectious disease doctor of some renown in Africa, and her Nigerian father was a senior-level rural-development expert with the World Bank in Nigeria.

Adaoma had never been to the US before Princeton but attacked the place with a fearlessness that, if I was honest with myself, I could only admire. A booming, make-people-in-the-restaurant-turn-and-look-at-you laugh, a thirst for learning, and a willingness to look for the good in everyone and give them the benefit of the doubt. She spoke excellent, accented British English that would have made the country's former colonial overseers proud.

Adaoma had long, straight, jet-black hair, dark black skin and bright eyes. She was shorter than me, about five-three. She radiated contentment, self-assurance and good humor. I was envious.

Back in our dorm room, she asked me, "So, when will I be seein' the handsome Mr. Findlay? I need to meet Prince Charming. You saw him at Christmas, right?"

"No. His dad's been in terrible health for years and took a downturn during the holidays. He had to be rushed to a hospital out of town in Spokane."

"Ah, too bad," Adaoma said. "No fun for you or him. What about after Spokane?"

"Brian only had a week at home because of basketball and other Naval Academy stuff and spent it all in Spokane at the hospital with his family."

"Are you two still not officially together, but kind of together, and kind of free to see other people? But maybe you're not doing that, eh?"

"Ah," I groaned, "can't I just have a pelvic exam instead of talking about this?"

This elicited a big laugh. "Sorry, woman, I left my stirrups in philosophy class, so you're going to have to talk about Brian."

I sighed. "I think he'd be fine with an official relationship and not seeing other people. Which is good because it would kill me to think of him with someone else. I just don't know if I want that kind of thing."

Adaoma nodded. "But it's not like you've been seeing anyone or dating around regularly."

At that point, I'd been out with Mark from Houston a few times, the son of a famous and staggeringly rich trial attorney. Mark affectionately called his father "the Mick Jagger of ambulance chasers," and he planned on law school after Princeton so he could practice with him. He was a nice guy, treated me well, we had fun together, and he badly wanted into my pants.

One night, with a slight assist from alcohol (just slight), I relented. We flew through the one-stoplight, blink-and-you'll-miss-it, town of sexual intercourse. He was practically shuddering, groaning and done before he had his pants off. Alas, once Mark had visited my town, he pulled out and headed for new vistas. I was fine with that. We were still friendly when we ran into each other.

Adaoma changed into her lime green flannel pajamas, then made popcorn. She put it into two bowls, got us Cokes out of our little refrigerator, and sat next to me on my bed.

"What are you doing tomorrow?" she asked.

"Library," I said. "Trying to keep up. Sometimes I wonder why I even try."

Adaoma shrugged. "You are plenty capable. I think you maybe just never had to struggle, and now you are having to a little. You try to be big and brash, but you have a confidence problem, I think. My mother always says that life is about struggle and challenge; the necessary elements of a virtuous life. I have faith in you, Alex. Just keep working, believe in yourself, and things will be fine. Besides, you must come back next year so we can room together again."

I laughed. "Yeah, I don't know what I'd do without a room covered in wild African sculptures and art."

"You need to do your part with our decorating. You've contributed nothing to these walls. Next year, bring something from your logging town. Maybe a big tree or a blade from a saw. And I must see this cheerleading uniform. It will go on the wall once you model it for me. Quite a species, the American high school cheerleader, it seems." With that, she let out a booming laugh and got up. "We need more butter and salt."

"You have a lot more faith in me with my two-point-one GPA than my parents do. They are beside themselves. It's like they think I spend all my time partying, having sex, and not studying. I mean, I've had sex all of three times: with Brian once in high school, last October with him, and then with Mark that one time."

Adaoma laughed again. "That is in the syllabus for every parent. You're going to be fine. I'm so glad the rich girl from Philadelphia kicked you out, so you had to come live with the loud black woman from Nigeria with the big nose and large ass. Ha-ha-ha!"

· · ·

I spent three weekends with Brian that summer, as the Navy took most of his time. It was good to see him, like we'd never been apart. With him, my assorted grievances and unhappiness at Princeton just melted away. Sex with him in June was a little better than the prior October but still not much different than our maiden voyage in high school, at least for me. Brian had studied up, had done all the things men were supposed to do to help the lady enjoy it, but to no avail.

Brian hinted at making post-college plans together, but I imme-diately shut that down; I just didn't want to think about it. In fact, I reiterated that we should be free to see other people. Why? I don't really know. Pretty quickly, I knew I didn't want that. I was just too proud, frustrated and thick-headed to admit it.

28

South Bend

JULIE: 1982 – 83

Julie returned to her one-bedroom apartment, exhausted. She'd finished her last two finals that morning. She was proud of herself for earning a total of twenty credits over the summer and in the fall, despite being in and out of the hospital in July and August with extreme morning sickness. She'd spent a week in the hospital again in September with an intestinal infection. She looked at the bare three-foot Christmas tree on her two-person kitchen table and resolved to decorate it the next day. Her C-section was scheduled for late next week, so there would be no time after that.

She worried about taking care of two infants and what the future might hold, but was tired of being pregnant and ready to move forward, come what may. Her mom's friend, who'd made it possible for her to come to St. Mary's, checked in with her almost every day and had already helped her arrange childcare.

She and Tim had spoken about once a week through the summer and early fall, but their call frequency diminished thereafter. She hadn't spoken to him in over a month. Yes, Tim was busy with basketball and school, but he'd managed to call her lots the past summer even when the Cal basketball team was traveling through Australia. She'd sent him a letter before Thanksgiving telling him they were targeting a C-section in mid-December but never heard from him. She tried not to think about it, but with each passing day was certain she'd be a single parent.

She'd just received her Chinese food delivery when the phone rang. *They must have forgotten something.*

"Hello."

"Hey, Julie."

She almost dropped the phone. "Tim, hi, it's good to hear from you. The team's at that Christmas tournament in the Bahamas, right? Must be warm in Nassau." She laughed. "It's snowing here."

"I know. I'm in the lobby. They wouldn't let me up, said visitors have to be cleared first."

Oh my god! Why is he here? To send me on my way? Cut all ties? Maybe I'll just beat him to it, tell him we both need to move on with our lives separately.

His presence at the door to her apartment was weird. She hadn't seen him since June. But he looked and smelled great, as always. She wished for a moment they could be back in high school before she was pregnant. They hugged awkwardly and struggled to make conversation as they shared egg rolls, sesame chicken and fried rice. "Good thing I'm eating for three. As you can see, there's plenty of food," Julie nervously joked. "And I'm huge, as you can no doubt see."

He kind of smiled. "Julie, you look great."

But still, he almost seemed afraid to touch Julie, let alone her stomach, to say hello to his daughters. Julie thought back to their Chinese food dinner that summer in Spokane when he'd returned from Poland. Back then he was relaxed and enjoying himself, but now he was quiet, nervous. In all the years she'd known him, he'd never shown any outward signs of stress or worry. *Probably another bad sign. Prepare yourself, Julie.*

With dinner finished and the minimal dishes washed, Julie and Tim sat together on the sofa.

"Ah, Julie. I just need to say some things, if that's okay."

Oh boy. "Okay."

"Well, first, I'm sorry. That hardly covers my sins, but I'll start there. I've not handled this whole thing with you and the pregnancy well. You have, I haven't. It's not an excuse, but the whole thing last spring and summer just knocked me for a loop. Then the coach changed his mind and told me freshmen needed to go on the tour to Australia. I'd figured maybe we'd have the summer to talk and sort stuff, but that didn't happen since you left just a few weeks after we graduated."

Julie sat, arms crossed in front of her chest.

"Alex was right. I was an ass, a shit, or whatever she called me. You know, I think about you probably a hundred times a day. I wonder what you're doing. I miss your laugh, that perfume you wear, miss you resting your head on my shoulder. I think about having a life with you and a family all the time."

He looked at Julie. "Say something, please?"

"Believe me. I know the idea of kids is lots to process."

"It is, sure, but mainly Julie I've missed you. Missed talking to you, just being with you every day."

Julie bit her lower lip before saying, "Tim, do you miss me or are you just homesick and lonely? You have a funny way of showing how you feel. You've been radio silent for like two months. You practically kicked me into the trash. I figured you've come here to cut me loose forever and even tell me you want nothing to do with the girls."

Animated and talking with his hands, Tim protested, "No! No! I know. I was stupid. Julie, please! I want us to be together – you, me, and the girls – forever, if that's what you want. Wherever and whatever it takes."

Julie sighed deeply. "So, when are you due back with the team? Can you stay until next week when they do the C-section?"

"Yes, I'd like to stay longer if I can. And I'm not going back to the team."

"What? Oh no. I don't want to be responsible for you not playing."

"Coach told the team last week he's leaving at the end of the season, being fired really, and he's the reason I went to Cal in the first place. Jarvis…"

"The assistant, right?"

"Yeah. He's likely getting the job, and he's no real fan of mine, nor me of him."

"So? You can transfer. Dozens of schools would want you. You were a high school All-American and Mr. Basketball in Washington junior and senior years, for god's sake. You'll just have to sit out next year to transfer."

He nodded. "Maybe, but I need shoulder surgery now, so I won't be playing for the rest of this year. We'll just have to see how that goes, whether anyone wants me after that."

"My gosh, what happened? Is it serious?"

"It's a torn rotator cuff. It's certainly not life-threatening or a big deal in the grand scheme of things, but it may not be good for my basketball career."

Julie sat up, leaned toward Tim, and drilled her eyes into him. "Tim, would you still be here now if you hadn't hurt your shoulder, if your coach wasn't leaving? If maybe Cal hasn't been what you'd hoped it'd be? If I'm just a consolation prize, you're going to be dis-appointed and unhappy. It's just a matter of time. And that won't be good for anybody. I'd rather have you break my heart now than in a couple of years when we can't make it work."

He shook his head, and she saw tears streaming down his cheeks – for the first time ever. "Julie, Julie. You and the girls are the prize, the best one. You will never be anyone's consolation prize. I love you and would be miserable without you. I'm scared as hell, but I've never been surer of anything in my life. I think we'll have a great life together. I think we should get married."

Julie reached for his hand. "I love you too, have known it since junior year. And I'm so glad to hear you say that. But I think we should wait to get married, at least for a bit. Let's see how it goes, see how you feel after you finish freshman year."

"That won't change, Julie, and I don't want to go back to Cal without you."

"No, you should, Tim. Finish the year. Try to come visit us here as often as you can, and let's see where we are in June. Okay? And in the meantime, we can spend the holidays together here."

He sat silently for almost a minute. "Okay, Julie, whatever it takes."

He reached for her, and she fell into his arms, the happiest she'd felt in months.

Later, after asking Julie to catch him up on the months of her pregnancy, Tim said, "Oh, uh, um, if it's okay with you, my mom would love to come out and spend January with you to help with the girls. She said she'd sleep on the couch or the floor if you don't have a couch."

"Oh, that would be great. She's always so good to me. I have no real idea of what I'm getting into with twins, I'm sure. How long have your parents known I was pregnant?"

Tim winced. "I told them in September. They wanted to call you right away, but I begged them not to, said I needed time to work things out with you. My god, they were pissed."

Julie nodded. "I was afraid of that. I'm sure they felt I'd messed up your life."

He sort of laughed. "Are you kidding? I got the biggest ass-chew-ing of my life from them. They called me irresponsible, heartless, immature and cruel to you. They said they hoped I would come to my senses and marry you as soon as possible. And by the way, Jules, I don't want to marry you because of them. I hope you don't think that."

29

Sally Horrigan: 1983 – 1984

GALWAY

Sally Horrigan entered the Quays in Galway's Latin Quarter, midafternoon in early January 1983. A large wooden, multi-floor pub, it had well over a hundred years of history in its Jameson and Guinness-soaked walls and floorboards. The day was overcast – cold even, for January – and the stoves and fireplaces scattered throughout were roaring, smells of wood and coal evidence of their efforts.

Sally quickly spotted Frieda in a quiet corner near a coal-burning stove. Frieda Lieberman and Sally Horrigan (née Hughes) had been friends since second grade, the two new kids on the first day of school. That Sally was Catholic and Frieda, Jewish didn't matter; they became the closest of friends. After graduating high school in 1975, Frieda went to the UK for university with plans to be a doctor, and Sally stayed in Galway to work. Now they saw each other every year around the holidays when Sally and her kids came down from Northern Ireland to visit her parents.

Sally and Frieda had a long embrace. After a bit of chatter, they went to the bar, ordered hot Irish whiskeys and returned to their corner by the stove.

"Look at you, Frieda! I've missed you so. How is it being the only female gynecologist and obstetrician in Galway?"

"Oh, it's fine, Sally. Good, really. But busy. How are you?"

Sally thought Frieda was eyeing her up with genuine concern. No surprise. Frieda had known her forever and was a doctor. She'd debated whether she should even come to the pub, given how badly off she was, but Frieda was her only long-time friend, and she needed someone to talk to.

Sally cast her eyes down and mumbled. "Hm, eh, suppose I've been better."

Sally was short, five-foot-two and had always been slight, with long, sandy brown hair and an attractive face. But she weighed only about eighty-eight pounds and looked hollowed-out and gaunt. Her hair was stringy, and her teeth were rotting from the stomach acid. Her eating disorder had gone full-on since she'd seen Frieda over a year ago. Lots of time on her knees in front of the loo or bent over sitting on it, bringing up or pushing out everything she ate.

Frieda moved her chair next to Sally and took both of her hands in hers. "Sally, you don't look good. What's the matter? Something to do with your grief about George? I know there was a bombing, an accident maybe, or maybe not. I didn't push for details last year knowing he'd passed, but my god, look at you!"

Sally had met George Horrigan in July 1975. She was seventeen, right out of high school. George was originally from Northern Ireland and had moved back when he was fifteen, but he still spent his summers in Galway with his widowed mother. Sally had told Frieda back then that it was love at first sight, and that within a month, the two of them were "doin' what we shouldn't be doin', bein' unmarried and all." Sally made a trip to confession every time afterward. However, no amount of Hail Marys quelled her love and lust for George.

After three months, Sally was pregnant. George and Sally married soon after news of the creation of their daughter, Tracy, and moved to Northern Ireland. Shortly after they'd married, Sally learned that George's family had been committed members of the IRA for decades. This shocked her, but she'd come around to it soon enough. George's family was from South Armagh, hardcore IRA country. George's father had been in the IRA. Unionist paramilitaries killed him in 1968, and after that, his widow gave up the IRA, moved to Galway with her kids, and tried to discourage George, her youngest, from the life.

Frieda leaned closer and lowered her voice. "What happened with George?"

Sally sighed, returning to her grief, always close by, its presence like a bad neighbor that wouldn't move.

"Mind you, Frieda, I only knew what happened because uh

George's brother, Otto, who's in the Provisionals in Belfast."

Sally knew that there would be no stopping once she'd started this story.

"Just about two years ago, George and I were livin' in South Armagh. He was in the Provisional brigade there. Tracy was five, Sean was three, and Fergal was two. And I was three months pregnant."

Frieda sat up straighter. "What? My god, Sally, what happened to the baby?"

Sally shrugged. "You know, the stress of it all. I was just a mess and had a miscarriage a couple of months later."

Frieda put both hands up to her mouth and shook her head.

"The Officer Commanding in South Armagh ordered George to lead two men to bomb the British Army barracks in the area. There were no devices available locally at the time, so they sent a bombmaker down from Omagh. The bomb was big and supposed to detonate in the boot of a car on a timer. George knew a man friendly to the Provisionals inside the barracks who would leave a back gate unlocked so George and his men could bring a car inside the fence, park it quick, and run away."

Sally's voice thickened and grew halting. She drained her whiskey, reached for Frieda's hand, and talked even faster.

"All went okay at first. They got the car inside the gate, but before they could get away, the bombmaker said he needed to check again that the bomb was correctly primed, something that shoulda been done before they drove to the barracks. But he was inexperienced and a drunk, and on that mission, he could barely function. And while checking the bomb, he set it off. Killing him, my George, their mate, and twenty soldiers in the barracks."

Frieda squeezed Sally's hand and whispered. "No!"

"After, the Provisionals celebrated George and his men as heroes, killed fighting for the cause. But it destroyed me, and once Otto told me the bomber was drunk when he detonated the bomb, I got so angry. I wanted a court martial for the bombmaker, even though he wuz dead."

"Did that come about?"

Sally shook her head, tears now streaming down her cheeks. "I wanted my George's name cleared of any mistake during the operation. Normally, somethun like that would get done, though it would all be secret. But this time, the bomber was the son-in-law of the Officer Commanding of the Omagh brigade, so nobody did nothin'."

Frieda wiped tears from Sally's cheeks with her thumb, then fumbled around on the small table for her whiskey and took another drink.

"Otto swore me to secrecy, told me I had to move on. That I couldn't say nothin'. But I couldn't. When I heard 'bout what happened, I had to get justice and couldn't just have 'em sweep it away with no consequence or conscience. I was mad and sometimes hysterical. I threatened to go to the media but didn't, and also tried to get George's men in South Armagh to help."

Frieda took yet another drink of her whiskey. "Did it help, Sally?"

The frustration, bitterness and sadness rushed into Sally like water in a charged fire hose. "No! 'Course not. I kept at this for musta been three or four months, but nothing happened. Finally, Otto come to see me, and said for the good of my children and my future, I needed to keep quiet. So I did. The Provisionals let me keep my job in the organization. I hated my job from then on, but I had babies to feed and no place else to find work."

"So, that was the end of it, then?"

Sniffling and stopping to blow her nose, Sally said, "I thought so. I was ready to move on, but wuz wrong. You see, George's family – not Otto or George's mother, but his other brothers and relatives – thought that by makin' a problem, I hurt the family's reputation and legacy. I didn't see it that way. I wanted justice for him. Anyways, George's family hated me then and tried to have me declared an unfit mother and take Tracy, Sean and Fergal from me. They didn't win, partly because George's mother sided with me; Otto had to keep quiet. But I had to fight them for months in court."

"Did the organization help you at all?"

"They suggested I get out of South Armagh, move to Belfast, and take a job with 'em there. So, last summer, I moved all-a us to Belfast."

"Well, Sally, that must have helped things, right?"

"I dunno. I was away from George's family, and that was good. But we was living in Divis Flats in Belfast. You know Divis?"

"No."

"It's a high-rise Catholic ghetto. Full-a all kinds of poor and strugglin' people, like me and me kids. I was working but didn't make hardly no money. I worried every week' bout feedin' me babies."

"Sally, why on earth didn't you move back to Galway with your parents and your mother-in-law? Why don't you just move now?"

"I think 'bout that all the time. I'm afraid-a what George's family might do if I move the kids outta Northern Ireland. I think they hope one day my babies will continue George's legacy in the Provisionals, but I'd rather die before I let that happen."

Frieda left to get refills on their hot whiskeys. Returning, she sat next to Sally and held her hands.

"Sally, your health – I can tell it's not good. What's happening? Are you harming yourself in any way?"

Sally was crying again. "I don't know. I'm just buried in blackness and sorrow, can't hardly function no more. Every day Tracy has to push me to get outta bed, feed everyone, and go to work. I hate myself for bein' so weak and useless to my wee uns."

"Depression, I think this is," Frieda said.

"And I don't know how it happened, but once I lost the baby, I just kinda had this thing about food and quit eatin'. And once I quit, I couldn't start up again. Now when I do eat a bit, I feel I have to just get it out a me."

"Oh my god, Sally, if not for you, then for your kids, you need to get help, mental and physical. Will you promise me you'll do that as soon as you get back?"

Sally nodded. "Will do my best, Frieda. But nothing I do is gonna help me with me money troubles. And I'm still paying the solicitors 'cause George's family is still trying to make trouble and take me kids."

After another hour, Sally and Frieda said tearful goodbyes and promised to be better at keeping in touch.

A month later, a postcard arrived at Sally's Belfast flat:

> Sally Dear
> Thinking of you every day. Be strong. As it happens, a friend of mine, Simon is his name, may be in Belfast soon. He's wonderful. I told him to look you up, and maybe you can have a pint or some tea together when he's there.
>
> Much Love, Frieda

· · ·

Simon surfaced in Sally's life in March of '83, introducing himself as she walked home from work one evening, saying he and Frieda were old friends from university days in England. He was a manufacturer's representative for a French company that sold tools to the shipyards in Belfast and was in town about once a month.

Sally had initially thought Frieda was fixing her up on a date. He was an attractive man, always well-dressed in business clothes, and much taller and older than Sally. He had an olive complexion and spoke English with what seemed like a funny accent, certainly not something from Ireland or the UK. He told Sally his father had worked for the UN, and he'd lived all around the world while growing up, including a number of years in the US.

They got together for a pint at Belfast pubs in May and July. Sally increasingly wondered what Simon's interest in seeing her was, but in August, she found out. They met for lunch on a hot, overcast Saturday at an Italian restaurant near Stormont in Belfast's government district. Seated at a four-person table in an isolated back corner, Simon ordered a whiskey, neat; and Sally, hot tea. Simon wore gray slacks and a white dress shirt; and Sally, a green crew neck cotton jumper and brown pants.

Sally's brows furrowed. "What's the occasion, Simon?"

He smiled warmly at her. "Sally, in getting to know you these past months, I must say your determination to care for and provide for your children is extraordinary."

Reaching for her tea, she said, "What choice I got, eh? My George would roll in his grave if we ever had to go on the dole."

"After we met last month, I couldn't get it out of my mind that George's family will maybe try to take your kids again. What bastards. How do you pay your solicitor's bills?"

"I been getting some money help from me parents in Galway."

Sally didn't tell Simon that financial support from her parents had ended two months prior. Her sister had been diagnosed with stage-three kidney cancer, and the free treatments she'd been having in first Galway and then Dublin weren't working. It had spread, and her last hope was experimental treatment in the US. While the medicines and doctors' fees were covered by the sponsors of the clinical trial, her living expenses in Boston were not. She had to check in with doctors weekly, so she would need to remain in Boston for the entire twelve-month trial. What little financial resources Sally's parents could spare now needed to go to her sister.

Simon continued, "That must be quite a stress on your parents and you. You know, Frieda is concerned about you and asked me if there was anything I might do to help."

Sally made a bit of a face. "I don't see that. What could you do for me?"

"I work with an organization that's always interested in mutually beneficial alliances and partnerships with certain individuals. In exchange for useful information, we often compensate the providers handsomely. There is limited risk for the people we work with and many benefits for them."

"This is all mysterious to me. What kind of financial benefits?"

Simon smiled slightly. "We could discuss the details, but say, for example, we might be able to match your current salary. We could be your second job, night job, as some say. I know you work for the Provisionals in their quartermaster's organization."

"Just who do you work for, Simon? The Brits? Because if so, you can forget that right now. They are enemies, for god's sake."

"Sally, please. I do not work with them. We have nothing to do with them."

"Then who do you work for?"

"Israel. I help protect the nation from its enemies."

Confused now, Sally asked, "How in the name of Jesus, Mary and Joseph could I ever help Israel? It's not like I'm involved with weapons in my job. I buy food and cleaning supplies for our locations and call the plumber when the loo's broke."

Simon shrugged. "Maybe you can't. But maybe someday you can. Perhaps in your line of work, there could be times in the future when you might learn something about events or people in the Middle East that would be important to us."

"And what if you pay me for months, years even, and I don't ever give you useful information?"

"That's fine. We just want to know that if you have useful information sometime, we can ask you to help us. We would NEVER ask or expect you to do anything that would endanger the Provisionals or their activities."

Sally furtively looked over her shoulder and whispered back, "Did Frieda tell you I worked for the Provisionals?"

"No. We learned that on our own. But don't worry, we would never tell anyone anything."

Sally sat for almost two minutes, swirling her tea in the cup. Finally, she looked at him. "No. I can't do it, Simon."

"Okay, that's fine. Regardless, I would like to stay connected and keep meeting every couple of months or sooner if you like. Just know that this is a standing offer. If you ever want a rethink on this, let me know."

Sally's response to Simon's gentle query the next month was still no. But by October, events had loosened Sally's tenuous hold on her children. The legal fight with George's family had restarted, and her solicitor's bills were unrelenting. Her parents were also desperate for any financial help she could provide to support her sister in Boston.

Sally knew nothing was ever free, and it would be riskier and more complicated than Simon was claiming. But she was desperate. By the end of 1983, the Mossad, Israel's foreign intelligence service, was paying Sally an amount equal to her monthly salary. All in cash, left for her on the tenth of every month at a rotating series of locations spread across Belfast.

Sally saw Simon about every three months in Belfast in '84, but their agenda never included business. It was as if the conversations about helping Israel had never happened. Meantime, the money arrived for Sally every month. At first, she needed all of it for her solicitors, but by the summer, she had again defeated George's family's attempt to take her kids. Thereafter, she shared half the Mossad money every month with her parents, who were now raising her sister's two children after she'd passed on in Boston even before the completion of the clinical trial.

30

Julie: March 1983

THE TIMBERLINE EXAMINER, MARCH 7, 1983

My Spot in the Bleachers by Shug Adams

Tim ("Ice Man") Delacroix, the best-ever player in the rich, decades-long tradition of Timberline basketball, and one of the best high school players to ever lace up sneakers in the state, "a generational talent" many said, is leaving Cal Berkeley for UCLA and an unknown future. Until injuring his shoulder last November, Tim had been a favorite for Pac-10 Freshman of the Year. Just out of high school, he led the Bears in scoring and assists on their fifteen-game tour to Australia last summer.

His shoulder needs surgery but should pose no problem for a return to his winning form. But it won't be at Cal, the winner in a frenzied two-year recruiting battle that captivated Timberline. Yes, the coach that recruited Tim will be leaving Cal at the end of the season, but the Ice Man's decision to transfer to UCLA as a walk-on without a scholarship is puzzling. Sources tell me he now has family considerations and has moved to Cal's LA rival because he got an ROTC scholarship. Financial considerations are apparently a factor in his decision not to wait for new scholarship offers from other schools. ROTC will certainly cloud his basketball future, as upon graduation, he will owe the US Army and Uncle Sam a five-year tour as an officer. Absent special dispensation, this will seemingly foreclose any kind of NBA career, a shame for sure.

Neither Tim nor his parents responded to my inquiries about his future plans. Everyone in Timberline wishes Tim well and hopes he can resurrect his promising basketball career. But now, possibly, it's dead in the water before it really begins. And that is a great disappointment for everyone.

31

South Bend

Julie called Alex in her dorm on a warm mid-March day, and Adaoma answered.

"Hey, Adaoma. It's Julie. How are you?"

"Ah, it's momma! I'm good. Are you getting any sleep with those twins?" Laughing, she said, "Alex said she bets your boobs are about to fall off feeding those babies all the time."

"It feels like it sometimes, let me tell you."

"We must meet sometime, Julie. It feels like I've known you my whole life. Here's Alex."

"Hey," Julie said, "Adaoma is so cool. You're lucky to have such a good friend." But before Julie could say anything else, Alex cut her off.

"Did you see that bullshit newspaper column in TL from Shug Adams? What a fucking hack!"

"Yeah, Tim's parents called and told us about it last week."

"He was in Indiana?"

"Yes. Berkeley's on spring break, and he's taking an extra week. He's out with the girls in the double stroller on a walk now."

"Doesn't that article piss you off?"

"Not me, really, I've decided," Julie replied. "I have such low expectations of the town, given my life there. I've left it behind, and I don't care. Tim was angrier than I was about it. He didn't take the guy's call but didn't have any idea he'd write an article like that."

"I should write a letter to the editor and rip him a new one."

Julie laughed. "Alex, please don't. There's no upside for you in that. Anyway, I was calling to see if you and Brian are going to be free Memorial Day weekend. Tim said he thinks Brian can get leave from Annapolis for a long weekend."

"Why, what's up?" "A wedding," Julie said, her smile practically visible through the phone. "I need a maid of honor, and Tim needs a best man."

"Holy shit! "You're doing it, finally. Awesome. Of course, we'll be there. I'm calling Brian as soon as I get off the phone with you. Where is it, and who's coming?"

"We're going to do it at a small chapel on campus here at St. Mary's. The wedding will be TINY: you, Brian, Tim's parents and two older sisters, and the friend of my mom's here at St. Mary's who has helped me so much. And, of course, Tim, me, Faith and Hope."

"I like it! I'm soooo happy for you and Tim."

"Me too," Julie said. "And Shug Adams did have it partially right. We're moving to LA this summer. Tim got an army ROTC scholarship and will be a preferred walk-on for UCLA basketball. I can hopefully work part-time and maybe squeeze in some classes in the three years we'll be there. Then we'll have a five-year military adventure."

32

Alex: September – December 1984

I called Julie from Princeton on a late September afternoon of junior year.

"Hey, sweetie, it's Aunt Alex. How are my babies?"

"Hey there yourself. I just put Faith and Hope down for a nap."

"I can't believe they're going to be two in December. And that you and Tim have been married for over a year. How's life as a twenty-year-old married hag?"

Julie laughed. "It's exhausting with the twins, but no complaints."

"Brian and I have the same fall break, and we thought we'd come out for a long weekend. We'll meet in Philly, fly out of there, and you guys can pick us up at LAX."

"Wow, that would be great."

"With Tim doing military business now, he and Brian will have even more stuff to talk about. They can go off and play soldier together while you and I drink margaritas and play with my nieces."

"Sounds like a plan. Tim and the girls will be so excited. When are you coming?"

"Three weeks."

"All right, it's on the calendar!"

* * *

Brian and I flew into town Friday afternoon in mid-October, and we hung out at Julie and Tim's rented townhouse in Culver City that night. Brian and I slept on the pull-out couch in the living room. We badly wanted to have sex but worried about Tim and Julie hearing since their bedroom was just off the living room. We decided to go for it but resolved to do it quietly because we didn't want the twins to wake up. I felt so close to Brian, happy to be free of Princeton's constant anxieties and irritations. It was like we were meant to be one unit forever. I could see myself as Mrs. Brian Findlay. That night, I thought he was all I would ever want and need. Everything would turn out amazing. I would get my shit together, and we'd both have great careers and would see the world. Happily ever after.

Our worries about waking the little ones were unfounded. Their room was right next to Tim and Julie's through paper-thin walls, and Tim and Julie had the same idea we did. This would mortify Julie, but I heard her finishing as I drifted off to sleep.

The next day, we went to the UCLA football game at the Rose Bowl. Julie and Tim's neighbors, a retired couple, babysat. After the game, Brian and Tim grilled steaks and vegetables while Julie made a salad and I played blocks with Faith and Hope. I loved it. They were so much fun, calling me "Auntie Alex." Though they were identical twins and hard to tell apart physically with their dark hair and uncanny resemblance to Julie, their personalities couldn't have been more different. Hope was bossy and talkative, telling me all about her day and what she liked and disliked. Faith was quieter, more like Julie.

By 22:00, everyone was asleep except Julie and me. We sat out on the tiny back deck with a nightcap.

"Those little ones of yours are beautiful. They look just like you, with a little bit of Tim."

"Thanks. I'm pretty proud of what we created, I must say."

"So, did Tim get a basketball scholarship this year after sitting out last year to transfer?"

"No. Technically, he's still a walk-on. His ROTC scholarship covers tuition, plus we get a monthly stipend for housing and expenses. And we still have my mom's MDW medical insurance until I'm twenty-five."

"Is the ROTC thing enough, money-wise?"

"We make it work, but it's tight every month. We decided to save my mom's money for emergencies and a college fund for the kids."

"How much do you work at that software company?"

"About twenty hours a week. Thank goodness for Mrs. Kowalski next door, who babysits every afternoon."

"How does Tim like hooping for UCLA?"

"He likes it. He's glad he's getting to play college ball for more than those few months at Cal, especially after the shoulder surgery. He may start this year, but we'll see. But as of now, he isn't sure if he'll play next year. I'm encouraging him to keep an open mind."

"I think Brian will end up playing all four years at Annapolis."

"Tim will be in Germany part of next summer doing Army stuff. The girls and I will stay here. Then the next summer, he'll graduate, get commissioned, and be gone all summer again."

"Back to Germany?"

"No. He's already picked the infantry branch. So that means infantry officer school at Fort Benning in Georgia and then maybe Ranger School in North Carolina."

"Will you and the kids go with him?"

"No, we'll stay here and move with him to his post when his training's done, sometime in the fall."

"Where will the army post you guys?"

"We don't know yet."

Julie went into the kitchen to get us another drink and brought a cheese plate onto the deck.

"New subject." I smirked. "How's married life?"

Julie sighed. "It's good, no, it's really good. But it's hard sometimes, you know. Every day isn't champagne, roses and unicorns. We're still learning about each other, learning how to disagree and fight constructively when we need to. The girls are great but exhausting."

"Okay then, that sounds complicated. So, how's married sex?"

Julie smiled and laughed softly. "I highly recommend it. How's-Serious-Boyfriend-Brian, or, I-have-Brian-but-we're-seeing-other-people sex for you?"

I made a face. "It's good with Brian. There really hasn't been anyone else for ages. And I'm still not very good at it. I'm afraid sex might not be my thing."

Julie smiled. "Maybe you just need more practice."

"I may have too many of my mother's genes, I think."

"Why do you say that? Were your parents not very intimate?" Julie asked.

"I don't actually know, but I just can't imagine my mother having sex, can you?"

"Hmm, now there's a thought. Let's try," Julie said, giggling. "Your mom's on top, drenched in sweat and riding hard. Panting and saying, 'Oh yeah, that's good, I'm almost there, I'm almost there, oh, oh, oh god, I'm coming! I'm coming! Ahhhhh, Ahhhhh!!'" Julie made a face and shook her head. "Nope, sorry, Alex, can't see it."

"Oh god, stop it, stop it," I whimpered, covering my ears. "That's such a disturbing visual. I need more wine."

"I don't know. Maybe she masturbates instead," Julie offered.

"No way!" I said. "I'm sure she could saw away down there for an hour and be more likely to start a campfire than come."

By that time, Julie and I were both doubled over with laughter.

When we composed ourselves, Julie said, "You know, though your mom has a severe sort of personality and is emotionally closed off, she's a very smart and capable woman. She wasn't ever very nice to me, and I always sensed this low-energy current of dislike from her. I was afraid of her. But make no mistake, I owe her much. And you. Literally, my life. I think about that almost every day, and I will always be thankful to both of you."

I shrugged and didn't say anything. Maybe I didn't want to give my mother any credit.

• • •

Everyone was up by seven the next morning. We went for breakfast at a diner in Culver City, where the girls loved the blueberry waffles with whipped cream. After breakfast, we all walked around Venice Beach. The guys carried Faith and Hope on their shoulders and found a face-painting spot. Next, we drove down to Manhattan Beach, the six of us crammed into Julie and Tim's lime green Challenger. I sat on Brian's lap in the back, in what little space remained next to the car seats.

"Tim," Brian said, "this is just wrong. For god's sake, get a station wagon or something. Two car seats don't belong in a four-hundred-fifty-horsepower two-door."

"Never," Tim said. "I'm gonna keep it and teach the girls to drive stick."

We staked out a spot on the beach around four. It was a beautiful day – sunny, seventy degrees with a sparkling blue sky and a breeze. The crowds were starting to thin. Tim and Brian took the twins down to the water to play, and Julie and I spread out a beach blanket closer to shore.

After a few minutes, Julie asked, "Now that you're halfway through Princeton, are you glad you chose it?"

"It sucks."

"Why do you think that? Has it not gotten better at all? What about Adaoma? I can't wait to meet her."

I looked down at the beach. "Princeton's not what I thought it would be. Some of the people are really interesting and nice, but a lot of them are elitist dicks and assholes."

"But isn't that kind of like life in general, sweetie?"

I put my sunglasses on and said, "Yeah, maybe. Probably. You know, I'm also just tired of my parents. Sick of their bitching about my major and my grades and plans after I graduate. My grades are shit. Makes me feel like a total ass hat. But I like my major, medieval studies, impractical as it might be. And as a bonus, it makes my parents batshit crazy."

"Your grades can't be that bad. You're one of the smartest people I know."

"Believe it. I'm on academic probation again this semester. I have to get at least a 3.0 GPA this semester to ease my cume above 1.8 to stay in school. I know what you're thinking. Have I tried my hardest and put my best foot forward academically? No, not even close."

"See?" Julie pointedly said. "So, you can certainly do it."

"Probably. It's just that it's been so much harder than I expected. Well, listen to me, the whiny little pussy bitch, saying, 'Wow, I was the smartest girl in school my whole life, and now I'm not.' I don't even feel sorry for myself when I think about it that way."

Julie put her hand on my shoulder. "You can totally do this. For a time, my life was one setback after another, and as hard as it is sometimes, you have to believe in yourself and keep trying. Keep fighting and moving forward."

"Yeah, yeah, time for another subject. How about this weather?"

"Okay, how are things with Brian?"

I turned my eyes from down the beach and looked at Julie. "I'd rather talk about my grades. Better yet, let's walk down to that cotton candy stand – the smell is reeling me in."

Back after a few minutes with our cotton candy and with a bag for the girls, Julie asked, "Why don't you want to talk about Brian? You seem so happy with him. Is everything all right?"

"I love being with him. We only see each other every few months, and usually just for part of a weekend. But that's when I'm mostly happy – not angry, worrying or feeling sorry for myself."

Sarcastically, Julie said, "Wow, that sounds terrible, Alex."

"He's talking about getting married or living together once we graduate. He's told me a couple of times he loves me, and I've just brushed it off and changed the subject."

"Then that's something you don't want?"

I threw up my hands. "I don't know. Sometimes I think yes, but then I think no. I mean, he's gonna be in the Marines for five years, god knows where. I don't want to be living in some shithole military town out in the middle of nowhere."

"Like I will be," Julie laughed.

"After all, I've got to make use of my medieval history degree. The working world will be panting for me to get out of school, I know."

"Do you love him? Do you want to make a life with him?"

"I don't know. I mean, yes, of course, in some ways. We've practically spent our whole lives together. Dating for what, the last six or seven years? But in terms of, yeah, he's the love of my life, who knows? I'm not sure I even know what that is or if I ever will."

33

Sitting on the blanket in the sand, Tim, Brian and the passengers on their shoulders barely visible far down the beach, I looked at Julie and marveled. She looked like a model now, almost unrecognizable from our days in Timberline. She had long dark chocolate brown hair blowing in the wind, soft, loose bouncy curls that dropped well below her shoulders with short bangs. A slightly oval face, subtle chin, rounded nose, full red lips and a sparkling toothpaste-commercial smile. She'd always had those luminous black eyes, today nesting behind prescription sunglasses. Since leaving high school, just two years ago, she'd also acquired a sort of low-key, confident presence.

"I gotta say, I'm proud of you," I told her. "You really have your shit together, a strong, tough, confident woman. Your life is like perfect."

She shook her head. "I'm so thankful for my life, Alex, for Tim, the girls and his family. And you. I'm happy, really happy now. For the first time in as long as I can remember, I'm not fearful and anxious most of the time. But my life isn't perfect; my marriage isn't perfect, Alex. Nobody's is. I have challenges."

"Like what?"

"I still have mental health issues that come up from the things in TL – not that often, but when they do, they can send me down this dark well and sometimes I can't get myself out." Julie took a deep breath, slowly blew it out and chewed on her lower lip. "I resisted this for years, but now I realize Tim needs to know some things about me that I've never told him. Things I haven't told you either."

I sat up straighter on the blanket. "Julie, what are you talking about?"

"You know Tim's aunt in Timberline died of cancer last May. She died on a Wednesday, and the funeral was Saturday. Tim was close to her, so he felt we all needed to go to the funeral. But I was reluctant.

I suggested that he go and I stay back with the girls."

"Why? Because of the money to fly up?"

"It was expensive, yes." Julie kind of laughed. "I mean, the available credit on our Visa is like a vanishing air pocket in a doomed mine. Tim thought it was just because I didn't like TL and was being a selfish baby. That wasn't it, but I didn't say anymore and just went along."

"What the hell are you talking about?" I asked, impatient for details.

Julie pulled her knees up to her chin and wrapped her arms around them. That trip last May triggered memories of bad things in Timberline a couple of months after my mom died."

"What?"

Julie's voice caught and grew quieter. "I was raped and beaten up. Not having my mom around didn't help with that, but the rape and the violence were mainly what drove the suicide situations. It still causes me problems. Doctors told me I had PTSD, like a soldier could get in war, but in different ways."

This hit me like a sucker punch to the gut. I couldn't believe it. Never could I have imagined this. A hundred questions started running wild in my head. I had to consciously tell myself to shut up and listen.

"Sometimes it comes rushing back and scares the hell out of me, just paralyzes me. Usually, I can get myself out of it. I take medicine regularly, and that helps me from getting too low. And it's much better now than in high school and when I was alone in Indiana. Remember senior year when I was supposedly out with a bad flu for a week?"

"Yes."

"I was really back in Spokane as a psychiatric inpatient. Annie Findlay took me, but Brian didn't know; she told him she had to go to Spokane to talk to his dad's doctors."

I was like some dumb pug fighter, standing there, this news like blows raining down on me. "My god, Julie!" I finally spat out. "Why didn't you tell me after it happened?"

Julie started to fight back tears. "So many times after, Alex, I crept across our room in your house in the wee hours of the morning, shaking. I'd sit on the edge of your bed, extend my hand, ready to tap on your shoulder to wake you up. But every time I pulled my hand back, afraid."

"Well… well, I mean, who the hell did this to you?"

"Win Blackpool."

"No!" I put both hands on my forehead and ran my fingers through my hair. Blows continuing to land on me, the hapless boxer. I slid over next to her – I couldn't have been closer without sitting in her lap – and put my arm around her. "Julie," I half-whispered and sputtered, "can you tell me what happened?" She wiped both eyes with the palms of her hands and began.

It was early February when you were back east with your mom on that college trip, and I stayed behind at your house. The basketball team had a bye that Friday night, and Fogg invited a bunch of people over to his house. I rode over with him and some others. Brian was due later but never showed up. Fogg took us in through the kitchen when we arrived, and his mother was there. She started talking to me about my mom, wanted to know how I was doing, that sort of thing. By the time we'd finished, Fogg and the others had left the kitchen.

Fogg's mom told me everyone was in the game room, which was somewhere in a back corner of that massive, multi-wing house. After a couple of wrong turns, I found it, but nobody was there. A few dim lamps were on, the only signs of life in the room. Fogg's mom had been mistaken about the location. I learned later they were in a whole different part of the house, far from me.

I turned to leave just as Mr. Blackpool came in. I'd probably said barely twenty words to him since I'd lived in Timberline. But after mom died, whenever I saw him at Fogg's or at a game, he was pretty talkative and always seemed concerned about me. He said hello to me. For the first time, I noticed he had a nose that looked like it had been broken before. He was wearing blue slacks, a bright white button-down dress shirt with diamond cufflinks, a Rolex watch and snakeskin cowboy boots. He asked me about my classes, how I was getting along, and how far I thought the basketball team might go that season. He said he didn't know if they had what it took to get to State with Tim in Europe. There was a strong smell of cologne, cigar smoke and alcohol coming off of him. I excused myself to go find Fogg and the others.

Julie stopped her retelling for a moment, took a deep breath, and wiped the beginnings of another stream of tears with the cuff of her red-and-blue rugby jersey.

I tried to sound soothing. "Julie, honey, keep going. It's okay."

As I was leaving, his hand landed on my right shoulder, and he spun me around to face him. Immediately, both of his hands were on my collarbones up around my neck. He practically lifted me off my feet and dragged me across the room. I was in shock. What was going on? Why was this happening? What did I do wrong? He pinned me against that huge fireplace, and I could feel the rough stones digging into my back. It seemed like forever before I could squeeze words out of my mouth.

I was gasping, "Mr. Blackpool, what are you doing? What's the matter? I'm sorry, what did I do? Please stop it! Please!"

He pressed me harder against the wall and started clawing at my underwear under my jeans. Oh my god, oh my god! I thought. I don't know where I found the strength, but I started really struggling. It was hard for me to scream because I had trouble catching my breath. I was begging him to stop. Then... then... he pulled my pants and underwear down, and his other forearm on my chest glued me against the stone wall like the bearskin above the fireplace.

He hammered away at me, first with his fingers, jabbing, poking, pulling, scratching and ripping. I kept struggling, and he got angry. The next thing I knew, still pinning me to that stone wall with his left forearm, the palm of his right hand rushed toward me like a rocket and smashed into my left eye. My head snapped back and slammed into the stones behind me. I heard something snap or pop near my face. Then... then, Alex, his pants were down, and instead of his fingers ripping at me, he was in me. He went on and on for I don't know how long. My god, it hurt. He was grunting, but then he was done. He stepped back and as he removed his arm, the one pinning me to the stone wall, I just slid down like an express elevator to the ground floor, hitting the back of my head on the stones on the way. The world was spinning and starting to go black. I was fading in and out. No part of my body seemed to be working.

I thought I saw someone else come into the room, but it was just a blurry shape at first. I threw up all over myself sitting there, I couldn't even think to turn my head to the side. Win and the other person spoke, and Win left the room, I'm pretty sure. The other person came over and helped me up, but I couldn't really walk. I hurt all over. I had a terrible headache, was dizzy, and there was blood matting up in my hair, running from there down my back. My left eye and face were throbbing and swelling up like crazy, and then I couldn't see out of my eye. I was nauseous, and every time I took a step, the pain in the area where he'd been down there doubled me over and made me scream.

"Who was that guy, Julie? Did you know him?" She didn't answer, too focused on trying to get through it, I assumed.

"Keep it down," the other person said. "We need to get you out of here. You're safe now." Next thing I remembered, I was in his car. We hadn't gone very far when I threw up all over myself again. Everything hurt so bad, my head, my face, my private parts. I was crying and moaning, and the smell of my blood and vomit was overpowering. The guy driving the car rolled the window down for fresh air and said we couldn't go to the hospital. "Too many questions," he said. But he told me I needed a doctor and that he could take me to the house of one who could help me.

I... I don't know. I just freaked out even more. Adrenaline took over I think. I didn't want anyone to know what had happened, didn't want anyone to see me. I started screaming, "No, no, you'll just kill me there, and nobody will believe me anyway," or something like that.

"Calm down," the guy said. "Nobody's going to kill you. Don't be crazy. You need a doctor."

But I was still hysterical. Screaming. "No, no, no...no doctor. The whole town will know!"

He ignored me at first, but I just went on and on. Finally, he got really mad, looked over at me and said, "You don't want to go to the doctor, fine. We'll discuss it later."

At that point, I didn't care if I died in the woods or beside the road, but I wasn't staying in that car. I told him to let me out. He resisted, and then I was screaming at him, blood pouring out of my head and everything. "Yes, yes, you will let me out of this car now, or I will tell people you did this!"

He looked panicked but didn't say anything. But he stopped the car right outside the Central side of the north tunnel, right by that phone booth on the side of the road. I got out, and he drove away. I was going to pass out, maybe for good, I thought, but I was able to make a call from the pay phone. I called the first number that came into my head: Brian's house. Maybe he was still home. But he wasn't.

I held up my hand, a feeble stop sign, a squirt gun against a raging inferno. Julie violently shook her head and said, "Please, Alex, I just want to finish this."

Brian's mother answered, and I was just wailing. Somehow, I managed to tell her where I was because the next thing I knew, I was lying face down in the snow in the woods just off the road, and Annie was trying to wake me up. She brushed the snow off my face and got me into her car.

I blacked out again, and when I came to, Annie and another woman were carrying me out of her car and into the Findlays' house. Brian wasn't home, thank god. I didn't want him to see me like that. Annie wanted to take me to the hospital, but again I started crying hysterically and saying, "No, no, no! Please, promise me you won't take me there! Nobody will believe me, and everyone in town will know."

Brian's dad was asleep, and Mrs. Findlay moved her younger kids to blankets in their tiny living room. She and the other woman carried me into the kids' bedroom and laid me down on the double bed. I remember Annie visibly winced and whispered, "My god," as she sat on the bed and held my hand.

I learned later the other woman was Gloria Rodriquez, a neighbor Annie had called. She'd been a nurse in the emergency and obstetrics departments of a major hospital in Mexico City for years. When her children were grown and moved to the US to Timberline and Spokane, Gloria and her husband had moved up to be closer to them and their grandchildren. She was unable to get licensed to work as a nurse in the US without expensive schooling she couldn't afford, so she worked on a loading dock in a fruit warehouse near the MDW terminal. Gloria provided medical help and advice to everyone in the Flats since many of them could never afford to see a doctor. People regularly gave her small donations to help her maintain and nurture a stock of medicines and medical supplies for the neighborhood.

Julie continued.

> Finally, though, I had to give in. Gloria insisted I go to the
> hospital. She felt my injuries were just potentially too
> dangerous, especially around my eye, and she also worried
> about my concussion and possible internal injuries. I was so
> upset, just bawling. Knowing my fears of going to the hospital
> in TL were justified, Gloria called a doctor friend in the ER at
> the hospital in Wenatchee, and then she and Annie laid me
> down in the back seat of Annie's car and drove me there in
> a snowstorm. Gloria agreed at least we wouldn't tell them
> about the sexual assault at the hospital. She felt she could
> treat those injuries with the medicines and supplies she had.
> I was back in TL the next day and moved in with Brian's family
> for like a week since you were back east.

"What did Brian think about you at his house? Did he know you
were raped? Did he ask you anything?"

"I'm sure he was curious. But I told him I'd had a hard fall on the
ice and would stay at his place until you and your mom got back. I
told him the same ice story I told you. Annie kept quiet, and fortunately, you guys never asked many questions."

I was a fucking idiot! "What did the hospital find?"

"I had two big gashes on the back of my head from when I hit
the stones on the wall. A lot of blood had clotted and matted in my
hair. Thirty stitches and staples to close those up, and I also had a
severe concussion, but a cat scan and X-rays showed no skull fracture
or brain swelling. The doctors prescribed bed rest for a week in a
dark room and gave me medicine for my near-constant nausea and
vomiting from the concussion."

How was I so obtuse to think she'd really just slipped on the ice?
"What about your face?" I asked.

"I had a fractured cheekbone but no detached retina or other
damage to my eye. As you saw, it was painful and really ugly for so long,
and I did eventually need surgery in the spring for my cheek as you
know. But the doctors were right. There wasn't any permanent damage."

I was afraid to ask in a way, but I had to know. "What about any
injuries, you know, from the rape part?"

"Well, it was all part of the rape, Alex, but down there, I was cut,
bruised, swollen, torn and bleeding. Gloria was sure there were no

lasting injuries to vital systems other than my mental ones, though the pain was excruciating for weeks. I needed help from Annie to get to the bathroom for the first couple days. Gloria came by every day to check on me and make sure things weren't getting worse."

The sun was almost down now, and Tim, Brian, Faith and Hope were headed our way. "Oh," Julie said, "here come the guys and kids. Time for me to pull myself together and stop crying."

• • •

Julie and I were pretty quiet the rest of the night, letting everyone else carry the conversation. I was shaken, in a fog, an anvil sitting in my stomach.

Tim gave his daughters a bath and teamed with Brian to read them a bedtime story after our late, hastily assembled dinner. Everyone was sleeping by 23:30 except Julie and me. Julie put the kids in sleeping bags on an air mattress on the floor of their room and put Brian and me in Faith and Hope's twin beds. I got a bottle of wine and curled up against Julie on the sofa in their living room. We sat silently for probably fifteen minutes. Julie finally spoke.

"Quite a mood killer, my story, eh? It felt good to tell you, though. I'd been keeping that in for so long."

I rested my head on her shoulder and said, "I don't understand any of this. I have so many questions. I feel so awful for you. I can't even imagine. What kind of shitty friend was I for not knowing something terrible had happened to you? Why wouldn't you tell me?"

"I was so scared afterward and ashamed, too," Julie answered. "I felt that somehow I had done something to provoke it, that it wouldn't have happened to someone like you. You wouldn't have let it. It must be something wrong with me, something I did. I thought you, Brian, Tim and the others would think I was some slut and cast me away forever."

"But why didn't you go to the police or something?"

"Oh, come on, Alex, you know the answer to that. Nobody would have believed me. How am I going to take on Win Blackpool and the whole town? Besides, I figured Win had the police in his back pocket, and I would have ended up dead after some 'accident' out in the woods. Though, of course, not long after, I was wishing I was dead."

"What was that like when you thought about killing yourself?"

Julie slowly nodded and whispered so softly I could hardly hear her. "First, I had these horrible headaches, like bad migraines, every day, and I had trouble remembering or understanding even simple things because of the concussion. Even with the medicine, I was always throwing up from the headaches. I finally had to get IV fluids a few times. It took several weeks for all of those symptoms to fade. My other injuries were painful, but very slowly, they improved. And my face was a hideous black-and-blue mess for so long, as you and everyone else saw. The eye surgeon told me I was lucky I didn't lose my eye."

"What was going on with you mentally?"

"There were bad dreams. They stalked me. Just a movie of blood and fear every night. I was tired all the time but afraid to go to sleep. I was paranoid that everyone I saw knew what had happened. I thought people looked at me funny and that the whispering in the back of geometry class was really about me and how I'd been with Win Blackpool and seduced him or something."

"Why didn't you try to get help?"

"Where, Alex? My injuries, the bad dreams and the paranoia just devoured me. The hopelessness grew every day and finally just did me in. I couldn't imagine any kind of happy future. I just wanted everything to go away. I thought of Win Blackpool whenever I heard a strange noise or saw a dark shadow, and it terrified me."

I took this in, didn't know what else to offer Julie at that point.

"I thought about killing myself every day afterward. The only good thing that happened was I got my period, so at least I wasn't pregnant."

"Yes, one good thing," I offered.

"Then, Alex, I just did it, don't know why I chose that night instead of another. I drove the knife below my wrist again and again. Started with the tip, pushed it in, and then split the underside of my arm in half like a melon. There was blood everywhere, fast, pumping out of me. I felt no pain, though, just a peaceful tiredness. Then after the knife in the cafeteria episode, it was off to Spokane where I realized I'd been broken into thousands of little pieces."

"But then you told Tim later, right?"

At this, tears started creeping out of Julie's eyes onto her UCLA basketball T-shirt, trailed by sobs. Violently shaking her head, she haltingly choked out, "Gosh, oh gosh. No, no, Alex, no. I was too scared. I still am."

"Why, for god's sake?"

"Oh, Alex, I couldn't bear it if I told him and it changed the way he looked at me or if it diminished me in his eyes. In some ways, that's the worst thing now about all of this. My life is finally in a happy place, so good. For a long time, I thought I would tell Tim at some point, but then I got to thinking, why tell him at all? Maybe I don't need to. But now, after our trip to Timberline last May, I'm going to have to tell him. This secret is devouring me again."

"So tell him. It will be fine," I said.

Julie shook her head. "I guess I hoped my life would be normal by now, you know, motherhood, apple pie and all that. But, clearly, Norman Rockwell will not be coming to paint my life anytime soon. And, shocker, right, my suicide muse Anne Sexton's poetry is not constructive, obviously, though it speaks to me, often when I don't want it to."

"What happened in May at the aunt's funeral?" I asked.

"The next day, I was waiting for Tim's parents to pick me up at this new café in TL after I'd met Annie Findlay for coffee. Tim was at the Barn with the girls. Annie had left, I was alone, and Win Blackpool and the other guy that was there that night walked in."

This other guy again? Who the hell was it? "What happened?"

"All the memories came flooding back. I broke into a cold sweat, and my heart raced. Then they spotted me, I could tell. Just that faintest look of surprise, sort of a double take. Win turned and left."

I shook my head in disgust. "Too bad you didn't have a gun. You could have walked over and shot the fucker."

"But before Win left, he whispered something to the other man. And then that guy walked over to my table and invited himself to sit down. He said hello, asked me how I was doing and wondered why I was back in TL. I told him and he didn't say anything."

"Julie, who was this guy?"

She gave me another stop sign with her hand. "Then he leaned over close to me, and no matter how I try, I can't forget this."

"What?"

"He said, 'It looks like you're doing well, Julie, and I'm really happy for you. You and Tim have twin girls now, so congratulations on that. Look, I won't keep you and will just get to the point. Since you just got back to town, you probably don't know that some women around here have recently made some allegations against Win Blackpool, accusing him of some, um, mistreatment.'

"I surprised myself and said, 'You mean like rape?' He didn't say anything to that, but then kind of threatened me. He said, 'It's not a police matter and won't be. But you know this is a small town, and dangerous talk can spread. Those women are not going to prevail and will end up the worse for it if they bring it up in any kind of public way.' I was shaking by then and feeling faint like I was trying to finish the Ironman triathlon.

"He said, 'I'd hate to see you get caught up in something like this, Julie, either of your own choosing or because someone finds you and talks you into getting involved. Do you understand? You deserve to be happy, and it will be best for you and your family to stay away from this. Go back to California and be happy. Forget about this place.' He left, and I just sat there shaking."

"What did you do after he left?"

"I had a panic attack and passed out, slid out of my chair and onto the floor like a Slinky. When I came to, Tim's parents were on the ground next to me, my head in my mother-in-law's lap. She looked scared and was rubbing my cheek. Others were standing around me in a circle. I finally convinced everyone I didn't need an ambulance or the hospital, that I felt better."

"And you just went back to LA after that?" I asked. "Like it never happened?"

Julie shook her head. "I wish. I tried to pack it all away like before and not think about it. But I couldn't. It kept eating away at me. By the summer, I was having more panic attacks, had some major depressive episodes, and by Labor Day, I found it hard to get out of bed in the morning. Tim was worried and confused, and finally, last month, he just boiled over and was yelling at me because I wouldn't go to a doctor. We had just awful fights about that, our worst ever by far, and that made it so much worse. He was right. I needed a doctor but not the kind he thought. He assumed I had a weird virus or something."

"What are you going to do?"

"To move past this, I know I need to tell Tim, just like I told you. But I'm terrified he'll think less of me."

"No, he won't, Julie. You and the girls are his whole world."

Julie shrugged, helplessly it seemed. "I hope you're right."

"But let me ask, I can't get this question out of my head. Who was the guy that drove you away from Win's house that night and threatened you in the coffee shop? Did you know who it was?"

Julie closed her eyes tight and began rocking back and forth on the sofa in their living room, her arms around her knees. "Alex, that guy was your dad."

It was all so surreal to me. I was in a fog. I didn't yet know what to do with the knowledge about my dad, but at that moment and for years afterward, I would be angry, consumed with fury to make Win Blackpool pay for what he'd done, no matter how long it took.

· · ·

Julie's revelations ruined my attitude for the rest of the fall semester. For the first week, I was sad; I felt betrayed and devastated by my parents, especially my father. Then rage took over, like steam building in the boiler of an ocean liner, propelling the ship forward with increasing speed. I forced myself to think in a disciplined way about how I would respond. Would I confront them? Ignore it? And what about Win? Did he just get to skate away from his savagery?

I talked Adaoma's ear off, whether in our dorm room, eating in the dining hall or out at a restaurant. I vented, questioned, ranted, speculated and kicked around revenge scenarios. She was a skilled listener, never judgmental, and always a voice of reason and wise counsel. Sitting in our room on a cold, rainy Thursday night, both of us leaning against each other on Adaoma's bed, we discussed different courses of action.

"Well, Alex, going to the newspapers in Timberline, even if they believed you, would likely hurt Julie most of all. Yeah, she doesn't live there anymore, but her in-laws do. And her husband is apparently some kind of a legend in the town. If people in town don't believe her, he will suffer too, though not as much as Julie. And if your dad would be willing to perjure himself in court, which it sounds like he might, it would just be Julie's word against Win's. You don't get to make this decision for Julie, Alex."

"Yeah, okay, I get it. And besides, Julie would never support me doing that."

Adaoma walked across our room and retrieved two Cokes and M&Ms from the fridge. She was wearing this ridiculously loud, crazy-patterned, African print blouse that always made me marvel at her willingness to wear stuff like that and call attention to herself. "We need fuel for all this strategizing, Alex. I think if you want justice administered to Win Blackpool, that's not likely. Horrible as it is, I'm sure he's done this kind of thing for years. Julie is sadly one of many, I bet. You may have to get someone to kill him to get the justice you seem to want. And that's not realistic." Chuckling now, she asked, "What's that game… Clue? Maybe Mrs. White with the lead pipe or Mr. Green with the rope could do it for you?"

I smirked at that. "No, it'd have to be Miss Scarlet 'cause Win would think he'd be getting up her dress. Then she could shoot him with the revolver and chop off his dick with the knife."

Sitting there munching our M&Ms and marinating in my revenge scenarios, Adaoma announced, "Alex, let's talk about something else. I have an adventure for us this summer."

"Okay great, I could use an adventure. What?"

"We can work for a nonprofit organization that operates medical clinics and field hospitals in Africa, Southeast Asia and Latin America. We'd have to interview for jobs, but I'm sure they'd take us on."

"How do you know about this?"

"My parents know the managing director. He's from Morocco originally."

"That's fine for you. You're pre-med, a bio and chemistry major. I doubt this organization is sitting there saying, 'You know, what we really need is a medieval studies person.'"

"There're lots of jobs, Alex: pharmacy, purchasing, finance, all kinds of stuff. You are a talented woman and could do most anything." She chuckled. "You need something like this, a chance to focus on helping others instead of nurturing your vendettas. I'm serious about that."

"Ah, I don't know. They'd hire you, but not me, probably. But it does sound interesting."

"How do you know they wouldn't take you? You go to Princeton, after all. Let's go for it. What? You going to spend next summer in Princeton again? You hated that last year. And at this point, I don't really see you going home to Timberline."

"That's not my home anymore."

34

Timberline

'd decided to confront my parents at Christmas about Julie. I was going to war, was going to ignite years of dry relationship grassland with a flamethrower. For those from Washington State used to seeing Smokey Bear signs cautioning people to prevent forest fires and showing the present fire threat, this would be the "Holy Shit, Run for Fucking Cover" fire danger level.

I got home from Princeton on the 21st of December, pretty sure I'd edged my cume GPA enough above the quicksand so I could return for the spring semester. My plan was to play it cool initially and have one final Christmas with my parents before having at them the day after. But too many snarky comments about my poor grades and lack of career focus from my mother and too much aloof indifference from my father led me to unleash the flamethrower early on the 23rd.

My parents and I were having lunch at the country club. Festooned with decorations and two large, lighted Christmas trees, the Gentlemen's Grill (women were allowed during the holidays if accompanied by a man) had a string quartet playing festive tunes like *Joy to the World*.

After we ordered, my mother jumped right in. "Alexandra, your father and I are concerned you're not making the most of your Princeton opportunity. Your awful grades, your unwillingness to get any kind of quality summer internship, and your horrible and immature attitude – it's all extremely frustrating. You're running out of time. It's already halfway through junior year."

"Really?" I snapped.

"Achievement is the most important thing," my father added. "And you're just not executing, haven't been since you left for college. Is everyone else at Princeton just better than you?"

"Maybe so."

"And," my mother said again, "it seems you're still seeing Brian. Is that just too big a distraction? Do you spend all your time pining for him or having sex?"

She didn't know shit. I'd slept with the guy from Houston once during freshman year, and since then, it had only been Brian, though we only managed to see each other every few months.

My mother continued poking around the nitroglycerin. "I mean, I hope you're not going to be like Julie. Instead of accomplishing something in life, she just chose to get on her back and put her legs in the air, and now look at her. She ruined her life and Tim's."

"She didn't ruin her life," I icily replied, as the notion of going off on them in the middle of the country club gained momentum. "And she didn't ruin Tim's life. They're good for each other, and they will do great."

"Oh?" my dad offered. "No college education for her and no prospects for him – maybe they can go on food stamps like the Findlays and live in the Flats."

D-Day. Let's hit the beach! I stood, took my full glass of iced tea and threw it in his face. "FUCK YOU!" I screamed. "YOU'RE A GODDAMN MONSTER!"

Every head in the place turned to our table, and the string quartet seized up. It was like a movie scene: my parents dropped their silverware and sat with their mouths open.

I sat back down but was still yelling. "Julie is building a good life despite what you, Win Blackpool, and what this town did to her. Fucking animals!"

Hearing Win's name snapped my parents back to reality, red alert for their damage-control instincts.

"Alexandra!" my mother hissed. "Be quiet, for god's sake. You're making a scene! What is this all about?"

I shouted, "I don't fucking care if I'm making a scene. And you know what this is about. Don't be a dumb, dishonest bitch with me."

"What did you say to me?" she shrieked.

"Angela," my father urged, "be quiet."

Pointing my finger at my father, I lectured, "You're an amoral, gutless prick. How many other girls have you helped Win Blackpool rape in this town? How many other crimes have you covered up? Like Steve Lonsdale killing Julie's mother. That whole company is corrupt and evil, and you're one of the reasons!"

Murmurs built around the room. I could see everyone whispering to one another. This was a train wreck rolled into a raging dumpster fire in a radioactive waste pit, and nobody could look away.

"Dammit, Alexandra!" my father shouted. "We're leaving. Let's go." He beat a hasty retreat, iced tea stains all over his bright yellow wool sweater.

Ho Ho Ho, I thought as we walked out. I knew I would never again set foot in the Timberline Country Club.

The battle went on in my father's BMW in the parking lot. My parents had nothing but rationalizations and excuses: Of course they felt awful for Julie, but their hands were tied. The police and DA in town would have never gone after Win, and Julie would have suffered the most. Yes, they should have told me. They wanted to but didn't know how. I was being naïve; they would have had to give up everything if they'd turned on Win, and wasn't I also a beneficiary of all that privilege and security? And on and on.

Back at the house, my mother snidely continued, "You have a lot of self-righteous gall criticizing us, Alexandra, slurping at the trough of privilege all these years."

"You're right, Mother. And I don't want any more of that. I'm done with both of you."

"Sure, Alexandra," my mother sneered. "So, you're going to pay for Princeton? Your tuition, living and travel expenses, everything?"

"Yes."

My father laughed at this. "Well, you may not have to pay to be there much longer since you apparently lack the capabilities and drive to stay in school and graduate, let alone succeed."

"Fuck you! I never want to see either one of you again."

• • •

My arson complete, I walked out of their house, shaken, and went to Brian's. I wasn't expected, and he was surprised to see me on the front porch of their tiny cottage in the Flats. Just looking at me, he knew I was a mess of anger, frustration and emotion. He reached for me, and I went to him willingly.

"Alex. Hey, what's the matter? Here, let's sit down out here for a bit."

I recapped the country club throw-down and subsequent battles in the car and at home.

"I checked," I said. "I can leave on a Greyhound bus three days after Christmas that will eventually get me to Princeton, and I know you're leaving to fly back to Annapolis around then. Any chance I can stay here? I know it will be a huge imposition for your family."

"Of course you can. But my dad's been having even worse problems with his back the past month and is most comfortable on the sofa in the living room, doped up in front of the TV. And as you know, that's my bed usually, so I've been sleeping out here on the porch in a sleeping bag. There's one for you too, but this porch only provides minimal cover from the snow and none from the wind."

"Fine," I said. "Thank you. Maybe we can zip the bags together and share body heat." I grinned.

We chatted a bit more before going inside so I could say hello to his parents and younger sisters.

Brian's mom, Annie, saw me, immediately smiled and came over with a hug.

"Hi, sweetie, what a nice surprise!"

"Uh, mom," Brian said, "Alex needs a place to stay until she goes back to Princeton a few days after Christmas, and I told her she could stay here. Don't worry. She knows all about the porch."

"I'm so sorry, Mrs. Findlay," I practically gasped. "I know you don't need someone taking up more space and another mouth to feed, but, but…"

"Shush, honey." Annie smiled, reaching for my hand and squeezing it. "You are always welcome here for as long as you want. We love seeing you."

Annie had no idea what had brought me to her doorstep, but she knew something was wrong and warmly took me in. Later, I would remember that as an act of humanity, class and grace, even amidst the grinding poverty always swirling around the Findlays.

"Now that you'll be with us on Christmas, Alex," Annie enthused. "You can open your present here."

Annie's "kitchen" was a stand-alone two-burner cooktop, a refrigerator, an ancient oven, a tiny sink and a dish drying rack. Under a small decorated tree next to the TV were seven wrapped presents: one for Roger, one for Annie, one for Brian, one for each of his three younger sisters, and one for me. There were two little bedrooms: one for Brian's parents and one with a double bed his sisters shared. Very small bathrooms off each bedroom completed the picture. At that moment, even with the verbally abusive nature of Brian's dad, Roger (he was asleep on the couch), I felt more warmth in that cramped home than I'd felt in mine for years.

Proximity to Brian made my Christmas of 1984 a happy one. A few days later, early in the morning, I kissed him goodbye, barely staved off crying, and boarded the Greyhound bus for a six-day, four-transfer journey to Princeton. I slept on the buses or overnighted in the terminals the whole way.

• • •

When I got back to Princeton, I gave the administration enough details to paint the picture that I no longer had any financial support from my family and needed to do it on my own. I had my family removed from all Princeton contact and mailing lists. The school found some grant money for me and a job in the library on campus. I also worked thirty hours a week in a restaurant in downtown Princeton. My senior year would be financed in a similar fashion.

In perhaps my most satisfying "Fuck You" to my parents, I got a 4.0 GPA that spring semester and would never get grades less than that at Princeton until graduation. My parents wouldn't know any of it. I decided I would need to skip the graduation ceremony the next spring since they might show up. Even years later, I had no regrets about cutting my parents out of my life forever. And they never made any attempt to contact me. They either knew not to doubt the longevity of my rage, or they didn't really care and were just as happy about the situation as I was.

35

Sally Horrigan: February 1985

DUBLIN

The Dublin weather was so nice. Warm and sunny with bright blue skies, nothing like the usual February day. Sally finished her business meeting the day before, but decided to be reckless and treat herself to a weekend in the city instead of going straight home to Belfast. She slept in on Saturday, then shopped for one small present each for Tracy, Sean and Fergal. Late in the afternoon, she carted her packages back to her bed-and-breakfast and asked for her room key.

"Of course, ma'am," the clerk responded. "And I'm told someone came by and left this for you as well."

It was an envelope; inside was a plain white A4 page folded in thirds.

> Hello Sally, hope you are well. Looking forward to seeing you this evening for dinner at 21:30 at the Steampipe.
>
> Regards, Simon.

The clock on the lobby wall said 16:30. Sally would have hours to fret and worry about this meeting. Anxious thoughts raced through her head. How did he know where to find her? This couldn't be some casual check-in, could it? Or did Simon just happen to be in Dublin? It had been months since she'd last seen him in Belfast.

Oh, god, I'm going to be asked to do something!

She stammered and sputtered but managed to compose herself to ask the desk clerk the location of the Steampipe.

"It's not far at all. Maybe half a kilometer from here, easy walk."

As she approached the Steampipe at 21:25, a tall figure in a black sweater, black wool pants and a charcoal Irish tweed flat cap walked up behind her and put his left arm through her right. She jumped and emitted a yelp. Simon.

"Sally, my dear, how are you? It is great to see you."

Simon walked with her, arm in arm, on a seemingly random course, up, down and through various streets and alleys. They made casual conversation, no business discussions, for what Sally guessed was over an hour. She had no idea where they were.

Finally, Simon led her down a dark, trash-strewn alley to a back door with a flickering red-and-black neon skull-and-crossbones sign – The Jolly Roger. The place looked closed, but apparently, it wasn't. Simon had a key. Inside were six small black wooden tables with four chairs apiece. Dark red wallpaper, peeling in places, covered the walls, and cheap-looking swords and treasure chests hung on them. The room was dim, bordering on dark. Neither customers nor a bartender were in sight.

"Sorry for the lack of ambiance, Sally. I needed to rent an entire small space on short notice. So the tired old Jolly Roger is our fate."

He pointed at a table. "Please, sit," and then walked behind the bar. "What can I get you to drink?"

Sally shrugged.

"Your pick, Sally. Scotch? Irish whiskey? Cider? A pint?"

"Cider, I guess, lovely," Sally finally said.

"Excellent. Jameson for me." Soon he returned to the table with the drinks and sat across from her.

"So…" he said.

Worried, Sally just wanted to get the meeting over with. "I'm guessing you want something from me, Simon, since you'd not've tracked me to Dublin and spent the last hour walking around to bring me here if we didn't have some business."

He nodded as he sipped his Jameson. "Sally, we need a small favor."

"You need a favor, or you expect me to do somethin'?"

"Of course, you don't *have* to do anything, Sally, but we were hoping you could get one piece of information for us, given our relationship these past years."

Reaching for her cider, Sally reflected. She knew this wasn't optional. She had her kids because the Mossad money had paid her solicitor's bills. All the money they'd paid her, money that had made her life and her kids' life bearable, would stop if she refused. And, who knew what other kind of problems they'd make for her if she said no?

"Okay, what is it you need?"

Simon smiled and patted her hand across the table. "Superb. We really appreciate it."

Sally leaned back, her arms crossed over her chest, and waited.

"Sally, we know the Libyans have been providing guns and ammunition to the Provisional IRA over the past couple of years. There have been three large shipments in the past eighteen months. The Provisionals send commercial fishing trawlers to Libya, and they return to Ireland with the weapons hidden below decks. Then your organization hides the guns in warehouses and underground all across the Republic of Ireland, moving them into the North as needed."

Sally shrugged. "I don't have no details 'bout that." This was technically true, though Sally had heard general outlines and rumors. She figured her boss Peter was involved because, at times, someone on the phone or in his office would reference shipments. In those instances and only those times, Peter asked her to leave the office for coffee or tea.

Simon continued, "Well, Gaddafi and the Libyans also give and sell weapons to the PLO."

"Who?"

"The Palestine Liberation Organization. They want our land and want to destroy Israel. They've been fighting us since the forties. They were based out of Jordan in the seventies and then moved to Lebanon. We invaded southern Lebanon in '82 and kicked them out of the country. They had to go to Tunisia, which is where they are today."

"So what?"

"We believe the PLO and Provisional IRA have the same contact in Libya, Toufik Al-Libi. He's Libya's Minister of Culture, and people call him Amin Almaktoba, the librarian. The CIA on the other hand unofficially calls him Toe-fuck. He runs all of Gaddafi's weapons sales and smuggling programs."

Sally made a face. "What's this have to do with me?"

Simon smiled. "Look, Sally, we know Toufik organizes big weapons shipments for the IRA and PLO at the same time. They usually load and ship the IRA one day and the PLO the next."

"Why?"

"More efficient. You only need to pay bribes once, only have a convoy of trucks into the port once, that kind of thing. Less for the spy satellites and informers in Libya to see."

"How often do these shipments go? Like every month?"

"Oh no, only three or four times a year. We need you because Gaddafi no longer uses his ports in Libya to ship to the PLO and the IRA. They go out of Tunisia now. The PLO weapons go to Lebanon and the Provisionals' to Ireland."

Sally shook her head and said, "You said the PLO has been in Tunisia since 1982. Why do their weapons go to Lebanon?"

"Good question. The PLO is planning a return to Lebanon and needs pre-positioned weapons for when they send people back in. We know a shipment is going out sometime this summer, one day for the IRA and the next day for the PLO. We just don't know when. And we don't know where in Tunisia it will originate because the coastline is over eleven hundred kilometers long."

Sally sat silently for almost a minute before standing and saying, "Simon, s'cuse me, but I need the loo."

While she was in the toilet, Sally's mind jumped about. How in the hell was she supposed to get this information? What if her boss wasn't even involved? How could she trust Simon and the Mossad not to take the IRA weapons too?

Sally settled herself back in front of Simon.

"Simon, how in the hell do you think I can get this information? I'm not involved in stuff like this. I buy soap and pay gas and electric bills."

"But we think your boss, Peter, is involved. We hope you might be able to get some details from him one way or another."

Sally snorted. "You mean just say, 'Hey, Peter, them Mossad people would like to know 'bout that big weapons shipment youse working on. Can you just hand me over the particulars?' I'm sure he'd think that's just grand."

Simon held up his hands in mild protest. "Sally, we just want you to do your best. We've invested quite a lot in helping you and are just hoping you can do us this favor. Anything you learn would be helpful."

Sally leaned back in her chair. She was gripping the table so hard with both hands she thought her fingers might dig into it and leave permanent marks.

"And if I do learn something and tell, then you can just take our weapons too, if youse right, and they get sent 'round near the same time."

Simon's hands were immediately up again in self-defense. "Oh, no, no, no, Sally! We have no interest in the IRA weapons and would do nothing to interfere. We care only about the PLO."

"But Israel is friendly with the Brits. Why wouldn't you just betray us?"

Simon firmly shook his head. "We are friends with everyone except Arab terrorists and the Iranians. We're friendly with the Americans, the Soviets, the Indians, the Warsaw Pact. Almost everyone. And nobody would ever trust us or work with us if we betrayed the IRA. You must believe me on that, Sally!"

36

Simon's news of her assignment ruined the remainder of her weekend and totally shut her down for the first couple of weeks back in Belfast. Every day, she expected people to show up outside her office and take her away: *Disloyal, traitor to the sacred cause… a tout.* She made little effort to find out what Simon wanted to know.

Sally didn't hear from Simon in March. Maybe, she hoped, things had changed, they got the information elsewhere, or the shipments had been called off. Deep down, she knew this wasn't likely, but she grasped onto that hope, barely clinging to the side of the lifeboat before she slipped underwater.

In early April, Simon brushed past her on a crowded Belfast street, seemingly not recognizing her. But later, in her coat pocket, she found a note:

Any news? Time is critical. I know you won't let us down.

Sally, beginning to panic, stepped up her efforts to find the desired information. Listening in on Peter's cryptic phone conversations at every chance yielded nothing. She looked at the papers on his desk whenever he stepped away, but it was as if she was five thousand meters above; all she saw were fuzzy images, impossible to know if they were what she needed.

A stroke of luck surfaced one afternoon when she was out for a lunch break with Rose, one of her mates in the Provisionals.

"I'll be glad for Good Friday and the Easter holiday. Work is just manic," Rose said, sipping her tea. Rose also had a low-level job in the Provisionals, but her cover job was with a small bakery. "How's it been for you?"

"Okay, I guess," Sally said, "but Peter's really been irritable lately. It's no fun when your boss is short with you and outta sorts. I hope I've not done something to get wrong with him."

"I'm sure not," Rose said. "I bet he's stressing over this big thing that's coming up."

"What big thing?"

"Well, I don't know a-course, but my sister's friends with Peter's wife, Aine; they're both from Sligo County originally. Aine told her Peter's been on the knife edge all year over some big deal they're working on. Anyways, Aine said she's looking forward to their August holiday because the business is supposed to finish in the first half of July."

That has to be it! Sally hoped.

"Hmm, well, it's good to know his mood might eventually improve, but that's still a few months away. Do you know what kind of deal?"

Rose laughed. "I got no idea, girl. But you and me both know, the less we know 'bout that, the better. I sure ain't gonna be askin' no questions."

Sally passed this along to Simon via a short note – *"first half of July"* – left in a dead drop, an empty can of Heinz beans in a trash bin behind a pub five kilometers from Divis Flats. Sally still needed to know where the arms shipment would be made and worried that she'd have no way to find out.

She was in the office she shared with Peter on a warm early May afternoon when he burst in and shut the door. *Oh, no! He looks awful. Frantic. Pale. Oh god, I'm found out!*

"Sally, I've just got some awful news. Aine's been in an accident on the motorway. A lorry spun out of control, crossed the road, and hit our car. They've taken her to hospital."

Sally jumped up, walked over to him, and put her hand on his shoulder. "Oh my god, Peter. This is terrible, such unlucky news. You must go see her right away."

"I know, I know. I must. But… but could I ask you to do me a favor? This must stay between you and me."

"Of course! Anything you need! What is it?"

"I've nobody else to turn to that I can trust, Sally. I hate to burden you."

"Peter, stop! Whatever you need. Anything. What is it?"

He sat down and motioned Sally to do the same at her desk. "This chap, name of Luka, will be calling me here today at 16:10. He's in Malta. We've worked with him before. You need to be here to take this call."

"Okay. What's it about?"

Peter ran both hands through his hair. Sweat had stained the chest and underarms of his pale blue shirt and was beading up on his forehead. "Oh, Sally, this… this is so, so important, but nobody must know about it."

"Don't worry, nobody will know. What is the call about, and what do you need me to do?"

"Okay, okay. Tell Luka I was called away for an emergency. Give him your name, call yourself, I don't know, Nicole, and tell him I asked you to take his call. He's going to say, 'The weather is grand lately here in the Med. How's yours?' And you must, MUST respond, 'Hardly matters. Rain lurks here every day.'"

Sally wrote that down. "Okay."

"Then he's going to say he has the figures for Project Watchtower. The figures will be the money we owe him for some transportation services. I need you to get the figures and find out the wiring instructions for the money. Tell him I will personally wire the funds next week, as we agreed."

"Okay, no worries. That's it? You want me to just get the figures? Do you want me to ask any questions? Like how did he calculate the figures? Do you know his figures are right?"

"No, no, don't worry about that. Don't ask any questions. None. Just get the figures and the wiring instructions."

He handed her a key and pointed at the center drawer of his desk. "Write the figures and the instructions on a piece of A4 and put it in the drawer. Then relock it and put the key in the pocket of my coat hanging on the office door here."

"That's it?"

He nodded.

"Now, get to Aine, Peter! When you have news, please let me know how she's doing. And don't give this Luka matter another thought."

After Peter left, Sally was nervous and distracted. She murmured a prayer for Aine, but her thoughts were on the phone call. What if it had to do with what Simon needed? It was 14:00, a bit over two hours before Luka would call. She tried to do work, make the time pass, but couldn't concentrate.

16:10, and the phone sat silent. 16:15, and still nothing. *Did I mess this up? Was I supposed to receive the call somewhere else? Was I supposed to call him? What if he doesn't call? This could be my chance to be done with Simon and his lot!*

16:17, and the phone rang. Sally wiped her sweaty hands on her blue skirt and reached shakily for the phone.

"Huh, huh, hello?"

"I'm looking for Peter," replied a man, speaking in heavily accented English.

"He's not here. Called away on a family emergency. He asked me to handle your call. My name is Nicole."

The man grunted. Suspicious, Sally was sure. He didn't say anything, and Sally had to again wipe her sweaty hands on her skirt one at a time, shifting the phone.

Finally. "The weather is grand here in the Med. How's yours?"

Carefully and deliberately, Sally replied, hoping her voice wouldn't quiver. "Hardly matters. Rain lurks here every day."

Another grunt at the end of the phone. More long silence.

What am I supposed to do now? Peter just said I was to take down information.

"So, Luka, is it? Do you have some figures for me? For Project Watchtower?"

"Twelve point five million Austrian schillings."

"Let me make sure I have that. Twelve point five million Austrian schillings."

"Ya."

"And the wire instructions?"

Sally took those down and agonized about what to do next. *Peter said no questions. But I need more information! Will he tell Peter if I ask questions? This is my best chance to get this information. I have to risk it!*

"Grand. So, Luka, just a couple of questions."

"What?" he barked.

"This twelve point five million schillings, help me recall, how does that compare to our past work with you on, uh, matters like these?"

Another grunt, almost like he expected her to ask this question. "Look, it's more than before."

"Yes, I know that, but help me understand how much more." *Is he going to wonder why I don't know the prior amounts and get suspicious?*

"About double," he said.

"I see," Sally said. "And that's mainly because…"

Luka was getting impatient. "Because there are now three trawlers, not two, and you need 'em in the busy season. The second week of July is much busier than November, like before."

"I know. 'Course," Sally said, hoping to keep him talking.

"And yes," he said, "before, they went from Tripoli, fifteen hundred kilometers from Ireland, and now it's only thirteen hundred from Sfax, but that doesn't make no difference. We done?"

"Yes, done," Sally said. "Peter will wire the funds next week, as agreed. Oh, sorry, just one more question I'm s'posed to ask. That second week of July, what day-a the week will your trawlers show up?"

"Peter told me it was Wednesday. Is it different now?"

"No, no, I was just s'posed to double-check. Everything is still the same."

Sally hung up the phone and wiped her hands on her skirt again and her face with the untucked hem of her blouse. She sat at Peter's desk for she didn't know how long, breathing heavily. *What if somebody heard me asking those questions? Oh god, what have I done? Calm down, Sally, just calm down. Remember what you need to do here. If our shipment is Wednesday, the PLO's will be the day before or the day after.*

She put the piece of A4 paper with the 12.5 million Austrian schillings figure and bank details in Peter's top desk drawer, relocked it, and put the key in his coat pocket on the door. 16:40. She headed out.

Her mind raced as she walked home. Tomorrow at lunch, she would go to one of the Belfast libraries, far from her office, to try to find Seafax, Sofax, Sumfax, Cpax whatever it was. Luka's accent on the phone was so thick, she worried she had misheard him and would get the location wrong. She knew Tripoli was in Libya, but that was all. *Simon had said he thought the weapons were going out of Tunisia.* She would start with a map of Tunisia at the library tomorrow.

· · ·

Two days later, at 23:00, Sally loaded a different dead drop for Simon, an unused post box at the side of a church being renovated in one of the Catholic areas.

"Second week of July, likely Wednesday 10th. Sfax Tunisia.
Don't know nothing 'bout details for the PLO part."

Sally had learned at the library that Sfax was a medium-sized city with a small port in Central Tunisia. She had also discovered that 12.5 million Austrian schillings was approximately 400,000 British pounds.

Peter returned to work the next week. Aine was badly hurt but would survive, thank god: a broken leg, broken arm and a punctured lung. Peter never asked about the call with Luka but nodded when Sally said, "I left that item in your desk drawer."

The rest of this was on Simon now, Sally thought. Her part was done. Besides, what harm would it do to the Provisionals if the PLO lost a weapons shipment?

37

Alex: June and July 1985

Tunis was sweltering and dusty every day. Adaoma and I shared a tiny flat with no air conditioning, one small bedroom with twin beds, and a fetid WC with a squat toilet at the end of the hall. Adjacent to that was a room with a rusting sink and shower, no hot water and low water pressure. Our neighborhood got daily doses of sewer gas in the mornings, thanks to over a million people regularly taxing infrastructure likely designed in 200 BC in what was then Carthage.

I loved it, though. The ancient medina was close by and always an exhilarating assault on the senses. It teemed with shoppers and aggressive, shouting merchants who called out, begging to negotiate with you to buy something. Their stalls held seemingly every type of food, clothes, jewelry and other items. The smells of spices suffused the air: saffron, turmeric, paprika, curry and others, and mingled with clouds of flavored tobacco smoke emanating from hookah parlors.

Adaoma and I went to the parlors several times a week. We sat on cushions and they brought us trays of different tobacco flavors to smoke in the ornate, bubbling water pipe – a big clear glass teakettle-like contraption with hoses and small nozzles, like octopus arms extending out to you. They also brought plates of figs and dates to eat while we smoked. Sitting on Lake Tunis near the Mediterranean, we often got cooling breezes that cut the heat and humidity, especially at night. Tunis was chaotic at all hours, and I learned to listen for the Muslim call to prayer five times a day and to fall asleep amidst the city's noises. I loved it! So different and absorbing. It was the first time in months I wasn't consumed with anger and sadness.

We were working for Relief Angels Global, the international charity Adaoma had told me about. We had interviewed by phone with five or six people at headquarters, and Adaoma got her parents to vouch for me (they'd met me only twice when they'd visited Princeton). We learned in February we'd gotten jobs! I was happy. The first evidence in a long time that I could actually succeed at something.

We got sent to Tunisia. Adaoma worked on the nursing side of the organization in patient care, and I worked in pharmacy supply, things like inventory control and working with pharmacists on fore-casting supply needs. After almost a month in a tiny regional office in Tunis, we would spend June, July and the first half of August living and working at a clinic site – tents in the desert outside Sfax, a small Tunisian port city about three hours from Tunis.

It was great to be with Adaoma for the summer. I now had another close friend to fill my life, a great addition to Julie and Brian. And the work was interesting and enjoyable. I'd found something I could see myself doing once I graduated: international charity and aid work.

38

July 10, Sfax

"July tenth, woman!" Adaoma boomed as we left the breakfast tent. "Can you believe we only have a month left before our summer is over?"

Adaoma was in her work uniform, royal blue surgical scrubs and blue-and-white Adidas. I was also in 'business attire,' the same surgical scrub bottoms and an orange Princeton hooded sweatshirt with a black tiger head embroidered on the front. I was wearing orange Nikes. Before noon, when the heat rolled in, I would shed the sweatshirt for the ratty blue-and-yellow UCLA T-shirt I had on underneath.

"Yes, it's gone by so fast. I'll be sorry to go. An extra month would have been just right. But I'm excited to go to Nigeria with you before we go back to Princeton. Can't wait to meet this big, partying, laughing family you're always talking about."

"Ah, it's just gonna be one week-long party, Alex. Friends, family and whoever else wants to come by."

It was 08:40, and we had twenty minutes until we had to start our shifts: Adaoma in the nursing wards and me in the pharmacy. Sipping coffee from Styrofoam cups, we sat on a bench outside the surgical tent listening to music on a small radio. The BBC soundtrack of the summer had been a healthy dose of songs like *Freeway of Love* by Aretha Franklin, *Sussudio* by Phil Collins, *Every Time You Go Away* by Paul Young, *Shout* by Tears for Fears, and Prince's *Raspberry Beret*.

The camp was twenty kilometers outside Sfax, about two hundred yards from the ocean and a small beach. There was nothing but desert, ocean and a small dusty access road around us.

Our compound was eight large, dark brown military-type tents. Separate female and male sleeping quarters with cots, a centralized unisex latrine with eight squat toilets and minimal privacy screens (still better than the Timberline High locker rooms), and shower bays on the other side of the building. The pharmacy, which consisted of a work table and numerous lockable cabinets and refrigerators, shared a tent with storage for everything else the camp needed. There was also a dining tent, a surgical ward, a nursing/patient ward, and a walk-in clinic.

I was so happy and said to Adaoma, "What a brilliant day!" It was sunny with a bright blue cloudless sky, a pleasant breeze and seventy degrees. "We have to go down to the beach after work."

Adaoma pointed. "Look at that. Our blokes have company today."

The day before, around 06:00, people had arrived and erected three large military tents similar to ours, though these were light blue with United Nations logos. A procession of trucks, two and three at a time, maybe twenty-five or thirty in all, unloaded at the tent off and on for hours afterward.

"What's the UN doing here?" I'd asked Adaoma when the tents first went up.

She'd shrugged. "No idea."

That Wednesday morning, three large commercial fishing boats had docked right off our small beach. I guessed they were seventy- to one-hundred-foot boats, each with a crew of eight or ten people. It was hard to get an accurate count since they were all moving around. While we were looking at the activities on the boats, more trucks, similar to those the day before, began arriving, and these drove on the hard sand right to the edge of the beach by the boats.

I turned to Adaoma. "I got up to go to the bathroom this morning around four. The tents were all shut up. But I saw armed guards, so there's something important in them. We should go over after work, introduce ourselves, and see what they're doing."

Adaoma wrinkled her nose and vigorously shook her head. "No, Alex. Very bad idea."

"Why?"

"They might be UN, but they might be something else too – smugglers, pirates, government officials up to no good. If they are really doing UN business, they will come over to meet us soon enough."

"Listen to you," I teased. "Miss People-Are-Good-and-the-World-Is-Happy, thinking ill of others."

"Ah, Alex. I've lived in Africa a long time."

"Okay, I trust your instincts."

"Time to go to work," Adaoma announced.

We stood and threw our coffee cups in the trash. I could hear far-off voices on the beach, unintelligible garbles of Arabic and maybe some English, too.

Then I heard something else, very faint but growing louder, coming closer. I first guessed it was more trucks rolling down the access road toward the beach, but no, it sounded different.

I recognized the sounds before I saw them. *Whop whop whop…* droning louder and louder. The ground began to shake and vibrate. Helicopters.

39

Sally Horrigan: July 10 – 11, 1985

Sally settled back in at her desk around 09:00 with a cup of tea. She had yet to see Peter. That was odd. Even when he had meetings all day, always in secret Provisional locations, he would swing by in the morning to check in and give her instructions or projects for the day. Maybe he was ill, or god forbid, his wife Aine had had some sort of complication from the accident. She was having a hard go coming back from it.

Peter burst into the office just after 13:00. He looked pale and physically ill. His hands shook as he tried to pick up a pencil from his desk.

"Peter, there you are. Did I miss you this morning?"

He said nothing and sat at his desk, his forehead buried in his hands.

"Peter, what is it?" Sally urged. "Has something happened with Aine? Peter! Peter! Can you hear me?"

Finally, he turned his chair around to Sally. "No, Aine is fine, thank you. It's just, just… well, we've had a bit of a business setback."

"Oh no, what?"

"It's best you do not know, Sally, and it's also best you say nothing to anyone about it. In fact, why don't you take the rest of the day off? We shan't be having any normal activity anyway."

Walking home, Sally passed a newsagent with the day's papers in the window. Seeing the date on one of the papers, it struck her. It was 10 July. Oh no, the information she'd provided to Simon: 10 July and that port town in Tunisia. But that wasn't going to affect the

Provisionals. Simon had promised. It was the PLO's weapons they were going to take the day before or after. Peter could be talking about anything. Nothing could have happened to the Provisionals' weapons. *Just carry on and forget 'bout it*, she told herself.

Despite her attempts at self-assurance, all that night, Sally expected a knock at her door. She imagined herself being taken away, never to see her children again. What had happened? Simon had assured her there would be no consequence to the IRA for her help. She slept fitfully and stumbled bleary-eyed into work the next morning. Again, no Peter, and this time she didn't see him all day.

Rose, her friend and IRA workmate, came by from her bakery cover-job late in the afternoon. She entered Sally's office and shut the door.

She looked over her shoulder and leaned in toward Sally. "Sally, you knows what's going on, don't ya? What ya know?"

Fear and bile rising in her throat, Sally shook her head.

Rose whispered, "There was supposed to be a big weapons shipment for us someplace over in Africa, but the Brits heard 'bout it and ambushed it."

Sally drew her breath in sharply. *Oh god, oh my god.*

"What happened?" she sputtered out.

"What I heard was we had three big fishing boats tied up on a beach with thirty to fifty of our men on them. We was just starting to load weapons when these Brit helicopters swooped in. They had a bunch-a soldiers, and they just cut our men down with machine guns and blew up the boats."

Sally's hand shot to her mouth. Rose patted Sally's knee.

"What else happened?" Sally croaked out, now looking over her shoulder too.

Rose said, "I hear the soldiers killed all our men. No chance for them to surrender or anything. Then these other Brit helicopters swooped in and fired a bunch of missiles or bombs."

Rose got really close to Sally's ear. "There's talk it had to be touts. You heard that?"

Eyes slammed shut, Sally shook her head as Rose kept whispering.

"I seen what happens when they think they been done in by traitors. Everyone will be under suspicion. Sally, they will sure be asking you about Peter. He was probably in the middle of the operation. Was he?"

"I… I don't know," Sally said. "He never said nothin' to me."

"Well, you got nothing to worry 'bout if Peter didn't tell you nothin'."

After Rose left, Sally was a wreck, barely able to make it through the end of work. Right before she left the office, a man with a birthmark on his left cheek and a large tattoo of an anchor on his left hand walked in. *Oh, me god, I bet it's Paddy Mac.* Paul McMahan, Paddy Mac, based in the Republic of Ireland, came in and shut the door. Sally had never met him, but had heard about him. He was supposed to be way high up in the Provisionals.

"Sally, how are you?"

Her heart was racing, and she was sweating even more than earlier. In no time, it was running down her sides from her underarms and flowing between her breasts like an alpine stream.

"Uh, uhm, I'm fine, sir, thank you."

"Good. Sally, I work with Peter. Have you spoken to him in the past day or so?"

"I, uh, well, I ain't seen him today. He came into the office yesterday afternoon. But then he sent me home for the day. We didn't talk about work or nothin'. He just sent me home."

Paddy Mac was expressionless. "I see. Sally, can you do something for me?"

She nodded eagerly, still terrified.

"I'm going to send some papers over to your house tonight. I need you to look at the figures on the papers and pull them together into a simple budget. I'll pick it up here first thing tomorrow. I hate to ask you to work on it at home, but it's important. Peter is busy and he usually does this for me."

"No worries, 'course. Happy to help."

"Lovely. What's your address? I know you live in Divis Flats, but I don't have your flat number."

He slid her a piece of paper. Sally, concentrating on keeping her hand from shaking, wrote her address and handed it back to him.

40

Alex: July 10, 1985

Adaoma and I looked up into the sun and saw three outlines. Helicopters swooping low, fast and loud over us with British military markings. They set down about two hundred yards away between the blue UN tents and the beach. Figures with guns jumped out even before the helicopters touched down on the hard flat sand. It seemed like there were dozens of them, some running toward the UN tents and others down to the men and the fishing boats on the beach.

Our camp, the UN tents and the boats on the beach each represented a point on an almost equilateral triangle with two-hundred-meter sides; the beach with the boats at the tip and our camp and the UN tents the points on the base.

Adaoma and I were still standing by the trash can outside the surgical tent. We watched, confused and transfixed. It all happened so fast. I saw muzzle flashes from the guns, followed by staccato pops of gunfire. Men on the boats at the beach and nearby in the surf started to drop.

The helicopter-borne figures also fired into the UN tents. Two men with guns ran out and, before they could return fire, dropped as if struck by lightning. A figure came running toward our camp, unarmed. He was coming closer and closer.

"Oh my god," Adaoma gasped, "that's Dr. Miller!"

Jonathan Miller, an Australian surgeon in our group, was in his early sixties and had been doing this kind of charity medical work for decades. What was he doing down at the UN tents?

"He must have gone to visit this morning," Adaoma said, incredulous.

One of the soldiers, about one hundred and fifty yards from us, saw Dr. Miller running away. The soldier dropped to one knee. We saw the muzzle flash, and Dr. Miller fell face forward onto the sand.

I was in shock. Adaoma had both hands up to her mouth.

Then I saw Dr. Miller move. He was still alive and crawling behind a small, nearby sand berm. I didn't think, wasn't even conscious of what I was doing. I just took off.

"Alex, no! No, no, no!" Adaoma screamed.

I ran toward Dr. Miller. The soldier who'd shot him was still kneeling, probably a hundred yards away from me now, but I was closing toward him and the doctor.

Another muzzle flash, and I heard a hiss whiz by my ear. I dropped to the ground and crawled frantically toward the doctor and the berm. *Another shot, and I'll be dead.*

But there were no more shots. When I reached Dr. Miller behind the berm, I saw that all of the armed figures, including my stalker, were running back toward the three idling helicopters.

Dr. Miller was screaming in agony, his light blue surgical scrub pants now dark red from waist to ankle. I didn't know what to do. I felt helpless.

"Alex, Alex!" he gasped. "Apply a tourniquet to stop the bleeding. I'm hit in the upper leg."

I took my Princeton sweatshirt off, but it was too thick to tie tightly enough. *Shit! What am I supposed to do?*

"Alex—" The doctor was now moaning. "In my shirt pocket is a penknife. Use it to cut strips from your jumper for the wound."

I grabbed the knife, cut off a sleeve, sliced a couple of strips, and managed to cinch them tight around his left leg just below the groin. *I did it! I did it!*

Dr. Miller leaned back against the berm, in pain and panting heavily. "Good, good… good on you, Alex, well done. Brilliant. Thank you. This was clearly not the morning for me to go introduce myself to those UN chaps or whoever they are."

The three helicopters lifted off and roared away right over us. I was afraid someone would shoot us from the air, but they didn't.

After a bit, I've no idea how long, I could still hear the helicopters. *Were they still circling around? Weren't they leaving?*

No! They were coming back. The ground shook again, the *whop*

whop whop of the rotors rolling in. Then I saw them – two of them. These were British, but different. The first three were green, and these were blue.

Then my world went black.

• • •

I came to after I didn't know how long. I could see, had my limbs, but was stone deaf. I struggled to my feet. Some sort of bomb had gone off. Maybe it had come from the helicopters. Death from above. The blast had thrown me about fifty feet from the sand berm where I'd been with Dr. Miller.

I stumbled back to the berm. The doctor was dead, I could tell; frozen, white as a ghost, his mouth half open. Either the shock wave had killed him, or maybe I hadn't got the tourniquet on right, and he'd bled out.

I looked toward our camp. *Where were the tents, our dozen tents?* It was like they'd vaporized into the seventy-degree air. There were burning bits of wreckage all around the radius of what had been our camp and many columns of black smoke. I didn't see any people.

"No, no, please, no! Please!" I was screaming, but I couldn't hear a thing.

I ran toward where our camp had been. "Adaoma! Adaoma! Adaoma, where are you?"

Now I saw bodies, whole and in pieces, everywhere. An arm lying on the ground, then a nurse with half her head blown away, some of the patients from the ward maimed, dead and scattered in a haphazard row like victims the Allies found at Bergen-Belsen in 1945. And blood everywhere, intermingled with the smell of smoke, oil, melted steel and what I later realized was burned flesh.

Screaming yet deaf, I raced around the camp. "Adaoma, Adaoma, Adaoma! Please, it's me, Alex!"

Brian told me once that when he was in kindergarten, he'd gone to the state fair with his mother and gotten separated from her. He was crying and a good Samaritan took him to the information booth at the center of the fairgrounds, where someone called over the PA for the mother of Brian Findlay to come to the information desk to meet her son.

Brian said he'd been terrified, afraid his mother would never arrive to take him home. She did, of course. But as I careened around that camp, I knew I could call and call, but Adaoma would never be coming back to me. Because as I stepped around a piece of burning wreckage from one of our vehicles, I saw her.

She was flat on her back on the sand, both her legs missing and nowhere to be seen, evenly sliced off as if done by a paper cutter for a school art project. She lay in a massive pool of blood, her upper torso spotless, her eyes wide open, and she had what I thought was a peaceful expression on her face. Sticking into the middle of the top of her head was a huge piece of metal, a splitting maul that had made firewood of her skull and beautiful brain.

I dropped to my knees, screaming hysterically, but nobody else was around. I kneeled next to Adaoma, then lay next to her, my whole body soaking up her blood. I kissed her on the cheek, wrapped my arms around her body, and passed out.

Hours later – I know this because it was far into the afternoon with the sun well past vertical and headed west – I regained consciousness when rescue workers lifted me onto a stretcher and carried me to a makeshift ambulance, the bed of a ramshackle Toyota pickup.

• • •

I spent the last two weeks of July in a disoriented haze. Though I had no physical injuries, I was taken to a hospital in Tunis for tests and rest. The leader of our organization, the managing director, came there to visit me and others from our team. Apparently, only about fifteen percent of us survived. Of those, some barely made it and others would live the rest of their lives in pain with orthopedic or brain injuries.

This was a scandal in the world media, the managing director had told me. The British were taking a beating for their carelessness and heavy-handedness. By and large, though, it seemed Margaret Thatcher's response was, effectively, "Well, fuck you, just go bugger off. It's the Provisional IRA's fault those innocent people were killed."

The managing director wanted to contact my parents, but I refused, said they weren't in my life and hadn't been for some time. He said the organization would give me a plane ticket back to the States.

"Where would you like to go?" he asked. "New York? That's closest to Princeton."

"No, Los Angeles."

After two days, the hospital discharged me to a hotel. Adaoma's parents came to visit me there. Shocked and consumed with grief, they were in far better shape than I was. Her mother saw me in the lobby and ran to me, wrapping me in a tight hug. I fought back sobs until I couldn't.

She stroked my head and rubbed my back.

"Shhh, shhh, now, Alexandra, darling, it will be okay. It will be okay." Faint lilac perfume, a scent I will never forget, enlivened her light brown skin. She wore a bright blue dress that stopped below her knees. Amidst her grief, she radiated concern and affection for me, and I could have stayed there forever.

"I'm so so sorry," I howled. "I couldn't save her. I failed her. I should never have left her to run to Dr. Miller. I wish it was me instead of her. Will you forgive me, please? I'm so sorry!"

Adaoma's mom was still holding me tight. "You were brave and courageous, darling. You didn't do anything wrong."

"No! No! I loved her so! She was one of the most important people in the world to me. I don't know what I'll do without her."

Adaoma's mom continued soothing me. "I know, baby, I know. You were so very important to our lovely Adaoma."

Sobs kept exploding out of me. "What am I going to do? I will miss her so. But I promise… promise you, that I will get even for her. I will make the people who did this pay. I don't care if I spend the rest of my life doing it."

Still holding me and stroking the back of my head, Adaoma's mother whispered, "No. No, sweet Alexandra, you must move on. Don't let this poison your dreams. Adaoma wouldn't want that. She was a beautiful blessing in everyone's life, and we must take her legacy with us. Always remembering, but always moving forward with goodness. Promise me… promise her, you will do that."

41

Sally Horrigan: July 11, 1985

A storm moved east across Northern Ireland off the ocean since Sally had been outside for lunch earlier in the day. Fast-moving dark clouds and blustery wind rolled across Belfast's streets. Normally it would be light until 22:00 in July, but now at 17:30, it looked like November. It would rain soon.

Walking home, Sally beat herself up for giving her address to Paddy Mac. She'd volunteered to stay at the office and complete the work, but Paddy'd said he wouldn't have the figures and papers till after 21:00 and didn't want to make her wait around. *Don't be worried. It's probably just like Paddy said.* Normally Peter would do the work, but he wasn't around, so she had to do it. Did Paddy know where Peter was? Was Peter in hiding? *Oh my god, could he be dead?*

Sally needed a shower. Sweating all afternoon in that stuffy office had soaked her clothes. Paddy had left after a few minutes, but it didn't matter; she was falling apart the rest of the afternoon. The cold wind felt good, but her body and clothes still stank.

She approached Divis Flats, and everything looked normal. Kids out playing, groups of men and women out smoking and, in some cases, drinking beer. In a dark corner off the west entrance, a young couple were entwined in each other's arms, passionately kissing, oblivious to the world. The sight of them made her sad and envious, bringing back warm memories of being wrapped in George's strong arms while he softly kissed her lips. They had done that all the time when they were courting.

Two men she didn't recognize sat outside reading newspapers, one in a red leather jacket and the other in a green sweatshirt. She briefly thought they were watching her, but told herself not to imagine things. Maybe they were visiting friends or had just moved in.

She entered the building as usual through the side entrance. The elevators were always slow and crowded, so she preferred to take the stairs. The stairway often smelled of urine and trash, but Sally would hold her nose and quickly walk up the five flights to her flat.

The stairwell was pitch black, the overhead light not working. *Hmm, maybe the electric is out.* She considered going back outside and walking around to check the elevator but decided to use the stairs. As often as she'd been up and down, she could do it in the black. It was deathly silent. *If the electric and elevator are out, wouldn't more people be on the stairs?*

Her left arm in front of her, she took a couple of steps. *There! That's it, the rail.*

As she put her foot on the first step, she felt rustling air over her shoulder. Suddenly, a hand clamped over her mouth. The person pulled her off the stairs and wrestled her against the wall. A dim flashlight clicked on, and her wide eyes adjusted in a few seconds.

Simon!

He put his finger to his lips, put his face so close to hers that she felt his breath on her cheek. He whispered, "You're in danger, Sally. I need to get you and your children out of Belfast. Now."

In a shocked daze, Sally shook her head. "No, Simon. Nobody suspects me. My boss Peter maybe, but not me."

Simon cut her off. "You'll never see Peter again."

"It was nothing I done anyways. I gave you information to get at the PLO. You swore nothing would happen to us, to the Provisionals. You did!"

"We don't have time. I'll explain later. Let's just say mistakes were made."

Sally closed her eyes and moaned. "Oh no, no, no. What have I done?"

"Listen to me! Men will be at your flat tonight to take you away. Did anyone mention that people might come by with work papers or something like that?"

Sally nodded and began to hyperventilate.

"If you're in your flat when those men come by, your children will be orphans. Understand?"

Sally's knees buckled, and she went down. She put her head in her hands and bent her face to the floor. Simon roughly pulled her up.

"Are your children in the flat?"

Sally began to focus, her children now the imperative.

"Yes, Tracy should have got Fergal at school, and Sean should be home from school too."

"Okay," Simon said. "Let's get up there." He pointed the flashlight at the stairs. "Come, quickly."

They ran up the five flights, with Sally completely winded when they reached the stairway door on five. She bent over, panting, with her hands on her knees, while Simon cracked the door to look for people in the hallway outside the stairwell.

"It's clear. Let's go."

As they were exiting, Sally heard two men talking and coming up the stairs from where they'd come.

"Shit," Simon said under his breath. "They're already here. Sally, we've got to get your kids and run." He said something unintelligible into a small walkie-talkie he pulled from his pocket.

Sally burst into her flat. *Oh, Hail Mary!* Her children were all there.

"Kids, come, right now, we have to get out of here. Right now! Hurry! Hurry!"

"Mum," Tracy said. "What is it? You look terrible. And who is this man?"

"We have to leave now. Come with me."

"But, Mum," Sean protested, "I just started my studies. I got me math exam tomorrow."

"Now, Sean! We're in danger, and this man is helping us."

Sally herded the kids and, after what seemed like hours but was less than a minute, got them out the door. The hallway outside was still clear. The men would be here any second. Simon pointed them to the other stairwell at the far end of the hall.

"Come, run. Everybody, follow me."

"But, Simon," Sally protested, "what if men are comin' up there too?"

"We'll have to risk it," he said. "They may have sent only two men, figuring it an easy job. Now come along, run!"

Simon, the kids, and Sally reached the stairway door at the other end of the hall. Sally looked back. The men still hadn't appeared from the other stairwell.

"Wait! Simon, you and the kids go on. I need to get something from the flat."

"No, Sally!"

"Simon, I must. You go down with the kids. I'll catch up."

Sally ran back to the flat, still all clear. She found what she needed on her bedside table, a picture of George, her and the kids, and grabbed it. On her way out, she took a large knife from the kitchen.

Sally exited her front door as two men in black ski masks came from the stairwell next to her flat. *The men from out front!* The one in the red jacket came after her, and the other in green ducked into the flat, looking for either the kids or incriminating evidence, Sally figured.

She took off in a panic, running for the stairs at the other end of the hall where Simon and the kids had gone down. She had to get back to them. She couldn't orphan her babies.

The man was closing in on her. She could hear him getting closer, his pounding feet and heavy breathing. Closer, closer. The stairway door was still about ten meters away when his hand landed hard on her shoulder, causing her to stumble. He was thin and unshaven, and had a large scar on his cheek. He smelled of cigarettes and raw onions.

You will only get one chance at this, Sally told herself. She swung the kitchen knife, aiming for his chest. The blade struck home midway up his abdomen. She desperately moved the blade up and down while the man screamed and screamed. He fell to his knees, blood pouring out of him. Sally left the blade in and ran for the stairs.

By now, the second man had left the flat and was rushing down the hall toward her and his fallen mate. He was somewhat obese, and Sally hoped he would lack speed and endurance.

She hit the stairs, scared and crying. She had to get down the five flights and find her kids. As she reached the fourth-floor landing, she heard the door open on five, the second man. On the third-floor landing, she fell, cradling the picture in her arms to protect it. She scrambled up and kept going, trying to go faster and faster without falling again.

Sally hit the ground floor, encouraged that the other man didn't seem to be closing on her. *But what if there were more men down here looking for her?* She burst out through a side door into the gray evening, completely out of breath and scanning for Simon and her kids. *Where were they? Where were they?* Panic would overwhelm her soon.

"Over here, over here!"

Ah, blessed Mary! It was Tracy, and she was with the boys and Simon about a hundred meters away, standing outside a maroon Ford sedan. They were all motioning for her.

With her last remaining strength, she ran toward the sedan just as the second man came out the same exit door. His eyes locked onto her, and he began running. People all around them were staring.

Sally made it to the sedan about twenty meters ahead of the man. Everyone was in the car. She jumped into the back seat with her kids. Simon was in the front, with a driver she didn't recognize. The car sped away from the curb before the back door even closed.

No one spoke as the car drove rapidly through Belfast. They were headed toward the shipyard, Sally realized. The car drove to a deserted part of the yard and stopped while Simon got out to cut a padlocked gate to let them through. Simon jumped back in, and the car roared ahead, squealing its tires. Soon it pulled alongside the water next to a cabin cruiser, about twenty meters long. Simon rushed Sally and the kids onto the boat, and the maroon sedan drove off.

"Get in and below decks quickly!" Simon urged. "Stay down there, away from the windows."

In no time, the boat cast off, and they were underway. Below deck were food, drinks, blankets and a change of clothes for everyone.

After a few minutes, Simon came down. "You are all safe and are going to be fine."

Tracy had lots of questions, but Sally shook her head and motioned her to be quiet.

"We've about ten hours ahead of us on the boat," Simon said. "Fortunately, the storm has blown through, and the seas should be calm." He gave each of the kids a pill to help them sleep, and they were out within fifteen minutes.

* * *

Sitting with Simon in the aft of the boat in her changed clothes and wrapped in a blanket, a defeated and shell-shocked Sally asked, "Where's we goin'?"

It was a clear, cool night with a full moon, the boat making twenty knots. Two armed men Sally had never seen were up top driving.

"We will put in outside Cardiff."

"Wales? We're staying in Wales?"

He shook his head. "No, a van will meet us at the dock tomorrow with your new passports and a suitcase of clothes for each of you. We will go to Heathrow and be on the afternoon El Al flight to Tel Aviv, your new home."

Sally put her head in her hands and started moaning.

After a bit, she whimpered, "I don't want to live in Israel! Me parents, me nieces and friends, they's all here. Will I ever see them again?"

Simon shrugged. "Not anytime soon, I suspect. I'm really sorry, Sally. The Provisionals lost thirty-three men to the British and will not soon forget that."

"They'll know it's me that touted them out since I went runnin'."

"They'd have known that anyway, soon enough. Why do you think those men came to your flat? You didn't see them bringing any work papers, did you? The Provos don't know yet what you've done, but if you stayed, they would have worked backward, questioned everyone, maybe even tortured you or threatened your kids to find out what you knew. It would all come out."

"You said this would never happen! Said it was all about the PLO, and the Mossad don't care about the Provisionals. What happened, Simon?"

He sat silently, staring at her.

"You owe me this! You done ruined me life and me babies' lives. Who you think I gonna tell?"

He helplessly sighed. "As I said, Sally, I'm very sorry this happened. I, the Mossad, we didn't expect this. We had every intention of doing what I said. Ignoring the Provisionals and just targeting the PLO when they came to Tunisia to get their weapons. And if that had happened, you'd still be in Belfast, and your life would be no different."

"But that ain't what happened, is it?"

"Right. Last November, the PLO took four of our soldiers hostage in southern Lebanon. They were conscripts, three of them nineteen and one twenty years old. When this happens, and sadly it's not a rare occurrence, the nation of Israel does everything in its power to get them back. We do whatever it takes. Always. We try to find and rescue them, but if we have to, we will trade prisoners or terrorists we have in custody for our people. We will trade fifty to one hundred prisoners for just a few of our soldiers. And we never stop trying to get our people back, even if it takes years."

Sally's tears had stopped, and she now looked resignedly at the moon and glass-calm sea.

"By this past May," Simon said, "we hadn't yet found the soldiers, and we got intelligence that a new, violent splinter wing of the PLO planned to kill them, publicly assassinate them on television in June. They weren't interested in a prisoner exchange. We circled back with anyone who might know anything about where they were: the British, the French, the Turks, the Soviets and other terror groups."

"So, how did this lead to casting me and me children out – betraying us?"

"The British knew something, had a bit of intel. Let's just say that in the past year or so, relations between MI-6 and the Mossad have been strained. They felt they'd helped us previously, and we hadn't sufficiently reciprocated. To help us here, we had to give them something."

"So, you gave 'em me."

"No. Not directly. We didn't tell them how we had the information. They asked, but we refused. But we tipped them off about the weapons shipment for the Provisionals, the date and the location. The arrangement we had was that they would send in the SAS and…"

"The who?"

"SAS. Special Air Service. Military commandos. The deal was supposed to be that they would only take or destroy the weapons and wouldn't fire at the Provisionals' men unless fired upon. The Provisionals would, of course, be furious to lose their weapons, but at least their men wouldn't be massacred."

"But that didn't happen."

"No. The SAS hit the boats, the trucks, and the two weapons tents and killed everyone in sight."

"'Course they did." Sally sighed. "Bastards!"

"This has been a disaster for the British in the media, and it's only going to get worse. After the SAS finished killing the Provos, they reboarded the three helicopters and lifted off the beach. Then two more helicopters with air-to-ground missiles came in and destroyed everything near the beach. Including a medical compound for refugees and the poor run by a big multinational charity. There were only two weapons tents, but this medical camp had a dozen tents that looked similar about a hundred meters away, and the Brits just blew everything to hell. Killed almost all the people in the medical compound."

Sally was angry. "This is not my fault, Simon. You and the Brits killed all those people, and you may as well-a just killed me an' me kids."

Simon leaned in closer and took her hands in his. "I know this is unexpected, an unlucky turn of events. But I assure you, you and your children will be one hundred percent safe in Israel. Nobody will ever know you're there. We will give you new identities, get you a nice flat and arrange a good job for you. Your kids will go to good schools. And you all can live in Israel forever."

Sally spat out, "How in hell are me kids and me ever supposed to settle in and live the rest of our lives there?"

"If you want," Simon said, "we'll take you back to Northern Ireland or the Republic of Ireland, but you'll be on your own. We won't be able to protect you, save for giving you some money. But there's a chance the Provisionals would find and kill you. Both sides of the Troubles have touts everywhere. They would never kill your children – they don't do that, but you, most certainly. You know this – you and your husband were in the Provisionals."

After several minutes, she finally spoke. "If it wasn't for the kids, I'd take me chances rather than live far away in a new place. Hide out in Ireland somewhere. But I need to give me kids their best chance for a future, at least till they are old enough to lead their own lives."

42

Alex: August 1985 – November 1989

In early August, I took Lufthansa from Tunis to Frankfurt, changed planes and flew to Los Angeles to collapse into Julie's arms.

She met me at LAX outside International Arrivals. I walked toward her with my head down as she rushed to embrace me, squeezing me tight. With one hand on the back of my head and the other rubbing my back, she whispered, "Alex! Alex, my god! Ever since I saw what happened a few weeks ago, I've been worried to death. I don't know what I'd do if I lost you."

I didn't say anything.

"And every time I think about Adaoma, I just cry. I so wish she and I had more than phone calls to get acquainted. What a beautiful person she was."

Back at their townhouse, Faith and Hope screamed "Auntie Alex" and ran to me as soon as Julie had retrieved them from the neighbor next door. Now much taller, they'd be three in December, and looking even more like Julie with their dark eyes and hair, they wanted to show me their new dinosaurs and for all of us to play with them. I did so half-heartedly for an hour, and then they lost interest once Tim came home. Back from his army duties in Germany for just over a week, they ran to Tim for hugs, shouting, "Daddy! Daddy! Auntie Alex is here!"

"Yes!" he said. "Isn't that so exciting?"

"Hi," I feebly said. "The unwelcome houseguest has arrived."

He hugged me and said, "Don't be crazy. You can stay here as long as you want. Brian's going nuts over all this."

"I know," I said, "but he's on that Marine amphibious ship all summer. I figured I'd see him somehow when we were both back at school next month."

"He called here yesterday. They were ending a port call in Okinawa, and he hoped we knew something. I said all we had was a call from your organization in Tunisia asking for you to be picked up at the airport today."

About two weeks into my stay, I was still in my pajamas and lying on the couch watching game shows. I hadn't moved since Julie had taken the girls to preschool that morning at eight. Just like every other day, I had roots growing out of my ass. That night, while Tim bathed the twins, Julie sat next to me on the sofa and pulled me close to her.

"I'm worried about you, Alex. I think you need some help."

I violently shook my head.

Julie continued, "As you know, sweetie, I'm no stranger to trauma and grief. It just eats away at you like aggressive termites. For the longest time, you think you can tough it out, and it will get better, but eventually, your house just collapses, things falling down all around you."

I rested silently against her shoulder and her bright yellow polo shirt. Her mellow perfume smelled calming.

"I have a good friend here. She's at UCLA getting a Ph.D. in clinical psychology and focusing on trauma. She's great, and I'm sure she would talk to you about Tunisia and everything else that's happened."

I shrugged.

"And, I don't know, maybe…do you think it might help you to talk about Tunisia with your parents?"

I didn't say anything for probably five minutes, and Julie knew not to ask again. Finally, I said, "I'll meet your friend, but as for my parents – never!"

"All right," Julie said. "I'll set it up."

Within a few minutes, I'd fallen asleep nestled into Julie's shoulder.

Let's just say I wasn't very open-minded or talkative during the sessions with Julie's psychologist friend, and I ignored the woman's recommendation to begin seeing someone when I went back to New Jersey.

• • •

During my semi-comatose month on Julie and Tim's couch, I resolved to spend my senior year at Princeton focused on getting done and out of there. I would study like a nerd because it would suck up lots of hours and help keep me from dwelling on Adaoma. I would be only marginally social and would hopefully find some way to put my rage, not my Medieval Studies BA, to a satisfying use come May 1986.

Going back to the room Adaoma and I were planning to share senior year was not remotely anything I could do, so I moved off campus. Lived in a tiny studio apartment above a diner in downtown Princeton. I worked thirty hours a week at the diner, went to class, studied, and smelled like fried food morning, noon and night.

And though I didn't realize it then, my return to Princeton in the fall of '85 also marked the beginnings, consciously or otherwise, of my pulling away from Brian. It started first with emotional distance and then progressed from there. He tried hard to help me process Tunisia and also hounded me to get psychological help, but I kept him at arm's length. He deserved better. Over the next two years, I would be closed off, unfaithful on occasion, cruel and distant. A complete bitch.

· · ·

The diner was busy, a mid-September football weekend, Princeton versus Penn. People were lined up out the door for breakfast, and one of my tables for four was being blocked by one person. He'd been there over an hour, had eaten, but was now just drinking coffee. The manager told me to hurry him along.

He was good-looking, either a student or a recent graduate, I figured. He had dark, wavy, longish hair, pristine skin and teeth, and a lanky frame. At the table, he asked, "Hey, uh, you… could I get more coffee?"

"Hmm," I said, "that could be an issue. You're occupying a table for four, have been here over an hour, and people are lined up down the street to get in, as you can no doubt see. They likely want breakfast before kick-off this afternoon."

"Really, now? You know, your service wasn't the fastest, so it's partially your fault I've been here for so long. I'm not going to be able to give you much of a tip because of that, and since you're running me out of here…"

"Tell you what, mister—"

"It's Paul."

"Okay, Mister Paul, I have an idea. How about I pay you a tip instead, and in exchange, you never come back here while I'm working?"

"So hostile. I see you working here all the time. That would mean I could never eat here."

"Gee, isn't that too bad?" I smirked.

A week later, I'd gotten my hands on a scarce ticket to hear Margaret Thatcher speak at a small venue on campus. I wanted to see the monster who killed Adaoma. This likely wasn't a good idea since I still grieved for her and relived that day often in my violent dreams. But, maybe like people who gawk at a car crash, I wanted to see and hear the British Prime Minister.

At the event, she gave a foreign policy speech, then took unscripted audience questions. After three or four of the typical variety on the Soviet Union, the ongoing Pershing Two missile furor and her wrenching privatization programs in Britain, the moderator recognized another student for a question. He got up a few rows ahead of me. It was the guy Paul from the diner that football Saturday.

"My name's Paul. I've been listening to your lies for the last hour. You lead a nation of murderers. Why do you think the fucking British flag has been known forever as The Butcher's Apron? You've always been nothing but goddamn colonialist occupiers. Africa, India, Malaysia, Singapore."

The audience was staring, electricity building in the crowd. Most found it curious, if impolite, a few shouted encouragement and many were angry, embarrassed by their fellow student. The moderator moved quickly to shut him down.

"Sir, sir, your tone is disrespectful, and I'm going to ask you to leave or be removed."

"Fuck you! You're just an accomplice."

Thatcher's security detail moved from the stage toward Paul, ready to drag him out or beat the crap out of him. Thatcher was stone cold, looking at Paul as merely a minor, annoying odor, something she'd stepped in.

As Thatcher's guys dragged him from the auditorium, he yelled louder.

"Fucking fascists. You're still running an apartheid state in Northern Ireland. You're a murdering bitch, Maggie! Bobby Sands,

Francis Hughes, Raymond McCreesh, Patsy O'Hara, their blood is on your hands! Burn in hell, Maggie! We missed you at Brighton last year, but it's only a matter of time for you."

Later, I learned that Paul's reference to Bobby Sands and the others was to Provisional IRA members who died on a prison hunger strike in Northern Ireland in 1981 after Thatcher wouldn't approve their demands for changes in prison conditions. And in '84, the Provos bombed the Tory Party conference hotel in Brighton, nearly killing the prime minister.

· · ·

Two weeks later, on a Wednesday afternoon, Paul was back at the diner, again at one of my tables.

"Hello, Alex. You weren't wearing your name tag the last time I was in. Maybe today I'll get some faster service, eh?"

"Maybe. But I wonder, are you going to have another mental breakdown today? Start foaming at the mouth and screaming about Margaret Thatcher? Will the police have to come and drag you out of here too?"

He smiled, proudly, it seemed. "You heard about that. How?"

"I was there. I hate Thatcher too, but after that night, everyone likely thinks you either have a mental illness, were drunk or are a terrorist."

"Maybe I am."

"Drunk? Mentally Ill?"

"Aren't we funny? No, a terrorist."

"Yeah, right."

"Maybe we should grab lunch or dinner sometime, Alex. Not here. Explore your hatred of Thatcher in more depth."

I shook my head. "Look – Paul, is it? You're good-looking, that's for sure, but my gut tells me you're an asshole. I've had enough of those in my life."

The guy was relentless. He came into the diner several times a week, also saw me in the library a couple of times and came over. "Just lunch," he'd say. "Have lunch with me. Then, I'll leave you alone." Finally, I gave in. Our first date, if you want to call it that, was lunch and then a demonstration on campus protesting Reagan and the Contras. Paul introduced me to some of his friends and, as the group of us were leaving, a photographer for the campus paper, the *Daily Princetonian*, snapped our picture. A few days later, we were on the front page: **"Concerned and active Princeton students attend the Contra demonstration,"** the caption read.

• • •

Paul and I started hanging out, at first occasionally and then most days. In November, I went to Boston with him for a long weekend to meet some high school friends of his. We stayed with his parents at their house in Southie. Paul thought we were kind of dating. I didn't. I was still with Brian, though we seemed to be speaking less and less. His final Annapolis year was really busy, and basketball made it even more so. I'd seen him over Labor Day, but I was still out of it, in a fog, depressed or whatever, over Tunisia. I wasn't in the moment. I'd given him sex, was happy to do it, but was like a mannequin – silent, wishing the whole time he'd hurry up and come.

Brian and I carried on through senior year, gasping toward the finish line. I didn't want Paul or anyone else – didn't want anyone, I'd decided. Didn't know why, but had pretty much quit producing movies of the future with Brian in my mind. Nonetheless, things would drag on until late '87, when I just had to end it.

Paul and I were never serious, though not because he didn't want that. We were great friends in my mind, but nothing more. I slept with him a few times, but as expected, it didn't do anything for me. I wanted no entanglements of any kind. Just wanted to get on with a new life.

I learned over my senior year that Paul's family were staunch Catholics, originally from Northern Ireland. Nine months or so into our friendship, right before our graduations, he disclosed that his parents were members of the Provisional IRA. His dad was a Boston cop, one of many working with the Provisionals. His job was helpful to NORAID, the Provisionals' fundraising organization in the US. The weapons trade was his dad's medium, and Paul planned to join "the family business" after Princeton while also working for an investment bank in its Boston office.

Over the course of my senior year, through Paul and his family, I met a couple of Provisional IRA members in the US and also delved deeply into the long, bitter history of Northern Ireland. Their cause resonated with me on its own merits, but also nicely dovetailed with my hatred of the British. I'd told Paul about Adaoma and Tunisia, and he only fed my anger, sharing tales of atrocities the British Army, police and Protestant militias committed on a daily basis in Northern Ireland.

It was perhaps inevitable that I proved receptive to an approach from Paul and his parents to begin to do "just a few small things" for the IRA cause. I needed a vessel to carry my anger and desire for revenge, and there it was.

• • •

After graduation in '86, I moved to Boston and shared an apartment with three high school friends of Paul's, all recent BC and BU graduates and, as far as I knew, not members of the Provisionals. I worked for an advertising agency as a junior copywriter, coffee fetcher and receiver of unwanted sexual innuendo and ass-pinching by certain lecherous married men in the office.

My night job was helping Paul with IRA things. It started as small-time stuff: Acting as a lookout while business meetings of whatever sort went on, and ferrying occasional messages from one person to the next. By the second half of '87, I'd started to do more, always with Paul or his parents. One time, the four of us buried weapons under a barn in Maine that the IRA had rounded- up on the west coast. Two months later, we went back, dug them up, and hid them in a tractor-trailer bound for Canada.

Another time, Paul's mother asked me to 'entertain' a potentially large financial donor for NORAID, a man from out of town whose money could buy lots of guns. She told me I needed to do whatever it took, whatever he wanted, to make sure he was happy.

"What exactly do you mean?" I'd asked her.

"Whatever he wants, Alex. He wants to go eat ice cream, you take him. He wants to put his dick into you, you let him. He wants a blow job or to shoot his load all over your tits, you love it and ask for more. Got it? I've probably fucked him half a dozen times over the years," she added.

I went to dinner with him and then back to his hotel room. Fortunately, I'd been feeding him drinks all night, and at the hotel, I slipped something into his Irish whiskey to get him to pass out, so I didn't have to have sex with him. When we woke up naked together the next morning, I told him he'd been amazing. He gave NORAID the money.

I worked with Paul, his parents and the IRA in Boston until early '88, when an opportunity arose for me to move to Dublin to help the IRA under an American cover. Paul's parents arranged this with a woman they knew, someone named Maeve, who I didn't meet until Maine at the end of '89. I spent my Dublin time helping the Provisionals as a low-level gopher: messenger, lookout and largely platonic, harmless hostess duties – eye and arm candy. I returned to the US in late '88 to arrange my death before going back to Belfast after a few weeks. I was there until I went to Maine in November '89.

PART 5

Pursuit and Revenge

43

Julie: 1994

Julie waited for General Moreland in a conference room and sipped bad coffee. On the burner too long, in her Styrofoam cup, the brew conformed with government specs the world over. This was already her third one of the day, and it was only 09:00. Worse, she already craved another cigarette. In her fourth year of devotion to this unhealthy vice, she'd taken it up in 1991 to try to soothe her anxieties when Tim deployed with the First Infantry Division from Germany, first to Kuwait for Operation Desert Shield, then to Iraq for Desert Storm.

She was in a soot-blackened office building a block off Princes Street on a warm June day. Edinburgh Castle loomed outside the conference room's casement windows.

Ralph Moreland exploded into the room. He wore a dark charcoal suit, a white shirt with American flag cufflinks, a lime green Hermes tie and incandescent black slip-on dress shoes. Save for his bald head, he didn't look like a former three-star general in the US Army. Julie wore a knee-length, dark blue-and-white pinstriped dress, blue heels and nylons, plus her ever-present tortoiseshell glasses.

"Delacroix… or Mitchell." He smiled and extended his hand. "I don't know which is right; the paperwork says Mitchell, but someone referred to you as Delacroix. Regardless, I'm Moreland. Great to meet you."

"Hi. I use both my maiden and married names, depending on the context. My maiden name, Mitchell, is a tribute to my mom, but my husband is Tim Delacroix. It's nice to meet you too, General."

"Call me Ralph, and I'll call you Julie. That work for you?"

"Yes, sure, General."

"Julie, it's Ralph, not general and not sir." He chuckled. "How the hell are you ever going to work for me if you can't follow instructions better than that?"

Moreland kept his suit jacket on and sat across from Julie at the end of the long table. "I'm going to get a coffee. Can I get you another? Christ, that stuff from the kitchen's awful. It's like black tar from a latrine. I bought an espresso machine for my office. I'll have my assistant bring you one, too."

"Sure, thanks, Ralph."

He reached for the phone on the table and punched in two numbers. "Hey, Alicia, can you bring us a couple of double espressos, please? Oh, let me give you our lunch orders. Usual for me."

He turned to Julie, the phone still cradled in his ear. "Julie, what do you want for lunch?"

"Uh, lunch? I thought we were only scheduled for an hour."

"Oh hell no, we'll be here most of the day. That a problem for you?"

"Um, no. That's fine. Anything's fine for lunch. I'll go with Alicia's recommendation."

"Alicia, you pick something for Doctor Delacroix. Thanks."

"Um, Ralph, I don't want there to be any misunderstanding. I'm not a doctor yet. I am still working on my Ph.D. dissertation. So, if that's an issue for this interview, I understand."

Moreland waved his hand as if to say "details, details." He leaned forward toward the center of the table. With his blue eyes and broad yet pointed nose drilling into her, he asked, "So, how much do you know about why you're here?"

"Not much. The people at the agency said they wanted to assign me to a new intelligence initiative but that I needed to meet you first. That's it, really."

The conference room door opened, and Alicia arrived with double espressos on bone china cups and saucers. She was an attractive, middle-aged woman in an expensive-looking black-and-red dress that stopped just above her knees. The sort of executive assistant one would typically find in CEOs' offices or law firms, but not the US government. After seeing her and Moreland, Julie thought, *I'm going to need a wardrobe upgrade if I work here.*

"Julie, this meeting is your interview to be CIA's analyst on a new pan-European secret terrorism task force. The President asked Sec Def, an old friend of mine, to spool it up, and he pulled me out of retirement to do it. The group will work to identify terrorist threats to Europe, Canada and the US. To the outside world, it will be the Center for Political and Economic Assessment, a multinational think tank affiliated with the University of Edinburgh. Our official confidential government name is the task force on Joint European Terrorism Policy Action and Knowledge, or JETPAK. Before you say it, yes, it's a stupid fucking name, but the British and French picked it, and as you know, everyone in government loves acronyms."

She laughed.

"The focus will be on existing and new terrorist organizations that operate in Europe. We'll also watch emerging groups elsewhere that can stir things up in Europe, Canada or the US. That'll include organizations on the subcontinent, the Stans, the Middle East, Africa and even places like Afghanistan, where guys with beards down to their knees screw and crap in caves and mud huts."

Julie loved Ralph's earthy candor. She guessed he was someone she could respect and learn from.

"Time to talk about you, Julie. All I know is you come very highly recommended by people I know at the CIA who are a hell of a lot smarter than me. You joined the agency in '91, right? Talent-spotted by one of your Ph.D. professors?"

"I joined in '92, actually. I'm getting my DPhil in Physics at St. Andrews. I finished my courses and passed my orals last year, and my dissertation should be done late this year or early next. I started with the agency part-time while taking classes but moved to full time last year. But since joining, I've been seconded to a joint effort with MI-6. They have a small office here, and I spend about a week a month in London working on nuclear issues."

"I'm told your dissertation is classified. What's it on? I'm cleared, so you can tell me."

"Miniature nuclear warhead technologies for next-generation missiles."

Ralph chuckled. "You're literally a rocket scientist. How'd you end up doing nukes and then terrorism at the agency?"

"I started graduate school in nuclear physics. I just kind of took to it. Then at St. Andrews, one of my professors pulled me into the weapons side. And then one thing led to another. I really like it, and that's the appeal of the CIA. Hopefully, my contributions will help keep the world safe, especially because we need to keep nuclear technologies away from terrorist groups."

"Let's talk about that," he said. "Give me a quick tour of the bad guys' nuclear weapons world."

As easy as talking about the weather, Julie jumped in. "You have two kinds of groups: state entities and terror groups, with all kinds of arms dealers and brokers in between; some overlapping, and some not. The state players are mainly North Korea, Iran, Iraq and Libya. Generally, they work to build capabilities and infrastructure that will allow the steady production of nuclear weapons, typically ballistic missiles. Most of the technology comes out of legacy Soviet weapons labs or the Khan network from Pakistan. There's also some technology leakage out of the US, France, the UK, India and Israel."

"What kind of stuff do the state guys want?"

"Highly enriched uranium – uranium-235 is the feedstock for uranium or plutonium-based weapons. Uranium out of the ground gets refined with acids and other methods into a dried powder called Yellowcake, but still, that's only about one percent U-235, and the rest of the stuff from the ground is uranium-238, useless for weapons. There's lots of Yellowcake floating around."

"And the implications of that are what, Julie?"

"Kind of limited. Because to make use of the Yellowcake, you have to enrich it, and part of that process is separating the U-235 from the U-238 using sophisticated centrifuges that spin at twice the speed of sound in these huge, often underground, centrifuge farms. For civilian power generation, you only need about five percent uranium-235, but for a weapon, you need at least ninety percent.'

Moreland's eyes bored into Julie, taking it all in as she continued.

"Nobody will sell these bad state actors centrifuges, so they need the plans to reverse-engineer them and make their own. Other technologies come into play here too. One example would be beryllium reflectors. Those basically help prevent neutron leakage from the chain reaction, which helps lower the amount of highly enriched uranium you need for a weapon. And making plutonium is even harder, more time-consuming and more capital-intensive than enriched uranium. And once you have enough weapons-grade material, you still need to fashion it into a warhead, for which you need detonator know-how and technology, among numerous other things."

"Sounds like terror groups can't really play in that game," Moreland offered.

"Exactly. They lack the money, patience, industrial capabilities, and science and engineering talent to do this. Terror groups want low-tech, off-the-shelf stuff. Ideally, a detonation-ready suitcase bomb they can buy, or possibly some tiny amount of highly enriched weapons-grade material they can fashion into a dirty bomb."

"And you find and get to these people how?"

"Mainly through the supply, rather than the demand side. We map and monitor the legacy sources of the materials – Russians, Ukrainians and Pakistanis – as well as the brokers and middlemen selling to terror groups. The clandestine sides of the CIA and MI-6 also have some of these people on their payrolls. Plus, the NSA can surveil their communications: phones, emails and the like. For example, by now, we've figured out their draft email folder scheme."

"Their what?"

"Ralph, let's say I'm a seller of materials, and you're the contact of a terror group looking to buy. You give me your email address and password. We then pass messages via the Drafts folder of your email account. Nothing is ever sent, but we nonetheless communicate back and forth. Thing is, you don't realize the NSA is still reading your mail."

"Got it. How about a quick break, Julie? Toilets are down the hall, and let Alicia know if you need another coffee."

"God, what I really need is a cigarette," she remarked almost unconsciously.

"Ah, those are a demanding mistress. Took me years to quit."

"It's an awful habit. My husband and kids hound me constantly about quitting. I've yet to endorse that plan, but I am down from two packs a day when I started to less than half a pack now."

"Smoked since high school? College?"

"Oh no, never before '91. My husband deployed for the Gulf War, and the stress ate me up. The smokes helped."

Alicia delivered more espressos, soft drinks and lunch: a turkey sandwich for Ralph and a salad for Julie. Later, dessert arrived: huge chocolate brownies with a single-malt scotch chaser. It was an Islay malt and wasn't for the faint of heart, Julie thought after her first sip. *Like choking on smoke in a forest fire.*

"Let's talk more about you," Moreland suggested. "Your family, college, where you're from."

"Okay. Married eleven years now and married young. I was eighteen. Four kids, two sets of twin girls, eleven and eight."

Ralph whistled. "How do you do it without losing your mind?"

"We manage, but it's crazy at times. My husband is very involved, and we get lots of help from my in-laws. They visit often and wedge into our tiny rental house. Eight people for one bathroom is cozy," she laughed.

"Where are you from originally? What about your family?"

"Only child. Never really knew my father. My parents met in college in Indiana. My mom was a senior at St. Mary's across the road from Notre Dame, and my father was a Notre Dame chemistry Ph.D. student. He was from a prominent family in India and divorced my mom when I was really young, to go back to India to marry a woman from another prominent family in Delhi. My mom took her maiden name, Mitchell, back and changed mine to hers from Singh. My father didn't want any contact with me, so that was that."

Moreland sipped his scotch.

"We lived in Chicago, and my mom worked for a railroad in middle management. They transferred her out to a small town in northern Washington State up by the Canadian border, Timberline, when I was a seventh grader."

"Is your mother still there?"

Julie shook her head. "No, she passed away."

"Sorry to hear that."

"Thanks."

"Where'd you meet your husband? Tim, is it?"

She nodded. "Middle school, but we didn't start dating until high school."

"What's his story?

"ROTC at UCLA, finance and marketing major. Played basketball for them, a starter, as a walk-on for a year. Graduated in '86, infantry and Ranger schools and all that, First Infantry Division at Fort Riley, an unaccompanied tour on the DMZ, and then we posted to Germany in '90. Desert Shield and Storm before finishing in England for a few months, Cambridge, before Tim left the army in June of '91."

"I heard your husband was in some crazy shit in the Gulf War. Won a bunch of medals."

"Just two: The Distinguished Service Cross and a Silver Star."

"Wow, the DSC is just a step down from the Medal of Honor. What went down in Iraq?"

Julie took a bite of brownie and mustered her courage for another run at the scotch.

"He was a captain, a company commander, and two platoons of a different company in his battalion got pinned down across the Tigris River next to a bridge and took heavy casualties. Their officers and NCOs had been killed or wounded, and there was a sandstorm, so no air cover. Tim led two platoons of his company in rubber boats across the river under heavy fire. They got to the other side, outnumbered five to one, but Tim and his men stabilized the situation, counter-attacked and evacuated their wounded back over the river. It all took about four hours."

Moreland nodded approvingly. "Ass-kicking stuff. I'll look forward to meeting him sometime." He kind of laughed. "If he played college basketball, he probably made a tall target for Saddam's boys."

Julie nodded. "He's six-five."

"You must have tall kids then because you're what? Six foot?"

"Ish."

"What's your husband doing now?"

"After the army, he and a UCLA friend found an investor to help them buy an old, closed soft drink bottling plant in Edinburgh. They founded a company a little over two years ago, Fun Natural Beverages, that develops and sells vitamin-infused drinks with funny, unusual flavors. That's how we ended up here."

"How's that going?"

"So far, okay. It's still a very small company. Time will tell, I suppose, but we are expanding into the major cities in Scotland."

"One last thing on your education. Your undergraduate is physics at Kansas State?"

"Yes. I stitched credits together from everywhere for that degree. AP high school credits, a summer at Gonzaga in Washington in high school, a semester and a half at St. Mary's in Indiana before I got married, some credits at UCLA, and finally, K-State, both in Kansas and by correspondence from Germany."

It was around three in the afternoon, and Julie craved a cigarette.

Moreland leaned back in his chair. "Julie, I've enjoyed getting to know you. As advertised, you're impressive as hell. This job is yours if you want it. JETPAK needs nuclear terrorism in its remit, and you're just the person to give it to us."

"Thank you. I've liked our conversations today, and the job sounds interesting."

Moreland added, "I've got a pretty good nose for talent. Over the years, I've been wrong a few times, but not many, on picking people for key jobs. And in addition to your obvious smarts, Julie, you know what I see in you?"

She swallowed. *Do I want to hear this?* "What?"

"Toughness, resilience and a fierce but humble spirit. Nobody's going to roll over you."

After a minute or so of silence between them, Moreland asked, "Well, Julie, do you want the job or not?"

"Yes. What happens next?"

• • •

Julie awaited General Moreland in the conference room where they'd first met six months prior. It was a cold, wet Edinburgh December day, and Julie was due for her performance review from Ralph. He burst into the room, poised to suck the oxygen out of it as always. After some initial small talk, Ralph got right to it.

"Julie, you're kicking ass, doing great. Everybody in JETPAK loves you. Well, that does it for my review of your performance. But tell me, how are you liking this?"

Julie laughed. "I really am, but I've gone from six cigarettes and a half dozen cups of coffee a day to like a dozen of each since I started here. But we all need something to work on, right?"

"Hey, I don't have much time," he said, "and also wanted to let you know your job's getting bigger. You'll keep the nuclear terrorism portfolio, but we are now adding the Provisional IRA to the remit. Given your history of working with MI-6 at the CIA, you're perfect for this."

"Um, okay, Ralph. Thanks. That's fine, but why me? I don't have any particular expertise in that area and don't think anyone expects them to be looking for nuclear weapons."

"We're mixing things up in JETPAK, getting fresh eyes on the group. MI-6, MI-5 and the British military have been fighting the Provisionals for so long, they may resist new ways of thinking. Let's just say they're steeped in confirmation bias."

"But why would they listen to me, then?"

Ralph smiled. "Because you're charming, smart as shit, and aren't going to let anyone bully you. Plus, you're from the CIA, and the British know that 'the cousins' are not to be dismissed lightly. Who knows – we may learn nothing new, but then again, we might. Meantime, you'll keep on with the nuclear stuff, too. You'll just need a few more hours in your day, that's all," he laughed.

Julie didn't mind this. It was a chance for new learnings, and she was confident it wouldn't take her long to get up to speed on the Provisionals. She would tap her relationships with the CIA, FBI, NSA and the different British intelligence agencies. However, taking on the IRA as extra responsibility also likely meant more coffee and cigarettes, and less time with Tim and the kids.

44

Alex: Junior Executive – 1995

Jennifer Nathan, i.e. me for the next few months, presented her US passport to the immigration official at Aeropuerto Internacional Benito Juarez in Mexico City on Valentine's Day, 1995.

Petra Müller had closed up her Berlin apartment in anticipation of a months-long absence. She explained to her ad agency employers that she had been diagnosed with a non-life-threatening medical condition and would need to go away on medical leave for three months to seek treatment. Klara Steinmetz had then taken a train from Berlin to Frankfurt. The newly created Jennifer had flown out the next morning.

I told the immigration agent I'd been visiting friends in Europe and now planned to do the same in Mexico before going to Montreal to take an intensive French course for three months.

A week later, I flew to Montreal and, late that evening, went to a dark, trash-strewn alley behind St. John the Evangelist Anglican Church on the Avenue du Président Kennedy. It was a bright, cold night, the stars almost overpowering the reflected glow of the city. I'd seen the two blue chalk right-to-left slash marks on the trash dumpster a few kilometers away – meeting confirmed. I went to the back of the church and waited. And waited, stamping my feet on the ground to ward off frostbite on my toes.

Finally, I heard the back door of the church open and saw a figure descend the stairs carrying a duffel bag. He came closer. Another priest, much younger than Pavel. Apparently, the Russians were using spies to help them nourish souls around the globe.

The priest came up to me, nodded, looked up at the sky, and in

English, said, "They say spring will come early this year." Sign.

"But I think it will come to Edmonton first." Countersign.

The priest looked at me and smiled. "Pavel sends his regards."

"And please convey mine to him, Father."

The priest handed me the all-leather duffel. "In the bag, you will find assorted beauty supplies as well as a dark blue padded box for expensive perfume. You will want to make sure that the bottle in that box doesn't break or become damaged."

I nodded and pulled a thick brown manila envelope from inside my coat. "And this is for you."

He smiled. "God bless you, dear, and have a nice evening."

Walking back to my hotel with the duffel bag, I wasn't cold anymore. My heart was racing, and I was sweating. If I dropped the bag and broke the perfume bottle, or if I was mugged and lost the bag, the polonium 'perfume' would kill me and anyone it touched.

What I'd given the priest would be the end of the defense attaché at the Russian embassy in Madrid, his days of selling secrets to MI-6 brought to a violent end at Lubyanka prison in Moscow.

• • •

The day after collecting the duffel, I boarded the train in Montreal, crossed into the US at Rouses Point, New York, and headed for Grand Central. My first time back in the US since Maine in '89, six years. From New York, I took Amtrak's Lake Shore Limited to Chicago and then the train to St. Louis, where I began setting up Jennifer Nathan's temporary life.

I paid cash to rent an apartment for six months in the Dog Town area, across the street from the two-bedroom, two-bath 1950s bungalow where Sally Horrigan, now Suzanne Harris, lived. I purchased a 1986 white Chevy Impala sedan with 106,000 miles, obtained the insurance, rented a storage unit nearby in the suburb of Brentwood, and bought two hazmat suits, paying cash for everything. I went to a gun show and legally bought a 9mm semi-automatic and several magazines. Jennifer Nathan already had a driver's license issued by the state of Wyoming and would not be there long enough to need a Missouri license.

45

'd returned from my Warsaw meeting with Maeve in December of '84 excited that after ten years, I'd be able to avenge Adaoma's death on that Tunisian beach, as well as the deaths of over thirty of our people. Back then, I'd had no idea how I'd do it or when, but once I joined the Provisionals in 1987, finding the tout had become one of my unofficial missions.

The Provisionals knew almost immediately after the attack at Sfax that they'd been betrayed, but they knew little else. The number-two person in the quartermaster organization, name of Peter, had been tortured for weeks, shot dead, and left in a Belfast street. Sally Horrigan, who worked for him, had disappeared without a trace. Thus, we knew who'd likely done it but not how and why. And more importantly, where was Sally Horrigan? The matter had long been consigned to the cold case bin, pushed out by other priorities once years had passed. But not by Maeve or me.

Right after I'd returned to Berlin from the Patricia Maguire business early in 1994, and before I met Maeve in Vienna in May, an acquaintance made contact in Berlin. "Omar" and I (Klara Steinmetz) had met before as a professional courtesy. He was one of the PLO's men in western Europe.

We met at a coffee shop in Berlin near the Ka-De-We department store. We sat outside under a table with an umbrella close to one of those stand-up heaters cafes use. We had the patio to ourselves since Berlin was in the midst of three days of steady, drizzling rain. Omar wore blindingly polished black dress shoes, a dark blue Armani pinstripe suit, a pale blue spread-collar dress shirt and an orange Hermes tie with light blue sailboats.

He was mid-thirties, I guessed, with black trimmed hair and dark smoldering eyes, and he smelled great: a mix of French cologne and fresh dry cleaning. He was hot. No other way to describe him. As he settled in at our table, I felt a tingle in a few places. I imagined him bending me over the table right there. I surprised myself, hadn't had thoughts like that in about three years. *Maybe there's life in the old girl yet.*

Speaking English, we made small talk and got down to business. Omar needed information and was checking to see if, by any chance, I could help.

"So, Klara, we hear a senior French diplomat in Paris might be open to recruitment."

"Oh," I said, "who told you that?"

He smiled. "You know I can't say. Just some friends in the east."

Turkey, I guessed. I had no knowledge of any of this but saw no harm in keeping him talking.

"This person, let's call him Mr. X, like many over the years in France, has Communist sympathies. And we believe he has particular ideological bitterness against the US, UK and French governments."

"Okay, and you think since he hates the British, we might have a relationship with him?"

Omar gave a sort of shrug. "Something like that," he said, waving at the server for two more espressos. "We think the French may soon deploy this man to Beirut, and it would be crucial if we could establish a relationship. Maybe he has money troubles or women problems we could help him with, or maybe he just wants to work against the West and make a difference."

The server delivered our coffees.

I took a sip. "You know, I have no idea if we have any sort of relationship with this person. That isn't my department."

"But you could find out, make inquiries, no?"

I waited. He wouldn't just ask for a favor and offer nothing in return. That would be like coming to high tea at Buckingham Palace barefoot, wearing a halter top and cut-off denim shorts with fringe.

After maybe thirty seconds and sips on our espressos, Omar continued.

"If you could make some investigation with your people, then I could perhaps undertake questions on something that might be interesting to your organization."

I grinned at him, tipped my head slightly, and raised my eyebrows. "Oh?"

He smiled back. "I assume you weren't with the organization then, but you may know that back in 1985, the Provisionals lost a weapons shipment and a number of men in Tunisia to a British commando raid."

Holy shit! My adrenaline was immediately flowing, but I tried to be calm.

"I'm aware. Touts betrayed us."

"It might have been just one person, a woman," Omar remarked.

Sally Horrigan. Alone and not with Peter?

"Go on."

"What you may not know is that she was perhaps working for the Israelis. And they may have moved her outside of Ireland after it happened."

Stunned, I said, "Why?"

Omar smiled again. Now he, too, spread his hands helplessly.

"I don't really know, but I could make some discreet inquiries if you might be willing to ask some questions about the French diplomat."

Our mutual tasks clear, we agreed to meet two weeks later.

This time we met at VHF, a recently opened café off Alexanderplatz near the TV tower in the former East Berlin. We sat outside, and though a bit chilly it was a beautiful sunny late afternoon day. Omar was again impressively attired, this time in a light gray double-breasted suit with a dark red tie, white shirt and cufflinks. And more of that musky cologne. Again, I surprised myself by half-seriously wondering if we could just make a quick trip across the city to my apartment to have sex before we discussed business. If there was no time for that, we could use a bathroom stall at VHF.

We opted for large pilsners, and once the server settled them in front of us. I began.

"As it turns out, Omar, we are familiar with this man in France you mentioned." I nodded at the day's folded *Handelsblatt* newspaper I had set on the table in front of us. "What we know about him is on a piece of paper in there."

Omar said, "I see."

"He is indeed headed to Beirut to run counselor affairs at the French embassy. I think you'll find he will readily share information about intelligence matters but won't help if he thinks it could directly lead to violence. He doesn't work for money and has no women trouble, just wants to support anyone trying to bring down the capitalist system. We can pass a message to him if you like. Tell him you'd like to meet in France before he goes."

"Yes. Thank you."

"And how were your inquiries?" I asked.

Omar looked around our table. There was nobody close by, but he leaned in a bit nonetheless.

"The Mossad is not the only organization with spies. We have people in Mossad and Shin Bet in Israel. Mossad co-opted the woman in your organization back in the eighties. She had money problems."

Puzzled, I asked, "Why Mossad?"

"Gaddafi sold weapons to us as well as the IRA, and the same people in Libya organized it all. Sometimes they scheduled the weapons shipments one after another. One day us, the next day you, or the other way around. That's why Mossad wanted someone in the Provisionals, figuring if they knew about your shipment, they could look for one of ours around the same time."

"Did Mossad just pick up the phone and call the Brits when they got the information in '85?"

"I have no detail on that, but for some reason, Mossad tipped off MI-6."

I jumped in. "So, this woman, Sally Horrigan, tipped…"

Omar shook his head. "I never heard that name."

"Fine," I said, "but who got her out of Belfast?"

"Mossad," Omar said. "They resettled the woman and her three children in Tel Aviv right after it happened."

"She's in Tel Aviv?" I asked.

He shook his head again and took a long drink on his pilsner. "No, the US. She stayed in Tel Aviv until 1991, but the family never warmed to life in Israel. Imagine that." Omar grinned.

"Where in the US?" I pleaded, the tenuous grip on my cool reserve slipping.

"There, the trail goes somewhat cold, sadly." Omar sighed. "All my sources could learn was that she moved to the middle of the US sometime in 1991, and then Mossad severed ties. They moved her there, and they all kept their Israel identities. Mossad bought her a small house and arranged a job for her. And that was all. After that, she was on her own."

"Well, shit," I said. "We'll never find her in the US." I chuckled. "Omar, you're just a tease, in more ways than you know."

Omar gave me the what-do-I-know shrug of the shoulders.

"I have two last pieces of information, Klara. This woman has three children at university: Tracy in Wales; and Sean and Fergal, in the US. And her new name is Suzanne Harris. We know nothing more. The Mossad files are closed. This woman is long past for them."

I smiled broadly. "This is great, Omar, very helpful. Thank you. One last question…"

"Yes?"

"Sally Horrigan, now this Harris, betrayed the PLO as well as us. Why doesn't the PLO kill her?"

Omar finished his beer and wiped his mouth with a napkin. "We just learned of her not long ago, basically by accident. We are consumed by much bigger actions – airliners, weapons and such. We can't afford to go chasing someone like her." Then he laughed. "Though, we won't be sad should something happen to her."

46

St. Louis

Pursuant to Maeve's instructions, after Poland I'd quickly researched ways to kill someone so that they would die in agony. I settled on polonium-210 and signaled Pavel for what turned out to be our '94 Christmas Eve date at the Prater in Vienna.

Discovered in 1898 by Marie Curie, polonium was one of the world's deadliest substances. In fact, the most toxic substance known to man if swallowed, inhaled or otherwise ingested. It was thousands of times more lethal than cyanide and four hundred times more radioactive than uranium. The Soviets weaponized it and manufactured polonium-210 at a secret Siberian site beginning in 1952. It was estimated that a tiny amount was equivalent to the radiation of 175,000 X-rays and could kill or sicken up to a million people in ideal circumstances. A few micrograms, like a grain of sand, would kill anyone who ingested it.

My St. Louis apartment overlooked Sally Horrigan's house across the street. I spent the first two weeks watching her, tailing her in varied disguises and tracking her movements. She worked at a local CPA practice Monday to Friday in the Central West End. On Tuesday, Wednesday and Thursday nights she worked at a hockey bar, The Blue Line, in Dog Town near the arena where the St. Louis Blues played.

Sally had a boyfriend who stayed with her every Thursday through Monday morning. He seemed to work from the house on Fridays, as he spent the bulk of the day on the phone and in front of a computer. Fortunately, Sally and her boyfriend didn't seem to know their neighbors or interact with them. The small house next to hers was even vacant, with a for-sale sign in the front yard.

There was an alley behind her house, my best bet for entry to minimize being seen by others. I didn't yet have a concrete plan but had an idea, a hypothesis. I had to get into her house to confirm if it could work. I needed her to ingest the polonium-210, but I couldn't risk others coming into contact with it. Putting it in a drink in a public place or even around her house wouldn't do, as I couldn't have visitors to her house – the boyfriend, or anyone else – picking up an empty glass with traces of it or coming into contact with stray traces on a counter or table.

I brought the electronics and surveillance expert from Maeve's team over to St. Louis for a few days to set up hidden cameras and microphones inside Sally's house. He stayed in a hotel and we met in a coffee shop on a Monday in March, the day before our planned entry to the house. I'd never met or heard of him before. He looked like a teenager, was rail thin with blond hair and talked a lot. A lot!

"What do you need?" he asked.

"I need video and audio in the living room, kitchen, bathroom and bedroom, but first, I need you to check for any security systems: cameras, motion detectors and that kind of thing in her house. I need all the stuff you put in to feed into monitors in my apartment across the street."

"That won't work," he said. "You'll have to get into the house about every five days to remove the storage disks and replace them with new ones. Then you can watch the disks you removed at your apartment. Where are we entering the house?"

"Off the back alley."

"Who is this woman?"

"Better you not know."

"Thought you'd say that, but ya can't blame a guy for askin'." He laughed.

We were in the house the next day. He detected no surveillance or other security systems. If we were wrong about that and Sally saw evidence of us in her house, she might run for it in a panic. In which case, instead of an elegant poisoning, I'd have to perpetrate a messy, seemingly random shooting or stabbing.

I looked around her house. Her boyfriend's name was Bob Krause. Bob had some toiletries in the master bathroom and a few clothes in the closet, but not many. Clearly, his primary residence was elsewhere. They'd maybe only been together about a year – I saw no photos of them together earlier than 1993. They'd been to St. Thomas that winter on a cruise and had their picture taken on the dock. They'd been to California the prior summer: his and her mouse ears in a photo in a Disneyland '94 picture frame. Also, lots of pictures of her three kids and an older one with Sally, three very young kids, and another guy. It looked like a family shot from years before.

I found the rolling garbage can in the single-car garage and sifted through it, making notes. Several empty wine and Irish whiskey bottles, four pairs of stained, beat-up panties with holes, takeout cartons for Chinese food, two empty Famous Barr department store shopping bags, various empty containers for spices, and other food and baking items. There were also a dozen plastic tampon applicators and four rolled-up used sanitary napkins.

I went back to Sally's master bathroom. No birth control pills but a diaphragm and spermicidal jelly, antacid, Tylenol, shampoo, two toothbrushes, a razor, shaving cream, toothpaste, mouthwash, hair dryer, hairbrushes and minimal makeup. I hadn't yet found what I was looking for.

Ah, there, in the bottom drawer of her vanity: a ninety-six-count box of Kotex super plus tampons with plastic applicators, a large box of overnight maxi pads and a box of panty liners. Tampons by day, maxis overnight, and panty liners for the tail end of her period was my guess.

Even if Sally only used three tampons a day, say for four days, that would be twelve tampons a month, minimum – more likely at least fifteen. There were forty-nine tampons remaining in the Kotex box. I took three of them and put them in my pocket.

Perfect. My hypothesis could work. I'd found my murder weapon. It would be the most expensive tampon in the world, in more ways than one.

Judging by the contents of her trash can, I guessed she was at or near the end of her period for March. Counting the months ahead at twenty-eight-day intervals, I had my windows for when it might happen. The half-life of polonium-210 was one hundred and thirty-eight days, so I would put enough into a few tampons to do the job, even if it took a few months.

I had a desk and chair in my storage unit in Brentwood, along with my two hazmat suits. I bought a box of tampons exactly like Sally's and began practicing. I needed to unseal the top of the individual tampon wrapper, slide the tampon partially out of the wrapper, and apply tiny drops of liquid – water in my practice runs – then reseal the wrapper with a tiny amount of glue with the tampon in it.

A super tampon would hold nine to twelve grams of fluid. I was going to apply as small an amount of polonium-210 as I could manage, but not enough to make the tampon expand in the applicator. I learned this as I practiced. I dropped the water right at the tip of the tampon since that was the easiest place to apply it and was also the part that would be farthest into her body. I used gloves and wore the hazmat suit in my practice runs since I would be wearing those when it counted. In no time, I'd burned through my ninety-six-count box and would ultimately go through three more similar boxes before I was confident enough to drop the poison in.

It was now mid-April, and Sally continued her weekly routine with no real variations. By my admittedly imprecise calculations – who knew if her periods were regular – she should be getting it again within a week. The audio and video from her house were unremarkable; she gave no signs of knowing she was being watched.

By now, thanks to the surveillance tapes, I'd learned some details about her kids. She had Tracy, a twenty-year-old daughter at college in Wales; and two sons, Sean, a college sophomore at Xavier in Cincinnati, and Fergal, a freshman at Boston College. Sally was thirty-seven.

On a Wednesday afternoon in mid-April, I slipped back inside Sally's house after she'd left for work and replaced the three tampons I'd originally taken. They now contained the poison that would kill her anytime in the next three months if all went according to plan. There was the same number of tampons in the box, so none had been used since March. Her trash cans also revealed no signs of a recent visit from Aunt Flo. Of course, the whole thing wouldn't work if Sally and Bob had recently decided to try to start a family and Sally was pregnant.

Sally left for work on Thursday but didn't return that night. And didn't return for the next several days. *Oh great. Was she with Bob somewhere?* He lived in Memphis, I'd figured out. He was divorced with two teenage kids who lived with his ex in the original family home. Maybe that explained why Sally never went to Memphis to see him. *Until now, maybe?*

Or had Sally gotten spooked and run? If so, she was already a ghost. I'd gotten lazy and careless. I should have kept surveilling her. If she was gone, my standing in the organization – everything I'd worked for – would be damaged. Could it even be fatal to me?

Would people think me untrustworthy – someone who purposely failed to deliver because they had other loyalties?

More importantly, I'd have lost my opportunity to avenge Adaoma. Nothing to do but wait and see if Sally returned.

47

Sally Horrigan: April 1995

Suzanne Harris (Sally Horrigan) checked into Chicago's Westin River North on a sunny, seventy-degree April day. She was giddy with excitement, looking forward to a mother-daughter long weekend with Tracy where they could share the room and talk and talk into the wee hours. She'd spent a weekend with Tracy between Christmas and New Year's in her dorm room when she'd come over from Wales to start her semester abroad at Northwestern, but since then hadn't seen her.

Tracy squealed with delight when Sally opened her hotel room door. She practically ran into Sally's arms, squeezing her for what seemed like minutes. After a long hug, Sally took a step back and said, "Ah, you look great, my darling!"

Tracy had her mother's eyes, sparkling, perfect teeth and a warm smile, but in most other ways, she looked like her father. Five-nine with auburn hair that dropped well below her shoulders, she had a roundish face with the warm, soft facial features of her father and a nicely proportioned body. Tracy had won a full tuition and living stipend fellowship at Aberystwyth University in Wales. She would return next fall to begin her senior year, and her plan was then to head directly to medical school.

"Ah, mam, it's so good to see you. You look great too."

"Oh, Tracy, it's been too long. I miss you something terrible. I think about you and the boys about fifty times a day."

Tracy and Sally went out to dinner Friday night, shopped and

"

walked around all day Saturday, and got takeout Chinese to eat in the room that night.

Tracy passed Sally a carton of lo mein and said, "So, I've got something to tell you. I've met a guy."

Sally smiled and raised her eyebrows. "Really? Good on you. Of course, I want to know everything, but I suspect you won't tell me."

Tracy laughed. "He's Irish. Name is Tom, and he's at Northwestern like me, doing a semester abroad. He goes to Trinity in Dublin."

"I'm so happy for you. Do you love him, ya think? I know it's early, but I knew with your da right off."

Tracy blushed and shrugged her shoulders. "Maybe. It feels like it, but we'll see."

"When do I get to meet him, sweetie?"

"Memorial Day weekend. Tom and I are thinking we'd come down to St. Louis. Besides, I need to meet this Mr. Bob, make sure he's good enough for you. I'm glad you've found someone who makes you feel special."

The next day Tracy and Sally checked out of the Westin, stored their bags with the bellman, and went to brunch at a small restaurant with a view of Lake Michigan on Navy Pier. After brunch, they sat on a bench at the end of the pier and looked out over the lake. Tracy touched Sally's hand and said, "Can I ask you something?" I've wanted to ask for a long time, but have been afraid."

Sally turned to look at her. "Of course. What?"

Tracy took a deep breath, gathered herself a bit in on the bench and asked, "I know you've always said we changed our name to Harris from Horrigan when we moved to Israel because Dad's brothers were trying to take Sean, Fergal and me from you. But why did we move to Israel? I mean, why not England or France or the US? You always said you got a good job in Tel Aviv, but I don't know – weren't there good jobs closer to Ireland?"

Sally had always known this day would come.

"I don't know, mam, it doesn't all quite fit together the more I think about it."

A breeze had kicked up off Lake Michigan, and Tracy's long beautiful hair was blowing into her face, but she sat, staring at Sally.

Just jump in and tell her everything. She needs to know this. "Tracy, when you and the boys was little, your da wasn't killed in an accident with a lorry like I always said."

"No? What happened then?"

"Your da was in the Provisionals. He was important, a man movin' up. But there was this operation, and a man on his team was drunk and didn't know his work, and he set a bomb off by mistake, killin' them all. A tragic accident. I still get upset thinkin' 'bout the unfairness of it all."

Sally crisply filled in other details: the military barracks, the drunk bomber from Omagh whose father protected him from facing justice, her inability to let it go, her eating and money troubles, troubles from George's family who wanted her kids and wanted to introduce them into that life someday.

Tracy looked stunned.

"My da was a terrorist?"

Sally violently shook her head.

"No! He was a soldier, fightin' for a cause he believed in – a cause his countrymen and ancestors had fought and died for, for generations. A fight for a united Ireland and freedom from the boot the British always held at our throats."

Tracy looked confused, even unbelieving. "But he killed people. Those soldiers in the barracks."

"We never talked 'bout the specifics of his work, but yes, that time, yes. But, sweetie, people die in war. They aren't murdered. They are the price paid for the hopes and freedoms of future generations. Your da did what he did and died for you and for me and the boys."

Tracy pulled her knees up to her chin and looked over them at Sally.

"Tracy, it was a cause I believed in, too. Your da and I were one in that regard. You know, all truth here, I worked for the Provisionals too.

"What? Mam, no!"

"Not anything like your da. I was just a clerk, keepin' track of a wee bit a money here and there."

Even though the wind was blowing harder at the end of Navy Pier, pushing clouds over the sun, Sally clearly heard Tracy's next quiet question.

"So, was my uncles trying to take us from you the only reason we moved to Israel?"

Sally sat for over a minute, silently staring out over the water, full of sailboats on this beautiful day. Down the way, an older couple was sitting on another bench holding hands with a radio tuned to the Cubs game. They were up three to two in the bottom of the seventh. Scents of popcorn and hot dogs from a nearby food cart wafted by.

"Mam?"

Sally closed her eyes. "I'm just gonna say this. I ain't proud of it and I'd give almost anything to take it back. But I can't."

Tracy, knees still parked under her chin, brushed her hair out of her eyes with her right hand and waited.

"My world ended after George died. Weren't for you and the boys, I'da just killed myself and gone to hell probably for that sin. I had no money, my health was bad, my sister was dying, and your da's family was after alla you. The Provisionals moved my job to Belfast to get us away from South Armagh, but it wasn't enough. The problems kept on, and George's brothers kept after you and the boys in the courts."

"I know it was really hard for you."

"Then this man Simon from the Mossad in Israel shows up one day and says if I just give a bit-a harmless information now and again, they'd pay me every month. It wasn't a lot of money, maybe, but it helped. I needed it."

"What kind of information?"

"It was supposed to be stuff to help Israel fight the PLO in the Middle East that would not hurt the Provisionals. I thought that's what I gave 'em – just one time only, mind you. But it turned out it made its way to the Brits, and they used it to kill over thirty of our people."

Tracy's mouth dropped open.

"Once it happened, this guy Simon shows up again and says the Provisionals are going to kill me 'cause they'd figure soon enough I was a traitor. And he was right. Remember, when he and I and you kids ran out of our flat in Divis with just our clothes and that man chasin' us?"

"But you said those were people dad's family sent to kidnap us."

"No. Was the Provos. The Mossad got us out of Ireland and had us in Tel Aviv within a couple of days, and we was there till I came here."

Sally paused, and after a few seconds, Tracy, still pulled up into a ball on the bench, said, "Go on."

"Simon and his people got us a flat, found me a job, and gave us all our new name and passports. We were citizens of Israel. I didn't want to go there – my parents was in Ireland, your cousins too. But we had no choice, Tracy; you gotta believe me. They was gonna kill me, and you and the boys've been orphans or sucked into the IRA life by your da's family. I'd-a died to keep you out of that. I never saw my parents again. But I did it all for you, Sean and Fergal."

Tracy scooted closer to Sally on the bench, wrapped her arms around her and rested her head on her shoulder.

"I believe you. But I feel bad for you. And I'll do nothing but worry now. The Provisionals, they could kill you."

Sally nodded. "I thought that all the time in Israel, but the Mossad swore nothing would happen to us there. They didn't want me to move to the US, but ya know, the boys wanted to come here, and I'da never seen 'em if I'd stayed in Israel."

"I see that."

"And ya know, it's been ten years. I hope that either they've forgotten or, if not, they won't be able to find me. I have a gun in my house in case someone wants to try and come for me."

48

Alex

Fortunately, Sally returned home after her weekend away. It was April, and depending on Sally's tampon/pad usage mix, I could be watching her until July unless she bought more or decided to quit tampons, change brands, or whatever. I went back into Sally's house to replace the audio/video recorder disk on the Thursday leading into Memorial Day weekend. As usual, I entered off the back alley using the key I'd made. After about thirty minutes I was in the master bath counting tampons – all as expected. I was about to head through the living room toward the back door off the small eat-in kitchen when a key turned in the front door, and a man and woman walked in.

"Hi mam. You here?" We're early."

Shit!

I ducked into the cramped walk-in master closet and closed the pocket door behind me. Extinguishing the light, I stood amidst Sally's clothes. I was able to partially see through the louvers in the closet door. The door to the master was right off the living room, as was the door to the second bedroom on the other side of the living room. The kitchen and back door sat diagonally across from the master via the living room.

I can't run out the front door because I don't know who might see me leave. Better to stick with the alley through the back door.

The woman, who I figured must be Sally's daughter Tracy, spoke. "I figured she would still be at work. I'll call her and let her know we're in." She walked into the master bedroom, sat on the bed, picked up the nightstand phone and dialed.

"Hey, where's the toilet?" the man asked. "I've had to pee since we crossed the river."

"Just use the bathroom in here, Tom." Then her voice changed tone. "Hi there! We got outta Chicago early and are here. Yes, we're at the house. Don't worry about us, we'll see you after work. Oh, you can? Grand, see you soon."

Tom returned and sat on the bed with Tracy. "Ah, much better. Did you get hold of your mother?"

"Yes, she'll be here in about fifteen minutes. She's leaving work early."

I checked my watch: 15:40. My nine-millimeter was in a holster in my back, but I wasn't going to run for the alley in a blaze of gunfire. These were innocent people and a Dodge City scene wouldn't do. I just needed Tracy and the guy to get distracted, so I could run.

Someone was opening drawers in the bedroom. Tracy said, "Oh wow, there it is."

"There's what?" Tom asked.

"My mother told me last month she keeps a gun in the house, and I just found it."

"What kind?"

"I've no idea. I hate guns, don't know anything about them."

"Hand it here. I target shoot."

"What? You never told me."

"On the farm at home. Trace, this is a nine-millimeter Glock semi-automatic."

"Is it loaded?"

"Yes, the magazine is here, but the safety's on. You pop the magazine out like this and then just click it back in. Then you put the safety on. Maybe you and I should go shooting sometime. I'll show you how. It's really very safe."

"Hmm, we'll have to see about that. I'm gonna make some drinks for all of us."

"Great idea," Tom said. "What are we having?"

As they left the bedroom, Tracy said, "Don't know yet. What are you doing, Tom? You're bringing the gun into the kitchen?"

"Why not? I want to look at it a bit more."

Great! Now he's sitting in the kitchen with a loaded Glock and presumably knows how to use it.

Hearing them clanking about in the kitchen, I wrapped a sweater from the closet around my face like a hijab, only my eyes visible. I pushed the closet door open, and looked out. They were only about thirty feet away in the kitchen, but I couldn't see them. I would need to count on surprise and run right past them, behind them, to get out the back door.

Face covered, I ran for it. But as I left the master, I tripped over a weekend bag they'd dropped on the living room floor just as the two of them walked into the living room. The guy still had the Glock. I went down hard, and my face covering dropped away. *You fucking idiot!*

Stunned, the woman stared at me for what felt like a half hour. "Tom, call the police! Call the police!"

I got up and ran past them out the back door. I flew down the alley, hit the first cross-street, and began a weaving sprint back to my apartment, with a few stops along the way to make sure nobody was watching. Soon police sirens, growing louder, rang in my ears.

By the time I'd slipped back into my apartment, two police cruisers, Sally's car, a sedan with Tennessee plates and a coupe from Illinois were either crowded into the one-lane driveway or on the street.

I didn't expect Sally to be spooked and flee in the middle of the night after all that, but I needed to make sure. I was up all night watching her house.

Now that Sally's daughter was in the house, I had to hope she wouldn't need to borrow tampons. Though I knew about collateral damage in war, I couldn't have an innocent person die because of me. There was nothing I could do but wait and hope for no tragic accident. I also couldn't shake the feeling that Tracy had burned my face into her memory as I fled the house.

49

Sally Horrigan

The police took a description of the intruder from Tracy and Tom, saying there had been a spate of robberies in the general area over the past few months.

Sally looked carefully for missing valuables and, finding none, thought that perhaps Tracy and Tom had surprised the thief before she could take anything. This was little consolation to Tracy, mindful of their conversation in Chicago. She told Sally she'd read more dangerous, darker things into the unexpected visitor, but Sally dismissed those worries.

Later, Sally, Bob, Tracy and Tom had a late dinner at an Italian place on the Hill and stayed up late, laughing and getting acquainted. Friday's plans included sleeping in, having brunch in Clayton, visiting Forest Park and the Central West End, and going to the Cardinals game that night. Sally awoke, put on makeup, brushed her teeth and hair and inserted a tampon. Her period had arrived yesterday, right on schedule.

Sally was on her second cup of coffee when Tracy emerged from the guest room with sleepy eyes, wearing a long Chicago Bears football jersey as her nightshirt.

"Hi, sweetie. Hope you and Tom had a good sleep."

"We did, thanks. Tom's getting a shower."

Sally enthused, "Even though it's going to be hot, I can't wait to show you and Tom around the city today."

Tracy nodded. "Us too." She picked up a cup from the table and walked to the coffeemaker in the kitchen. "Uh hey, didn't expect this, but it seems I got my visitor last night, a few days early this month, for whatever reason. Do you have any tampons? Can I bum a few from you? I'll get some when we're out later."

"Of course, in my bathroom, bottom drawer. Use as many as you need. I got pads too, if that suits you better."

Tracy wrinkled her nose. "Oh no, Mum, tampons only unless it's overnight."

"Okay, let me go get a few for you since Bob's still asleep in the bedroom."

"Grand, thanks."

• • •

Sally, Bob, Tracy and Tom were eating at a busy restaurant in Clayton later that day, Friday. Brunch entailed a massive buffet with seemingly endless breakfast offerings as well as fruit, pasta, roast beef, vegetable, casserole and shrimp dishes. Sally told Tom and Tracy how she'd met George all those years ago and had everyone laughing with stories of how their first two dates had ended badly. On the first, Sally had found George "too fresh," and on the second, George's former girlfriend saw them in a pub and made a scene. Telling these stories felt good for Sally. She'd finally reached the point where any mention of George didn't hit her with sadness. And it was good that Bob enjoyed the stories, too.

Tom then told everyone about his family near Cork and how he'd seen Tracy in class at Northwestern and had told himself, "I must meet that woman."

Mid-afternoon, as they were finishing brunch, intense stomach pain doubled Sally over. She cried out and dropped to her knees. Tom, Tracy and Bob hustled her to the car and quickly drove her home. She began vomiting before they could get back to the house, and she spent the rest of the afternoon throwing up every twenty or thirty minutes. At first, she thought it was just food poisoning, but the vomiting continued, and by evening, explosive, bloody diarrhea had also begun.

50

Tracy Harris

After midnight on what was now Saturday morning, Bob and Tom carried Sally into Bob's car and rushed her to the ER at Barnes Hospital. Doctors gave her IV fluids, Cipro for any infection, and Zofran to try to quell her vomiting, but these didn't help.

After four hours in a bed in the ER, Sally's blood tests came back, showing plunging white blood cell counts. Though the cell counts were not consistent with severe gastroenteritis, the doctors admitted her to the hospital, suspecting a severe infection of some sort. By late afternoon, the severe gastrointestinal symptoms persisted, and Sally had developed painful ulcerating blisters all over her body, including in her mouth, nose, eyes, ears, vagina and rectum.

The following Saturday, a week later at this point, Sally was still in intensive care. After steadily ruling out one condition after another, specialists at Barnes began to tell Tracy they wondered about radiation poisoning. They passed a Geiger counter over Sally, but nothing registered.

"So, it's not radiation poisoning?" Tracy asked one of the doctors.

"It's highly unlikely to be that," he said. "Only a few exotic forms of radiation won't register on a Geiger counter."

"Like what, doctor?"

"Well, alpha radiation for one, but in thirty years of medicine, I've never seen it affect anyone. Alpha radiation only comes off of things like plutonium, polonium and americium."

"So, we're no closer to an answer then," Tracy said, discouraged.

"Tracy, we still suspect a particularly virulent antibiotic-resistant infection or some kind of rare virus."

"Will you be able to pinpoint it before it kills her?" Tracy asked, her eyes glistening.

"We hope so, of course. But honestly, Tracy, we don't know."

Within two weeks, still in the ICU, Sally was lapsing in and out of consciousness. Bob (Tom had returned to Chicago after a few days) tried, usually unsuccessfully, to get Tracy and Sally's sons, who had rushed home from college, to leave their mother's side for twenty-four hours to rest.

Most of Tracy's days were spent worrying about her mother and trying to keep her positive and comfortable. She also tried to provide support to her brothers. The doctors were great and assured her they hoped to solve the mystery and save her mother. Tracy prayed for that countless times a day; she couldn't imagine life without her mother. She tried to push all negative thoughts away but felt she was losing the battle, feebly trying to stamp out flames of panic as the blaze engulfed everything around her.

Tracy couldn't shake the nagging questions. Did this have something to do with the woman who'd broken into the house on Thursday? And what about her mother's history with the Provisionals?

51

Alex

Around 02:00 in the early Saturday morning of Memorial Day weekend, lit by street lights, I saw Bob and Tom carry Sally out the front door and lay her down in the back seat of Bob's car. Tracy jumped in the back with her, with Bob driving and Tom in the passenger seat. Had the polonium done its job? Bob and the boyfriend Tom finally returned to the house late Saturday afternoon. *Where was Sally? In the hospital, hopefully, but what about Tracy? No!* I was frantic. My stomach was jumping. Was Tracy poisoned now? *Damn! What if I killed her too!*

I called around to all the hospitals in town, saying I was a friend of Suzanne Harris, and I'd heard she'd been admitted to the hospital and asked if they could connect me to her room. No luck until I called Barnes Hospital, who confirmed she was a patient but would disclose nothing else other than she wasn't receiving visitors or taking calls. Then I called all the hospitals back, asking if a Tracy Harris had been admitted. No, at least not yet.

I figured Sally had used one, maybe two, of the poisoned tampons. That meant one or two remained, hopefully still in the box and not in Tracy or in her purse. I had to get back into the house to replace the whole box of tampons with new ones and also remove the hidden cameras and recorders. When I was sure nobody was home, I ducked into the house and got everything done.

I called the hospitals every day asking about a patient named Tracy Harris, relieved every time I heard there wasn't anyone there with that name. I finally spotted her back at the house on Wednesday with her boyfriend, five days after I'd seen her last.

52

Tracy Harris

Tracy, eyes moist on the kneeler in the hospital chapel, prayed for her mother to live on a Wednesday morning in mid-June. She was in the chapel at least once a day and had been ever since Sally had taken ill. Tracy prayed to Jesus, Mary and St. Jude, the patron saint of lost causes, for a miracle. Her mother had been in the ICU for almost three weeks and was slipping away. Tracy knew it. Bob still came to the hospital every day for several hours, but he mainly left the field to Tracy, Sean and Fergal, perhaps Tracy thought, feeling himself an intruder into their anguish.

The next evening, Thursday, near midnight, Sally's children slept, the three of them piled into a small loveseat in her room. Tracy sat between Sean and Fergal, their heads resting on each of her shoulders. Suddenly, loud alarms on equipment attached to Sally wailed. Two nurses rushed in, called a "Code Blue," and soon, more nurses and two doctors arrived.

Tracy and the boys stood on the loveseat to see over those working on Sally. Tracy had her arms around each of her brothers.

"It's okay, Sean, it's okay, Fergal," she sobbed. "We said our goodbyes early today, and every day before that since we knew the end could come anytime. She knew we loved her with everything we had."

The boys cried softly, and then Fergal yelped, "Why is this happening? What are we going to do?"

With that, Tracy cried harder.

Lost amid clouds of grief, Tracy insisted on an autopsy. But this failed to find the root cause of Sally's sickness. Her death certificate read, 'Cardiac arrest and multiple organ failure resulting from a potent infection or virus of unknown type or origin.'

53

Alex

The three kids returned to the house early on Friday morning. Tracy was crying; the two boys looked stunned. I called Barnes and asked the operator to put me through to Suzanne Harris's room. I got the nurses' station in the ICU.

"Oh my god, she died! What… why, um, how? Oh, I can't believe it! My goodness, she was my close friend, and I was hoping to come see her, but they always said she couldn't have visitors. What did she die of? What happened?"

"I'm sorry, Mrs… um, what was your name?"

"Landry, Alice Landry. Suzanne and I used to work together, and we are great friends. Oh my god, this is just awful, so unexpected."

"Mrs. Landry, I'm very sorry, but I can't give you any information on her condition. She passed away last night. Perhaps you can talk to her family for more details."

"Yes, wow, okay, thank you. I will speak with her daughter."

I left town within twenty-four hours. Cleaned out everything from the apartment, sold the car for cash to a mom-and-pop lot on the Illinois side, started a late-night dumpster fire to burn the wooden table and chair from the storage locker, and sank the hazmat suits in a weighted trunk as well as the tiny remaining amount of polonium in a locked lead container. Dropped them in the Mississippi River a hundred miles south of St. Louis around two in the morning.

54

Alex: June – November 1995

In addition to the polonium I got in Canada, I'd asked Pavel to place a small amount in a secure container in locker 473 at the Gare du Nord in Paris. I had other plans for that. I retrieved it later that summer and brought it to Berlin.

I spent the summer of '95 reintegrating into my life in Berlin. Petra Müller returned to work from her three-month leave of absence. I explained to curious coworkers and neighbors that I had gone to Switzerland for three months to have some "woman surgery" (less likely to get questions about something like that) and had recuperated with family near Zurich. "Mir geht es jetz viel besser, danke." *I'm feeling much better now, thank you.*

That summer, so as not to be in one place too long, Petra Müller moved house, as the British say, from her flat in the Mitte district to another in the Kreuzberg area of Berlin. Kreuzberg was part of West Berlin before the wall fell in '89 and the epicenter of the punk, techno and counter-cultural art and music scene for decades. It was slowly giving way to a gentrifying hip bar, restaurant, club and gallery scene.

In mid-October, a flyer arrived in my post box advertising a show by the Lipizzaner Stallions in Vienna on 21 October through 28 October. My signal from Pavel for a meeting on the first day of the performance at our usual time and place. When I'd met with Pavel over six months before to request the polonium, I had asked for something else, information on the whereabouts of a particular individual whom I thought traveled to Europe regularly.

I didn't tell Pavel why, but I did say that for reasons particular to my organization, this information request needed to be "off the books." In exchange, I told him that the IRA had a low-level tout in the British embassy in Casablanca, who was working with a Soviet diplomat there to embezzle money from Russian embassy accounts. When he asked why the IRA would burn one of its own British informers to have the Russians track the individual I'd mentioned, I gave him no information, saying only that this was for a larger cause.

• • •

I met – well, Inge Marstellar met – Pavel at his church in Vienna, at our usual spot, at 03:00. I saw he had a suitcase packed near his desk.

I asked, "*Sieht aus, als wolltest du wohin?*" Going somewhere?

"Yes, I'm going to a Catholic bishops' academic conference in Madrid." He smiled mirthfully and said, "It's about the book of Ecclesiastes and how we must better understand that things are not always what they seem."

I grinned. "I can't imagine that, Father."

Pavel got right down to business. "Inge, my flight is at six and I need to tidy up some paperwork regarding the repair of our stained-glass windows before I go."

"Okay, sure."

"It seems this person of interest to you, or to your organization, perhaps, comes to Helsinki every three months. He sits on the supervisory board of a local company and attends its quarterly meetings."

I raised my eyebrows and gave Pavel a little grin.

"He flies in the afternoon before the meeting and has dinner with other board members that night. Afterward, he entertains two prostitutes, together, in his hotel room. He's in meetings the next day from 07:00 to about 16:00 and then stops at an old seafarer's bar down the street from his hotel and drinks alone."

"What does he drink?"

"Johnnie Walker Blue. I can't imagine anyone else who drinks there could afford it, so they must have it especially for him."

"Okay. Then what?"

"Back to his hotel room and he leaves the next day.

"Anything else?"

"The next scheduled board meeting for this organization is in November."

"Does he travel alone?"

"He seems to, though we can't be positive about that." Pavel grinned. "This man of interest to you, or to the Provisional IRA let's say, he sounds like a lost soul. Perhaps you can bring him to confession, and I can help him? Maybe if he unburdens himself, I will understand why he is so interesting to you. What do you say, Inge?"

I chuckled. "I don't think so. He will need to find salvation without you."

• • •

The streets of Helsinki transported me back to Timberline. I didn't want them to, but the memories crashed in, like cops knocking a door off my mental hinges with a battering ram.

I closed my eyes and the sounds, smells and images of Timberline came rushing sweetly back. It was late afternoon in TL, cold mist amidst dimming light, battleship gray sky with no clouds. A stiff wind carried the smell of wood smoke and approaching winter. It was November 1, 1981 – what seemed like three lifetimes ago, someone else's life – but no, it was mine, fourteen years distant. I was walking from Timberline High's main building across campus to The Barn. The first day of basketball practice, and the magical smells of basketball season in that regal, majestic arena wrapped me in a warm embrace.

The sounds of bouncing balls, shoes squeaking on the wooden floor, the coach's whistle, and then, of course, yelling directed at my friend, Fogg. "God damn it, Blackpool, quit screwing around and get your head in the game! I'm not gonna be putting up with your shit all season."

Brian, Tim, Fogg and the others were kicking off their senior season as defending state champions. It was also the first day of winter cheerleading practice upstairs in The Barn near a railing overlooking the court. After a winless football season, everyone was ready for basketball. Anticipation hung in the air with the winter fog and mist.

I was in the Katajanokka section of Helsinki, surrounded on three sides by the Gulf of Finland, a mile or so from the Lutheran cathedral in the center of the harbor. It was a largely residential area, lower-income housing with assorted street-level retail. There was also a prison; its high brick walls and armed guard towers had housed Finnish criminals since 1837. Past the prison around a sharp corner, two of Finland's ocean-going icebreakers bobbed in the whitecaps of the harbor, resting for the coming working season.

A quarter mile farther along the waterfront was a relatively nice section of two- and three-star hotels, small restaurants and hole-in-the-wall bars. My destination loomed ahead, *Karhun Kaareva*, roughly translated as the *Bear's Lair*. I'd been there yesterday and the day before, making and double-checking arrangements.

I was disguised – poorly as it turned out – as Bridgett Schmidt, a German living in Helsinki who didn't speak much Finnish. Fortunately, Niklas, the bartender at *Karhun Kaareva*, spoke German. I'd told him I suspected my boyfriend, a much older man, was having an affair and planned to meet his mistress at the bar two nights hence. With some financial inducement, I persuaded Niklas to let me lurk behind the bar that night in the shadows to see the mystery woman.

If Pavel's intel was correct, the target, Win Blackpool, would arrive before 18:00, sit alone at a two-person table in front and drink Johnnie Walker Blue from an unopened bottle the bartender would have for him and leave on the table. Win would return to his hotel up the street after an hour or two.

Tonight, the beginning of the end for Win if all went well, I was behind the bar at 16:00, but by 18:30, he was thirty minutes late. *Where the hell was he? Not coming?* The bartender asked me in German if maybe my boyfriend didn't really have a mistress, or maybe he did and was already off with her. "Vielleicht schrauben sie schon." He laughed. *Probably they are already screwing.*

I checked the bottle of Johnnie Walker Blue with its drops of polonium in the backpack at my feet. I'd spent only two weeks in Berlin after getting the information from Pavel in Vienna. That was all the time I had. I practiced getting the liquid in the bottle and resealing it. As in St. Louis, I'd practiced in a small rented warehouse space. The biggest challenge was getting the bottle resealed without looking like I'd used a chainsaw to do it. I burned through ten bottles of the stuff practicing.

Plan A was to replace the bar's unopened bottle of Johnnie Walker Blue with mine when Win ordered. If Win didn't show or opted to drink wine or beer, I would need Plans B or C – opportunistic, messier and much riskier for me – at Win's hotel up the street or somewhere else close by. I had a sealed hypodermic with a massive dose of fentanyl and, if all else failed, a nine-millimeter Sig Sauer with a silencer. Why Plan A and not B or C, anyway? Because, like Sally Horrigan, Win needed to suffer horribly.

The bar was smoky, filling up, but not that noisy – an older, quiet-conversation sort of clientele. *Hold My Hand* by Hootie and the Blowfish was playing at light volume on the sound system. At 18:45, Win Blackpool walked through the door alone and sat by himself at a table in the front by the window. He wore a gray suit, white shirt and a bright green tie loosened at the neck.

I looked over at Niklas and nodded. He walked over to me and, in German, said Win was a regular in the bar but only came in a handful of times a year and always expected a new bottle of Johnnie Walker Blue. He seemed surprised that this could be my boyfriend, he'd never seen him with a woman and certainly not recently. But before he could ask me anything, he turned his back to take an order from someone at the bar. I quickly replaced the bar's unopened bottle of Johnnie Walker Blue, its only one, with mine, Johnnie Walker Blue Polonium.

I needed Win to open the bottle, pour a glass – just one – and drink deeply, imbibing the justice I'd sought since 1984 when Julie told me her story on the beach in LA. By 19:30, he'd had two glasses and poured a third. More than enough.

Just then, a man and woman, each in business suits, walked in and ordered beers at the bar. The guy said something like, "Ah," tapped his companion, and pointed at Win by the window. Win saw the Finnish couple and motioned them over. *Dammit!*

Then another individual entered the bar and walked straight to Win's table. *Hmm, now what's he doing here?* It was Steve Lonsdale, an executive colleague of my father's at Blackpool Industries. Lonsdale, the head of human resources, who, drunk again, had broadsided Julie's mother and killed her that snowy night in Timberline in December 1979. Also the guy responsible for the death of the nineteen-year-old girl in the botched Oregon abortion. He'd probably continued ruining the lives of countless others. Lonsdale was as corpulent as ever: probably six-five and over three hundred pounds, sweat pasting his comb-over to his forehead like bad wallpaper. *Justice times two, maybe?*

Win, apparently thinking I was a waitress, waved to catch my attention at the bar and motioned for three more glasses. He stared at me a bit too long, his mental wheels turning like I was familiar, but he couldn't place exactly how. I'd been hurried and careless leaving Berlin and wasn't heavily disguised, wearing only a brunette wig over my blonde hair. I acknowledged Win's request and retreated behind the bar to get more glasses.

I told Niklas that the people at Win's table needed three more glasses. He started to ask… I knew what he was thinking. How could Win have asked me for more glasses and not recognized me, his supposed girlfriend?

I gave Niklas no time to finish his question and quickly walked from behind the bar toward the short hallway that led to the bathrooms. On the way, sitting at the last table before the bathrooms, I saw someone else I recognized in my peripheral vision.

This has the potential to be a clusterfuck.

I need a diversion, I thought as I stood at the bathroom sink. I saw my answer in the overflowing trash bin in the ladies' room. I peeked out the door and saw Niklas deliver the three extra glasses to Win's table. Nobody moved to take them. The Finnish couple were still finishing their beers and talking to Win and Lonsdale. I actually hoped Lonsdale would pour himself some Johnnie Walker.

I hustled back behind the bar, grabbed the squirt bottle of kerosene Niklas used to start coals in the two fireplaces, stuffed it under my shirt, and went back to the bathroom. I poured the entire bottle into the trash can full of paper and lit it on fire. Immediately the can was ablaze, belching flames and smoke. Outside the toilet, I pulled the fire alarm and ran into the bar area, yelling and waving my arms. Smoke was now pouring out under the bathroom door.

"Feuer! Feuer! Ausgang, schnell!" I screamed.

Niklas, confused, pointed at the front door and started herding people out. But Win and his companions weren't moving.

I ran up to them and yelled, "Out, out!" in English. Then swept the still-empty new whiskey glasses onto the floor, shattering them. Finally, Win and his guests slowly got up and began moving toward the front door.

The smoke was much thicker now. I put on thick gloves from my backpack, re-corked the Johnnie Walker, and carefully placed it in the lead container in the backpack.

Win was almost out the door when he saw this. He headed back toward me, shouting.

"Hey, stop right there! What are you doing? Who are you?"

I ran for it. Grabbed a bar towel and wrapped it around my face as I moved through the choking smoke to the back door. Flames were climbing the walls of the ladies' toilet and had already spread into the bar area. A pile of construction materials inside by the back door near the bathroom was also burning. Out the door, I emerged into a back alley, the European-sounding sirens of the approaching police and fire brigade drawing close, a freight train in full alternating whistles rounding a bend for the station.

Before I could break into a sprint, someone hit me in the forehead with something and knocked me down. Falling forward, I used my body to protect the backpack with the polonium bottle. Sprawled on the ground, I wiped the blood running down my face from the fresh cut on my forehead and looked up.

Steve Lonsdale stood before me, holding a piece of two-by-four in his left hand. *I'd lost track of him, a mistake.* He'd hit me with a piece of lumber from the construction scrap pile inside, where a storage room was being converted to more seating. He was panting heavily and had a gun pointed at me. It looked like a .22. Whether he could hit anything accurately, I didn't know.

"I don't know who the hell you are or what you're doing with that bottle you stole off the table," he snarled, "but we're just going to wait until the police get here, and you can explain it to them."

Now sitting on the ground, I stared up at him, mute like the moai statues on Easter Island. Obviously, I couldn't let him keep me there waiting for the police. Could I get to the holstered Sig Sauer in the small of my back and draw on him before he shot me? Doubtful. I'd have to bet on him missing at point-blank range. Bad odds.

Get him talking, distracted, then roll over, go for the gun, and take your chances. You have to get out of here. "Steve Lonsdale, still a pig, I see. Killer of Julie Mitchell's mother and who knows how many others."

It took him a few moments to process this. "Hey! You're Alexandra Davis, Mike's daughter," Lonsdale sputtered. "What are you doing here? You died years ago."

"Obviously not, Steve. I came to kill Win Blackpool. And I did. Now I'll get to kill you too."

Nervous now, shaking his gun at me a little, he said, "What? Win just walked out the front door. You're fucking crazy. The police will be here soon."

The back door swung abruptly open, and the man I'd seen back by the toilets stepped toward Lonsdale and hit him in the head twice with another piece of two-by-four, this one with a protruding nail. On his way down, Lonsdale fired a shot that hit me in the left arm just above the elbow. The force rolled me onto my side from my sitting position, and the intense, burning pain began immediately.

Lonsdale was on all fours, trying to gather himself. I was about five feet from him and whipped the Sig from my holster and fired. Lonsdale's head exploded in red mist and brain matter.

Now arriving, watermelon dropped on the pavement from the fifth floor.

Heart racing, I shakily stood, my arm throbbing. The man who'd hit Lonsdale asked, "Wie geht's, Inge?" *How's it going?* "I was afraid I'd lost track of you in the commotion inside. And, no surprise, you don't really look like the Inge I remember from Vienna."

"Pavel! Was machst du denn hier?" *What the hell are you doing here?*

"I was curious about this man you needed the information on and wondered what interest you could have in him. I was afraid you'd be spreading more of that poison around because, as you know, we can't let it be traced back to us. So, I decided to drop by. I wonder if you'd be so kind as to return the whiskey bottle with whatever remains to me?"

Happy to be rid of it, I handed over the lead-lined case from my backpack, and Pavel put it in his.

Nodding down at Lonsdale's near headless corpse, Pavel noted, "Unexpected developments. And who is this, Inge?"

"A story for another time, Pavel."

The squealing tires and the sirens ceased outside the front of the bar. Faint reflections of their flashing lights blinking into the sky were visible from the back alley.

I looked at my arm. Luckily, it was a through-and-through – the bullet had hit no bone, muscle, or anything vital. I quickly wrapped a scarf from my backpack around the wound. I had to get out of there.

As he bent down to Lonsdale, Pavel said, "Inge, just a suggestion, but you may want to take his watch and wallet, perhaps make people think it was a robbery. I'll tell the police I came out here to get away from the fire and discovered him already dead."

"Yes, right." I reached down, got the items, and stuffed them in my pack. Before running away, I said, "Thanks Pavel, I owe you big time."

He kneeled next to Lonsdale and took a cross, a bottle of holy water and a priestly vestment from his backpack. He made the sign of the cross and started reciting prayers.

"What are you doing?"

"I must give him the final sacraments, Inge." Then he grinned and said, "I'd do the same for you, though I can't promise what would happen after that. That wouldn't be up to me."

55

Helsinki and Tallinn

My plans to slip comfortably out of the bar and onto a 23:45 overnight ferry to Stockholm long gone, I ran for the harbor, two miles away. Almost hourly ferries to Tallinn in Estonia or Riga in Latvia were now the best bet.

I stopped on the pier by the sleeping Finnish icebreakers, breathing hard, trying to catch my breath. My arm really hurt, but adrenaline and the improvised bandage were holding up. Not seeing anyone nearby in the dark amidst the heavy wind-driven snow and whitecaps on the Gulf of Finland, I took my large purse from my backpack, transferred some items to it, then threw the backpack into the water.

I took off on a dead run for the harbor and a ferry, any ferry. I got to the harbor and saw there was a departure to Tallinn at 20:20, twenty-five minutes from now.

I went into the ladies' toilet at the ferry terminal. It was cold and damp, with flickering fluorescent lights, puddles of water, slush and melting snow all over the concrete floor. A woman who looked drunk was throwing up in one of the sinks, her friend holding her up.

I entered a stall, locked the door and sat on the frigid seat, trying to calm down and think. I re-wrapped my bandage as I came to grips with my poor planning before I'd left Berlin.

Bridgette Schmidt couldn't go to Tallinn because she had no passport, Finnish or otherwise, one of my varied careless errors when leaving on this mission. Bridgette was only a concoction for Niklas at the bar, but still, I should have had a German passport for her as a backup. If things had gone according to plan, in and out of Finland only, I wouldn't have needed any passport since Finland had become a member of the EU ten months prior. But Estonia would require a passport.

As backup, I'd assumed Inge Marstellar would be going to Tallinn instead of Bridgette. But as I dug into the false bottom of my purse to get her red wig and Austrian passport, they weren't there. Forgotten in Berlin. *So sloppy!* Had the personal nature of this mission, the chance to finally settle up with Win Blackpool, led me to be careless?

The only passport I had was Petra Müller's. Risky, but there was no choice. Tallinn was the fastest way out of Helsinki. I stashed Bridgette Schmidt's brown wig in the false bottom and took out a white blouse and black dress slacks. I changed out of my jeans and red sweatshirt and also hid them in the purse. My shoes. *Fuck!* I'd forgotten another pair, so I would have to go with the ones I had worn in the bar. I put my parka back on and exited the toilets.

At 20:15, five minutes to departure, I stood amidst the heavy snow and wind on the back deck of the ferry, facing the city and the Lutheran cathedral. The PA came to life for the captain to announce, first in Finnish and then English, that the weather in the Gulf of Finland was deteriorating and that they were going to wait thirty minutes for an updated forecast before deciding whether to depart or cancel the sailing.

If the ferry didn't go, I could stay in Helsinki and get out to Tallinn or Riga the next morning, or I could rent a car in the morning and drive to Sweden. Neither were ideal since there were possibly security cameras outside the bar and witnesses who might connect me with the fire and maybe even Steve Lonsdale. Every minute I spent in Helsinki, and Finland, for that matter, was risky.

I heard them first, then saw four police cars, lights and sirens going, pull up to the ferry terminal. I went inside and downstairs to an eating area on the fifth deck. It was about half full. I ordered an espresso and took a German newspaper, the *Frankfurter Allgemeine*, out of my purse. I sat alone at a two-person table near the center of the room and read the paper. No getting off the ship now until the cops finished their business, whatever it was.

21:30. So much for the captain deciding within thirty minutes whether to sail. Two police officers walked into the café and began making their way around the room, talking to everyone and checking passports. Looking down, I noticed my shoes – the low-top, lace-up hiking things. *How did I not notice this when I put them back on in the toilet?* Wedged in among the tied laces, the tongue and the eyelets, were Steve Lonsdale's blood and brain matter. The two-mile run through the snow had scrubbed the bottom and sides of the shoes clean, but not the tops.

No time to run to the toilet, I was next up for a chat with the cops. *Do I take them off and try to tuck them behind me, or am I better off leaving them on and just hoping they don't notice?*

The cop came over, and I was in my socks rubbing my feet, the shoes tipped on their sides under the chair. I started to get up, but the cop motioned me to stay seated. He asked a question in Finnish. I shrugged, smiled, looked confused and shook my head.

The cop asked, "English?"

I smiled slightly and kind of shook my head. "Wenig, wenig." *Just a little.* "Auf Deutsch?" *Do you speak German?* The cop was maybe thinking I was the only German he'd ever met who couldn't speak English.

The cop shook his head and pointed at the passport of someone at the table next to me.

"Ja, ja." I had already taken it from my purse and handed him Petra's passport.

The cop looked it over, handed it back, then made a face as he pointed at my feet. He touched his own shoes. In English, he asked, "Your shoes, where?"

I smiled, the clueless German, and rubbed my right foot with both hands. "Ja, meine Füße sind sehr kalt." *Yes, my feet are very cold.* I made a sort of shivering motion. "Verstehen Sie?" *Do you understand?* We went back and forth for a few seconds, his inability to speak German, my savior. Finally, he grunted in exasperation and moved along to the next person.

The ferry sailed for Tallinn at 22:05. Once we left port, I went into the toilet to wash Lonsdale off my shoes. Rough seas meant we didn't get into Tallinn until well after midnight. In my hotel, I crudely stitched up my arm with the medical kit I always carried. I'd see my doctor in Berlin for a more elegant fix. I gulped Ibuprofen and Acetaminophen for the pain, but it hardly took the edge off.

The next morning I took the first ferry to Stockholm, and from there would take a train to Copenhagen and then another to Berlin. I never learned what the police were looking for on the ferry in Helsinki, but I couldn't be sure it wasn't me.

Though the mission was sloppy and hadn't gone like clockwork in the bar, I was able to keep Win's Finnish visitors away from the

Johnnie Walker and also get the polonium into him. And with an assist from Pavel, I'd given Steve Lonsdale what he deserved. A bonus.

On the ferry to Stockholm, the end of 1995 approaching, I realized that within a span of six months, I'd accomplished two major goals: I'd avenged Adaoma with Sally Horrigan and earned huge credit in the Provisionals in the process. And with Win Blackpool, I'd struck a blow at my parents, the whole corrupt system in Timberline, and most importantly, had made him pay for what he'd done to Julie.

But though I'd given Win his frontier justice, it made me sad I'd never see Julie again. I missed her so much sometimes, it hurt. I'd cast her out of my life back in '88 with that letter. I was sure it hurt her, but sorrows and setbacks never defeated Julie. She always just kept moving forward, one foot in front of the other, with a resolute faith that things would always get better and work out.

Back in '88, as I'd done with Brian, I'd told myself it was for the best, that I didn't need Julie either. I would find new things to fill the temporary holes she and Brian left in my life. The truth, though, I now realized, was that I was the brief ripple in the pond that disappeared, likely forgotten and not missed, a ferry disappearing from shore into the horizon.

PART 6

Doubts and Disbelief

1996 – 2000

56

Julie: November 1996

Julie hadn't expected the call she received at her in-laws' house the day before Thanksgiving, but she agreed to the meeting. Now thirty-one, thirty-two in a month, she was more curious than anxious about seeing Angela Davis again. Angela suggested lunch the Saturday after Thanksgiving at the Timberline Country Club.

On Saturday, the hostess took Julie to a table tucked away in a back corner next to a floor-to-ceiling window that looked over a golf green enveloped in cold, dense fog. *Particularly gloomy, even for TL*, Julie thought.

"Is this your first visit to the club?" the hostess asked Julie.

"Yes. I like the decorations."

"This used to be the Gentlemen's Grill," she half-whispered. "Women couldn't be here without a man. But, last year, they moved the Gentleman's Grill to a new bar area downstairs. And now any members can eat here. 'Bout time, I say."

Julie smiled.

The Club Grill already had its Christmas materials up, including a large, decorated Douglas fir in the center of the room. A roaring wood fire burned in the stone fireplace, and Christmas carols played softly over the sound system.

Angela greeted Julie warmly. She was mid-sixties, Julie figured, but surprisingly looked older and even a bit frail. However, she was as smartly dressed as Julie had always remembered her. She wore gray herringbone wool slacks, short black heels and a black shawl-collared cashmere sweater. Angela was very thin, and her hair was still dark but with ample flecks of gray. Her features hadn't really softened over the years, and her narrow face still housed a largish, pointed nose and chin. This triggered a memory for Julie. Upset with her mother once, Alex had said that when she saw Angela's face, it reminded her to go outside and look for the ruby slippers on her feet sticking out from under the house.

The server took drink orders, and Angela began. "Julie, you look fabulous – just stunning, really. But I could tell when you left town all those years ago that you were going to grow into a beautiful woman, just like your mother."

"Oh, thank you, Angela. You look good yourself."

"I ran into Tim's mom in town last month, and she mentioned that you, Tim and your kids were coming for Thanksgiving. I'm sure you're wondering why I asked you here, and I'll get to that shortly, but indulge me if you would and catch me up on you and your family. You're in England now, if I understood Tim's mom, and moved there from Germany?"

"Yes, we moved five years ago but are in Scotland now, Edinburgh."

"I'm sure your in-laws told you how proud Timberline is of Tim. He and Brian Findlay were already basketball legends here, and now they're also war heroes from the Gulf War. Brian Findlay won the Medal of Honor in the Marines? And Tim won a bunch of medals, right?"

"Brian won the Navy Cross, one step down from the Medal of Honor, and a Purple Heart. And yes, Tim won a couple of awards, too."

Angela smiled slightly. "And are you working? Don't know how you'd manage it with your kids."

Julie laughed. "Our lives are crazy with the kids, but I love it."

"How many kids now?"

"Four. Faith and Hope, our first set of twins, will be fourteen next month, and Lauren and Charlotte are eleven."

Angela reached over and touched her hand in what Julie found a surprisingly affectionate gesture. "So, in '85 you were, what, twenty-one with four kids? How did you not lose your mind? How did you pay for it all?"

Julie grinned. "I have Tim too, and he's great with the kids. I was an only child and didn't have an extended family, and Tim has two older sisters and lots of extended family. A big family just kind of felt right for us. It's exhausting and financially challenging, but we make it work."

"What are you doing now, other than shepherding your brood?"

"I work for a research institute at the University of Edinburgh."

"Oh, what do you do for them? And, I'm sorry, I'm not sure if I ever knew this, did you finish college?"

"I did. Undergraduate and master's degrees in physics from Kansas State. Then I got a Ph.D. in nuclear physics – a DPhil, as the British call it – at the University of St. Andrews in Scotland. I just finished it not long ago."

"My god, and you did this with four kids while working?"

"I was just part-time at the research institute for several years, but I am full time now. And we've had so much help from Tim's parents with the kids."

Angela shook her head. "Amazing."

They continued light chatter throughout lunch. Though her conversation was a bit clipped and terse at times, Julie couldn't get over how happy Angela seemed to be to see her.

• • •

The server cleared away their lunch dishes and brought coffee and a small plate of holiday cookies.

Angela took a drink of coffee and looked across the table at Julie. "I'm sure you wonder why I asked you to lunch, and I appreciate your willingness to meet me. I felt I had to take the opportunity to try and see you."

"Why?"

"Julie, I have ovarian cancer – stage four."

Julie touched her lightly on the arm. "Oh, Angela, I'm so sorry. That's awful. How's it, uh, um…"

"What's the prognosis? The doctors in Seattle are trying some clinical trials, but you know it's always tough when that's all they have left. If cancer gets me, it will be one more thing Mike and I had in common."

Julie winced. "I heard about that. When did he pass?"

"Year and a half ago. Lung cancer. He was stage four when they found it. Dead two months after the diagnosis. He was never even a smoker."

"I'm sorry, Angela. That must have been horrible."

She said nothing to that. "Julie, my condition has made me reflect on my life: the ups, downs, wins and losses."

"I can understand that."

"And one of those losses was you. All those years ago, I had an opportunity to help you, show you kindness at a minimum, and perhaps even render some advice or wisdom. I actually should have loved you enthusiastically, laughed with you, wrapped my arms around you every night, soothed and encouraged you. But as I suspect you knew then and have long realized since, I wasn't capable of that. Not then, not later. I don't like that about myself now, but it's the harsh truth."

The server arrived with coffee refills. Angela took a cookie from the plate, bit off half and bored her eyes into Julie.

"Julie, you may not choose to believe this, but initially, I didn't know what happened to you, what Win Blackpool did to you. He did lots of monstrous things in his life, but I could never have imagined, nor could have Mike, that he would rape a sixteen-year-old girl, a friend of his son's, no less. It wasn't until that summer when you and Alexandra were in Spokane that Mike told me."

Julie took this in silently.

"I used to sometimes think that had I been there, I'd have done the right thing for you that night: taken you to the hospital, disclosed what happened, cared for you, fought for what was right, and defended you from Win and the backlash. But if I'm honest, I wouldn't have done that had I been there or in Mike's shoes. We had too much to lose. That's neither noble nor honorable, but it's the truth."

Revisiting this was so unexpected, shocking really – to be again pulled back to those grim days. But Julie wanted to hear it all.

"Mike was mad and scared that night, too. Now, that's no excuse. He was the adult and the parent, and hadn't been through what you had. Mike never did well in highly personal situations, let alone hysterical ones. He was emotionally closed off in ways, like me. That's one reason we never had much of a relationship with Alexandra."

Julie chewed her bottom lip and hoped her hand wouldn't shake as she reached for her coffee.

"Mike left you by the side of the road in the woods, trauma-tized – like a slasher movie, for god's sake. I'm thankful Brian's mom was home to get the call from you that night, and that she had the compassion to take care of you."

"Yes, she didn't kick me out of her house," Julie acidly noted, surprised by her flash of resentment.

Angela pursed her lips. "Once Mike told me everything, I knew you couldn't come back to live with us. Win was adamant about that.

But I didn't realize the state of Washington would put you in a foster home with that crack whore in your junior year."

Julie was still feeling spiteful. "Why would you care? I was out of your house."

Julie noticed Angela didn't seem upset by her snide comments, as if she expected them.

"After whatever the hell her name was did everyone a favor and OD'd, I lost faith in the state's ability to get you in a good foster situation for senior year, so I felt I needed to intervene. I learned about the Tanners. They had been foster parents for many kids in the past, but had stopped doing it some years before. I quietly asked around and heard fantastic things. I approached them and asked them to take you in. Once I told them about you, they were happy to do it, but I paid them also – I wanted to make sure they had ample resources for whatever you needed. The Tanners agreed to reach out to the state and ask about you."

Another unexpected revelation. Julie had liked living with the Tanners. They'd been great to her – the first normalcy she'd had since her mom had died. She still corresponded with them. But, if Angela expected any credit from her for that, given her much bigger failings in the aftermath, Julie wasn't about to give it.

"And, Angela, did Mike tell you about his encounter with me in '84, when I was up here for that funeral?"

Angela sighed. "Yes, he made a mistake. 'Leave that poor girl alone,' I told him, 'let her get on with her life without all the baggage from here.' He could have just lied to Win and said he'd spoken to you."

Julie excused herself for the restroom. Walking back to the table, the fresh scent of the Christmas tree and the music, *Hark the Herald Angels Sing*, took Julie back to Christmases with her mom in Timberline: their two stockings hanging on the fireplace of the tiny bungalow in Central with a large fresh tree in the living room. That seemed like so long ago, another lifetime, but the film still ran vividly in her mind.

Settled back at the table, Julie asked, "I hadn't realized Mike died before Win Blackpool. How are things at the company now?"

"Not good. It has too much debt, operational and legal problems. They're the biggest employer in town and have already started laying people off. As I'm sure you know, Win brought Brian Findlay in when he got out of Harvard to help Fogg prepare to run the company someday – Brian has Mike's old job now. But Win died too soon. I hear Brian's very capable, though Fogg isn't, and it may be too late for the company."

"I never heard. How did Win die last year?"

Angela shrugged. "Nobody ever really had an answer. Some thought a weird virus, and others thought some sort of industrial poison he came in contact with at a Finnish paper mill. He was in the hospital in Helsinki for a couple of weeks, and then they flew him to Seattle. It didn't matter. He just kept getting worse."

Julie nibbled at a cookie.

"Then on that same trip, Steve Lonsdale got robbed and killed."

"I heard that also. I appreciate your honesty, Angela so I'll be honest too. I can say I'm sorry about Mike. Sorry for you, for him, despite what he did and didn't do that night almost seventeen years ago." Then icily Julie added, "But I'm not sorry about Win or about Lonsdale, since he killed my mother. That's not very Christian of me, but that's how I feel."

"So, you knew Lonsdale was drunk the night he hit your mother? And that Win had the police cover it up? Alex told you?"

"Well, he had Mike cover it up, right? But yes, Alex told me in '84 when I told her about Win raping me and Mike's role. I'm curious, Angela, did you or Mike ever talk to Alex again after '84?"

"No."

"Did you try?"

"Not really, though Mike and I went to her Princeton graduation. We were hoping to at least see her, maybe begin some conversation. She wasn't there. I suspect you knew that."

"I did. But Alex began pulling away from me a year or so after Princeton. I think the whole Tunisia nightmare was tough for her to deal with."

"What are you talking about?"

Julie filled her in, but Angela had no comment, other than "Oh, we never knew."

Angela reached for another cookie and looked down at it before saying, as if to the cookie, "Julie, I think you know motherhood was not my thing. I never wanted it – never wanted to be in Timberline. I thought Mike and I would live in major cities and both have really big careers. Instead, Mike got sucked into Win Blackpool's world and we ended up trapped here."

Julie made a skeptical face. "Angela, you weren't trapped. You could have left anytime."

"When I ended up pregnant with Alexandra, I resolved to make the best of it, to accumulate influence and power in Timberline. I also decided to build her into an achievement machine, someone who would never settle for what I did."

"You did a good job. Alex was one of the smartest, most driven people I ever knew."

Angela sighed. "I suppose I should have cared more about all her non-academic activities: the Girl Scouts, the theater group in high school, and the cheerleading. But I just saw them all as so frivolous – a complete waste of my time and hers."

Julie debated internally, but decided to ask the questions. "Did you love her? Do you miss her?"

Angela took a deep breath and was quiet for a few seconds, but it seemed like forever to Julie. "I miss her terribly. The chance to see how her life would have turned out, to talk to her about the places she'd been and the people she'd met. Since they never found her body, sometimes I foolishly wonder if she's alive, off living some secret life. I hope so."

"What about my other question? Did you ever love her?"

"Yes, Julie, of course I loved her, but in a parental, obligatory sort of way. Nobody is supposed to say this about their children, but I loved Mike more – not equally, but more. I could always, if I had to, imagine my life without Alexandra, but never without Mike. Mike was the one I couldn't wait to see when he got home, to hear about his day. He and I were partners; he would tell me about the issues at Blackpool, and we would strategize together on how best to manage the situations. We were a team. I never missed Alex as much, never watched the clock to see when she would be home from school or from her activities."

Julie took this in. Angela had always been a direct communicator, bordering on brutal. Still, her willingness to admit her feelings toward Alex was surprising.

Angela went on. "And I never had any empathy for Alexandra. I expected her to achieve and to meet the very high standards Mike and I had set, and growing up, she did, brilliantly. She made us proud and was a great credit to her parents. But once she got to Princeton, I expected her to keep achieving and meeting our standards, and when she struggled, it made us angry. I felt she needed to suck it up and get it together."

Julie interjected, "Princeton was unpleasant for Alex overall, I think. But she had a four-oh GPA her last three semesters. She did achieve, like you expected."

"And, Julie, I also had no empathy or sympathy for you. Intellectually, I thought I could conceptualize what you were going through, felt you just needed to pull yourself together and get on with your life. But I had no idea, still don't. And when you ended up pregnant, whatever sympathy I had vanished. It confirmed the verdict I'd already reached: You were an inferior, damaged version of Alexandra. You were not someone I wanted associated with my family and certainly not someone I was going to invest any time in."

Though not surprising, the starkness of Angela's views about her then was still shocking for Julie to hear so many years later.

"I have to ask," Julie replied, "I've always wondered. Did you think twice about saving my life that night? Was it because you cared about me, or was it more because you didn't want the embarrassment of having some troubled girl die in your bathtub?"

Angela pursed her lips, thought briefly and said, "Both reasons, as harsh as that sounds."

"Well, regardless of your motivations, I literally owe you my life. I will be grateful forever for what you did for me that night, Angela."

They parted ways in the parking lot, and Angela actually reached out to hug Julie. They swapped addresses. Angela was spending most of her time in her condo in Seattle near her treatments. Before getting into her car, Angela turned back toward Julie.

"Julie, I am profoundly sorry for how I treated you – for my errors of commission and omission all those years ago. It's one of the biggest mistakes and regrets of my life. I spent all those years working on Alexandra, building and honing her into someone who would go into the world and do great things. It didn't turn out that way, but the person who would do that, you, was right in front of me, and I couldn't see it. You've overcome massive obstacles, things that would have defeated many, most even, to build a full life. I'm proud of you."

57

Alex: 1996 – 1998

If 1995 was a big year for me, '96 was slow. Apparently, we were running low on touts hiding in Europe. Though I did kill a former bombmaker for us who had sexually molested underage boys and touted for the RUC, telling them where we'd hidden a cache of Semtex. He'd fled from South Armagh to Nice, France. I watched him for three weeks and then took him out. It was all very routine: I ran him over in a stolen Audi at two in the morning as he stumbled home from a bar. I was disguised and also wore a balaclava. Just to make sure, I backed up over him and ran forward over his body again after the initial hit.

Maeve also sent me to Croatia to begin what would be half a year of negotiations with shadowy elements of the military and domestic arms suppliers. We were looking for automatic rifles, ammo and plastic explosives – tons of it –but why the Provisionals' quartermaster organization wasn't doing this was beyond me. I (as Klara Steinmetz) made four trips to Zagreb in the last six months of '96, and we finally got an agreement on terms. Maeve then basically said, "Never mind, but keep up the relationships." The quartermaster organization in Ireland had decided the timing wasn't right. Or had Maeve?

• • •

I left my ad agency office just before 22:00 on a Wednesday in July of '97, my office days now longer since my March promotion. I now led media buying in Central and Eastern Europe for a small marketing communications firm. Work offered a nice distraction and different kinds of challenges from my work for the Provisionals. Especially since little was happening other than Nice and my occasional trips to Croatia.

It was a twenty-minute walk to my flat, and given the warm night, the bars and restaurants on my walk home were lively and crowded. As was my habit, I crossed streets frequently, doubled back often, and did various other things to identify anybody watching or tailing me. In all the years I'd been in Berlin, I'd never spotted anyone, but it was essential tradecraft nonetheless.

I was about halfway home when I saw him. I scolded myself for taking so long to spot the tail. I altered course and began moving away from the direction of my flat. I could have lost him if I'd wanted, but decided to confront him. I'd met him before, after all.

I led him into a less-congested neighborhood, cautious to not move too quickly and make it hard for him to catch up. The crowds were thinning, but not so much to make him obvious behind me. I arrived at a small dead-end alley with only three hole-in-the-wall bars and poor lighting.

He followed a couple of minutes later, hesitated briefly and turned down the alley. He'd walked about ten yards when I stepped from the shadows behind him and put a gun in the small of his back.

"Otto, for being such a feared member of the Provisionals, your tradecraft sucks," I calmly said. I had neither seen nor heard of Otto since that night with Patricia Maguire over three years before.

"Maybe I wanted you to see me, Petra."

This gave me pause. "Why?"

"Gerald Morrissey sent me to meet ya. You're in danger and he wanted me to warn ye. But this isn't a short conversation. Maybe we could get a pint somewhere?"

After searching Otto for weapons, we sat in a bar not far from the alley, crowded but not too crowded. Irish whiskey neat for Otto and a glass of Bordeaux for me.

"Before we get into your agenda," I said, "I've a few questions."

"Of course, uh, Petra. Do I call you Petra?"

"Yes. When did you start following me?"

"Two days ago. Got the word from Gerald to come make contact. All he told me was where you worked."

Otto sipped his whiskey and lit an unfiltered Camel in the smoke-choked bar, his bald head rosy, gleaming and sweating. "Not many people in the organization know you even exist, Petra, and those that do know very little about you, including Gerald Morrissey. Maeve has seen to that.”

“That's good, right, since the organization seems to be crawling with touts?”

Otto nodded. “You may not realize it, but you're quite respected, even feared, in the Provisionals, and are known to be close to Maeve.”

“I'm not that close to her.”

“As close as anybody, 'cept maybe Gerald himself.” Otto looked quickly around to make sure nobody was nearby. “The Provisionals are facing some major change soon, and Gerald wants me to try to find out what side of that change you might be on. If you's to choose, who would it be?”

“What?”

Otto held up his hand. “In a few weeks, Gerald will announce a new ceasefire 'tween the Provisionals and the British and Protestants, and though many's failed in the past, people think this one will stick. The Americans are leading serious negotiations to end the Troubles in Northern Ireland and have a real power-sharing between Catholics and Protestants. This would eventually lead to the disarming of the Provisionals as well as the Protestant militias. And the British Army would leave.”

I had seen some news stories to this effect, but Maeve had yet to say anything to me.

Otto continued, “Some in the Provisionals will never accept this. It will be an unforgivable betrayal to them. They will work to scuttle any negotiations and continue armed struggle. They've already begun a new organization for that, the Genuine IRA. It's just forming, but they'll build it from now.”

I caught the server's attention and ordered another round for us.

“So, how does this relate exactly to me, Otto?”

He looked at me for a few seconds, trying to figure out whether this was a real question or not. It was. “Well, Maeve is sp'osed to be one of the two or three people driving the formation of the Genuine. She may even be the leader.”

“You don't think she'll see that neither side will ever give up, and that imperfect as it may be, some sort of settlement is the only solution?” I asked.

Otto dove into his new drink and shook his head. “I knew her a bit in Belfast growing up. Her family's originally from South Armagh, dating back generations, but her mam and da moved to

Belfast –Andersonstown – when she was wee and then went to the US. I would see her around Belfast most summers with her family. They were hardcore Republicans, always hated the Protestants and the British. But even as a kid, there was something 'bout Maeve, I don't know, an icy kind of coldness. Not evil really, more like soulless, and you got the sense she'd do anything to get what she wanted; would cut 'yer heart out if you was blocking the goal box."

"But what about now?"

"Tis no matter, my opinion, but I think she'll fight forever, to the death. Will never agree to power-sharing in Northern Ireland. Will only accept a united, Catholic Ireland."

He took a drink, wiped his bald head with a napkin, and continued.

"I got lotsa blood on my hands these past twenty-five years in this war. And as you know, plenty-a people on both sides fear me. But Maeve is in a class all her own, my opinion. I've seen few people as capable and none more ruthless."

I nursed my Bordeaux and, after a minute or so, asked, "And I'm in danger how?"

"Because if you haven't already been asked, Maeve will ask you to continue the fight with the Genuine, though probably with you back in Northern Ireland or the Republic, not Europe. And if you turn her down, she may conclude you know too much and are a risk to her."

"And if I join her?" I shot back.

Otto looked into his whiskey, swirling the liquid in his glass. "I thought like you once. If you join her, you'll have the forces of the British, Irish and Northern Ireland governments united against you, relentlessly focused on keeping the Genuine from becoming established enough to erode a negotiated settlement in Northern Ireland."

I sipped my wine.

Otto went on. "And I think you'd best prepare yourself to do grisly things if you go with Maeve and her lot."

"Like what? Isn't that what I've been doing?"

"No, you killed touts – a military necessity. With the Genuine, it will be the killing of innocents, bombings with no warnings, and assassinations in Northern Ireland and Britain – not just of touts but of politicians and others that just disagree with them. The Genuine will need to build its reputation as a harsh organization to be feared, respected."

"And what about you, Otto? Obviously, you're going with Gerald Morrissey, Sinn Fein and the disarmament, but why?"

He grimaced and again wiped his profusely sweating bald head with a fistful of napkins that wilted against the challenge. He became a bit emotional. "This is tearing me guts out. I was one of the first to join the Provisionals in '72; Gerald and I joined together. I fought most of my life for a united Ireland. It was a war for a just cause. I believed in it, every bit of my being. I still do. But we failed, miscalculated maybe. All we could ever get to was a stalemate, not victory, and that's all it'll ever be. So, why keep fighting? Why continue the violence, economic destruction, heartache, and fear people live with every day? I think a settlement is the best hope for the Catholics in the six counties now. Our population will grow faster than the Unionists over time, so we'll gain more political power in the long run."

"And in the dark of night, between you and the mirror in the loo, how does that thought sit with you, Otto?"

"God, it breaks my heart, ya know? When I think about things I done, the people I killed, maimed, threatened, and terrified, and it's all for what? You may already know that my nickname in the organization is the Reaper. And I also had loss, plenty of it. Mates, men under me, my brother George, even his widow, Sally Horrigan."

Shit!

"I know you killed her, Petra, can't prove it but I just know. You're a hero to many for that, and I understand – the code and all, orders from Maeve – but Sally's was a tough lot. You know, Gerald Morrissey knew nothing 'bout that til it happened; it was all Maeve, learning the information, not sharing it with anyone, and sending you to kill her."

Surprised, I said, "That's not what she told me."

"You expect her to tell you the truth?"

Wow, Morrissey didn't know! "I… I don't know."

Otto finished his thoughts. "Every night since 1972 I say the rosary, and I go to mass every morning. I always ask for understanding and forgiveness, because I was in a war, fighting for a just cause. I always hoped that when it was my time to wait in purgatory, the scales would balance out in my favor, even though it could be close. Now I don't know. But the past is past, and all I can do now is what I think is right, just like I always done."

I reached across the table and squeezed his hand. "I understand. I feel bad for you. But if you hadn't fought all those years, and fought well, the Catholics wouldn't have any kind of bargaining power in truce negotiations. The Brits would keep screwing them like they've always done."

"Yeah, I know, 'tis good-a you to say it, but it's still a hammer blow. Anyways, Gerald Morrissey sent me to see what you think. D'ye think you'll go over to the Genuine or no?"

I ignored his question. "So, should we keep in touch in the future?" I asked.

Our meeting over, we set a secret means to keep in contact periodically, and to reach each other should an urgent need arise. I didn't sleep that night, couldn't get Otto out of my head – his warnings and predictions, but also his personal anguish and regret. I knew that could be me.

• • •

I loved Christmas season in New York. Even though I disliked much about Princeton, I always appreciated its proximity to the city. I'd last been there twelve years prior, December of '85 – not a happy time, my emotional wounds from Adaoma and Tunisia still raw. I wondered if my sadness about her was like phantom limb pain for someone who'd lost an arm or a leg. You think she's there, can almost feel her, but you look and she's not. A cruel mind game.

I briefly considered trying to contact Paul Reilly while I was back in the States, but dismissed the idea. Too much history.

I met Maeve in a junior suite at the Pierre Hotel near Central Park on a snowy Wednesday afternoon. She wasn't staying there, she told me, but didn't want to meet in a public place or at her hotel. As always, I'd been summoned on short notice, and Jennifer Nathan, i.e. me, had returned to the US for the first time since St. Louis over two years prior. As usual, Maeve was elegantly dressed. A dark yet electric green dress, matching heels, and her green fedora tossed nearby on the sofa. Also a gold Rolex and massive diamond earrings. I wore charcoal gray slacks, a red wool turtleneck and a black ankle-length wool overcoat that I tossed on the second sofa in the living area.

"Ah, love, there you are. Appreciate you rushing over on short notice."

"No problem. You're looking festive."

"You too, look at us all red and green. The Christmas twins."

I laughed. Our room-service lunch was there when I arrived and we chatted for half an hour about fairly typical stuff. She wanted an update on my contacts with the Croatians, when I'd last spoken with Pavel in Vienna, and her team's ongoing efforts to locate a couple of low-level touts who'd fled Northern Ireland for Europe or the

Middle East.

Maeve went to the mini-bar and removed several small liquor bottles – vodka, bourbon and Irish whiskey. Pointing at me, she asked, "For you, love?"

"Vodka, please. A shot."

"Ah, grand. I'll have the Maker's Mark. So, Alexandra, what do you hear over in Europe about the peace talks?"

I shrugged. "Not much. It's not a real topic of conversation there."

"Hmm, suppose so. Well, I think Gerald Morrissey is going to sell us out, down tools, and quit fighting. I can't imagine a larger betrayal. I've known him his whole life, and in the past ten years, he's transformed from a fearless general to a gutless wanker."

"Why does he want to sue for peace?"

"He says we're at a stalemate with the other side, that further fighting will be counter-productive and cause undue suffering."

"I think that's bullshit," I said. "The British will eventually give in, just like they did with all their colonies. Eventually, the people of England will lose their taste for battle and suffering. Besides, over the long term, generationally, the Catholics have demographics on their side. They'll grow faster and eventually be a majority in the six counties."

Maeve eyed me. "You're soon going to have a choice to make, love."

"About what?"

"Gerald Morrissey and the rest of Sinn Fein are going to gut the Provisionals for a peace deal. Only a matter of time. Have them shut down and disarmed. But lots of people in the organization aren't accepting it, and a new organization is secretly forming, the Genuine IRA. They're going to take the fight to the Unionists, the RUC, MI-5 and the British Army. And it's going to be harsh and bloody, back to the days of the seventies and eighties. Morrissey's wobbly; he lost his taste for blood and victory at any cost years ago but tried to hide it for a long time. The British are buying him off, filling a Swiss account with who knows how many millions to sell his people out."

"So, my choice is downing tools, as you said, or the Genuine IRA? How do I know they'd even want me?"

"Trust me, love, you'd be wanted. It's totally your choice, but if you don't continue the fight, you'll need to stay out of Northern Ireland forever. You know too much, and some in the organization could see you as a security risk."

Some in the organization? You mean you, right, Maeve?

"I think I can guess where you will come out on the Genuine, right, Maeve?"

"So, love, give it a think and let me know what you want. I'll support you, regardless; either help arrange a path into the Genuine or get you a safe exit."

"What's the timing on the Genuine, and any sort of official break from the Provisionals?" I asked.

"Unclear now. We need to see how these peace negotiations play out. The US is driving this, and the Labor Party in London will be more willing to sell out the Unionists than any Tory government ever would be, so I think it's likely."

"I see."

Maeve added, "I'd think something may happen with the Genuine next year sometime."

I honestly don't know what I think about the Genuine right now, but I sure as hell need to keep my options open. Maeve will know this, so my answer won't surprise her. Who knows if she'll believe me, though?

"I'm with you Maeve. All in."

58

Alex: 1998

The emergency "Bat Signal" from Otto appeared as a voicemail on my mobile in October. An update on "mam's fight with the bowel cancer" with some of the follow-on details signaled a late-night meeting outside Berlin in a park near Potsdam.

It was cold for October. An air mass from Russia had dropped temperatures into the teens, reminding me again, unwillingly, of Timberline. Otto was cold, and I wasn't. He wore Nike trainers, blue jeans, a button-up shirt and a dark green rain slicker. He had no hat or gloves. I was head to toe in black, with a knit ski hat, gloves, boots, jeans, sweater and wool waist-length overcoat. We met on a park bench away from streetlights at fifteen minutes to midnight. Sitting on opposite ends of the bench, we grunted recognition at each other.

"What's up?" I asked.

"Other than freezing my arse off, I need to understand what you know about Ballycastle. We know it was the Genuine."

"Well, that's more than I know."

"Don't lie to me, Petra. A bombing with over thirty innocents killed, three hundred wounded, no phoned warning. The heat on this is harsh. It could scuttle the whole Good Friday Agreements after six months. The Genuine needs to be smart about things like this."

I asked, "Just what do you think I can do?"

"You can tell me the people involved. The Provisionals need to take these people down or the Brits and the Unionists won't believe we will ever disarm and stop the fighting."

"I told you, I know nothing about it."

"And I don't believe you."

"Then you can fuck right off, Otto. I'm maybe willing to share some things with you about what I might know, but it's nothing about Ballycastle. And in exchange for things I know, you will need to share information with me."

Agitated, he sighed. "Understood. Look, we know you're with Maeve in the Genuine, in the quartermaster's organization. You're still here in Germany, but responsible for weapons supplies from Europe and the Middle East, and Pints O'Toole covers North America."

I burst out laughing. "What the hell kind of name is Pints O'Toole? Who the fuck is that?"

"Frank O'Toole. He spends a lot of time in the pubs."

"That's news to me. I don't know or do anything outside my little world. The only person I deal with is Maeve, and she isn't one for over-sharing. But yes, you're right about my remit. Now, your turn to answer a question from me. How does Maeve fit into the Genuine?"

He looked at me like I was mental. "You're serious? That's a real question?"

"Yes."

"She's one of the people who stood the organization up. Gerald Morrissey thinks she runs the whole effin' show."

"How could Morrissey not know for sure who runs the Genuine?"

"In the years leading up to Good Friday, there were seven people in the Provisional leadership, the Army Council. Gerald Morrissey was one, Maeve another, and five other blokes. Maeve and two of the others broke away to start the Genuine. The three may lead it together, or one of the three might be on top, and Gerald thinks that's Maeve."

"How many people are in the Genuine now?"

"Estimate now is maybe only around fifty, with probably three-quarters of them in South Armagh. That place is like a whole other country."

"You told me Gerald and Maeve have known each other their whole lives. Do they still speak?"

"No."

"If the Genuine's such a threat, why doesn't Gerald have Maeve killed?"

Otto chuckled. "If only it was that easy. Good Friday is not popular with a lot of people in the Provisionals, even if they're not in the Genuine. And while lots in the Provisionals may find the

Genuine's tactics too harsh, they'd never support selling out their own countrymen to the Unionists and Brits. Gerald's living on the knife edge."

"So, what's he trying to do other than make himself king or king-maker?"

Otto frantically rubbed his hands together to warm them. Taking pity on him, I took my gloves off and handed them over.

"Ah, thanks, that's good on ya. Over time – it'll be years – he hopes he can shift most Catholics in Northern Ireland into relying on political power with Sinn Fein more than military power using the Provisionals to advance the cause. But not now; it's too soon. So, while he won't support the Genuine, his ability to actively work against them is limited."

"If I knew who in the Genuine did Ballycastle, and again I don't, what would Gerald do with that information? Tip off the Brits?"

"Aye, likely, but I'm guessing. Touts are everywhere, so people would suspect others for touting, not Gerald."

I sat, silent, waiting for Otto to tell me more.

"So, uh, Petra, are you committed to the Genuine and the blood they're going to spill?"

I shook my head. "I'm not answering that. You should assume I am, but that said, I'm willing to keep our communication lines open in the future as we've been doing."

"Aye."

I grinned at Otto. "Are you sure I can't persuade you to join us in the Genuine?"

He rubbed his bald head. "No. Killing innocents and children is not for me. But nothing will be too much for Maeve and her lot for the cause."

• • •

At first, being excluded from the planning for what would be Ballycastle had pissed me off. Like Maeve was just taking my joining the Genuine for granted. In May of '98, I'd met her in London to take my oath for the Genuine. She'd alluded to a major operation in Northern Ireland that would "tell everyone the war wasn't over after the Good Friday Agreements," but offered nothing else. But once it happened in August, an 'own-goal' for the Genuine if there ever was one, I was thankful I'd known nothing. Also, thankfully, the explosives used were stolen from a British Army depot in Northern Ireland. The Semtex I'd gotten from the Croatians wasn't used, but it likely would be in a future operation, I knew.

After Ballycastle, the Genuine went to ground, practically dark. Larceny and other fund-raising activities continued, as did building weapons-procurement networks. But all active service operations, bombings or assassinations ceased. I spent the next year cultivating weapons networks in Croatia, Belarus, Serbia and Algeria. I closed two deals with arms traders in Croatia: a couple of hundred AK-47s and Glock nine-millimeter handguns, as well as a dozen RPGs and a few mortar launchers. The mortars and rocket propelled grenades troubled me a bit, seemed like weapons of escalation, but not much different from bombs, I decided.

The Croatians shut down our Semtex supply, the Ballycastle heat too much. The weapons dealers didn't care, of course, but their sources in the Croatian military did. I spent much of my time in '99 working to re-open that spigot. I saw Maeve twice between October '98 and August '99.

Building the Genuine's weapons networks fed my rapidly growing doubts about the righteousness of the organization's cause and my role in it. Otto had sent a message some months after we'd met in Berlin. We spoke on burner phones, and he passed along that once the Genuine resumed operations they would focus on soft targets in England and previously untouchable areas in Northern Ireland, even including St. Paul's Academy, the private high school in Belfast where most British elites sent their kids.

"Why would they do that?" I'd asked Otto.

"They think people have become numb to the killing of those in the RUC and British Army, and only spectacular killings of innocents in England and Northern Ireland will pressure parties to scuttle Good Friday and push to drive the British out."

"That's crazy," I said. "It won't work. Will turn the whole country against them."

"It's also a recruiting tool for hardcore former Provisionals who might jump off the sidelines and join them. And you can't underestimate how much hatred people like Maeve have for the Unionists and the British."

A few weeks later, information from Otto on another phone call sent chills down my spine.

"You ever heard of an arms dealer from Croatia with the name-a

Radko?"

Yes, if you count half a dozen meetings with him. "No," I lied. "Why?"

"We hear Maeve's trying to buy highly enriched uranium through him."

What the fuck! "For what reason? The Genuine's sure as hell not going to detonate a nuclear bomb in Northern Ireland."

"A-course. Word is Maeve thinks the Genuine has the technical expertise to fashion the uranium into a dirty bomb they could sell to other terrorists for tens of millions of pounds."

Shit. So, is that why Maeve told me to set up another meeting with Radko? And she's obviously keeping me in the dark about this new twist.

"I haven't heard anything," I said.

If all of what Otto said was true, that was repugnant and not what I'd signed up for back in 1987. I saw myself as a soldier in an important cause – not as a terrorist, serial murderer, nuclear proliferator, or killer of children. If I just kept on with it, reaping whatever benefits came to me and rationalizing or pushing away my doubts, I'd be no better than my parents.

I was also lonely – crushingly so. Maeve had been right about that back in Vienna. Work for a cause in isolation from other aspects of life isn't enough for most. I feared I could end up like Otto years down the road: alone (he'd never married) with only regrets and self-recrimination to keep me company in some depressing flat. Or I could end up back in prison for life. Or dead.

I'd dipped my toe back into the dating scene in Berlin with unsatisfying results. I couldn't get Brian out of my head. I wasn't able or willing, I realized, to be open to other possibilities until I knew whether I had really closed that door forever over ten years ago. I was sure I had, but maybe needed to be kicked in the head with the cold, hard reality of it.

So, if the Genuine life was not going to be for me, how would I exit? Disappear and hope Maeve and her mates couldn't ever find me? Or would I work against them and do what I could to mitigate the carnage they planned?

Ultimately, I decided to work for a safe exit for me and to work against Maeve and the Genuine until I found it.

59

Julie: December 1998

Since joining JETPAK, Julie had spent roughly a third of her time on the Provisionals and now-emerging Genuine IRA, and two-thirds on groups selling or buying nuclear weapon components. The organization assembled for its weekly Monday morning staff meeting, with General Moreland presiding.

"Okay," he began, "before we dive into our items, just a quick check to make sure everyone has directions to the Christmas party at my house tomorrow night." He looked around the table. "Everyone good?" Nods of agreement all around. "Not to be Mary Poppins here, but just want to remind everyone that if you're in no condition to drive home at night's end, please call a taxi and charge it to the office."

As in most places in the intelligence world, nobody used their real names in their working lives. Everyone had a cryptonym, "crypt" for short. "Marcel," from French intelligence, sat on Julie's right and turned to lightheartedly ask her, "Laurie—"

Laurie, as in Laurie Partridge, was Julie's cover name; she didn't see a resemblance, but colleagues back at Langley did and she'd had that name since joining the CIA. It could have been worse. A friend of hers was a fast-rising Navy pilot, Stephanie Jobbe, as in robe. And since flight school, her call sign had been "Blow."

"…my dear friend Laurie, your husband seems a good sport, a grand gent. I was wondering if you'd consent to let him fuck my wife after the party if I'm too disabled by drink to do it myself."

Annette from MI-6 jumped in. "That would be your greatest

Christmas gift to Sophia ever, Marcel. A moment of ecstasy for her after twenty years of crushing disappointment in bed."

Everyone laughed, and after it died down, Julie replied, "Marcel, you're my good friend, but I'm afraid that won't be possible. Just a bridge too far."

"Ah, pity," he sighed, laughing. "I'm sure he'll be vigorously engaged with you after the party, anyway."

The group next went around the table, each person sharing updates or new information from their respective portfolios. Julie spent most of her time on nuclear smuggling and terror items, but closed with some IRA news.

"A friend of mine in the FBI tipped me off last week that a gun runner for the Provisionals in the US died in a shootout with New York state police near the Canadian border. I have a call with the people in the Bureau later today to learn what they've found out. I'm assuming he'd either gone over to the Genuine side or was maybe working with another unknown faction in the Provisionals opposed to disarmament."

• • •

Later that day, Julie was on the phone with her friend at the FBI. After some quick pleasantries, they began.

Julie asked, "So, what have you learned in the past week about our dead gun runner? Were they the Genuine IRA's guns?"

"Yes. We have an informer on the fringes of their people in the US. He tipped us they had guns, ammo and military-grade mortars stashed in an underground warehouse in the woods, ten miles from the border. We showed up with the state police and surprised the guy and some others as they were loading trucks to move material into Canada. They chose to fight, go out like Butch and Sundance. The leader had body armor, but a trooper hit him with a head shot."

"What do you know about the guy?" Julie asked.

"Not much. Name's Paul Reilly. Family is originally from Derry in Northern Ireland, but he grew up in Boston. Dad was a Boston cop, retired a few years ago, and mom worked too. Lots of family in Northern Ireland."

"Did he go to college? Where did he work?"

"Believe it or not, our boy graduated from Princeton in 1986. Economics major. Phi Beta Kappa and everything. He worked for a small banking firm with offices in Boston, New York, London, Dubai and San Francisco. They aren't saying anything. Said he was a good employee, a loner, who did his job well."

Julie kept asking questions. "What do we know about his Princeton days? Activities, people he knew, that kind of thing?"

"Nothing. The guy was a cipher. Check your inbox. Just sent you a picture of him and a group of students that ran on the front page of the student newspaper. They were at some campus demonstration their senior year, but there are no names in the caption. This is all we've been able to turn up on the guy at Princeton other than things like his transcript. We're trying to ID and track down the other people in the picture, but no luck yet."

Julie turned to her computer, opened the file, scrutinized the picture, and gasped. "Oh, my god!"

"What?"

"I… I know, well knew, one of the people in the picture."

"Really? Which one?"

"The blonde, second from the left."

"Who is it?"

"Alexandra Davis. We grew up together in Washington State and were close at one time, including through college."

"What's her story now?"

"We lost touch in '88, and she died a few months later in a car accident in Maine. I never heard her mention anyone named Paul Reilly."

"Well, that's one less person we need to track down. Hell, we don't even know if they knew each other; could have been just a group of strangers standing together."

Seeing Alex in the picture was a jolt. It had taken Julie several years after Alex died to banish her from her mind, and also to forget the letter that had mysteriously ended their friendship.

Julie checked back regularly with the FBI on the Reilly investigation, but they turned up nothing more about his time at Princeton, or anything else for that matter. Maybe Alex and Reilly knew each other or maybe they didn't, Julie reasoned, though in her business she'd learned to never believe in coincidences. Regardless, there was nothing connecting Alex to the Provisionals before she died. And the FBI had found nothing suggesting Alex and Reilly had ever seen each other after Princeton.

60

Alex: December 1999

Alex disembarked from the Eurostar at London's St. Pancras Station on December 9, the Semtex explosives secreted in the hidden compartment of her rolling bag. She moved down the long escalator to the tube, took the Victoria Line to its southern terminus, Brixton, and walked the mile to Dover House, her two-star hotel.

Maeve had sent a postcard to Alex at her Berlin flat the prior month that simply said, "Missing you." This was a signal to go to a combination locker in the Dresden train station and retrieve the contents. In the locker was an envelope with a single sheet of paper inside.

> Hi, looking forward to your visit on December 10. It would be grand if you can get fifteen kilos of that cheese (I know it's a lot, we're planning a raging Christmas party!) from your friends in Croatia and bring it with you. See you soon. Say hello to Peter in Zagreb for me. He's a good bloke. Oh, and we've moved recently; see new address below.

> Best, Sean

Returning from Dresden to Berlin, Alex contemplated the letter. Fifteen kilos of Semtex. Jesus! Was that for one bomb or several? If one, it could take out a whole city block. Less than a pound had brought down Pan Am 103 over Lockerbie a decade earlier, and the Provisionals had used two fifteen-kilo bombs in 1996 to try to drop the Hammersmith Bridge in London. They'd easily have succeeded if the bombs hadn't been partially disarmed in time after the Provisionals phoned a warning. Alex had always found the Provisionals' practice of phoning warnings about bombs just and necessary to spare innocents. It troubled her that Maeve and the Genuine could be departing from that.

The Provisionals always had Semtex on hand, oceans of it at times, accessible in either Northern Ireland or the Republic of Ireland. But the Genuine did not as of yet; it lived a hand-to-mouth, as-needed existence in terms of weapons. Alex was making progress building the group's supply lines and stocks, but it was still early days.

Alex spent the rest of November working contacts in Serbia for Croatian Semtex, since the Croatians themselves weren't an option. *Christ, Maeve thinks it's just as easy as going out to get a quart of milk.* Finally, a deal was made and money went to Belgrade with a pickup location agreed. Alex would retrieve a locked rolling black suitcase from long-term baggage storage at the Prague train station. Flying to London was out of the question. Since the early 1990s, the Czech manufacturer of Semtex had added a chemical marker to the product that made it discoverable by bomb-sniffing dogs. The train wasn't riskless by any means, but better than passing through an airport or a border checkpoint in a car.

• • •

Walking from her hotel to Sean's through the gray fog and drizzling rain just after nine the next morning, Alex saw that the character of the area confirmed her research: lower income, a mixture of apartment blocks and small row houses with lots of small bodega-like retail and storefront businesses. It was multi-ethnic: Caribbean Blacks, North Africans, other Muslims, Indians and Whites walking about everywhere. A miasma of mashed-up international food scents penetrated the gray weather.

Alex wore black gloves, blue jeans, a white wool turtleneck fisherman's jumper and a black Barbour waist-length wax cotton raincoat.

Sean's place was a row house with four steps up to the porch and a one-car garage below. She rang the bell and knocked repeatedly. Finally, two eyes peered through a torn pink curtain and filthy window. The door unlocked and opened to a late-twenties man of medium height with red hair, freckles and a patchy red beard. He had black glasses, blue eyes, a pointy sort of chin and was wearing a white Chelsea Football Club T-shirt and loose-fitting blue boxer shorts, his junk and red pubic hair visible through the fly.

"Sean, so good to see you! It's been too long. Peter from Zagreb sends his regards." Alex had long-mastered speaking English with a slight German accent. She couldn't have anyone tagging her as an American.

He eyed Alex suspiciously, but then grunted and said, "Yeah, he's a good bloke. Uh, come in. Didn't think you'd be this early."

He was English, neither Irish nor from the six counties in the north, judging by his accent. The house was small, with a cluttered living room area and a tiny galley kitchen with dirty dishes overflowing the sink. It smelled like fried food, beer and cigarettes. Alex briefly flashed back to her studio apartment in Princeton her senior year living above the diner.

"You've, eh, got the package?" he asked.

Leaving her gloves on, she handed over a heavy dark gray backpack. Needing to get him talking so she could learn more, Alex hoped that sound tradecraft wasn't Sean's strong suit.

"Um, Sean, sorry to bother, but you know, I froze my arse off walking over here. Could I get a spot of tea or coffee to just warm me up?"

"Uh, sure, okay, course." He walked over to the kitchen, rattled about, and put the kettle over the gas flame on the ancient white stove.

"Tea or coffee? What ya prefer?"

"Coffee, please. Thank you!" Coffee might take longer, she figured.

Sean returned to the small, cluttered table and sat down across from Alex while waiting for the water to boil. Alex suddenly felt the presence of someone else. Across the room, a woman walked out of the bedroom, wearing a black camisole and nothing else. She was thin with brown straight hair, medium height and attractive in a rough-hewn, flannel-shirt-and-boots sort of way. Alex thought she might be the hairiest woman she'd ever seen. Her underarms hadn't been visited by a razor in months, she had large amounts of visible dark hair below her knee all down her calf and her bikini line, buried in an ocean of dark hair, would be as elusive as the Loch Ness Monster.

Lighting a cigarette and walking toward the bathroom, the woman asked, "Who the hell is this?"

Sean shrugged. "Just a bit of business. Won't take long."

"Fuck," the woman grumbled, "the sun's hardly bloody up."

As she walked to the bathroom, Alex saw a bright green tattoo of a palm tree covering her entire right ass cheek.

"Sorry, the missus," Sean said. "She's lovely, really. Just a bit off in the morning."

Both of them now drinking coffee, Alex asked Sean, "You lived here long?"

"Few months. We moved down from Manchester. Activity gonna be pickin' up around London, they say, and needed me here."

"What's your trade? I mean, other than making bombs."

"Plumber."

"Let me tell you," Alex began, "it was not easy getting the things you needed in time. A little more notice would be better in the future."

"Shite, no need tellin' me that. I wanted this stuff two weeks ago. All I got now is a fuckin' week. I'll be livin' on edge every minute."

A week, Alex told herself. *Exactly a week? Is December 17 the date?*

"So, is it one bomb?"

"Aye. Will be quite big."

Jesus. If I was staying in the Genuine, the first thing I'd do was get rid of this guy. His tradecraft is appalling.

Alex figured she knew the answer to this, but asked, anyway, "Must be a vehicle bomb. No way you could easily get something that size inside somewhere, eh?"

Sean got animated. "Yeah, it's brilliant. My idea, really. We use the Semtex in combination with a fertilizer bomb. The Semtex, the detonator and the brains of the bomb will be in the cargo bay of a BT service van, and the fertilizer will be in secret compartments we're building on the sides, underneath, what have you. Out of sight. You wanna see the van?"

Unbelievable! He says "we," so he has help building the bomb.

"Ah, sure. I'd love to learn more about how we set these things up."

He took her down the steps to the tiny garage. Inside was a small yellow British Telecom service van: a two-person cab with two vertical doors in the back into the cargo space. Sean turned away from Alex briefly to pick some tools up off the floor, and while he did, she quickly took a penknife from her pocket and scratched a roughly six-inch lightning bolt into the paint on the back left door. She assumed the license plates might be different or removed later.

Alex kept fishing. "You can't leave this on the street for long without getting attention. Are you parking on a side street?"

He shook his head. "Loading dock in the back by the delivery entrance."

"How long will you, or whoever, have to get away? It'll be chaos once the warning's phoned."

"No warning," he said. "Am supposed to set the timer for exactly thirty-seven minutes, don't know why. But I ain't doin' that. Am setting it for forty-five minutes to give us more time to get away."

"Hmm," Alex muttered.

"It's a good ten kilometers back here, and with traffic, it'll take me at least a half hour."

Thoughts ran quickly through Alex's mind. *He's building the bomb and delivering it. Wherever it's going, with no phoned warning, the casualties will be horrific. Don't ask where he's putting it, too obvious, could make him suspicious, though he seems a bit dim.*

"You're right. It seems odd to insist on exactly thirty-seven minutes."

"All I was told was, 'we're gettin' it right this time,'" Sean said.

Walking back upstairs to the main level, Alex asked, "You're not Irish, Sean. English, right?"

"Aye. From Yorkshire, up north. My father was a miner in the coal pits around there, shop steward. In '83 and '84, when fuckin' Maggie Thatcher crushed the miners, it sent our family onto the dole – forever, it turned out, for me, mum and dad. When the Provisionals almost killed Thatcher on the loo takin' a shite with that bomb in Brighton in '84 , my dad said, 'Now that's noble work, fighting for workin' people and stickin' it to the likes of Thatcher.'"

"I agree. It's courageous and important work you're doing."

Sean tilted his head at Alex. "And what about you?"

"A similar story, but a long one, and I must go."

Sean walked her to the front door as his wife, still with no pants or underwear, exited the bedroom again and walked into the kitchen. She snorted at Alex and said, "You still fuckin' here?"

"Good luck, Sean," Alex said. "May God be with you."

61

Walking back to her hotel, Alex's mind raced. *A week to get the bomb ready… December 17? Ten kilometers from the house. Going to get it right this time, vehicle bomb, thirty-seven minutes…why that? And no warning. You can't phone an anonymous tip to the cops now because Maeve and everyone in the Genuine leadership will suspect you. Same reason you can't just take out Sean. You've got no clue how to disarm a bomb, even if you see him leave it and drive off. Best bet is to phone a warning once Sean parks the BT truck. Maybe the Brits will have time to disarm it, or maybe not, but hopefully, they can get the people away. They'll have to clear the area for blocks around.*

A thought came to Alex back at her hotel. She researched it on the internet and a local library, checked dates, details and distance. *That's it! Has to be.* The biggest uncertainty now was the date. Did Sean purposely give her the wrong date, or would it really be the 17th, as history would dictate? That would be just like Maeve, to do it on the exact date. Harrods department store in Knightsbridge, seven days from now. But what time? Would it again be 9:51 am, just before they opened? Alex guessed yes.

On December 17, 1983, the Provisional IRA left a vehicle bomb parked outside Harrods. The Provisionals phoned a warning at 9:14 am, thirty-seven minutes before detonation. Confusion after the warning led to an incomplete clearing of the area, and the bomb killed six people and injured over ninety. But with no warning, Maeve and the Genuine were upping the stakes, going for massive casualties. Alex hoped Sean was wrong, that the Genuine would phone a warning, but she knew that if left up to Maeve, there wouldn't be one.

Sean had said he'd be working until the last minute on the bomb, so Alex figured it likely until sometime Thursday or even through the early hours of Friday morning the 17th. Every night that week, at 18:00, 20:00 and 23:30, Alex donned a black niqab she bought near her hotel, along with a pram and some blankets to stuff inside. Covered from head to toe with only a narrow slit for her eyes, she was ostensibly a Saudi woman walking her baby.

The light was on in the garage each night, and Alex could see two or three shadows moving through the small dirty window in the garage. *If it's just two people, it could be Sean and the missus – Chewbacca with a palm tree tattooed on her ass. But if three, there are others.*

Thursday night on the 16th, around 23:45, twenty yards from Sean's house, Alex froze and ducked behind a red Royal Mail post box with the pram. The garage was open, and the BT van was still there. *Were they getting ready to leave?* There were two other men with Sean. He exited the garage and began walking toward her, closing the distance… fifteen yards, ten. *Great, walking his dog.* A small, leashed lap dog began barking furiously in Alex's direction. *IRA Bomber Randomly Stabbed by Saudi Mother While Walking His Dog.* Alex doubted that headline would play well with Maeve.

Now less than ten yards from Alex, Sean stopped and talked to the dog. "Ah, quit yappin'. It's late. You had your piss; let's go. I still gotta fix the tire before we go tomorrow mornin'." He turned with the dog, walked back to the house and closed the garage door.

Tomorrow is the 17th. Has to be tomorrow. He's ready to go. Of course, if Harrods isn't the target, I'll be fucked and will have failed.

• • •

The next morning, in a niqab and gloves with the pram, Alex sat in a small park-like grassy area a hundred yards from the loading dock at the back of Harrods. She'd walked the neighborhood between 07:30 and 08:30 and settled on a bench with an Arabic-language newspaper. She'd found a call box close by, as well as a backup she could use to phone the warning once Sean arrived with the BT truck. Would Sean set the timer for forty-five minutes like he said, or would he be afraid to disobey orders and set it for thirty-seven? She would have to assume thirty-seven.

09:05. A BT service van drove down the street toward Harrods. *Is this the one?* No, it continued past and didn't stop.

09:15. Two BT vans drove up behind the loading dock at Harrods and parked on the street. A man in BT-logo'd coveralls exited one of the trucks, and then a man similarly dressed exited the other. The two men met between the trucks and started talking.

09:20. The men walked away from the trucks to a cross-street at the back of Harrods, away from Alex, obscuring her view. To keep them in her sights, she put her newspaper in the pram and walked quickly with it in the direction of the BT men.

09:23. A tan Vauxhall four-door covered with dents stopped next to the men and they climbed in the back. A woman was driving. Sean's supposed wife? Alex had only a partial view of her face, but thought it was her. Then she saw nests of dark underarm hair under her loose-fitting white blouse. Had to be her, Alex told herself and wondered if she was still not wearing pants or underwear. Then, out of a doorway on the other side of the street, Sean jumped out and into the passenger seat of the Vauxhall.

09:26. Alex waited until the Vauxhall was out of sight, took the pram, and ran to the BT trucks. She reached the first and checked for the six-inch lightning bolt she'd scratched on the back left door. Not there. Reaching the second truck, she saw her mark. The closest BT red phone box she'd scoped out was a block away. She threw the pram in a roll-away trash bin at a construction site nearby and went on a dead run for the phone box.

09:30. Running. *If they set the timer on the bomb at 9:15 and they set it for thirty-seven minutes, 9:52… 10:00 if it's forty-five minutes.* Panting, she reached for the box, dumped coins in and realized it was out of order. *Fuck!* The next phone was another block away. Breathing harder, she reached it at 9:35, dialed 999 and got an answer.

"There's an IRA bomb in a BT service van parked behind another BT van on the street at the back of Harrods by the loading dock. It will take out the whole block. You've got to get people away!"

"Who's calling?"

"Fucking listen to me, okay? There is a bomb at the back of Harrods in a BT service van that will detonate between 9:52 and 10:00. You understand? Get help to the site."

Alex ran back toward Harrods, second-guessing herself the whole time. *There won't be enough time before it detonates. I should have just taken Sean out when he was walking his dog. I should have phoned in a tip days ago. To hell with what would have happened to me with Maeve. I should have run straight to the BT trucks when they parked.*

09:45. *Seven minutes!* She reached the front of Harrods, sirens now screaming and approaching from all directions. It looked like at least a hundred or even more people were lined up outside the doors, waiting for the 10:00 open. Alex, still in her niqab, ran along the line shouting.

"There's a bomb! There's a bomb about to detonate! Get away! Get away! Run!"

Realization, then panic began spreading through the crowd. Alex kept running down the block, shouting to anyone in earshot. She did the same at two side entrances, scattering another few dozen people.

• • •

10:30. Having tossed the niqab many blocks away and changed clothes, Alex stood as Jennifer Nathan, along with several dozen curious onlookers, two blocks from the front entrance of Harrods. She had blonde hair, green-and-white Adidas Stan Smiths, faded jeans, gloves and a blue-and-orange New York Knicks letterman's coat. It seemed every emergency vehicle in London surrounded the store: police, fire, ambulance and other services she didn't recognize.

The Times of London
Saturday 18 December 1999

MASSIVE HARRODS BOMBING STOPPED

Scotland Yard explosives experts disarmed a bomb on Friday hidden in a British Telecom service van parked near the back of Harrods in Knightsbridge just prior to the store's 10:00am opening. At an afternoon press conference yesterday, a Scotland Yard spokesman said that ordinance disposal experts had rendered harmless a "rather large yet crude" device prior to detonation. The spokesman would not speculate about who planted the bomb. The spokesman also confirmed that a warning about the bomb was phoned into the 999 emergency service in advance, but he refused to say when the call was placed and from where.

Unnamed sources within the Metropolitan Police described the bomb as "massive," capable of "taking out city blocks, killing hundreds, and injuring scores more." The sources furthermore stated that the ordinance disposal squad disarmed the device with "hardly any time to spare just before 10:00am," and only because its unsophisticated design allowed for quick dispensing.

Yet another mystery surrounds an apparent Saudi woman who ran among the crowds queuing to enter Harrods before the opening, warning of a bomb and urging people to flee. She wore a black niqab, a Muslim female dress garment that covers the body from head to toe with only a narrow slot exposing the eyes. According to several witnesses in the queue, the woman spoke excellent English but with an accent. One person stated she sounded like an American.

John Aldridge, a terrorism professor at King's College Department of War Studies, suggested that those behind the bombing could be associated with Middle Eastern terror groups, citing things like the 7 August 1998 bombings of the US embassies in Kenya and Tanzania by Islamic terrorists that killed and injured hundreds. More likely, however, Aldridge suggested, were interests related to several violent offshoots of the Provisional IRA, with the Genuine IRA the largest and best known of these.

The Genuine IRA formed in 1997 in response to the disengagement of the Provisional IRA, stalwarts of the Troubles since the early 1970s, from armed struggle following the Good Friday Agreements of April 1998. The Genuine IRA has been largely dormant since it perpetrated the August 1998 bombing in Ballycastle, Northern Ireland, that killed or injured over 300. Aldridge believes that the Harrods effort could signal the group's return to armed action.

Aldridge noted another factor pointing to IRA interests: "In terms of date, time of day and phone warning, yesterday's events were exactly sixteen years since the Provisional IRA detonated an explosive outside Harrods just before store opening." That event in 1983 killed six, including three police, injured almost one hundred and caused extensive property damage. The bomb failed to fully detonate in that incident, preventing much greater injury and loss of life.

As is its custom, MI-5 refused to offer any comment or statement on yesterday's events at Harrods. Scotland Yard and the Metropolitan Police both confirmed that an active investigation has commenced and that no resources will be spared to find the perpetrators.

62

Julie: December 1999 – March 2000

22:30 on December 23, and Julie cleared her desk, locked her files and headed home. She'd be back early on the 26th. Since Harrods, she'd slept on a sofa in an office conference room every night but one. There were showers in a health club across the street, and she saw Tim briefly early every morning when he brought her a change of clothes.

Earlier that day, she'd given JETPAK an update on the Harrods situation.

"Harrods, where are we?" Moreland asked to begin the meeting. "We've now confirmed it's some element of the IRA, right?"

Julie had a few PowerPoint slides if needed, but typically didn't use them to brief. "Yes. The Metropolitan Police got a tip: The bomber was a plumber from Yorkshire with red hair, supposedly named Sean. Scotland Yard found his parents, sweated them, and they said he rented a row house near Brixton. Scotland Yard arrested him and his wife there. They were too daft to get out of town, apparently."

"He admitted to building the bomb?" Beatta from German intelligence asked.

Watson from MI-5 chimed in, "Yes, but that's all we got. Sean and his wife were both stabbed and killed in their respective holding cells within hours of us taking them in."

"Unfortunate," Beatta said.

"Completely bollocksed-up by the locals," Watson snorted. "A total fucking howler."

Nodding at Julie, Moreland said, "Go on."

"So," she said, "by Provisional standards, though large and capable of horrific damage, the bomb was very unsophisticated. That's the only reason we were able to disarm it so quickly. We were incredibly lucky."

"Why so unsophisticated?" Marcel from French intelligence asked.

"We know the identities of the best bombmakers in the Provisionals over the past ten years: who they are, signatures of their work and the like. But MI-5 is confident they stepped back after Good Friday. So, I believe it's the Genuine or some other splinter group out of the Provisionals, and they're having to use bombers learning on the job."

"Then about a quarter of them will be dead in a year, I'd guess," Watson added.

"What else?" Moreland asked.

"The warning was from a pay phone a few blocks from the BT trucks. The woman was panting, out of breath on the call, so she could have been running from somewhere near Harrods to the phone. And she didn't use code names like the Provisionals always did when phoning warnings."

"What?" Beatta asked Julie.

"In the years leading up to Good Friday, a man always called a specific number and used the name Tom Milford. This is how authorities could distinguish a real warning from a fake. Since this didn't seem to have that organization or order, it's another reason to suspect a splinter group like the Genuine."

Watson from MI-5 jumped in again and nodded at Julie. "Agree with Laurie here. Plus, the call was shambolic, poorly organized. Why not have a person waiting by the call box to phone the warning at a set time? Makes me wonder if the woman who called went rogue and decided to alert us, even though maybe the Genuine didn't plan on issuing a warning."

Julie added, "And I'd bet the woman shouting to everyone about the bomb outside Harrods was the one who made the call. The Metropolitan Police ran simulations and confirmed that if someone ran, they could have placed the call and gotten to Harrods about the time the woman showed up."

"There are cameras everywhere in London," Olaf from Norwegian Intelligence chimed in. "Don't we have footage of the niqab woman at Harrods and between the store and the call box?"

"No," Watson said. "Something or someone took several of the cameras offline. We're working to see if they still captured anything we can recover. Nothing on that yet." He looked at Julie. "But CIA's got voice analysis on the call."

"Yes. We're certain the caller is an American, likely originally from the west coast. The voice was muffled, like the person was speaking through a face mask, ski hat… or something like a niqab."

"Anything else?" Moreland asked.

"So far, nobody thinks this is a Middle Eastern or Islamic act of terrorism. There is no chatter on that so far at Langley, and MI-6 and the French haven't heard anything either."

Moreland nodded.

Julie noted, "I think history points to some version of IRA fingerprints here, whether the Genuine or another offshoot. This was the same date, same location, same time and similar MO as the Provisionals in '83."

"We need to catch or kill these assholes before they try again and succeed," Moreland told the group. "Merry Christmas, everyone."

• • •

Though brief, Julie needed the two days off for Christmas. She spent them in a blur of activities with Tim and their four daughters, now seventeen and fourteen. Julie, Faith, Hope, Lauren and Charlotte made and decorated Christmas cookies on Christmas Eve Day, and Julie prepared their traditional fondue meal on Christmas Eve. Meanwhile, Tim and the girls made the desserts for Christmas Eve and Christmas. Tim still easily fit into his elf suit, as did Julie in her Mrs. Claus attire. Faith's boyfriend, a German from Düsseldorf she'd met at the international school and whose father worked in asset management in Edinburgh, had come over to join them all for dessert and then returned to his house around 23:00.

Around 02:00 and still awake on what was now Christmas Day, Julie and Tim drank champagne as Julie leaned against him in bed.

"You saved Christmas for us this year, babe," she said. "You got no help from me, what with work."

"Not true," he said as he lightly massaged her shoulders. "You made dinner tonight and will cook tomorrow, and you made cookies with the girls."

"Oh, please," Julie laughed. "You got the tree, decorated the house and shopped for everyone's presents. Oh, and the basketball team had two games this week. It's so good of you to keep coaching the school's club even after Hope decided not to play this season."

"Yea, well, I know Hope's glad she doesn't play anymore; she's spared reliving all those childhood moments when I coached her different teams."

"Maybe that's why Faith quit basketball too, a couple years ago, to focus on soccer year round," Julie teased.

"Probably. Well, I'm glad in a way that Lauren and Charlotte have decided to give up sports for high school and focus on music and other things."

Julie reached behind her shoulder to hold Tim's hand. "It's been almost two years now since we sold the company. Do you miss it? Are you tired of just consulting, lecturing and taking care of the girls?"

Tim shrugged. "Sometimes, but we'd have been crazy to turn down that offer from Coke. Because of that, we've got college for the girls funded, and we were able to buy this house, small as it is."

"True that. I think we all liked moving from a three bedroom, one bath flat to a house with four bedrooms and three baths," Julie said.

"I'm fine for now," Tim said. "They're still after me to teach that financing the start-up enterprise class down at the business school at Cambridge two days a week. Faith and Hope will be off to college in a year, so I'll have more time to do it."

Julie sipped her champagne and put the glass back on the nightstand. "I'm pretty sure Faith will get in at St. Andrews, but it might be a close call for Hope to get into Cambridge. But LSE's a good backup."

"Yes," Tim added. "The London School of Economics is a good alternative. I was kind of surprised neither of the girls wanted to look at schools in the US. But I'm happy about it."

"Me too."

"Oh, one more thing," Tim noted. "Not to dent your holiday cheer, but I heard last week that Charlotte is smoking."

"What? Who told you?"

"The school. She and her friends are doing it right on the grounds and in the bathrooms. Very brazen of them."

"Damn! She's fourteen. Did you talk to her?"

Tim nodded and, sort of grinning, said, "Yep. What do you think her response was?"

"No!"

"Yes. Her answer was, 'Mom does it all the time, she's a total chimney, so why can't I?' Now, I told her that comparison was invalid, but don't know how much traction I got with that."

Julie shook her head. "I need to talk to her. I suppose her sisters have known but weren't going to rat her out."

"Correct."

Julie sat silently for a couple of minutes. "I really need to quit. Can't believe I've been smoking for almost ten years."

"It's been a while," Tim concurred.

Julie rolled onto Tim and nestled her head into his neck. "To give me another incentive to quit, what would you think about revisiting our conversation about having another baby? It's been a year since we talked about it. We've always wanted to try for a boy. I just turned thirty-five. Hopefully, the machinery still works. I know yours does," she giggled.

After a few seconds, Tim muttered, "That would be a big age difference between the girls, but I've been thinking about it too. "And yes," he smiled. "I could be persuaded. Your "machinery" down there works just fine, so I bet you could get pregnant again."

Julie smirked. "Hmm, well then…."

• • •

Julie was back in the office at four in the morning on the 26th. She turned on the office lights, started the coffee and found a padded manila envelope on her desk with a note attached: "Got this two days ago, what little we could salvage from the cameras around Harrods. This is as good as we can make it. Haven't looked at it yet. Best, Watson."

Julie slid the DVD into a machine in her office. The video footage, from one camera in front of Harrods, was choppy, out of focus and short, about thirty seconds long. It was a distant panoramic view, though the woman in the niqab could be seen running in front of the store, talking with her hands and shouting at the people queuing for the opening.

After fifteen minutes of playing and replaying the video, it hit Julie. The woman's gait as she walked and ran reminded her of Alex. She never would have made the connection were it not for seeing Alex in the photo of Paul Reilly at Princeton.

Two potential coincidences now. Despite that, Julie found the chance it could be Alex just too far-fetched.

January 2000

Even before Harrods, Julie had decided the best way to decode the Genuine IRA or other offshoots of the Provisionals would be to follow the weapons. The old saying was that an army marched on its stomach, but Julie knew terrorists didn't do anything without weapons. Over many months, she'd become an expert on the Provisional IRA's historical weapons suppliers, smuggling tactics, successes, failures and key people in those areas. Possibly someone from that area had moved to the Genuine.

This, of course, had led her to the British debacle in Tunisia in the summer of '85. Julie had heard the gory details of Adaoma's horrible fate from Alex when she lived with them that month in Los Angeles. After reading the files and talking to people at MI-6, Julie knew Alex had, inadvertent or otherwise, at least a peripheral connection to the Provisional IRA. Two coincidences – Paul Reilly and the woman in the niqab who walked and ran like Alex – and now maybe a third. Too many.

But what was the Tunisia connection? Was Alex already in the organization that summer in Tunisia, working in the medical clinic compound as cover? Or, perhaps, had the British destruction of the camp and death of Adaoma been the radicalizing incident for her, ultimately leading her to the Provos? Or was it all nonsense? Just ghosts Julie was chasing.

The Mossad had tipped off the British about Tunisia but not told them their source. MI-5 assumed it was someone with the *nom de guerre* Peter, a senior sort in the quartermaster's organization, who, after Tunisia, had ended up dead in a Belfast street, shot behind the ear. Julie had asked the Mossad three months prior about this and had been stone-walled. She'd shared her frustrations about this with General Moreland at the end of November.

"I think I can help with that," Moreland had said. "Danny Yatom runs the Mossad and I've known him for almost thirty years. I also saved his ass in Beirut in '82. He owes me. It'll give me a good reason to call and catch up with him."

• • •

Julie was hanging her coat on the back of her office door early on a frosty mid-January morning when Moreland knocked, walked in, and dropped a thin manila folder on her desk.

"Hey there. Don't want you to think I forgot about you on the Mossad thing. There wasn't much in their files, Danny said. Their source wasn't that guy Peter, but a Belfast woman named Sally Horrigan who worked for Peter. Unfortunately, Sally's controller in the Mossad back in '95, a guy named Simon, was killed in an undercover op by Hezbollah in Damascus last year, so there's no chance to learn more."

"Okay, thanks."

Moreland continued, "Horrigan was the tout. The Mossad didn't have useful informers in that area in the PLO at the time, so they looked at the Provos, knowing Gaddafi shipped weapons to them, too, usually one after the other. The Mossad didn't care about the Provos, only wanted the PLO weapons."

"Why did Horrigan do it?"

"A widow with money trouble after her husband, also a Provo, blew himself up."

"Why'd the Mossad tip off the British? They usually keep things to themselves, hoard information, as I've learned all too well."

"The Mossad needed help in Beirut, so they traded their Tunisia intel for that. They didn't give up Horrigan by name, just said they had a source."

Julie opened the folder after Moreland left. The 'file' was one typed sheet of paper with bullet points. Not an official Mossad document, it had no markings. She read it over.

- After Tunisia, the Provisionals suspected Sally's boss, "Peter," and possibly Sally. The Mossad had no interaction with Peter. Knowing her exposure, Sally's controller arranged an immediate ex-fil out of Belfast for Sally and her three children. The Mossad resettled them with new identities and Israeli passports in Tel Aviv, where they lived safely for a number of years.
- Sally later insisted on leaving Israel and returning to either Ireland or the US. She chose the US. The Mossad opposed this but resettled her and then cut ties in the early 1990s. Sally had a daughter and two sons when she left the Mossad's protection.
- Sally Horrigan, new identity… Suzanne Harris, reportedly died of an illness in the US in the mid-1990s.

Julie spent the next few weeks waiting for the FBI to see what they could learn. They confirmed a Suzanne Harris had died in St. Louis in June of '95. The FBI had gotten copies of her medical records, and her daughter Tracy had also gotten them. The daughter had returned to university in Wales at the time and finished her medical degree. She was now in London, an infectious disease specialist and attending physician at a hospital.

Julie secretly listened in on a call to Tracy she'd asked Special Branch to make. As CIA, JETPAK and an American, Julie couldn't credibly introduce herself to Tracy without exposing her affiliations. The man from Special Branch introduced the reason for the call and after initial pleasantries, Tracy moved to the subject first.

"Inspector, I'm certain the IRA killed my mum."

"Why?"

She recapped Sally's role in the Tunisia bit, said she was in an impossible situation. "But the Provisionals would have thought her a tout, and they kill touts," Tracy said.

"Even years after Tunisia?"

"Yes, I think it just took 'em ten years to find her. And, it's just too much of a coincidence that somehow me mum contracted radiation poisoning in St. Louis out of nowhere."

"What makes you think that?"

"Ever since, I've done lots of research, first on her symptoms, then the autopsy records, then finally on all kinds of different poisons. I'm sure it was polonium."

"That's pretty sophisticated for anyone. The only people in the world that have that are Russia, the US and Israel."

"And," Tracy added, "the day before she gets sick, we catch this woman in Mum's house. Another coincidence? I hardly think so."

Julie sat up sharply in her chair, almost losing her grip on the phone cradled in her neck. She messaged the Inspector: "Need details!"

"Could you please explain that further, Tracy?" he asked.

"I'd just got into St. Louis from Chicago with Tom, my boyfriend then – husband now. Mum was still at work. A woman was hiding in the house. We must have surprised her. Not ten minutes after we got there, she ran right past us, heading for the back door. But she tripped on our luggage and fell down. When she fell, it knocked her headscarf off, and I got a look at her. The police came, didn't really pay attention and just said there had been break-ins in the area. Mum didn't think much of it since nothing was missing, but even before Mum took ill, I had a sinister feeling about it."

Julie sent another instant message to the Inspector: "Send sketch artist?"

"Tracy, could you still describe this woman if I sent a sketch artist down to see you and your husband? I know it's been years ago."

"Of course. I still cry for me mum probably once a week. I miss her so. I can't prove it, but I think that woman in the house had something to do with her death. I will never forget her face as long as I live."

Tracy was going to be tied up out of London for medical work the first two weeks of February, but the Inspector arranged a date in late February for the sketch artist to meet her and her husband.

• • •

Julie was preparing to leave the office on a cold, rainy Friday evening in January when Phil called her on her mobile. Phil was with the CIA's clandestine service and worked under NOC, or non-official-cover. Instead of masquerading as a low-level state department foreign service officer at a US embassy with the full diplomatic immunity if something went wrong, NOCs had no ostensible tie to the US government. They had nothing but their covers and wits to keep them out of prison in a foreign country if something went wrong.

Phil, an American Ph.D. clinical psychologist, practiced with a small group of Austrians in Vienna and served a largely upscale clientele. His 'night job' with the CIA was tracking arms networks, many of which operated in and out of Vienna, and this had connected him with Julie early in her agency days.

"Hey, Laurie. It's Phil." Phil had only ever known Julie by her cryptonym.

"Well, hello there."

After a bit of small talk, Julie asked, "What's up?"

"I've got an asset in Zagreb, our crypt for him is Felix. He's an arms dealer, the main bridge between some terror groups and a corrupt cell in the Croatian military. We pay Felix, and our deal with him is that we don't care about his conventional arms smuggling activities, but he passes on anything he knows related to WMD."

"Okay."

"In the past year, these Croatian contacts of Felix have sourced highly enriched uranium, and they're looking to move it to the highest bidders who can turn it into a dirty bomb."

"Hmm. Where'd they get it?"

"It's Ukrainian stuff. Been floating around since the fools gave up their nukes in '89."

"The prospective buyers, the usual suspects?" Julie asked.

"Yep. Al-Qaeda, Lashkar-e-Taiba and other Pakistani, Middle Eastern and Southeast Asian groups. But there's a new entrant, and that's why I called. Have never run into them before, and wondered if you've heard of them playing in this space."

"Oh. Who?"

"This new offshoot group from the Provisional IRA, the Genuine IRA or something like that."

Julie, who'd been standing by her desk, immediately sat back down and prepared to take notes.

"Why the fuck would they want this stuff?" Phil asked. "I can't imagine them detonating a nuke in their backyard. They think they can mark it up and sell it to others?"

"That would be my guess," Julie said. "They probably have the ability to make a dirty bomb if they have the enriched uranium. So, who is Felix dealing with from the Genuine?"

"He said at first it was this one woman, supposedly a senior person in the IRA. But since '96 it's another woman, named Klara. Klara buys conventional weapons from the Croats via Felix. Felix sounded out the first woman, the more senior one, when he heard about the uranium a few months ago and she's interested. But she told Felix not to tell anything to Klara, the other woman from her organization."

"I need a picture of Klara and the other woman if possible. Can Felix get one?"

"Probably, he won't be happy about it, but I'll tell him he needs to find a way. But the next meeting isn't until April, and it's with Klara on conventional arms business. There's no meeting set yet on the uranium."

"That's fine. Get me a picture of Klara in April, and a picture of the other woman whenever you can. And thanks, Phil. Always great to hear from you."

February 2000

Julie had a senior MI-5 man in Belfast on the phone on a gloomy pelting-rain Tuesday early in the month. Her colleague, Watson, had made the introduction. The MI-5 man on the phone had served off and on in Northern Ireland for close to two decades. Another investigative thread Julie was pursuing to learn about members of the Genuine IRA and maybe the woman in the Harrods video, was to see who had been imprisoned in Northern Ireland from the beginnings of the Provisionals in the early '70s to the present day. Prisoners would have photos and records. Today some would be dead, others would have left active service in the Provisionals years before, and still others would have stood down with the Good Friday Agreements. Any people unaccounted for in those ways would warrant further investigation.

Julie introduced herself and the purpose of her call, and the man asked, "What do you need?"

"A cigarette," Julie joked, "but I'm trying to quit and am five weeks without one."

"Good on you, and best of luck with that."

"Thanks. Hey, I'm looking at prison records in Northern Ireland from 1970 onwards to see who was locked up, when they were let out, that kind of thing. But I can't find records on anyone in Northern Ireland, male or female, from 1990 to '94."

"Yes," the man growled, "that was a big cock-up. The government changed prison and RUC computer systems beginning in '97, in preparation for Y2K and other upgrades. And in that process, they lost the digital records from the old system for '90 to '94. So they had to re-enter the data from paper files in storage, but it turns out there'd been a fire years ago that destroyed maybe half of the paper records from those years. The paper files that weren't destroyed are being re-coded into the new system, but there won't be any records from the burned files. The project is behind schedule, but it's supposed to be done in three months."

"Okay, thanks. Just curious about a related subject since you've been around Northern Ireland for so long. Did MI-5 lose any of their own people in Northern Ireland between '90 and '94?" Julie asked this on a hunch, expecting little. If someone had gone to prison for killing a British MI-5 figure, it would be in the records. Anyone in the Provisionals who had done it may have been relatively high up, so possibly they'd be candidates to join the Genuine. She had a small team working that angle, but the '90 to '94 information was, of course, missing.

After a few moments, the man said, "Well, we did, actually. Our guy in Londonderry, Magnus Herrington."

"What happened?"

"It wasn't IRA-related. Unseemly business… cock and fanny trouble."

"Excuse me?"

"Ah, right, sorry. His mistress shot him when she got tired of him beating her when he was blind pissed."

"What happened to her?"

"Went to prison, a couple of years maybe, then got out."

"That crime isn't in the system, so it's either being coded-in now or the file is ashes, right?"

"Yes. Special Branch, along with the RUC, questioned the woman. I could probably get the name of the Special Branch interrogator for you if you want to make inquiries. The RUC guy is dead, ambushed by the Provisionals with two others outside Londonderry on Christmas Eve three years ago."

Three days later, Julie was on the phone with Samantha Byrne of Special Branch. After a bit of introductory chat and explaining how the incident was not in the computers, at least for now, Julie asked Samantha about her interrogation of the killer of Magnus Herrington.

"You and an Inspector Walsh of the RUC interrogated the killer of Magnus Herrington, correct?"

"Yes, in spring '92."

"She was his mistress, I heard, killed him in self-defense?"

Byrne snorted a bit. "That was her story. I didn't believe it. Planted by the Provisionals, I'd bet my flat."

"What made you think that?"

"Just a feeling. Yes, I don't doubt he roughed her up when he was falling-down drunk. And he did smack her about a bit that night, broke her nose as I remember."

"But you thought she was a Provo?"

"Still do. Her story just seemed a bit too convenient, too coincidental. How is it this random American girl ends up with MI-5's guy in Londonderry after only being in Dublin a few weeks? The only thing I couldn't reconcile was if you're in the Provisionals, why do you kill your source? I figure maybe the gal just got tired of him, figured fuck it, don't care what the Provos think, I'm sick of this."

"Excuse me, you said she was an American girl? What was her name?"

"Ah, let me think. From California. Molly? Yeah, Molly Fitzhugh."

"From California?" *Western US accent on the woman in the niqab at Harrods.*

"That's another part of her story that didn't sit well with me. Supposedly a daughter of Irish parents from Galway who'd lived most of their lives in the States. She allegedly grew up around Los Angeles and went away to some fancy boarding school out there. Then wanted a gap year in Ireland before starting university."

"I assume you checked her story out."

"'Course. Called California and this woman, supposedly her mum, confirms the story. Called her boarding school too and had 'em send me a copy of her high school yearbooks and records. Wouldn't ya know, she was never there on picture day."

"And she went to prison, right?"

"Yes, I think it was supposed to be year and a half, though they may have let her out after a year, what with overcrowding and all in Northern Ireland. I wanted to press the woman on the Provisionals, really squeeze her to see if we could learn more, but London just wanted it to go away – too much embarrassment and they were tired of Magnus, the sot."

"Don't suppose you have any files on the case? A picture of her?"

"Ah now, you're unlucky there. Everything got lost in the Y2K digitization, so I am afraid you'll have to see if her paper records survived that storage warehouse fire. If you find the file, there will be pictures."

Byrne called Julie a week later. She'd remembered that some of the women in Maghaberry prison were let out under group supervision one day a month to do charitable work in the community with the Catholic church. To participate, the local police and local parish needed a picture of each woman. If this Molly participated even once, there should be a picture of her in the files of the local church. Getting no cooperation initially from the RUC in Maghaberry to check local church files, Julie enlisted help from her MI-5 JETPAK colleague, Watson. Properly incentivized after a request from MI-5, a search was now ongoing.

Julie couldn't tell Tim much about her work, but late one night in their living room, and with few other details, mentioned the horrible way Sally Horrigan had died. Tim had said, "That sounds like Win Blackpool." That hadn't occurred to Julie, but if Blackpool and Horrigan had been killed with polonium, that could tie Alex to both of them. After all, it wasn't like people were killed that way every day.

Working with the FBI, Julie had experts review the medical files and autopsy records of Win Blackpool and Sally Horrigan, and while not definitive, it was plausible that polonium could have killed them both.

On the last day of February, the sketch of the woman Tracy and Tom had seen in Sally Horrigan's St. Louis house finally arrived. Viewed online, the rendering wasn't as definitive as Julie had hoped. The woman in the picture in 1995 could be Alex. The eyes and nose were similar, but the hair was different, and the face longer, more angular and more aged than Julie remembered or would have expected.

63

Alex: April 2000

The summons from Maeve to meet her on short notice, this time in London, was not unusual, Alex thought. Yet this time, something bothered her. She couldn't point to anything specific, but just had an uneasy feeling.

They met on a sunny but blustery Wednesday afternoon in mid-April at a closed, under-renovation pub a few blocks off Bayswater near the Notting Hill Gate tube stop. Alex – Klara Steinmetz, in this instance – had flown in that morning from Berlin.

Alex made her way to the alley entrance to the pub and to the open rear door. Maeve was seated at a table near the kitchen. Not surprisingly, construction workers were nowhere around.

"Ah now, love, how are you?"

"Fine, thanks," Alex said. "Looks like you're working today. Client meetings?"

Maeve grimaced and said, maybe more tersely than necessary, "I'm always working."

"Right. What's up?" Alex asked.

"You're seeing Radko this month, right? Finalizing the AK-47 and ammo arrangements?"

"Yes, meeting him next week in Zagreb."

"Brilliant. Be sure to let me know what happens."

"Always," Alex said. *Come on, you didn't have me drop everything to come to London, so you could ask me that.* In that regard, Maeve didn't disappoint.

"So, love, I want to revisit your trip to London last December."

Just then, two ugly men in construction worker clothes and poorly disguised bulges in their pants – guns – entered the pub.

"Pay no matter to them, Alexandra. I'm meeting them when we finish our business."

Shit! Stay calm. If you fuck this up, you won't make it out of here alive. Maeve will also have a gun, likely in her suit coat pocket, waistband, or purse. I'll have no chance.

"Okay, sure."

"Who was in the flat when you took the Semtex to Brixton?"

"The guy Sean and a woman he said was his wife."

"Did she say anything?"

"She bitched about how early I got there and walked around with no pants or underwear on."

"What did you do with Sean?"

"Handed over the backpack with the Semtex."

"Then what?"

She'd maybe talked to him before she had him shiv'd in jail. I can't say that I just handed over the package and left.

"I froze my ass off walking over to the flat, so I asked for a cup of tea or coffee. He made coffee for both of us and we sat at his kitchen table and drank it."

"What did you talk about?"

"He gave me a bit of his background, asked about mine, but I changed the subject."

Maeve's eyes locked onto Alex like a radar. No time to squirm or hesitate.

"Then you left?"

Careful here. Think.

"Uh, no. He asked if I wanted to see the truck he would use for the bomb, and I said yes. Couldn't believe it. His tradecraft was fucking awful."

"Then what?"

"He showed me the truck, told me it was a Semtex-and-fertilizer bomb, how they were setting it up in the van, that kind of thing. Then we went back upstairs, and I left."

"Okay, grand, love. I must go."

Maeve stood, picked up her purse, and cast a sideways glance at the two men.

"Oh, just a couple of other things, Alexandra. At the flat, did

Sean say anything about the plan, the mission? Time, dates, location, anything like that?"

It would be my word against his.

Alex struggled to remain icy and calm; her nerves were eating her alive and her stomach and intestines were on fire with the stress. "No. He couldn't have been that much of a fuck-up, could he?"

"And you left London after seeing Sean, or did you stay?"

What does she know? Anything? That I stayed in London for a week? Could anyone have seen me later when I wasn't in the niqab? This is awful. I'm gonna throw up if my stomach doesn't calm down.

"I flew out that night. Back to Berlin for a day and then to Moscow for three days for meetings with Pavel and some tourism. He'd been called away from Vienna. We were comparing notes on arms dealers in Turkmenistan and Serbia."

Maeve furrowed her eyebrows. "Now don't take this wrong, love. You know how these bits go, but would you happen to have any proof you were in Moscow?"

"What's this about?" Alex asked.

"The Genuine is doing an investigation of the Harrods business, trying to see what went wrong. Typical after-action stuff. Did that woman just happen by and look in the vans? Did the Provisionals sabotage us? Did Sean or someone on his crew bugger us? Since you were one of the last to see him, I need to ask."

"So, I'm under suspicion?" Alex chuckled.

"No, no, love, not at all. No worries. I just need to ask the questions, to be thorough."

Alex grinned, reached into her purse and handed over a passport, Inge Marstellar's, and a bill from the Kempinski Hotel in Moscow. "I've been waiting for you to ask. Would have been disappointed if you didn't. As you'll see, the dates and passport stamps confirm I was there."

Thanks, Pavel!

For those favors, Alex had burned a potential new arms supplier for the Genuine, who was also selling weapons to Chechen separatists. Russian Spetsnaz commandos killed him within a week.

Maeve smiled. "Brilliant, love, you never let me down."

As she was walking out with her two thugs, Maeve turned and called back to Alex.

"We're going to be making a trip to Turkey next month. Just a few days. Details to come within a fortnight."

"Okay."

Maeve fixed Alex with a hard stare, seemingly smelling her disloyalty and treachery. "Alexandra, the coming months will be ones of great opportunity for us, but will also be testing and dangerous. This is no time to go soft, understand?"

"Of course."

Alex stood and waited, expecting Maeve or her henchmen to come back and give her one behind the ear. After ten minutes they hadn't returned, so she barely made the toilet in the bathroom before she threw up and her bowels melted down.

PART 7

We Meet Again

64

Julie: April 2000

I t was the third week of April, around noon on a Wednesday, and thoughts raced in Julie's brain: Emotions, questions and facts, all screaming to be processed. *Why would she do this? When did she start? At Princeton? How many people has she killed? I've got to explain all this to Moreland and the team. Is this why she sent me that letter and banished me from her life years ago? Or if that wasn't it, had she really grown to dislike me for whatever reason?*

Phil had left her a voice mail on her CIA phone just after 03:00 that morning. "Hey Laurie, it's Phil. Check your email when you get this." He meant her CIA inbox, not her JETPAK account, and Julie had immediately opened Phil's message. Six photos. Presumably, Felix and his Genuine IRA weapons buyer: Alex? Disguised it seemed, but Julie could see a resemblance in her eyes.

Two hours later, a package with a 1993 picture of Molly Fitzhugh from Maghaberry prison finally arrived at her desk. The local authorities had taken their time looking through the church's photos. It was Alex; she had no doubt. The woman had dark, short hair, but the face was Alex's, only four years after she'd supposedly died. Whether or not she was the woman at Harrods, Alex had been a terrorist for years. And now she was with the Genuine, trafficking in guns, ammo, and maybe even nuclear materials for dirty bombs.

JETPAK assembled Friday for Julie to update everyone on the recent flood of information. Using an overhead with bullet points, she first recapped both her history with Alex and the elements of the hypothesis that now pointed to her as a member first of the Provisionals and now the Genuine IRA.

- CIA asset has confirmed Molly Fitzhugh/Alex (photo is her prison intake picture from 1993) is weapons buyer for the Genuine IRA. Is dealing with a broker, "Felix," who is sourcing material from a Croatian military faction. She met Felix this month.
- Genuine IRA now seeking enriched uranium (Ukrainian origin) from the Croatians via Felix. Plan could be to build a dirty bomb to: 1) Sell to other terrorist organizations for tens of millions of pounds? Or to: 2) Use it in London or elsewhere?
- Russia is the likely source for the polonium that killed Sally Horrigan. French asset in Russia, embedded in the SVR, says Provisional IRA working with the SVR since mid-90s, extent unknown. Account for SVR managed by SVR Rezident in Vienna.
- CIA Vienna station has hundreds of pictures of Vienna rezident, a priest. Xmas Eve '94 picture outside Prater amusement park shows him speaking with a disguised woman that could be Molly Fitzhugh/Alex, but this is unclear (see picture).

Watson from MI-5 jumped in to cover the remaining bullet points.

- Two of the three top people in the Genuine IRA are now known. The third (and the leader?) = woman with *nom de guerre* "Maeve." Shockingly, nothing known about her despite apparently being a long-serving senior member of Provisionals and on the Army Counsel. Supposedly largely known only to Gerald Morrissey, head of Sinn Fein and the Provisionals.
- Morrissey won't cooperate with us in any way regarding Genuine IRA. Believes he can manage the situation, despite its threat to him and his objectives.
- Former senior source in the Provisionals that opposes the Genuine says he hears "Maeve" has a short list of close confidants, one of whom, a woman, rumored to be a protégée. Could it be Molly Fitzhugh/Alex?

65

Julie: May 2000

Saturday morning, 6 May, 07:00, and JETPAK had been hastily assembled, summoned by Moreland the night before. Nursing coffees, everyone talked among themselves, looking for clues to the unusual emergency meeting. Moreland walked in at 07:00 sharp.

"Hey everyone, thanks for coming. I've got some close-hold information that we all need to be aware of. You'll also need to brief the highest levels of your governments. Look, I don't know why this came through this channel, but yesterday the US State Department got a tip from Ireland's Foreign Ministry. Gerald Morrissey will be meeting with the leaders of the Genuine IRA at the Ciragan Palace hotel in Istanbul on 10 May."

"What for?" Watson from MI-5 asked.

"Some sort of summit meeting, Morrissey's idea. He will supposedly offer the Genuine significant political power within Sinn Fein to push their issues, but in exchange require them to disarm, fold up."

"They'll never do that," Watson opined.

"Agree," Annette from MI-6 chimed in.

"Morrissey likely thinks his long relationships with the Genuine leaders will allow him to persuade them," Watson scoffed.

"Be that as it may," Moreland replied, "we'll have the leader or leaders of the Genuine, including presumably the mysterious Maeve, all in one place."

"To be killed," Julie offered. She guessed what was coming. Professionally, she was happy about it. Her job – JETPAK's job – was to hunt terrorists and prevent future attacks. But personally, she couldn't help but wonder if somehow Alex would be caught up in it, and she didn't know how she felt about that.

Moreland nodded. "The SAS has been spun up on this and will hit the hotel. It'll be a total shit storm because the British aren't giving the Turks a heads-up."

"Wait, wait," Olaf from Norwegian intelligence said as he held up one hand. "The British military is going to launch a secret attack on a five-star hotel in downtown Istanbul in order to kill these Irish terrorists?"

Moreland nodded. "As I said, total shit storm. The British will not be talked out of this."

"Rightfully so," Watson commented.

Moreland went on. "The SAS's only instructions are to avoid shooting innocents and Gerald Morrissey. They are to take out every member of the Genuine and even Morrissey's people if they can't be distinguished from the Genuine. Everyone shot on sight."

"When in doubt, kill everyone," Julie remarked. That's a bit of a blunt instrument, don't you think?"

"Yes it is, but the Troubles traumatized the British government for thirty years," Annette offered. "They'll do anything and take whatever blowback to snuff out the Genuine while it's still in the crib."

• • •

Julie was alone in her office afterward. She'd known better than to ask Moreland after the meeting if she could accompany the SAS as an observer. It was a military operation, and her request would have been a non-starter and shown either poor judgment or that she was too personally invested in the Alex angle. She would have liked to go to satisfy her curiosity, to confirm without a doubt whether Alex was in fact alive and close to the leaders of the Genuine. She also wanted to set eyes on the supposed Maeve. Was she, in fact, at the top of the organizational table? What did she look like? What was she like?

Had she been able to go, she knew she wouldn't have tried to save Alex or tip her off. She was a terrorist who'd killed god knew how many people. She'd made her bed, and if she was in Istanbul that day, the SAS would see to it that she slept in it, permanently.

66

Alex and Julie: May 8 – 10, 2000

Alex

Maeve messaged Alex on May 3rd and told her to fly to Istanbul five days later. Told her to check into a hotel of her choosing on the European side of the city. Alex was to meet Maeve on the afternoon of the 9th at a coffeehouse in the Pendik neighborhood, across the Bosphorus Bridge, officially the 15 July Martyrs Bridge.

Alex arrived at the coffeehouse on time at 14:45. The shop was dark with a brooding vibe, the small lamps on each table barely cutting into the gloom. The smell of Turkish coffee was strong, and tobacco smoke hung thick inside the café, the signs and scents of a forest fire drawing near.

Alex saw Maeve, who wore red pleated wool slacks, Italian red leather shoes, a blue-and-white blouse and a red fedora with a navy stripe. Never knowing what to wear for her meetings with Maeve and conscious of being overdressed in a grubby hole-in-the-wall coffee house, Alex wore black Nikes, black jeans and a gray polo shirt, and had a small blue backpack. Turkey would be Alex's first and only trip as the heavily disguised Dutch woman, Kara DeJonge.

Alex walked to Maeve's table, isolated near the back with nobody around.

"Right on time, as always, love." Maeve smiled.

"How are you?" Alex asked.

"Grand, but I'm pressed for time, so we need to get to it."

"Sure."

Maeve reached into her large black leather Coach purse and extracted a box gift-wrapped in red-and-blue happy birthday paper with a white bow and ribbon. Alex knew better than to touch the package.

"Alexandra dear, your present is a .45 caliber Sig Sauer P220 with four magazines and a silencer. You need to bring that with you to the Atatürk conference room on the second floor of the Ciragan Palace hotel tomorrow morning at 06:20 sharp. You know the hotel?"

"Yes. The one on the Bosphorus across from Yildiz Park."

Maeve nodded. "It's one of the nicest hotels in the world, so be sure to dress appropriately. I'd recommend a purse rather than a backpack."

"Fine," Alex said, resenting Maeve's possible dig at how she was dressed.

"If there's anyone outside guarding the Atatürk room, our colleagues will take care of them before you get there. I'll be in that room meeting with Gerald Morrissey. Your job is to step in and kill him. I'd do it myself, but his people will search me before letting me into the room."

Fuuuuuuucccckkk. It's a mob hit.

"Then you're to drop the gun and magazines there, and the two of us will go down the escalator and out a back door by the pool. We'll climb down the bank across from the pool to the edge of the Straits and a boat will pick us up. We'll go to the Asia side, split up, and you'll make your way back to Berlin. Clear?"

Alex sat in silence, processing. Finally, she replied, "No. It's not clear, Maeve. If I'm going to assassinate the leader of Sinn Fein and the Provisional IRA and become one of the world's most wanted terrorists, you're going to have to answer some questions for me."

Maeve stared hard at Alex through tense, closed lips before snorting, "Ah, now, really?"

"Really."

Maeve sighed. "I figured as much, love."

"Thank you. What's the story?" Alex asked.

"Gerald Morrissey reached out in April, asking me to meet him in town tomorrow. He's here on Sinn Fein political business with economics and political people in the Turkish government."

"What's he want to talk to you about?" Alex asked.

"He's trying to shut down the Genuine and wants me to help him do it. He thinks he can persuade me."

"Why not just tell him to fuck off? Why kill him and bring all that heat down on us?"

She leaned forward across the table, eyes blazing. "He's a risk to me, a risk to you, to all of us. He sold out every Catholic in Northern

Ireland with the Good Friday Agreements, and he'll sell out the Genuine next. We'll all go to prison, or worse. He's got the smell of the traitor coming off him everywhere he goes."

"So, we kill him. Well, I kill him. Then what?"

"We expose his corruption, that he was bought off, the Swiss bank accounts for him and a couple of others. Plus, he never wanted a strong leader under him, so with him gone, there won't be anybody any good to keep the Provisionals supporting the Good Friday Agreements and giving up the armed fight. We'll either reconstitute the Provisionals or the Genuine will take the lead. And we'll scupper Good Friday."

Alex wrinkled her nose and sipped her espresso. "And what happens to me?"

"We have big plans for you, love, in Ireland. You wrap up your life in Berlin, bring Petra Müller to a close, and take a senior role, either in the Genuine or the Provisionals, whichever goes on."

Doubt it! More likely, you hang me out to dry as a disavowed rogue assassin. Alex worried Maeve was beginning to doubt her loyalty and reliability over the past year, but if so, why bring her into this, other than to get her to kill Morrissey and then sacrifice her?

"How well do you know Gerald Morrissey?"

"Our grandfathers fought together in the IRA decades ago. Our mums were pals; the families were close. My family started in South Armagh but moved to Belfast briefly and then the US. I'd see Gerald every summer as a kid when we went back to Belfast from the US. He spent his junior year in high school in the US, living with me and my family. We were lovers my first two years of university, even though I was in Washington, DC, and he was in Belfast. Then he broke it off with me to marry a Belfast girl, and I met my husband not long after."

Hmm, hell hath no fury?

"We were both active in the Provisionals, and he was a great help to my career. He wanted me to fly under the radar, not be well-known to many in the organization, and to manage the Provisionals' affairs outside of Ireland and the UK once he rose up to leadership. He put me on the Army Council."

"And you still want to kill him."

Maeve sighed, took a deep breath, and blew it out. "It's not like he just wanted to retire, fade away and let the rest of us continue the fight. No, he sold us out. Undermined what people in Ireland have been fighting and dying for since 1919. Thought he could just make it all go away, that only he knew best for the Catholics in Northern Ireland.

And he did it for his own greed and political ambition. Unforgivable."

Maeve's eyes narrowed and bored in across the table from Alex. "In or out, love?"

Like "out" is really an option. If I say no, I'll be dead before I get out of Istanbul.

Alex waited a few seconds. "In."

• • •

Back at her hotel, Alex took one of her three burner phones and called the emergency number to contact Otto. It went to voicemail, as she expected.

In a Northern Ireland accent, she said, "Tommy? Tommy? It's Erin. Ma is really sick in hospital and doing poorly. You need to call me just a soon as ya get this."

The plan for the next day was still on since Maeve hadn't called her before 22:30, asking for a car service the next day at noon and then apologizing for a wrong number. Supposedly, Maeve and Morrissey were going to make eye contact from across the bar at the Ciragan Palace at 21:00 and not speak. This would be confirmation that the meeting was happening the next morning. No call from Maeve meant Morrissey was at the hotel. Unless it was all a ruse, and Alex was going to show up at the conference room in the morning so Maeve or her associates could kill her. But why bring her here just to do that when Maeve could have killed her in London last month?

Late that night, still fretting that Otto hadn't called, Alex reconnoitered the Ciragan Palace hotel and its spacious grounds. The back of the hotel backed up to the Bosphorus Strait in view of the Bosphorus Bridge. A huge swimming pool and deck with tables, chairs and umbrellas sat adjacent to the hotel's outdoor restaurant, a typical resort setup. A lighted promenade ran between the edge of the hotel grounds and the water. A gentle embankment led down ten or so feet from the promenade to the water.

It took five minutes to go from the main entrance up the escalators to the second-floor suite of conference rooms. She found the Atatürk room in the far northwest corner.

Alex planned to arrive tomorrow at 06:10, and when she got upstairs, she would duck into the women's toilets just across from where Maeve and Morrissey would be meeting. She had no idea if Morrissey's bodyguards would be splayed out dead, bleeding on the dark blue carpet, when she got there or if Maeve's people would have dragged them away.

Alex guessed the other people on Maeve's team would enter the hotel via a service entrance. She decided to go in the main doors, a headscarf covering everything but her eyes from the security cameras in the lobby. She would wear dark gray slacks, a black silk blouse, black flats, short dangling silver earrings and a dress watch. The gun, ammunition clips and silencer would be in her large black leather purse.

Still no word from Otto. What am I going to do? Shoot Morrissey? Shoot Maeve? Be a no-show and flee?

• • •

As Alex left her hotel the next morning, another of the three burner phones rang.

"Erin? Erin? It's Tommy," Otto said. "I just got your message 'bout Ma. Sorry it took so long."

"Listen, Tommy, you need to get a message to uncle Morrie." *Please make the connection, Otto!* "I think he's got some business meeting this morning, but he needs to skip it and get to Ma. It's really bad. D'ya understand? Can ya get word to 'em?"

"I, uh, um, I really don't know, the short notice and all. Be tough to get to him real soon, but I'll try."

He won't have time. Morrissey could already be in the meeting room.

Alex walked through the main entrance of the hotel at 06:05. That early it was quiet, almost silent. She saw two people at the front desk in hotel uniforms, one looking directly at her. Three members of the housekeeping staff, two women and a man, were changing the flowers in the massive vases scattered around the lobby, and yet another, a man, was setting up an elaborate silver coffee and tea service with large urns.

Alex noticed a woman off to the side of the lobby, bent over, head and face covered with a scarf, stretching out for a morning run. She wore dark blue Adidas capri running pants, red Adidas shoes with white stripes and a light blue hooded sweatshirt. Three men in dark business suits were also spread around the lobby reading newspapers: one *Le Monde*, another the *Financial Times*, and the third the German business paper *Handelsblatt*.

Taking the escalator to the second floor, Alex checked her watch: 06:10. Ten minutes until she would kill Morrissey.

Julie

Julie felt the Smith & Wesson .357 Magnum revolver and holster push against the small of her back as she bent over and stretched out in the lobby in her Adidas ensemble and head scarf. She wasn't sure why she'd brought a gun. She had no plans to shoot anyone, but if the unexpected happened, it couldn't hurt to have one. She'd debated whether to bring the revolver or a nine-millimeter. She shot expertly with both, but opted for the revolver – less risk of jamming. She got through airport security in London and Istanbul with the gun using US government documents and ID.

Coming to Istanbul was a bad idea, she knew. She was likely risking her spot on JETPAK and maybe her entire career with the CIA. Coming basically to sit in the bleachers to watch a top-secret SAS ambush. Moreland would be livid, and her JETPAK colleagues would lose respect for her, thinking she was too emotionally invested in seeing, killing or talking to her former childhood friend. They'd be right.

Julie couldn't fully explain it, but she wanted to see her, at a distance; the woman who'd lied to her and cast her away. Julie had told Tim she had to go to Istanbul on business, but characterized the trip as routine meetings, and left out the SAS and Alex pieces. She hadn't lied but had been deceptive. He would be furious when she apologized and 'fessed up afterward, but she couldn't tell him she was putting her life in danger to just maybe see Alex and Maeve. If Julie had thought her life would be endangered in Istanbul, she wouldn't have gone. She owed it to her family to be there for them: Tim, her four daughters and their newest child, two months along and traveling in her belly with her to Turkey.

Scanning the lobby, none of the varied people working or reading were SAS, she knew. They would crash into the lobby in body armor and start shooting. Therefore, they were possibly random guests, but more likely people that belonged to either Morrissey or the Genuine… or both. It was possible some of the hotel staff in the lobby were also not who they seemed.

With only her eyes visible, she looked back under her left arm while stretching, bent over her right knee at the woman who entered the lobby at 06:05. The woman wore a headscarf covering her face, but Julie knew immediately, her eyes, walk and body structure told it all. She almost gasped. *Oh, my god! Alex! It's all true. I was right!* Before her mind could wander back into the past with Alex, she reminded herself, *You can't think about that now. Pay attention!*

She watched Alex go up the escalator and disappear. Julie first decided to wait near the bottom of the escalator, figuring it too risky to venture upstairs, since there was going to be a violent confrontation with the SAS. Then she told herself she'd seen Alex, so instead needed to get out of the hotel before the commandos assaulted. But she didn't do either. Julie rationalized that Maeve could already be upstairs and potentially escape down a fire staircase rather than come back down the escalator, especially once the SAS started shooting. She needed to lay eyes on her in case the SAS didn't kill her. That could help JETPAK hunt her down.

As for Alex, Julie didn't need to see the SAS gun her down. But, if Alex had been the woman in the niqab outside Harrods, then she was working against Maeve and the Genuine. What would Alex do once all hell broke loose?

Julie rode the escalator to the second floor and scurried to hide behind three huge ceramic planters in an open area outside several meeting rooms. Two men were sitting in chairs outside a conference room in a far corner.

Alex

On the second floor, Alex snuck quickly into the ladies' toilet about fifty feet across from the Atatürk room. She saw two men in chairs sitting outside the room. Were they Maeve's or Morrissey's? Sitting on the toilet peeing in one of the four floor-to-ceiling stalls with louvered dark wooden doors, she screwed the silencer onto the Sig Sauer. She inserted a magazine and put the other two in the front pockets of her slacks before returning the pistol to her purse on the floor.

She rechecked her headscarf in the mirror above the sinks to make sure only her eyes were visible. She wondered if the men outside the Atatürk room, whomever they belonged to, would shoot her as she left the toilets.

06:18. Cracking open the door, Alex saw nothing had changed. The same two men sat outside the conference room door. She exited, stepping into the small recessed hallway that led to the ladies' toilets. The hotel's elevator music soundtrack had awakened: *Rhapsody in Blue* wafted down from the ceiling speakers.

Suddenly, the Atatürk room door opened and Maeve emerged to talk to the two men. *Okay, so they're hers.* Alex made eye contact with Maeve, who shook her head and walked toward her.

Back inside the bathroom, Maeve mouthed, "Are we alone?" and Alex nodded.

"He confirmed the meeting last night. We saw each other," Maeve said. "And now he's twenty minutes late."

"What do we do?" Alex asked. "Wait or abort?"

Maeve, brow furrowed and deep in thought, finally spoke. "He's never late. Abort. Let's go."

They walked outside to the conference room door. Maeve sent her two men away down the fire stairs, and she and Alex headed toward the escalators.

"How many people do we have here?" Alex asked.

Maeve nodded back toward the fire exit. "Those two and four in the lobby, one a hotel employee. Assume you saw the blokes reading the newspapers?"

"Yeah." *What about the woman stretching out*?

"The two from here will collect them and they'll exit the front. We'll go out the back toward the pool and meet the boat in the Straights."

Alex and Maeve were roughly twenty feet from the escalators when Gerald Morrissey and three men in dark suits eased into view, riding up. Morrissey, just hanging up his mobile phone, saw Maeve and Alex and barked something to his men. They pulled guns from their jackets and started firing.

Morrissey jumped the median between the up and down escalators, ran down and vanished.

One of Morrissey's men dropped Maeve as she and Alex ran behind a large garden planter. Alex pulled the silenced pistol from her purse, returned fire, and quickly hit two of the men, disabling but not killing them. She and Maeve crouched behind the planter as Maeve wrapped a scarf around her wounded wrist.

Where was the third man? Alex looked around, but he wasn't there.

"Come on!" Maeve barked.

Alex ran with her. As they neared the down escalator, the third man rose up, holding an Uzi submachine gun; he'd ducked behind a sofa a few yards away. Before he could fire, Alex hit him with two shots to the chest. *If he's wearing a vest, he'll live, and if he isn't, well, he put me in an impossible spot.*

Before they left for the first floor, Maeve commanded, "Drop the weapon. We don't want them to see you with it." Alex complied.

On the way down, they heard screaming, shattering glass and

automatic-weapons fire. Reaching the first floor, Alex saw four bodies, the men with the newspapers and a hotel employee with a gun in his hand. They were right inside the hotel's main entrance, blood pooling around them on the blue-and-white marble floor. The guys upstairs with Maeve also lay in pools of blood near the front desk. Six members of the SAS, assault rifles up, were scanning the lobby for more targets. Shattered glass covered the lobby like an ice rink, one of the massive stained-glass windows next to the front doors completely blown out.

Julie

Julie had seen everything, crouched down behind the planters nearest her. After taking pictures of what were presumably Maeve as well as Alex with her phone and waiting a few moments for Alex and the woman to run down the escalator, she rose from her hiding place to hustle after them at a safe distance.

She saw the man with the Uzi whom Alex had shot begin to crawl along the floor for his weapon a few feet away. As she ran down the escalator, the man, weapon now in hand, raised it and centered her in the gunsight. He unleashed a volley of automatic fire and Julie screamed.

Alex

Alex saw the SAS men far to her left, milling about the lobby, surveying their damage. She and Maeve ran out a back door, past the pool and the outdoor restaurant, and crossed the promenade. The boat – a small speedboat with a blue blinking light on the bow – was waiting, framed by the Bosphorus Bridge, the bright blue water of the Straits, and clouds tinted pink and orange from the rising sun.

Reaching the bank before Alex, Maeve said, "Let me get down there first, love, to give the password. To make sure this is our guy."

Who else would be here at this spot at 6:30 in the morning?

Maeve clambered down the bank. Before speaking to the man in the boat, she turned sharply back toward Alex, who was halfway up the bank five feet away. Alex saw the nine-millimeter pistol Maeve pointed at her.

Will she go center mass or headshot? I have no weapon. I'm dead.

"You mean I'm not coming with you?" Alex sarcastically asked.

"No, you're not, love," Maeve sneered, ice in her tone. "You worthless bitch. You're no better than all those people you've spent the past years killing. A tout."

"Maybe, maybe not," Alex calmly replied. "But I'm not a terrorist, which is what you've become. You talk about the unfortunate collateral damage of war, and I can see that – hell, I believed it. But mass casualty bombings of innocents like Ballycastle and what you tried to do in London aren't that."

"So, it was you who phoned in the warning in London. I never would have believed it until one of our informants said MI-5 was saying it was an American that made the call, too excited apparently to conceal her voice. Very surprising lapse in tradecraft for you, Alexandra. You're one of the best I've ever seen in that regard."

Alex shrugged. "Desperate times, desperate measures."

Maeve went on. "I still wasn't sure, didn't want to believe it. But after this business today, I know it's all true. It would be too risky for me to try to shoot you behind the ear like we prefer, so I'll just assassinate you from here."

"For what it's worth," Alex said, "I tipped one of Morrissey's people that he might not want to come to the meeting with you, but he just got the message on his phone coming up the escalator. Why else would he hang up the phone and have his guys start shooting? He sure as hell didn't have time to plan whatever that mess was out front. Someone else sold you out on that."

Hate burning in her eyes, Maeve hissed, "I only wish we had more time and privacy, so I could torture you myself, to see how else you've betrayed us. I'd pull your fingernails out first, then break your fingers, rough up your lady bits down below with sharp objects, then cut your tits off one at a time with an electric saw. I've done that before. Once that happens, you don't have much time left."

Alex stood silent and still, ready for death. She was sorry she would never have a chance to try to reconnect with Brian, maybe even make a life with him. She wanted her last thoughts to be of Brian, Julie and Adaoma – the only people she'd ever loved unconditionally.

Maeve squinted her left eye to sharpen her aim and moved her finger more squarely over the trigger. "Burn in hell, you traitorous cunt."

Alex closed her eyes and heard the shot.

**The Times of London
Wednesday 11 May 2000**

Tourists Killed in Shocking Assault at Luxury Istanbul Hotel

Local sources and police in Istanbul have confirmed that
at least seven European tourists were shot and killed near
the entrance and also by the pool of the five-star Kempinski
Ciragan Palace hotel on Tuesday. The killings took place at
approximately 06:30 local time. Witness accounts indicate
that there were five or six assailants wearing ski masks and
body armor who fled in two waiting cars after the killings.
Police have not released the names or nationalities of the
victims and speculate that robbery could have been the
motive. An investigation is underway.

• • •

**The Times of London
Wednesday 15 June 2000**

SAS Implicated in Istanbul Ciragan Palace Killings

Several anonymous British and Irish government sources
indicate that six Special Air Service (SAS) commandos carried
out what was originally believed to be a botched robbery-re-
lated tourist shooting on 10 May in Istanbul that claimed at
least seven lives. Two sources from within the UK Foreign
Office, one in London and one in Dublin, have now stated that
the victims of the attack, citizens of both Northern Ireland
and the Republic of Ireland, were not tourists but, in fact,
members of the Genuine Irish Republican Army, a 1997 violent
offshoot of the Provisional IRA.

According to sources, senior-level informants embedded
within either the Genuine IRA or the Provisional IRA, alerted
the US government, who then notified the Foreign Office, of
plans by the victims to travel to Turkey for a secret meeting.
British authorities dispatched the SAS to Istanbul to track and
kill the suspects. A confidential source within the Republic of

Ireland's Home Office separately confirmed these accounts. At press time, neither the UK Ministry of Defense, MI-6, nor MI-5 had responded to repeated requests for comment regarding these matters. The official spokesperson for the Irish Home Office said, "We will have no comments on this matter, now or in the future." The names of the attack victims remain closely guarded by British officials.

Speaking last night on the BBC World Service, Andrew McDonough, Head of the Ireland chapter of Amnesty International, said,

"This appears to be a monstrous act perpetrated by the British government. At least seven people were shot on sight by the SAS in another sovereign country without warning. They had no opportunity to surrender or to receive the rights accorded to the accused by modern, civilized nations. The British administered the cruelest form of premeditated street justice; they were judge, jury and executioner. There needs to be a thorough inquiry into this matter by the British, Turkish and Irish governments."

The incident has caused a bitter, escalating row with Turkey. Turkey's Foreign Minister summoned the British Consul General in Ankara to receive a formal protest over what it termed "outrageous, disturbing extralegal killings by the British on the soil of a sovereign nation and NATO ally." Opposition party figures in Turkey are calling it a "blatant terrorist act." Some believe it possible, if not likely, Turkey will expel a number of British diplomats in retaliation. To date, the British Foreign Office has declined to comment on the shootings, as well as current relations with Turkey.

One senior member of the British Foreign Office, speaking without attribution, told a Times reporter that, "Whoever approved this operation had to be mental. This will cause a storm that will blow for months and drag in the US and other European allies."

Alex

Disoriented and in shock, Alex opened her eyes. She was alive. Maeve lay dead on the riverbank in front of her, the top of her head missing and her bloodstained navy blue fedora, with its bright blue stripe, lying upside down a few feet away.

Feeling she was going to faint, Alex frantically looked around. There! Up on the bank, a woman, the one stretching for her morning run in the lobby. She stood with two hands holding a gun, smoke still curling out of the barrel. *No, no! Impossible!* But before Julie Mitchell could say anything, Alex ran to the boat, jumped in, and it sped away.

67

Julie: July 2000

Julie and Tim were taking a break from painting on a mid-July Sunday afternoon. They were converting their guest room into the new baby's quarters – their son would be another December baby like his two much older sisters, Faith and Hope.

Julie, a splotch of blue paint on her cheek and wearing an old torn and stained St. Mary's College shirt, returned from the kitchen with two ice teas and handed one to Tim. They sat on two folding chairs in the new bedroom.

"People might be back sleeping on air mattresses or on the couch when they come to visit now," Tim said. "Though it's usually just my parents a couple of times a year, or Brian now and then. I think he's coming for a week in September. I just heard from him."

"Great. He can stay in Hope and Faith's room since they will be gone."

"That's right. Faith has to be at St. Andrews for orientation the third week in August. And Hope leaves for Thailand right after that."

Julie pursed her lips. "I have my doubts about this gap year thing for Hope, but, of course, she doesn't want to hear that from me. I know she was disappointed not to get into Cambridge, but she had lots of other good options."

"It'll be okay, Jules. Lots of kids do this over here, and it can help them before college. If it helps her in getting into Cambridge, then great. And if not, I think she'll be happy going to LSE. Besides, Help the Children is a great global organization. She can't help but learn things and gain new perspectives, living in a tent and working in a refugee camp for a year."

Tim reached over and squeezed Julie's hand. "What happened to Alex's friend Adaoma isn't going to happen in Thailand. And she'll be home for Christmas for two weeks right after the baby's born."

Julie nodded. "I know." Then she laughed and said, "Charlotte and Lauren still think Hope's nuts for doing this."

"So," Tim said, "when Brian comes to visit, are you going to tell him about Alex?"

Julie sighed. "No. I wouldn't even if I could. He has no way of knowing she was 'The Woman Who Got Away' as the press dubbed her. If Alex wants to reach out to him, then that's on her."

Tim knowingly smiled. "He wouldn't be hard for her to find. She could just look him up on the internet."

Julie asked, "You think he's going to be able to save Blackpool Industries?"

"I don't know. He's been CEO now for a couple of years and inherited an incredible mess. He's got to restructure the company in bankruptcy, settle all the securities, tax and environmental criminal and civil cases, and help the government prosecute the executives who caused all the problems. Including Fogg – I think Fogg's going to prison. He will not escape this – his hands are very dirty."

"Like father, like son," Julie observed.

"What are Alex's options going to be?" Tim wondered. "Any news on that front?"

"She killed the MI-5 guy in Northern Ireland, but she served her time for that. And now we know she played a role in killing Patricia Maguire, the single mother with nine kids, in Northern Ireland. But Gerald Morrissey owes her his life, so he could probably make sure she's included in the general amnesty for all sides in the Good Friday Agreements. But she might have to live in Northern Ireland permanently, so she might always be looking over her shoulder if what's left of the Genuine IRA wanted revenge."

"But there's nothing left. You cut off the head of the snake in Istanbul. On your secret tryst with Alex and Maeve." Tim smirked.

Julie grinned. "Well, at least you've transitioned to teasing from disbelief and anger over that. You and Ralph Moreland. I thought that would take forever."

Julie knew that the only reason she'd kept her job on JETPAK was that she'd killed Maeve. General Moreland had bluntly told her so. The SAS wouldn't have reached the back of the hotel and the Straits before Maeve had escaped on the boat. Julie figured some might wonder if she'd let Alex go afterward, but Alex had no gun and Julie had had no reason to shoot her, or any other unarmed person for that matter, in that situation.

"What other options might Alex have?" Tim asked.

"She could just vanish, disappear somewhere in the world behind a fake identity. Obviously, she's quite good at that. The problem with other options is the dead bodies outside Northern Ireland. She killed Sally Horrigan in the US, Win Blackpool in Finland, and likely Steve Lonsdale. But they found a gun on Lonsdale in Helsinki that had been fired, so maybe there's a self-defense claim there. We don't know, but she also likely killed other IRA touts around Europe these past years.

"Wow," Tim said. "The Good Friday amnesty wouldn't cover that?"

"No, it only applies to crimes committed in Northern Ireland."

"Got it," Tim said.

"Another big unknown is that in late '89 in Maine, the Provisionals killed a supposed American tout for MI-6 with a bomb that also took out a young single mother as collateral damage. And MI-6 lost one of their senior guys in that operation, too. If Alex was involved in that, especially in killing the MI-6 guy, then the British would push for capture and imprisonment, probably for life."

"How will you know if she was involved?"

"We probably won't," Julie answered. "Maeve is dead, and even if Alex was involved, she might be the only survivor of that operation. And in addition to the body count she was an arms trafficker for the Genuine too."

"So, life on the run is her only option?"

Julie shook her head. "Maybe not. She saved hundreds of people around Harrods, tipped off Morrissey that he was in danger, and also contributed to the death of a violent terrorist – Maeve, who was trying to get a dirty bomb and also plotting to kill many more innocents by various other means. I'm sure the Russian secret intelligence service would have her, as might the CIA and MI-6, but for the British to be a landing place, that likely depends on the Maine thing."

"Knowing what she's done, to others and to you all these years ago, would you like to see her again?" Tim asked.

Julie thought silently for almost a minute. "Yes. I would, regardless of whether she's in prison or out in the world."

68

Alex: July 2000

Small and spare, maybe eight by eight, my room worked for me. A small lamp sat atop a weathered wooden nightstand next to my twin bed. A bare overhead bulb, a small, three-drawer dresser, and a ratty wingback chair with faded and ripped green upholstery filled the room.

A small closet held no clothes to speak of; my circumstances didn't require them. A raincoat, a winter coat and a week's worth of tan and light blue robes, the uniforms of my new trade, were spread across the hanging bar. Two narrow rectangular windows ran across the top of my room. They opened and at night, I could smell the flowers in a nearby park.

The communal bathroom for our floor was twenty yards down the hall: three sinks with mirrors and a like number of stalls and showers with a curtain. I was on the top floor, the third, with about ten other women. Ten more occupied the second floor. There were fewer on the ground floor because it also included the kitchen, dining area and storage. The building and rhythms of daily life were quiet, always. Nothing to distract me from my hungry longings for Brian and a new life with him.

Two locked suitcases sat on the floor of my closet. One with the few meaningful personal effects I'd collected and transported over the past twenty years: pictures of Brian, Adaoma, Julie and Tim and their kids, plus a few of Princeton and Tunisia. The other suitcase had clothes from my prior Berlin life. The closet also held a locked duffel "go-bag," with the equivalent of $30,000 in various currencies, and two nine-millimeter pistols with six ammo magazines each.

There were multiple passports in the bag, too: Alexandra Davis (US, expired); Petra Müller (Germany); Inge Marstellar (Austria); Jennifer Nathan (US); Alyson Flynn (Ireland); Klara Steinmetz (Germany); Sydney MacNaughton (United Kingdom); Prudence (Prue) Fuller (South Africa); and my newest, Natasha Chugunov (Russia), most recently used on a flight to Moscow from Istanbul.

On a daily basis, though, I carried only my picture ID card – Sister Angeline.

I'd been here less than a month and expected to stay for another six or so – one of the nuns at the Sisters of Saint Agnes Carmelite Convent in a marginal area of Vienna. Except for my lack of detailed Catholic knowledge, I fit in with my sisters, and they asked very few questions. I faked-it-till-I-made-it during prayer sessions in the cozy first-floor chapel with stained-glass windows across the front of the altar. Otherwise, I was like everyone else: I cooked, cleaned, did laundry and worked in the community.

I'd arranged this with Pavel before I went to Turkey. He'd asked few questions. I needed a place to disappear, to hide from the Genuine IRA as it sorted out its fate with the remnants of the Provisionals and the British and Northern Ireland authorities.

In exchange for his help – professional courtesy, after all – I gave Pavel the details of my Croatian and Serbian arms suppliers who also supplied Chechen terrorists. I'd also alerted him that the head of the SVR rezidentura in Zagreb was spying for MI-6; the Brits had turned him when they caught him in a homosexual affair with a Croatian local they'd dangled.

Though I couldn't be sure if the Genuine could ever find me, I was now a tout. The best outcome for my future would be either elimination of the Genuine IRA before it gained strength, or a substantial reduction in its capabilities and support from the people of Northern Ireland. People were tired of the Troubles, weary of violence, death, economic struggle and uncertainty. I thought a decent chance existed over time they could become nothing but a fringe, nuisance outfit, and thus unlikely to find or pursue me. Of course Sally Horrigan had thought that too.

And most importantly, Maeve was dead.

I also needed time to sort out the other issues of my past. If I'd only worked for the Provisionals in Northern Ireland, it was likely I could fall under the general amnesty for the soldiers of the Troubles on both sides. But my fighting for the Provisionals' cause, as well as my own personal scores, had led to three deaths in the US, two in Finland, one in the Netherlands, plus the pedophile in France.

Gerald Morrissey, the head of Sinn Fein but also still the unofficial head of the remnants of the deactivated Provisional IRA, owed me. Could he shelter me with immunity in Northern Ireland if I were to live there permanently? Provide cover if my past life were to someday be of interest to authorities outside Ireland?

Alternatively, Pavel was offering Russian citizenship and diplomatic immunity if I worked for Russia somewhere as Natasha Chugunov or someone else. It was hard to see the appeal of that, especially since I wouldn't ever work against the US or Germany, but one always needed options. Similarly, the CIA might offer a safe harbor, either in the US or internationally, as might MI-6. I'd had nothing to do with the disappearance of their guy in Portland so long ago.

Or I could simply disappear, go black, and create a new life.

My priority was the best, safest path back to Brian, if he'd have me. I had never wanted anything more in my life, I was certain, and I even thought about having a baby or two with him. I also wanted, if and when possible, to talk to Julie again, though it seemed she was now hunting me, so that conversation might not go well. But someday, I'd love to know what path led her to be standing on the banks of the Bosphorus Strait in Istanbul that day, in a position to kill Maeve and save my life.

Also, someday, I wanted to tell the children of Patricia Maguire and Sally Horrigan what I knew and what I did. There was much to do and big obstacles to overcome, but I had decided to follow Julie's life example, at least up until the time I cut her out of my life. Like her, I would not give up and would just keep putting one foot in front of the other every day, with faith that things would get better. The Genuine and my past were not going to defeat me.

I didn't think about Timberline much in the convent, even though I had nothing but time. People in TL likely considered my life to be a tragedy, a life cut short too soon in a sad car accident. Maybe, they might have speculated, I could have achieved great things like Brian and Tim did in war, athletics and life. Someday, Timberline would carve impressive statues of Brian and Tim to honor them. There will never be a statue of me; if people knew the truth, I'd be an embarrassment, a disgrace to the town.

But my story isn't over and I also think it's more nuanced and fluid than that, like trying to sculpt a statue of me out of the ever-shifting mists of Washington's North Cascade mountain range.

Acknowledgments

This novel has been a project of mine for more than five years, and I'd like to thank a few people now that the finish line is near. Thanks to Cynthia Burwinkle, my first reader who offered helpful comments and support. My developmental editor Margaret Lucke had many helpful suggestions for Sculpting the Mists and was also a steady source of optimism and advice. I also offer heartfelt thanks to Dr. Paula Machtinger, PhD, who helped me get back on a good path and was a constant source of encouragement throughout the process. My adult children Meredith, Edward and William have been hearing about this book forever if you ask them, and I'm sure they are ready to learn about a new project by now. Finally, my deepest thanks are to my wife Amy - all of this would mean nothing without her.

www.ingramcontent.com/pod-product-compliance
Lightning Source LLC
Chambersburg PA
CBHW030057310726
48970CB00004B/1042